Justine Ettler was born in Sydney in 1965. A graduate of Sydney's University of Technology, she is currently completing a Ph.D. at Macquarie University with the assistance of an APA scholarship, and planning a third novel.

Justine's second novel, *Marilyn's Almost Terminal New York Adventure*, is forthcoming from Picador.

D1596384

The River Ophelia

JUSTINE ETTLER

PICADOR
Pan Macmillan Australia

First published 1995 in Picador by Pan Macmillan Australia Pty Limited
St Martins Tower, 31 Market Street, Sydney

National Library of Australia
cataloguing-in-publication data:

Ettler, Justine.
The River Ophelia.

ISBN 0 330 35670 4.

I. Title.

A823.3

Typeset in 10/14pt Sabon by Midland Typesetters
Printed in Australia by McPherson's Printing Group

In memory of Linda Goldsmith

Acknowledgments

Thanks to: the Brown and Marnie family, Camilla Nelson, Edwina McLachlan, Gabriel MacKenzie, Kate Grusovin, Shelly Cox, my friends in Seattle, Richard Wu, C. and C., everybody at Picador, everybody at Hickson Associates, my family and Julian.

I woke up alarmed
I didn't know where I was at first just that
I woke up in your arms
And almost immediately I felt sorry
Cos I didn't think this would happen again
No matter what I could do or say just that
I didn't think this would happen again
With or without my best intentions
LIZ PHAIR, 'Fuck and Run', from *Exile in Guysville*

'Can I abuse you some more now?' he asked sweetly. 'In the car?'

    'What do you want to do?'

    'Gag you? That's all, I'd just like to gag you.'

    'But I want to talk to you.'

    He sighed. 'You're really not a masochist, you know.'

    She shrugged. 'Maybe not. It always seemed like I was.'
MARY GAITSKILL, 'A Romantic Weekend', from *Bad Behaviour*

It seems years since you held the baby while I wrecked the bedroom.
SINEAD O'CONNOR, 'The Emperor's New Clothes' from *I Do Not Want What I Haven't Got*

Contents

Sade

1

I MET SADE AT A PARTY. I WAS STANDING NEXT TO THE fridge reading the assembled crowd face by face when a man with porcelain blue eyes motioned for me to join him from the other side of the room. I walked across the kitchen, eyes taking in the empty bottles, dirty glasses, overflowing ashtrays, puddles of spilt drink, crushed overturned beer cans, empty cigarette packets, corks, chip packets, dirty plates, finger-smeared dip bowls, broken plastic cups, brown paper bags, bottle openers, twist tops, matchboxes, cardboard six-pack containers, plastic bags and a single drop earring in the shape of a gold heart submerged in a wide white wine glass half filled with water, and then followed him through the French doors and out into the garden. He said his name was Sade and handed me a joint.

'So what do you do?' I said, dragging on the joint. Sade was incredibly good-looking with hard eyes, long lashes, a prominent nose, a broad forehead, full pouting lips, the sort of lips I loved kissing, a strong jaw line, the kind of jaw line I loved slapping, and thick dark curly hair.

'I work for a magazine,' he said, blowing smoke rings.

'Which one?' I asked, curious.

'*Playboy*,' he said, his voice a sullen monotone. The smoke rings disintegrated into wisps of grey.

'That sounds like fun,' I said.

'I hate it,' he said, his voice quiet but firm.

'Why's that?' I wanted to know.

He offered me the stub of the joint. I shook my head and watched him toss the butt into a bush, the orange tip spiralling through the air.

'It's killing me,' he said, dispassionately.

The butt glowed red for a few seconds and then faded and turned to ash. He glared at me. I didn't know where to look.

'Why's that?' I ventured.

He took a few deep breaths, expelling air through his nose in hard jets. 'I'm underpaid, over-qualified, and chronically frustrated,' he explained, his voice icy and controlled. 'My work is repetitive, boring and meaningless. I am totally dissatisfied. The only people who think writing for *Playboy* constitutes an interesting occupation are people I meet at parties. People like you.'

Sade fell silent. I shivered a little in the cold. Summer was drawing to a close and there was a chill in the air. I couldn't think of anything to say.

On the other side of the French doors everybody was eating and flirting and getting drunk and talking about work and real estate and children and who's fucking who. Meanwhile all around us suburbia laboured on, quiet tree-lined streets, rows of dark terrace houses, people watching videos and drinking beer late into the night.

'What about you, Justine?' he said, his voice even and calm. 'What do you do?'

I looked at his neck caught in the warm glow shining through the French doors. His skin was pulled taut and smooth across clearly delineated strips of muscle and soft-looking cushions of flesh. A few small dark freckles dotted the lubricious olive surface.

'I'm writing an honours thesis,' I said, 'or I'm supposed to be writing one. I'm not really doing anything, though.'

He nodded and looked at me but not into my eyes. 'And what's your thesis about?' he asked, his eyes watching my lips.

'Sex and death,' I said, smiling.

I watched his face, waiting, but he didn't smile back. Instead his eyes stared straight into mine. They were wet, round and dark. I shivered again.

'It's cold,' I said, taking a few steps towards the door. I reached out and was just about to turn the handle when something made me pause and look back. He was standing right beside me, his hand mirroring mine, both of us frozen and with our arms outstretched on the doorstep. Smiling, we dropped our arms to our sides.

Soon my eyes were sinking down his face as my head inched towards him, slowly, jerking from my neck. I kissed him, crazy and brave, just the outer lips touching at

5

first, and then inside. My body folded into his and I reached for his tongue with mine, his arms firm around my waist and me hanging around his neck. The kiss continued, too delicious to stop. The word 'love' flew round and round in circles in the back of my mind.

I didn't want to stop kissing Sade. When I finally stepped back I was overwhelmed by sickening waves of anxiety. Desperate, I immediately wanted to start kissing him again but he was already opening the French doors. Marvin Gaye's 'Sexual Healing' blared from the stereo and the kitchen was full of people dancing and rubbing their pelvises together and smiling too much. They looked like they were on drugs but they could've just been drunk. Watching their awkward gyrating bodies I started to dry-retch. Everywhere I looked I saw white rolls of fatty flesh bulging out of collars, jeans, and tight midriff tops. Without saying anything, Sade and I walked straight through the intoxicated dancers and kept going until we'd walked out the front door. I followed Sade across the street to his car and then stood shivering, still thinking about the people dancing in the kitchen and feeling sick, and waited for him to unlock the passenger door to his beaten-up white Renault.

As we hurtled through the deserted streets I squeezed my legs together and pushed my finger through a hole in my pocket and inside the elastic of my underpants. I felt incredibly happy. Minutes later waves of inexplicable joy bubbled up the back of my throat as we sat side by side in silence, the car stopped at a red light.

'I can't stand the suburbs,' he said, looking around

him. 'I just can't relate to well-maintained lawns, lead-light windows, landscaped swimming pools, groves of fruit trees, birds waking you up in the morning, having to drive to the corner shop, mortgages, dogs barking at you from behind six-feet high fences, their teeth huge and yellowed, foam dripping from the corners of their mouths, their hackles raised and every dog for miles joining in, lawn-mowers on the weekends, children screaming at each other and stealing mail, neighbours trapping you with long-winded complaints about local developments, police knocking at the door conducting awareness of domestic violence campaigns, pagodas, speed humps, flowerbeds and TV sets flickering from the other sides of greasy windows in empty rooms.'

I was starting to wonder whether Sade's list of complaints would ever end when the lights changed and the car lurched forward, the tyres squealing on the tarmac and Sade silent, frowning behind the wheel. We sped through miles of streets lined with freestanding bungalows and cottages, the pavements dotted with small trees and bushes.

At some point he made a left-hand turn, too fast, into a dark side street. The headlights shone straight into a group of boys riding skateboards and bikes on the wrong side of the road. Sade swerved the car and slammed on the brakes and the rear end swung around, sending us into a spin. When the car finally came to a standstill we were on the other side of the road, the bonnet of the car pointing into a grass and cement driveway. Halfway up the driveway was a children's size pram, caught in the white glaring light.

'And that's another thing about the suburbs,' Sade said as we sat a little breathless in the stationary car, 'children. I can't relate to children, I can't imagine what possesses people to have them, or once they've had them, I can't imagine what convinces people to keep them.'

Sade looked for the boys in the rear-view mirror but the street was clear. He backed the car around so that we were facing in the right direction again and accelerated, the tyres screeching on the tarmac.

The city skyline came into view in the distance to our left. Soon it started to rain. Huge drops of water splattered the glass and the windscreen wipers groaned, swishing the water away. I couldn't stop chewing my nails. I wanted to run my hand along Sade's thigh but he seemed a long way away in the car and he was staring out the window and humming to himself under his breath. I ran my eyes across the dashboard and over the items on the shelf just above my knees. Among the cassette tapes, folded maps, sunglasses and empty cigarette packets was a black lace bra with a tiny red bow.

Suddenly my mouth was dry and I couldn't get enough air. I felt crushed and squirmed miserably in my seat. The lights changed and we drove off into the rain. Still breathless and writhing, I wound down the window and hung my head out into the cold night. As my head cleared I became outraged. I wanted to grab the bra and throw it out the window. I wanted to scream at Sade and hit him across the face. I wanted to throw myself out of the speeding car, tumble-roll into the wet, sleek gutter and go running off into the night. Instead, I pulled my head in, closed the window and, ignoring the bra, stared at the road, heart pounding in my chest. I watched Sade from the corner of my eye as he wound his window down, wound it up again and switched the demister on. He looked over at me sideways and then back at the road.

'Where would you like to go?' he asked me, his voice so deep, so honeyed, so soft it sounded insincere.

'I don't know,' I said, 'anywhere,' and shrugged my shoulders. I took a few deep breaths, calming down.

'You're a great help,' he said, his voice sarcastic now, and we both laughed.

Still smiling he suddenly pulled the car over to the side of the road and swung into a U-turn, foot to the floor, that had the tyres yowling and me holding onto the edge of my seat. We circled around looking for somewhere to park. Warehouses, dilapidated terrace houses, empty lots surrounded by cyclone fences, cafes, rows of shops, more parking lots, more warehouses, all sped past the steamy glass. Finally a car pulled out and Sade reversed in at top speed. My head hit the back of the seat as Sade slammed his foot on the brakes and it took me a few minutes to recover, sitting in the front seat while Sade stood on the pavement jiggling coins in his pocket, waiting to lock the door.

'I'm sorry,' he said, his voice extra soft, 'did I frighten you?'

I looked over at him and his eyes were round and bright and watching my face and his lips were sadly turned down at the corners.

'I'm OK,' I said, my voice catching in my throat,

9

warmed by the fact that he'd noticed.

Sade's hand clutched at my sleeve but I shrugged him off, still concerned about the bra. Then laughing, I spun around on my heel and threw my head back, the rain splashing into my eyes and my heart singing and singing. He started walking towards me and I went skipping up the street away from him and twirling around on my heel. He followed me, running a little, his shoes slapping on the footpath, and then grabbed me by the wrist and stopped me, pulling me towards him so hard he crushed my hand. He twisted my arm behind my back and held it down against my thigh. I squirmed in his grasp, unable to get away, and giggling said, 'You're hurting me.' He let go a little and kissed me hard.

'I'd never hurt you,' he said, still holding my wrist, squeezing again, 'you know that, don't you?'

I nodded stiffly and refused to look him in the eye, my arm hurting where he held it twisted against my thigh.

'It's only a game,' he said, letting go and laughing. 'I don't know, Friday nights always make me want to rape and pillage.'

I laughed too and turned around to face him. I considered retaliating but I decided not to. I wanted him too much.

'Can I buy you a drink?' he said, smiling. 'I'd love to buy you a drink if you'll let me.'

'Sure,' I said, wiping the rain from my face, 'let's go.'

We walked along the street at arm's length heading towards a group of people assembled on the footpath outside a nightclub.

'Do you know,' Sade said, his voice edgy but cold, his

eyes glaring, 'that as a result of recent law reforms the police are permitted to press charges in cases of domestic violence where they've been called in more than once to settle domestic disputes even if the victim of the violence doesn't want to press charges? The state now has the right to come inside the family home in domestic disputes and actually act on the part of individual members, no matter what they want to do, no matter how they feel about it. In other words, under the new legislation, victims of domestic violence may be delivered from their mutilating husbands only to end up in the hands of the police. And that is not a good thing, believe me. It's outrageous, it's terrifying, it's an absolute disaster.'

I felt a frown crack along my face and nodded in silent complicity. I was furious. I was frightened. I was totally out of control. I really wanted him.

After the nightclub I let Sade drive me home even though we were both a little drunk and he was definitely too drunk to be driving. Sitting in the car outside my building I was just about to ask him about the bra when he kissed me so I invited him upstairs for a coffee.

We plodded arm in arm up the six flights of fire stairs to my flat. I rarely used the lift. I hadn't even managed to lock the front door behind us when Sade grabbed me and started tearing all my clothes off. He kissed me hard and I tasted blood in my mouth. He dragged me to my bed and ripping my underpants in half pushed me down on the bed and fucked me, plunging right in up to the hilt so that it hurt. My head hit the bed-head with each thrust. I didn't come but was very close as he held my hips onto him and thrust in harder than before, moving me up and down on his cock in fast jerks as the warm jets of sperm went shooting up inside.

At some stage between fucks I went to the bathroom. As I bounced from wall to wall down the hallway I noticed blood dripping from my chin onto my hand. I ran my tongue around my lips. There were two cuts, one on the inside and one on the outside and two streams of blood. In my bathroom mirror the cuts didn't look so bad.

Back in bed I lay awake unable to sleep, listening to Sade's light snores. I couldn't stop thinking about him. Finally I fell asleep thinking of his small, square, golden hand. I was the dead leaf precariously balanced in the middle of his open palm.

The next morning Sade woke me up early, his cock between the cheeks of my ass. After he'd finished fucking me we went out for breakfast in a cafe. I was so tired I could barely focus on the newspaper I was trying to read. My head was sinking down towards the top of the table when Sade reached across the clutter of plates and tapped me on the shoulder.

'What?' I said, blinking, my face turning red, my head clouding with pleasure because he wanted my attention.

'I don't want to sleep with you any more,' he said. 'I want us to be friends.'

I had to try not to cry. I had to try not to cry because his face was so serious, so sorry and so calm.

'Why?' I squeaked.

He looked down at a patch of floor, pensive. 'It's hopeless,' he said, finally.

12

'But why?' I said, louder this time, feeling my hands clench into tight fists, the blood rush to my face.

'I don't know,' he said, looking at me, shrugging his shoulders.

Tears ran down each cheek. 'It's not hopeless,' I said. 'That's just an excuse. You don't love me.'

Frowning, he looked down at the floor again. He shook his head.

As I gazed dejectedly through the rest of the newspaper I noticed a story about a woman who had cut off her husband's penis with a large kitchen knife after he'd raped her one night. The crime wasn't premeditated and the woman, having driven straight off in her car, nearly died of fright when she looked down into her lap and noticed what was lying there in a pool of blood. Nearly gagging she picked up her husband's penis and threw it out the window. It was later found by police in a field next to the road. A team of surgeons eventually sewed it back on. I wondered whether or not the woman would go to jail.

Sade dropped me home in his car and kissed me a passionate farewell.

'Will I ever see you again?' I wanted to know.

He shrugged his shoulders and sped off in a cloud of exhaust fumes, leaving the air pungent with burnt rubber.

I spent the day in bed with the blinds drawn. Finally I looked outside and it was dark. I made toast and jam for dinner. I sat down to eat at my round dining table. I held a book in my hand and every so often I nibbled at a corner of the toast. The toast was dry and papery in my mouth and scratched my throat when I swallowed. Tears ran down my cheeks and dripped onto my toast. I concentrated on the page in front of me. I couldn't get past the first sentence. I put the book down on the table. I carried the plate to the kitchen and scraped the toast into the rubbish bin. My wrists were thin and pale.

My lounge room doubled as both study and dining room. The dining table took up one half of the room. My desk and bookcases took up the other half. The dining table had been bright orange when I bought it although I'd painted it black since then. Now the black paint was chipped in a number of places and the bright orange showed through. The paint I painted it with wasn't gloss, it was matt, and every time I wiped it with a cloth the cloth ended up smeared with black. The surface of the dining table was littered with application forms, rent receipts, contraceptives, sunglasses, my wallet, dirty mugs and glasses, half-read books, my diary and address book. The desk was oak but had been painted black when I bought it. I'd started stripping it with paint stripper a few years ago but never got beyond the top of the desk. The wood was unsanded and stained with the residue of cups of coffee and tea. The surface of the desk was littered with drafts of my thesis, piles of books, a stapler, my hairbrush, baskets full of correspondence and bank statements, two dictionaries (one French, one English), two speakers attached to my Sony Walkman and an amplifier I stole from my parents when I first moved out of home, cassette tapes and a pile of exercise books full of notes neatly scrawled down the right-hand page of every opening. The carpet was an indistinct grey and the nylon surface was smooth with dust and grime. The filthy, grey-carpeted floor between the desk and the table was littered with piles of unsorted photocopies and correspondence, old newspapers and neatly folded clothes I no longer wore but wasn't quite ready to throw out. I had two chairs, both small, wooden, painted black, with ill-fitting pillows whose torn stained covers leaked feathers all the time. The bedroom was tiny and square and my queen-sized futon almost filled the entire space. The bedroom and lounge-room windows looked onto bare-limbed trees and the street below. The small modern kitchen and original bathroom provided glimpses of the city skyline. The ceiling in every room but the bathroom was coated with cement rendering. The ceiling in the bathroom was made of moulded plaster. I spent two-thirds of my student's grant on rent.

The phone rang. I ran to answer it, listening for his voice. When it wasn't Sade I hung up. I just didn't have anything to say.

The book I was reading was written by a French libertine marquis during the time of his imprisonment in the Bastille in 1787. In the novel a pair of sisters were first orphaned and then evicted from their home. One became a prostitute and the other begged for mercy from wealthy, corrupt and powerful men. The novel chronicled the adventures of the virtuous sister. She was captured, tortured and abused by a series of interchangeable sadistic aristocrats. As I read I thought about Sade. I hated him. I held my wrists out before me, pale side upwards, and imagined running a bath, opening a packet of razor blades, slicing deeply into the flesh, and passing out in the warm water. Later someone

15

would find me dead in a cold bath stained with my blood. I crawled into bed early and closed my eyes. Soon I was fast asleep.

When I awoke the next morning the phone was ringing. During the night I'd wrapped a feather-down quilt around my head because of the draught that blew in through the gaps between the window frames and the windows. In my arms I held a small foam pillow to my chest. My head lay on a feather pillow I'd bought at a supermarket for ten dollars. The sheets on my bed didn't match each other or the pillow cases and were both stained blue and red from being washed with other clothes. A checked pink, green and brown woollen blanket was draped over the feather quilt. I was wearing a large white T-shirt also stained blue and red, a pair of ripped black cotton briefs and a pair of lime green socks I shoplifted from a department store a few years ago and no longer wore because of the colour.

The phone continued to ring unanswered. I forced my eyes open and staggered into the other room. I picked up the phone. It was cold in the lounge room and I switched the electric bar heater on and sat on the metal top.

'Did I wake you?' Sade wanted to know, his voice tender, sweet.

'Yes,' I said.

'I'm sorry,' he apologised. 'Anyway, how are you?'

'Fine,' I said, carrying the phone into the bedroom and lying back in bed and closing my eyes, 'and you?'

'This place is driving me crazy,' he said and I listened to

him complain about the people he worked with and about not making enough money.

Sade earned four times the amount of money I did on my grant. When he finished complaining I asked him if he'd ever thought about getting a different job.

'What good would that do?' he barked. 'Sure, I could leave *Playboy* and get a job with another magazine, a women's magazine, *Cleo* perhaps, or better still, I could try and land a job in New York along with all the other mugs. You don't seem to understand. No-one could pay me enough money for the work I do. What's more I could work in the company of the greatest minds of the twentieth century and still feel superior. Work is for unadventurous, unimaginative, obsequious fools,' Sade concluded indignantly. Lowering his voice he added, 'Sometimes I wonder about you, Justine, I really do.'

'Oh well,' I said and looked out the window at the street below. The sun shone cold white light through the bare-limbed trees.

'Are you alone?' he asked, his voice quiet, distant.

'Yes,' I said, a little annoyed. 'Who else would be here, Sade?' I asked.

'I don't know,' he answered. 'Can I see you later?'

'Sure,' I said, rearranging the pillows.

'I'll call you,' he told me.

'Fine,' I said, hung up the phone and climbed under the covers once more. I tried to go back to sleep but it was impossible, I was too excited about Sade. I climbed into a cardigan, a pair of jeans and another pair of socks and filled the kettle with cold water and placed it on the electric stove. I washed out a dirty glass and put a tea bag inside. I waited for the water to boil. I was cold and blew onto my hands to get warm. I poured boiling water into the glass. I added a dash of milk and threw the tea bag dripping into a plastic bag hanging on the handle of the kitchen door. I carried the tea to my desk, pulled the heater close and opened one of my notebooks. My mind was totally blank. Somehow the day passed and it was as if I hadn't been there at all.

The next thing I knew it was 8 p.m. and Sade still hadn't called back. I fought off the urge to call him at home because I thought I'd go to pieces if I called and he wasn't there. On an impulse I dialled his number and counted the rings. I counted all the way to twenty before hanging up.

Tears filled the corners of my eyes but I made myself stop. If I started crying I'd probably cry all night and then I wouldn't be able to eat or sleep. I started writing an angry letter instead. It ended with questions which I instinctively knew he'd never answer. When I'd finished I lay down on the carpet and started to cry.

I sat up and wiped the tears from my face. I went into the bathroom and had a cold shower. I sat wrapped in a towel at the desk and read the angry letter. I ripped it into tiny little pieces and threw them into the air like confetti, laughing maniacally. I dressed in black cut-off jeans and a black T-shirt and walked barefoot to the bottle shop and bought a bottle of vodka. I walked back home taking swigs from the bottle. I opened the door with the key and sat on the floor next to the phone and dialled Sade's number again. No answer. I took another swig of vodka. I turned on the TV with the remote control. I drank more vodka. I muted the sound. I dialled Sade's number. I held the bottle to my lips and swallowed. I counted twenty rings and hung up. I stood up, put my hands over my face and screamed, 'You fucken bastard, you fucken bastard, you fucken bastard,' at the top of my voice. I wanted to hurt someone, to get very hurt.

It was late. I couldn't sit up any more, I couldn't follow what was happening on TV, I didn't care. I fell back onto the carpet and laughed as the breath was beaten out of me by the floor. My eyes found the TV although now everything was happening sideways. I started crying again, I started laughing, stopped. I pictured Sade fucking someone else and thought, I don't care. I tried to picture what was happening inside my mind but all I saw was the view from the underside of a carriage on a Ferris wheel, or the sideways view from a roller coaster. Suddenly I felt very sick.

2

SADE LAY FLAT ON HIS BACK ON THE BED, HIS ARMS AND LEGS tied to the wooden frame with silk stockings. I considered holding an iron over his face and ironing his head flat to the sheets. The steamroller effect. I'd hold the iron over his squashed porcelain blue eyes, full mouth and smooth prominent nose and then press it down with all my might. That's for hurting me and fucking me around, I'd say between clenched teeth. I felt marginally better and leaving him there went into the bathroom and ran a steaming hot bubble bath.

The bathroom was the nicest room in my flat. The bath was deep and long enough to lie down in. It was so long that I had to rest my feet on the bottom to stop myself from floating away. It was white and stained blue beneath the taps. It stood on little cast-iron feet. I often read in the bath, hanging the book on a railing just above my head when I wanted to wash my hair. I had a nozzle on a long cord for wetting my hair. There was no shower. The floor was tiled in small oblong dark grey tiles with a deep green and white border. Most of the floor was covered by a bright blue rug with white, red, yellow and green stripes. The wall was tiled white with a dark grey border up to my waist and then painted white. The ceiling was an original ceiling. It was made of moulded plaster and painted white. The fixtures and fittings were all original, including the taps. The toilet was large and made of greying white china. The surface of the cistern was deep enough to double as a shelf for my make-up. The sink was white and stood on a white china stand. The basin was square and deep. The metal coating on the plug-hole had worn away and the grille and hole were an ominous dark brown. The window opened out onto a view of the city skyline. Sitting in the bath, only the single decorative spire of an art deco building was visible. Turning my head in the opposite direction I could see Sade lying in my bed. He was moaning beneath the gag I'd tied over his mouth.

I hung the book I was reading over the rail and slid down beneath the bubbles. I held my nose with one hand and closed my eyes tight. When I surfaced all the bubbles had floated down towards my feet. I swished them with my hands so they covered the entire bath. The water was cold so I let some out through the plug and then added more hot. The steam drew sweat from my scalp which ran in trickles down my brow and the sides of my face. I read some more of my book. I was still reading the book by the French libertine marquis. I was still at the beginning. The virtuous sister was looking for a job. She went to her dead mother's dressmaker who told her to fuck off. When she

21

asked the pastor for help he offered her food and board if she'd fuck him. The virtuous sister fled. The bath was cold again and I was ready to get out. I put the book on the rail and dried myself with a clean towel. I covered myself with moisturiser. I chose some clothes to wear and without a word or glance at Sade, left my flat, and headed off in search of a cup of espresso coffee.

I spent the rest of the afternoon going from cafe to cafe, window shopping, sitting on park benches and watching people walk their dogs—the crap oozing out onto the freshly mown grass in long coils, watching people exercise their children—their high-pitched screams frightening away the birds and making the dogs bark, and, as the day faded into night, I found myself going from bar to bar, asking for the house white by the glass and slowly drinking myself into an absolute stupor.

By the time I returned home I was quite drunk. The first thing I did was rush into the bedroom to check that Sade was still there. The room was empty. Rubbing my bleary eyes I wondered how he had got out without a key when I'd dead-locked him in. I dialled his number. I dialled it incorrectly twice but with my third attempt he picked up the phone on the second ring. We said hello, rather he said, 'Hello,' and I said, 'Hhh'llo,' everything was very friendly. I asked him if he wanted to get together, or at least that's what I thought I said. He said he did and that he'd call me back. I went to the fridge and poured myself another glass of wine. I wasn't sure exactly what was going on. I waited a long time for him to call back, a whole bottle of wine, before I left my flat and took to the streets once more.

22

I buzzed on his flat but there was no answer, so swaying a little and stinking of wine, I checked the number of the building against the number Sade had scrawled on the back of a drink coaster and given me sometime over the last few days. Satisfied, I hung around the entrance to his apartment building waiting for someone to leave or turn up with a key. I didn't have to wait long. I made my way in a long smelly zigzag up the six flights to his floor and down the long carpeted hallway to his front door.

'Sade,' I begged in a little-girl voice, 'please sweetheart, can you hear me?'

I was slurring my words. I was incredibly drunk. Soon I was lying on the carpet outside Sade's great big wooden door. Soon I was writhing in pain. Each thread of carpet seemed to dig into my soft sodden flesh with a stabbing knife-like intensity. I lay twisted and whining like a dog. The door loomed hugely above me. It was made of wood, solid wood. It wasn't a veneer, although it was stained a deep honey brown. It was shiny.

Somehow I knew Sade was inside and that he wouldn't open the door when I knocked. I knocked just the same. He didn't open the door. All I wanted to do was to climb into his bed, I just wanted to be in his bed and I never wanted to leave. It was cold on the sharp carpet and I wanted to have my skinny little head stroked. Tears rolled down either side of my face.

'Sweetheart, it's me, are you there?' I slurred. 'Sweetheart, please let me in. Sweetheart, can you hear me?'

I was crying so much my eyes felt like two swollen holes in the juicy wet flesh of my face. I looked at my fingers and the long thin whiteness of them made the tears come faster. I scratched the wood with my fingernails. Scratched long lines up and down the length of the door. I imagined how great Sade would look with long fingernail scratches dug up and down the sides of his cheeks.

'Sade,' I cried, 'I want to come inside. Open the door. Sweetheart? Can you hear me? Open the door.'

I lay on Sade's doorstep for a long time. My eyes were wet and they wouldn't stop being wet. I didn't know what I'd done to deserve this. I didn't know why I felt like this except that I always ended up feeling and acting like this. Was this really me?

'Just say hello, please Sade, just show me some sign that you know I'm here,' I pleaded between sobs. 'Tell me to go away, tell me you don't love me, tell me I should go and have my head examined, but don't ignore me. I don't know what to do, sweetheart. I'd like to feel free to go home and go to sleep but I can't, something holds me here. Please, pretty please, pretty pretty please with sugar on top and covered in Grand Marnier, please open the door. I'm dying out here.'

I heard footsteps, feet in socks, on the other side of the door. I lay my head flat on the doorstep and looked at the feet. The feet were standing still. I could hear Sade listening on the other side of the door. I watched the green socks for the slightest movement. I stared at the fuzz. Green slime oozed out from holes in the toes and a bit came trickling out under the door. It smelled like a swimming pool and I licked it up.

'It's me,' I wanted to cry, 'it's me.' I wanted to leap up and

24

say, 'It's me, don't you recognise me, don't you remember me
from before? Don't you love me any more? Remember
the other evening kissing on the doorstep while the party
raged inside?' But I didn't. The listening socks thought I was
crazy. The green ooze said, 'Go away from my doorstep you
greasy scum.' The carpet pricked the inside of my head.

I decided to wait just a little bit longer. The socks listened
from the other side.

'Sweetheart,' I cried again, 'will you please let me in? It's
me, I want to come in, can I please come in?'

'Stand back from the door,' Sade said, his voice cold, distant.

I crawled back, dragged myself up into a sitting position,
head lolling and nose dribbling. My head smacked hard
against the wall.

'Let's go for a walk,' he announced.

I didn't answer. This just wasn't what I wanted. I felt sick.
I just hadn't wanted the door to be closed like that. I just
hadn't wanted to be shut out. I just wanted to be able to
come and go anytime I pleased, in and out the door.

I vomited green and orange slime onto the carpet outside
Sade's huge wooden door. I watched him stride away
from me down the corridor, his nose in the air. I dragged
myself to my feet, wiped my face on my sleeve, and followed
him swaying and stumbling down the stairs, through the
vestibule and glass and brass doors and out onto the
chilly night-time street. We walked around the block a
few times but it wasn't any good. I couldn't stop crying and
Sade wasn't saying anything, wasn't comforting me like I
wanted him to. Finally I walked away without a word

and made my way back home, still crying. I unlocked the door to my flat and crept into bed and crying and still stinking of vomit, instantly fell asleep.

When I woke up the phone was ringing. It was Sade. He asked me how I was. I said I was asleep. I carried the phone back to bed and crawled in under the feather quilt.

'So what have you been doing?' he asked, his voice warm and friendly.

'Sleeping,' I said, thinking about the piles of books I'd collected to read for my thesis that lay untouched, pushed to the back of my desk, its wooden surface completely hidden beneath the clutter. 'And you?'

'Me too,' he said.

I turned over to the other side so I could see out the window. The sky was grey and a strong wind dragged at the few remaining brown leaves on the mostly bare-limbed trees.

'How's work?' I said, changing the subject.

He moaned. 'I'm just so tired,' he said.

'Late night?' I asked.

'Not really,' he said. 'I went to bed at around two-thirty. I just can't stand being here, the people, it's just unbearable. My boss wants me to write a feature on women, haemorrhoids and anal sex, you know, the inside story. I've been trying to tell him the whole idea is wrong for *Playboy,* that it's been tried before with little success but he's determined and won't listen to me. He thinks it'll be a big seller and that we may even break into a new readership.'

'Did you go out last night?' I asked, sitting up in bed, the covers sliding off my shoulders.

'Sort of,' he said, his voice quiet and far away. 'After you stormed off, I had a late dinner, a drink or two with a friend from work, and then went to a party and did a few lines.'

'Who'd you go out drinking with?' I wanted to know.

'I don't know,' he said.

'What do you mean, you don't know?' I said, indignant.

'I mean I don't have to tell you,' he said, smug.

'Why not?' I pressed on.

'Because it's none of your business, that's why,' he quipped, and hung up the phone.

I left the phone off the hook and walked around my apartment in circles saying, 'Fuck you, Sade,' over and over again. I stood still and thumped my thighs with clenched fists and shouted, 'You're such a creep,' at the walls. Then I started crying again. 'Why don't you love me?' I sobbed, snot running out my nose onto the carpet. 'Why don't you want to be with me?' I lay down on the bed and shrieked into the pillow. I sounded like I was being stabbed to death. I shrieked over and over again and then cried some more. The pillow was wet. I pulled at my hair, tearing out whole handfuls and screamed into the dark room. I fell down on the bed. Then I sat up on my knees and hit my head against the wall. 'I don't want any more, I don't want any more,' I moaned.

After a while I lay still and quiet, watching shadows flicker on the painted walls.

I had a shower, threw my clothes from last night into the dirty washing basket and picked up the phone and dialled

Sade's number. I apologised. He said that was OK. His voice was warm and soft. He asked me if I had any plans for the evening and I told him I didn't. He said he might be working but he'd call me later.

I hung up the phone and crawled back into bed. I couldn't get back to sleep, however, and kept wondering who Sade had been out with the night before. I pottered around my flat all day, reading the paper here, looking through my notes there, but deep down I was really just waiting for Sade to call. By late afternoon I'd opened a bottle of wine and was sitting watching TV with the sound turned down and reading the book by the libertine Marquis at the same time. This time I read about the other sister, the one who surrendered herself to vice, the one who delighted in crime and who became one of the most wealthy and powerful women of her time. The first thing she did as an orphan was check herself into the local whorehouse and then familiarise herself with all the trappings of her new trade. But humble whore was not enough for such a zealous and ambitious devotee, and in no time at all she became first a courtesan, and later the wife of a respectable and wealthy member of the French nobility. She murdered him and inherited all his money before moving on to her next husband, and then on to her next, each marriage having a similar outcome, and a similar financial reward. I put the book on the floor and crawled into bed, too drunk to read or watch TV.

By eight o'clock I couldn't wait any longer and I dialled Sade's number. He sounded happy to hear from me and suggested we go out to dinner. He picked me up in

28

his car and I immediately looked for the bra on the shelf but it was gone and I was relieved. We drove at breakneck speed to a bistro where we ate too much food and drank too much wine. I couldn't stop smiling at Sade or leaning across the table to kiss him on the cheeks and lips.

After dinner he drove me home in his car. We drove through red lights and over median strips and skidded to a halt outside my flat. We sat in his car and kissed. I watched Sade's face. He saw me watching him and stopped kissing me. We stared out our windows. I looked up and down the street not really seeing anything. It didn't look like Sade wanted to come upstairs.

'Is there someone else?' I asked, waiting for him to turn around.

He shook his head and kept staring out the window.

'Do you want to come up for a cup of tea?' I said, almost believing him.

He nodded for an answer and we climbed the fire stairs to my flat. Once inside we stripped off our clothes and fucked on the lounge-room floor among all my papers and books, both of us moaning and grabbing handfuls of each other's flesh. Then Sade fucked me up the ass and I came, his fingers in my cunt, his sperm spraying into my intestines. Later, he lay next to me in bed snoring lightly and I lay awake beside him watching his shoulders rise and fall, watching his hair curl around his neck, listening to the air rattle down his throat and come wheezing out through his nose. I moved closer across the bed until my breasts touched his back and the mound of my cunt pressed against his ass. I kissed the back of his neck. I knew he didn't love me. I wished I didn't love him. I reached my hand around him and pressed my palm flat against his chest. I thought about leaving him. Soon the sound of his soft wheezy snores sent me to sleep.

When I opened my eyes Sade was gone. I spent the following day in bed waiting for him to call. I didn't get up until a little after six. It looked like Sade didn't want to see me any more again. At seven I finally called him at work and he said he was sorry for not calling me all day but that he'd been busy, that he was working late and that he'd call me later. I didn't believe him. I was furious. I went out and bought a newspaper at the shop across the road. I read an update on the woman who'd cut off her husband's penis. She'd been acquitted. I jumped up in the air and screamed hooray. I played loud music on my stereo. I danced around my lounge room laughing. I collapsed on the floor sweaty and smiling, the music still pounding out through the open windows and onto the crowded street below.

The euphoria took a long time to wear off. By the time I was angry with Sade again I had a plan. My hands trembled and my stomach had butterflies. I had the whole scheme worked out in my head. I reminded myself, gesturing theatrically in the otherwise empty and now quiet room, that I had a mission to accomplish and on no account was I permitted to contact or communicate with my quarry. I had become a spy. I was going to find out if Sade had been lying to me once and for all.

I made myself one final cup of tea and drank it from a tall heavy glass, pacing restlessly around my lounge room. I checked that I had the right change. I counted out into the palm of my hand the exact money for a pot of tea, change for a telephone call, and a wad of notes for cab fares. I emptied the glass, took the phone off the hook and left.

I sat at the window table in the cafe across the road from his apartment block. From where I was sitting I had a clear view of everybody as they came and went through the swinging, brass-handled, glass double doors.

I ordered a pot of tea and opened a magazine. I found my eyes glazing over and my mind wandering. I tried to remember some happy times, times untainted by cruelty or complaint. I couldn't.

I sipped my tea, sighed, looked around at the other customers, watched the waiter clear tables and then turned back to the window just in time to watch Sade go in through the wide brass-handled door, his worn rust-coloured briefcase tucked under his arm. I finished my tea, placed the exact change on the table and left.

I walked past his apartment block on the other side of the road and watched the lights come on inside his apartment. I found Sade's car. It was parked in a side street. I walked back to the main road and stood in a doorway smoking a cigarette.

The lines that ran between Sade's apartment, his car and the doorway where I was standing formed a triangle. By leaning forward I could see Sade's apartment further down the road with little chance of him being able to see me. This was one line. Another line ran between me and the car. Anyone standing at the car could see me but it was unlikely that they would be looking this way. This was another line. The line that ran between Sade's apartment block and the parked car was another line. This was the longest line. Anyone who walked along this line, anyone walking from the car to Sade's apartment block could see me standing over here in the doorway. That is, they could see me provided they had a reason for looking over. It was a risk I chose to take. I checked the time, slid my hands in my pockets and waited. It grew dark. I smoked more cigarettes.

An hour later Sade bought a packet of cigarettes at the milk bar on the other side of the road and then walked down the main road across from me and turned into the side street where his car was parked. He didn't look over. I'd gambled and won. I waited for him to get inside before hailing a cab. I was almost laughing when I told the driver to follow that car. The driver laughed for me and we sped off. It soon became clear that Sade was going into work like he said he was going to do. I should have been relieved but I was not.

I handed over the money to the driver and walked around the building, looking for Sade's window. I smoked more cigarettes. I walked back around to the front of the building. I tried the door but it was locked and I knew I wouldn't get in unless I rang for security or followed someone in who had an electronic card. I was getting scared again although I didn't know why, so I lit another cigarette. The match blew out in the wind and I was still trying to light the cigarette when someone walked up right beside me and scared me half to death.

'Pardon,' she said in a heavy French accent. She held out

a lighter and asked me if I spoke French which I didn't and she frowned and pulled her mouth down at the corners. 'Ah, well,' she said and took a cigarette from my packet when I offered it to her.

I asked her if she was waiting to meet someone and she nodded and handed me a drink coaster from a bar I went to sometimes. On the back of the card was Sade's name and phone number and the address of the building. She was watching my face intently and so I kept my feelings to myself.

'Here,' she said and pointed to the ground with her hand.

'Yes, here,' I said, nodding stupidly.

We dragged on our cigarettes.

'You too?' she asked ambiguously.

'Me too,' I said.

I looked at her in brief glances and meanwhile I was keeping an eye on the doors to the lift inside the building just in case Sade appeared for his little rendezvous. Her hair was jet black and tight curls fought against the hard line of a short bob. Her eyes were dark and the whites incredibly bloodshot. Her jeans were tight and her breasts pointed beneath a loose white shirt. She was wearing deep cherry lipstick and too much mascara.

In the meantime someone had opened the doors with an electronic card and so I asked them if it was OK for me and the French girl to come in too. Inside I left the French girl standing in front of the directory, and went in search of a women's toilet.

I sat on a toilet with the lid down, smoked a cigarette and

tried to work out my next move. It never occurred to me that my suspicions were true, that there really could be someone else in Sade's life. My initial plan had been to see what Sade got up to when he said he went to work but I never expected it would be something like this, a secret rendezvous with a mysterious French woman. But was he fucking her? I was determined to find out but I had to think of a way of doing so without letting him know. I thought of phoning Sade and hanging up once he'd answered the phone, imagining I could tell what he was up to from the way he said hello, but I realised that he would probably guess it was me ringing and not answer the phone. This was the best way to find out if they were fucking, but it meant Sade knowing I was checking up on him, which was the last thing I wanted to do.

I dropped the cigarette with a hiss into the bowl and walked back outside. I circled the building once more, looking for a lit window. Not finding one, I walked back to the front of the building, my heart pounding against my chest. I told myself to calm down. I couldn't. I ran the few blocks to where I'd seen Sade park his car just a few minutes ago but his car was gone. I crossed the street to a public phone booth and called Sade's number at work. There was no answer.

I felt like crying, giving up, and getting drunk, and struggled not to come undone while the phone continued to ring unanswered in Sade's office.

On an impulse I thought of checking the bar from the drink coaster on the way back to Sade's place, and climbed into another cab. Halfway there I changed my mind and directed the driver straight to Sade's. The lights were on inside his apartment but the car wasn't there. I was starting to feel a little crazy and desperately wanted to go and get drunk but I didn't want to fuck up my chances of finding out what Sade was doing without him knowing. I paid the driver and stood in an unlit doorway across from Sade's apartment. I smoked more cigarettes and finished the packet. I bought another packet and returned to the doorway. I tried to think clearly and go over everything that had happened so far in my mind. My original plan had been to follow Sade to work, stay for the duration, follow him from destination to destination and ultimately home. If Sade hadn't gone to work I had intended to follow him to the first destination only and then return to the cafe where I'd wait for him to arrive home. I decided to stick as much to my original plan as was possible.

I returned to the cafe and ordered a pot of tea. Four pots of tea and another packet of cigarettes later and it was closing time and Sade still hadn't arrived home. I had a headache from all the tea and the cigarettes. One of the waiters called out to ask if I wanted a lift somewhere and I shook my head.

I stood in a public phone booth across the street from Sade's building and pretended to be having a conversation with someone. In the meantime I kept track of people going in and out through the security door. After half an hour or so I saw a woman in a long black coat come striding down the corridor towards the security door. I hung up the phone, dashed across the road and by the time she opened the door I was standing at the buzzer and I said, 'Hi, it's me,' as if someone was just letting me in and walked through the door just as she was leaving. We nodded hello and the huge brass-handled door slammed shut behind me.

I used the fire escape instead of the lift or the main stairs and ran up the six flights to Sade's floor. I was so puffed I had to lean against the door and catch my breath. Everything inside me seemed to be about to explode, blood pounded in my ears, coloured lights flashed before my eyes. I heard the lift door slam and jumped a mile which brought me back to the immediate present. I began to calm down. Then, holding my breath, I opened the door to the fire escape and made my way down the long corridor to Sade's apartment on tiptoe. A floorboard creaked beneath the carpet and I froze, but then nothing happened so I kept going. It flashed across my mind that I'd finally gone totally crazy, that my obsessive personality was finally absolutely out of control. I was seventeen again, walking into the shrink's office and sitting down in the huge leather armchair. The shrink looked me in the eye and said, 'Well,' and I started babbling and telling him all about my ridiculous behaviour. I left the office laughing and then went into a large department store and shoplifted an angora jumper. I did this over and over again.

I was standing outside Sade's door and I pressed my ear against the wood panelling. The TV was on quite loud. I heard no voices or movements. Nobody was home.

I looked at my watch. It was 2.30 a.m. I decided to go home. All of a sudden I was desperately tired and had to catch a cab the few blocks home. I crawled into my dark empty bed and fell asleep. The next thing I knew it was six o'clock and I was awake, absolutely wide awake. I checked the time. It was early, it was earlier than I normally woke up, much earlier than I'd ever been awake before. I was sitting at the table and shivering as cold bolts of sensation coursed down through my body. It was 6.45. I'd been asleep for three, maybe four hours. I climbed back into the same clothes and hurried out the door.

His car was parked just outside the apartment block, way out from the kerb and at an odd angle. I went back to the public telephone and stood there pretending to have a conversation, again waiting for someone to open the security door. I walked up the fire escape but this time I was dead calm. I stood outside the door, ear pressed to the wooden panelling. I heard voices inside. I retraced my steps and went back to the public telephone. Should I call, or should I buzz on the door? I decided a phone call would be less confronting.

'Hello,' he said, picking up after three rings.

'Hi Sade,' I said, 'it's me.'

'Oh hello,' he said, uninterested.

'How are you?' I said, smiling.

'Fine, and you?' he replied mechanically.

'Fine,' I said, cold.

'What can I do for you?' he wanted to know, business-like.

'Good question,' I said, dead-pan.

'Actually, I'm just about to run out the door,' he said, his head away from the phone.

'What are you doing?' I demanded.

'I'm just about to go out and grab some breakfast,' he announced.

'I was just about to propose that we have breakfast together,' I suggested.

'I'm going now,' he told me.

'That's all right, I'm ready,' I told him.

'You're up early,' he said, provoking me.

'I had an early night,' I said, weary.

'Good for you. Look, I'll just ask Juliette,' he said, triumphant.

'You'll just ask Juliette?' I asked, my heart sinking.

'Dr Lorsange is my therapist and she's been helping me with the story I'm writing about the psychological aspects of haemorrhoids for *Playboy* and we were at it until late last night so she decided to spend the night here because I was too tired to drive her home,' he said, enjoying himself.

'Ah, Juliette Lorsange,' I said, trying not to sound too freaked out.

'Hang on,' he said, almost laughing.

'Sure,' I said, assuming Juliette was the Frenchwoman I met last night outside Sade's office. I couldn't quite hear what they were saying. She laughed.

'Hello,' he boomed.

'Yes,' I answered tentatively.

'Juliette doesn't think she'll come so I'll pick you up in, say, fifteen minutes,' he said, his manner brisk and efficient.

'Tell Juliette I'd love to meet her and convince her to come,' I pleaded with him.

'She doesn't want to,' he said firmly, 'she wants to go home and get changed.'

'Well maybe I'm the one who should have breakfast at home,' I said, my head pounding, 'I don't want to intrude.'

'No, you're not intruding,' he explained, 'Juliette has to get to work.'

'OK, then, breakfast,' I agreed. 'I'll meet you at your place.'

'Don't bother, sweetheart,' he told me, 'I'll come and get you.'

'No, it's no trouble,' I said. 'I'm calling from across the road anyway.'

Silence from Sade.

'Hello?' I asked, smirking.

'Yes,' he answered, 'I'm still here.'

'So I'll meet you outside your place,' I said, my head spinning, panicking that there might be a back entrance to the building.

'Sure,' he said bitterly, 'whatever.'

There was a bench across the road from Sade's apartment building and after I hung up I sat on it. I crossed my legs and drew my coat around me in the chilly morning air. I watched them walk towards me. Sade talking, smiling and gesturing with his hands, Juliette wrapped in a full-length overcoat, her long blonde hair in a wispy French plait and puffing on a cigarette. Every so often Sade looked up, a quick furtive glance, and not seeing me looked away. I smiled out of the side of my face—Sade hadn't been fucking the French woman all night, he'd been hard at work with

Juliette—and was about to laugh out loud when suddenly I felt my breath go shooting out of me as Sade grabbed hold of Juliette's long blonde plait and pulled her towards him, kissing her hard on the lips on the other side of the closed glass door. He held the door open for her and she hurried off, not looking at me and disappearing inside a cab. Sade watched the cab drive away and then looked around for me. Seeing me his face paled.

'So, breakfast,' I called across the traffic.

He shrugged, weaving his way between the cars. He sat down beside me. We watched each other for telltale signs. I saw Sade look at my breasts.

'Of course,' I said, 'we could always stop off at my place first for a cup of tea?'

I didn't even manage to lock the door behind us before we were fucking standing up, clothes around our ankles, me pressed up against the wall. We crawled into my bed and dozed off before fucking again. Soon it was twelve and we still hadn't had so much as a cup of tea. I wanted him to stay, I wanted to be with him for a long time but then I realised I'd never experienced what a long time was like and I wasn't sure I really cared enough to find out. I gathered his smooth ass and held it cupped in my hand.

Finally Sade took me out and bought me lunch at around three. Then he dropped me home and went to work. Dazed, I was still smiling as I rode up in the lift. But by the time the doors opened at my floor I felt tense and irritable. The sound of the door slamming closed behind me couldn't have been more final had it been the door of a prison cell. I looked at my life and hated it, hated everything and immediately burst into tears. I felt totally ripped apart. Somewhere in the back of my mind I sensed people lived differently, lived without feeling like this, but it had been so long since I'd felt other than ripped apart I couldn't be sure there was anything else any more. I looked down at my feet and watched a familiar deep jagged-edged chasm of blood go tearing through the grimy grey carpet of my lounge room. I knew from experience that it was impossible to suture it back together.

3

I was sitting in a bar smoking cigarettes and drinking scotch. I was buying glass after glass and gulping them down. It was a lot of fun. I looked at my watch. It was 8.30. I was waiting to meet the professor from the French department who was co-supervising my thesis and he was late and I decided that I'd have one more scotch and then leave. I wasn't sure why I was meeting him. It was just one of those things. I'd wanted to fuck him at some point, or at least I think I did, and now I was sitting in the university bar slouched in a low deep lime-green vinyl chair, my feet resting on a round pine-veneered sticky smeared coffee table drinking the house scotch straight up with two cubes of ice to a glass. I shuffled up to the bar and ordered another drink from the barman. He was totally fuckable with his long dark brown curly hair tied back in a short thick ponytail, revealing a deep widow's peak. His eyes were deep set, deep blue and hugely round. His lips were full and pouting. His nose and the round curves of his cheeks were lightly dusted with rust-coloured freckles. Each time he smiled he blushed. He was definitely fuck material, if a little too feminine for my taste, and I was definitely still thinking about fucking him when, drink in hand, I swivelled around unsteadily on my heel, slopping scotch onto the brilliant vermilion and purple swirls of carpet, and came face to face with Bataille, who was smiling a crooked smile and slouched deep into his pockets. I stopped dead in my tracks. He said, 'Hello Justine,' and I nodded hello and then sat down in the lime-green chair again while he bought himself a drink.

He placed his glass down on the coffee table and dragged a purple vinyl chair over from an adjacent table so our chairs were side by side. He sat down with a loud plop onto the low deep seat, sipped at his drink and eyed me over the top of his glass. Placing the glass down on the table again he smiled. He removed his glasses, leaving them on the table, and held his face in the palms of his hands. He sighed, dropping his hands onto his lap. I waited for him to say something but he didn't and I found myself staring at his face. He had dark brown eyes which looked large without his round gold-rimmed glasses. His eyes were very wet and soft and he looked like he might be about to burst into tears at any second. At the same time they seemed to smile at me and his full lips were drawn into a wide smile. His nose was long, thin and curved. Sharply flared nostrils stood out at either side at the tip. His face was long and his cheeks and chin were covered in thin bloody lines, some still wet with blood, others had turned into dry dark scabs. I counted the exposed strips of flesh on the

43

side of his face nearest to me and there were seventeen cuts of varying lengths running up and down his pale white skin. They looked like they were made by a razor and I was just about to recommend a really nice moisturiser I used to shave my legs when he reached over and ran his hand along my thigh. He picked up his glass again, still smiling and took another sip of his drink. It looked like he was drinking vodka with grapefruit juice although I couldn't really be sure. He was wearing a baggy black T-shirt with black jeans and black boots. I looked down at his arm. His skin was very pale and his arm was covered in fine black hair. The skin from the back of his hand all the way up to his elbow was covered in a rhizomatic network of thin red scratches. They looked like they were cat scratches and I was just about to ask him about them when he lifted his hand to touch his face, bent all but his forefinger into a fist, and picked his nose. He rolled the snot into a ball and flicked it onto the floor. I finished my scotch and stared down at the carpet roughly at the spot where the snot landed as if I hoped to see it against the swirling technicolour backdrop.

'Let's get out of this cesspit,' he said, suddenly leaning over to kiss me on the lips and probing my mouth with his warm tongue.

I felt hot cunt juice flood my black lace body suit, fill the cotton lining, spill out the sides and go trickling down the insides of my thighs. I followed him outside. During the walk to his car I discovered that Bataille also knew Leopold, a fellow student I had allowed to rape and assault me most of last year. At his car I watched him fumble with the keys to the car door.

'This is my wife's car,' he explained, turning red, emptying his pockets. 'She's the most fantastic person, you know. She earns more money than me, she has a higher degree from the Sorbonne, she speaks five different languages, she's a marathon swimmer and she's an excellent cook.'

I watched him remove a dirty handkerchief, a black leather wallet, a handful of change and a huge ring of keys from his jeans pocket.

'Damn,' he said, returning them to his pocket, 'I can't find my car keys.' He started on the other pocket. 'What was I talking about?' he asked.

'Your wife,' I reminded him.

'My wife,' he continued. 'Yes. Not only is she fantastically intelligent and fabulously successful at what she does but she also has the most amazing body, great legs, tight little ass, huge tits with dark nipples that get incredibly hard. I've slept with a lot of women in my time you understand, I've had a lot of lovers, I've had every sort of kinky sexual experience there possibly is to have, but no-one else has ever come close to my wife. She's the fuck of a lifetime.'

I watched him empty a black notebook, two pens, a pair of sunglasses, and a watch from his other pocket. Finally, digging deeper, he pulled out a set of keys attached to a miniature Eiffel Tower.

'The most incredible thing about her, though, is that she adores me,' he went on in a lecturing tone, fitting the key in the door, 'she really cares about me, and she hasn't got a jealous bone in her body. She knows everything about me and she doesn't mind. I think she actually gets turned on by

45

the fact that I fuck around. She told me once she masturbated to an image of me fucking one of my honours
students. She's cool, she's really totally cool.'

He opened my door from the inside and I climbed in.

'Does she have a name?' I asked, thinking that Bataille
was probably making it all up.

'You don't want to know her name,' he said, starting up
the motor. 'It'll only give you something to become fix-
ated on. You'll become obsessively jealous and start
giving me a hard time, I know, I've seen what happens to
girls like you before. You go to pieces under the pressure.
You just can't compete with her, she's too good.'

We took off into the dark university grounds without
any lights. I had to remind Bataille to switch them on and even
then he had to pull over to the side of the road and go over
the steering column with a tiny torch which he kept on the top
of the dashboard. Then when he still couldn't find the indi-
cator I reached across the car, pushing him aside, and
turned the lights on myself. I was covered in sweat by the time
we started out again. We reached the gates and he drove
straight into the traffic without stopping at the stop sign.

'Hey,' I said, grabbing his arm, 'you were supposed to
stop.'

He slammed his foot on the brakes and we skidded to a
standstill. The car behind us blasted its horn.

'Damn,' he said, turning the key in the ignition and
switching off the lights. 'This never would have happened if
my wife was here. I can't drive without my glasses.'

'Well, put them on,' I said, trying to sound helpful but
starting to become impatient.

'I can't,' he whined, 'I left them on the coffee table in the bar.'

'Well, let's go back and get them,' I said.

'But we can't go back because I can't drive without my glasses, it says so on my licence,' he said helplessly.

'OK, then I'll drive,' I said.

'You can't drive,' he said, 'the insurance, the car, it's all registered in my wife's name. If anything happened and she found out I wasn't driving the car there'd be hell to pay.'

'I thought she was cool about your infidelities,' I said sarcastically.

'It's one thing for me to fuck around but it's another thing if another woman drives her car,' he explained. 'She would feel humiliated, she would feel that I'd replaced her. She drives me everywhere you know, she's the most fantastic driver, and I only borrowed the car so I could drive you around. Don't you see,' he said, raising his voice, 'she doesn't mind so long as I drive, but if you drive, well she'd go out of her mind.'

He seemed so innocent and helpless I couldn't help leaning over and kissing him. His lips didn't kiss me back but his breath quickened and he swallowed loudly. He was bleeding from one of the cuts on his face and I licked the blood from his chin. He started to whine.

'OK,' I said, leaning back. 'Let's go.'

Still whining he nodded and climbed out of the car. He left it to me to lock the doors and waited on the footpath.

'It's going to get towed,' he moaned, 'it's going to get towed and she's going to kill me.'

'It's not going to get towed,' I reassured him. 'See this

note I've pinned beneath the windscreen wiper? Well, it explains everything and you're not going to get towed, OK?'

I wiped my hands on my jeans and took his hand, the cat-scratched hand, in mine. With my other hand I hailed a cab. I directed the driver to the bar where Bataille ran in for his glasses. Then I asked him where he wanted to go but he just whined at me so I told the driver to drive around the block a few times. I held his limp hand in mine. He lay his head down in my lap and sulked.

'What's wrong?' I said, feeling like his mother.

'I want to go home now,' he said and closed his eyes.

I gave the driver Bataille's home address. Bataille smiled beatifically and moaning, drew my hand down and pressed it to his groin. Beneath the thick denim I felt his cock, bent in half but hard. I lay down beside him and unzipped his fly. His cock hard in my mouth, his hands pressed the back of my head urging me to draw him deeper and deeper down the back of my throat. We pulled up in front of a row of elegant terrace houses and the driver demanded payment for the fare. I watched Bataille fumble through his jeans pockets for the money and then paid the driver myself. Soon we stood on the pavement outside Bataille's house, his fly still undone and his huge throbbing purple-veined hard-on sticking straight out.

'Would you like to come inside for another drink?' he said, his eyebrows provocatively cocked.

For an answer I took his hand and slid it inside my jeans and used the tips of his fingers to probe beneath my body suit. My cunt squelched around his fingers and thumb, the surface slippery as stewed peaches, the consistency as flexible and toned as a piece of tender juicy raw fillet steak.

I followed him beneath the chandeliers and down a long dark winding carpeted hallway to a huge bedroom with an en suite.

We undressed in the middle of the room, just letting our clothes fall off our bodies onto the floor where we stood. A pungent, vaguely chemical odour emanated from his groin and wafted around, driving me crazy with desire. I waited for him to make the first move, his cock huge and standing straight up, and my cunt lips hanging loose and wet and the walls inside already squeezed hard together. Suddenly he lunged at me and speared me on the end of his tool. I gasped as he slid in all the way up to the hilt.

It took three thrusts and I was just about to come when a wide-hipped, hard-faced, middle-aged woman who would have been handsome if she'd been a man, appeared in the doorway and said hello.

'This is Justine,' he said, pausing between thrusts. 'I'm just helping her make a few finishing touches to her honours thesis.'

'Nice to meet you, Justine,' she said, frowning and not quite looking me in the eye. 'I just wondered,' she went on, looking at Bataille again, 'whether you wanted chicken or fish for dinner?'

'Fish,' he said, and I felt his cock twitch inside me and was unable to repress a high squeaky moan as my cunt gratefully squeezed back.

49

I listened to her heavy footfalls as they faded down the long corridor. The floor was still rumbling when Bataille thrust inside me again.

'That's my wife,' he said as he sucked my nipple red and hard, 'isn't she fantastic?'

He drew the rest of my tit inside his mouth and chewed on it like it was a piece of meat.

'Fuck, fuck, fuck,' I shouted and came.

He stopped thrusting for a few seconds and slid out of me so I could recover. Then I grabbed his balls in my hand and squeezed them hard. Lots and lots of white lumpy come spurted up onto my stomach.

Bataille collapsed on the bed and I dressed and started to leave.

'Give me a call when you're ready for me to look over your thesis again,' he called after me.

On the street once more I hailed a cab and sat in the back seat, my cunt throbbing, delightfully sloppy on the smooth vinyl seat. I was smiling. As we inched through the peak-hour traffic I understood I'd graduated my honours year before the fact and passed with flying colours.

When I got home the phone was ringing. I ran to pick it up but when I did there was no-one there. I rang Sade's number but he wasn't at home or at work. No doubt he was busy fucking Juliette. I took the phone off the hook and picked up the book by the libertine French Marquis. The virtuous sister was recounting her final tortures. It was the eve of her execution. Her cunt and ass were sewn shut by the judge and then she was fucked through the stitching until the bonds either broke or were torn from her flesh. The libertine eventually came deep inside her bleeding asshole. The next day the virtuous sister was saved from the guillotine only to die when a bolt of lightning struck her through the heart. Asleep, I let the book slip from my grasp as my head fell back onto the cool soft pillow.

I spent the following morning ringing Sade's number every half hour. I felt utterly crazed. I lay down on the floor listening to Eric B. turned up loud, dialling Sade's number, waiting for Sade to ring. I considered going back to the bar for the barman and dragging him off to some secluded spot and fucking him brainless, no exchange of phone numbers, no complications, but I wanted to save all my cab fares for Sade.

Bored, I started reading a new book. I picked up a biography about the French Marquis. I read how he allegedly abused a widowed pastry-maker and poisoned a group of prostitutes during an orgy at a brothel in Marseilles. The pastry-maker accused the Marquis of offering her a job as a domestic to lure her to his home. Once there, he bound, raped and beat her, and then made incisions into her thighs and buttocks into which he poured melted wax. The prostitutes claimed that he distributed an aphrodisiac called Spanish fly amongst them and then attempted to sodomise them.

Towards evening I looked up Juliette's home number in the phone book. I circled the seven digits with a pen and then tried Sade's number once more. There was no answer at Sade's, so I rang Juliette. Her answer machine left another phone number and explained that she'd flown interstate on business this morning. That didn't help me find

Sade. I looked up the phone numbers for the airlines and asked the agents to check every flight that morning to every major city for a reservation under Sade's name. Every so often I'd encounter an agent who refused to help me because I was asking them to risk their job by infringing the privacy act. I explained that it was an emergency and quickly invented a story. Even so, some agents still refused to give out the information so I hung up and then kept calling back until I got onto an agent who would help me and then I started again. There was no record or flight reservation under Sade's name.

It was growing dark outside. I dialled Sade's number and let the phone ring until it stopped. I hadn't eaten anything all day. If Sade wasn't with Juliette and he wasn't at home or at work, then where was he? Exhausted, I lay down on the carpet and cried until I stopped. Then I took two Normison and went to bed. I was almost asleep when the phone rang. I ran to answer it but when I picked it up there wasn't anyone there. Puzzled, I slowly placed the phone back on the hook.

I went back to bed and started reading the biography but the words swam all over the pages and I couldn't follow what was going on. I stared at the painted cream wall. I hated Sade. Then I climbed out of bed, dressed, and walked the few blocks to his apartment building. I sat on the bench across the road waiting for him to come home. The big hand on my watch-face crept towards twelve. I was out of my mind. I walked around the block smoking cigarettes, hearing the rattle of Sade's gear change in every car that passed. I bought more cigarettes. Back at Sade's I noticed that the light had come on in his kitchen.

I rang his bell and he let me in and then stumbled immediately into bed. I undressed and joined him. His breath stank of alcohol. He pushed my head down on his cock which was hard and told me to suck it. I held his cock firmly at the base with one hand and cradled and squeezed his balls with the other. I ran my tongue over the surface of his cock. It was rough. I pulled his cock out of my mouth with my hand and stared at it hard. It was covered in what felt like dried cunt juice. I sniffed his groin for hints of something foreign. Would he let me suck his cock if it had been inside someone else just hours before? I didn't want to suck his cock but he grabbed my shoulders, forced my face against his groin and commanded me to suck it again. I resisted him, tensing up my shoulders and holding my body rigid and he told me to go fuck myself in a low voice and stormed out of the bedroom. I lay writhing and abandoned in Sade's bed with a thousand images of Sade fucking Juliette running through my mind. I took a handful of Sade's sheet and stuffed it inside my mouth.

Sade stood in the doorway watching me and laughing. He sat down on the edge of the bed and offered me a handful of round white pills. I stared at them, not understanding. He said I could have a pill or else I could snort some in powder form if I preferred. The stench of alcohol on his breath was now mixed with vomit and I wondered if Sade had just been sick in the bathroom. Before I could decide he wrenched open my jaw and forced me to swallow two of the pills. He gulped down the remaining pills and then looked around for something to wash them down. There was a bottle of mineral water on the bed-head and he grabbed it, unscrewed the lid and drank noisily, water spilling out over his lips and running down his chin, dripping in even plops onto the bed. He offered me the bottle and I took a sip and handed it back to him. He finished the water, belched, and then held the bottle in his hands, slapping it onto his knees like a baseball bat and grinned at me idiotically. He threw the empty bottle onto the bed so that it landed inches from my head. Soon after he left the room.

The drug started to take effect and I started to ache between my legs so I grabbed a pillow and rammed it up there, pushing the cotton-covered feathers inside my wide open wet throbbing cunt. My cunt continued to ache despite the pillow and I looked around for something harder, for something more satisfying. I picked up the empty bottle and rammed it neck first up my cunt and that felt a little better. I started whimpering and lay writhing on the bed, on the verge of an orgasm, but unable to bring myself to a climax. When I next looked up Sade was sitting next to me on the bed, saliva dripping from the corners of his mouth. He stood up abruptly and started pacing around the room. He looked at me, shaking his head and smiling horribly. Suddenly he reached down and grabbed the bottle from my cunt. He continued pacing around the room and slapped the empty bottle hard against his hand.

'You're all the same,' he muttered while I struggled to catch his words. 'You're just after one thing and one thing only.'

He stood still just behind me. I craned my neck to see what he was doing. Suddenly he whacked the bottle against the wall and it broke clean in two. Then he leapt up onto the bed and waved the bottle, broken edge first, in front of my cunt.

'Do you still want it?' he demanded, while I screamed and wriggled away from him along the wall. He grabbed my ankle with his free hand and pressed it down onto the bed. Unable to get away I lay still, holding my breath.

'Oh fuck it,' he complained, tossing the broken halves of the bottle into his laundry basket. His face cracked into a wide dazzling smile.

Then he took hold of my other ankle and pulled me along the bed towards him. Next he pinned my shoulders to the bed and thrust his cock in my face. He told me to suck it. I opened my mouth and sucked greedily at the swollen head of his cock. In spite of everything I was going to have to fuck him. I couldn't help myself. I just had to get him inside me. And I had to do it soon.

It didn't take long for us to come, we were both on the verge by the time he was inside me. He wasn't wearing a condom and he didn't pull out when he came. I realised I'd risked getting pregnant again but didn't want to think about it now. I hadn't wanted to think about it for a long time. All I wanted was for Sade to scream at me, hit me, throw me out on the street and then fuck me again, the tears still damp on my face. We spent the rest of the night fucking. As I was leaving the next morning he handed me a novel and told me to read it. It was written by an American and it had received a lot of coverage in the press at the time of its publication due to the provocative nature of the story. Apparently the novel depicts a man raping, torturing and brutally murdering dozens of men and women but mostly women. I thanked him and walked home in a daze.

I went to bed and spent an uneasy four hours in a sweaty sleepless state. It wasn't until I sat down at my desk, the biography open before me, that I remembered about Sade's cock the night before. Who had he been fucking? I asked myself. I went back to the biography of the Marquis. The author was making a point about how wilful misreadings of the Marquis' life and work by contemporary writers and theorists have transformed him from a figure of horror into a figure of admiration. I didn't know what I thought of the Marquis myself. His writing horrified, entertained and fascinated me at the same time. I had even felt like I'd gained some insight into myself as a result of reading his work. I didn't know what to make of that.

I went into the kitchen feeling totally drug fucked and thinking that I needed to dry out for a while. I had to start taking care of myself so I made a cup of imported herbal tea that tasted and smelled like peach-and-apple cordial. I leaned against the counter drinking the tea, staring out the window at the city view. In the foreground the sloping hills surrounding the Art Gallery looked too green under the blinding blue sky. Along the path which divided the hill in two, people crawled like cockroaches, only slower. I loved taking Ecstasy but I hated coming down. A chill went through me. I almost called Bataille and begged him to come over and fuck me and beat me around the head a little, but at the last minute I pulled myself together and told myself to think clearly.

I knew the dried cunt juice wasn't Juliette's. This meant that Juliette and I weren't the only people Sade was involved with. There was someone else. Or maybe even a series of somebody else-s.

My hand automatically reached for the phone and dialled the first three digits of Bataille's number before I managed to take control of myself. My whole body was trembling with excitement and confusion. One wave of panic followed another. It was difficult to breathe. I lay on my back on the floor, arms flopped out from my body. My palms sweaty and the fingers slightly cupped, faced upwards. He was fucking someone else. A thousand scenarios went running through my head. Short wide-hipped blondes with golden brown skin and high fine eyebrows, nubile twenty year olds in black ass-length shorts and black midriff tops with flat stomachs, elegant long necks, fine-boned shoulders, too much make-up and no qualms about casual sex. In my mind I imagined him fucking every single woman I'd ever seen him with and even some I had not. There was no point in asking Sade. Now that he'd lied to me about Juliette I clearly couldn't rely on the conventional modes of communication.

I sat up and went through the huge pile of notebooks that were all I had left of my six years at university. I found a tattered old spiral notebook, half travel diary, half operating instructions for a broadcast standard video camera. In the middle were a dozen or so blank pages. I wrote a list of all the women Sade could be fucking and everything I knew about them. First names, surnames, references to where they lived or worked. I felt like I was finally getting on top of the situation. It was easier to breathe and I could even think of making something to eat. But as I stood up a fresh wave of anxiety welled up from the pit of my stomach and brought tears to my eyes. What if he was fucking someone right now?

I went to the telephone and dialled Sade's number at work but before the call connected I hung up. Panting, it occurred to me that there was no rational explanation for what I was doing. I wasn't sure where all this was taking me. I was just doing. I was just trying to avoid something very dark and frightening. Something that could really hurt me. Sitting on the carpet with one hand still on the phone, I managed to control my terror of this unknowable thing for just fifteen seconds. Blind to what and why I dialled Sade's number at work. There was no answer. I tried the number again and hung up on the twelfth ring. I started coughing and ran to the kitchen sink as nausea choked my throat. I didn't throw up but I had to stand there for a while until my stomach calmed down.

I spent the rest of the evening trying to find Sade, not eating. Finally I swallowed a handful of Normison and crawled into bed a wreck and closed my eyes. The images of him sleeping with other women pressed in upon me, sleeping or awake. He's in love with someone more beautiful, sweeter than me, someone sexier, someone more fun, someone easier. It was my fault he was fucking someone else, it was because I was unlovable and impossible. And now he had gone to someone else who could do it, someone

58

else who could make him love her, someone else who could make him stay. In my mind the other woman was blonde with smeared blue almond-shaped eyes, honeyed clear skin, a natural beauty spot and dressed in a black silk voile shirt worn loose over tight black jodhpurs.

I woke up at five covered in sweat in the middle of a nightmare about Sade. He was having an orgy with five pastry-makers. He gave them each a tab of Ecstasy and then told them to suck his cock. Each pastry-maker did amazing things with his cock combining sucking with chewing, licking, tasting, kneading, stretching, rolling, pulling and punching. Then I walked into the room and started beating Sade's head in.

I ran a bubble bath and sat shivering on the rim watching it fill up. I considered hiring a private detective, hiring someone to monitor all of Sade's movements, maybe a team of private detectives. The detectives could record when he arrived at work and when he left, who he lunched with, who he went out drinking with, where he went late at night and who came and went from his apartment. They could fill his bedroom with hidden cameras and microphones, they could watch from windows in adjacent buildings using binoculars and telescopes, they could put a tracking device in his car, they could intercept his mail, they could go through his garbage, they could comb his flat, go through his private papers and documents and they could deliver all the information they collected and reports they made to me. Better still, I could work with them. That way I wouldn't miss seeing anything. And when we caught him fucking someone else we could follow her home. Then we could collect information about her. I could try and work out why he was fucking her. And then I could work out what to do about Sade.

I collected the biography from the bedside table and plopped into the bath, my plump buttocks parting the mountains of bubbles and slapping hard against the water. My eyes stared not seeing at the page and meanwhile sordid scenario after sordid scenario played through my mind. I saw him calling up a twenty year old he'd picked up in a bar and asking her to come over for a drink late last night. I saw them fucking all night and him waking her up the next morning with another hard-on which he jammed straight into her perfect full-lipped large white-toothed mouth. I saw him sneaking out late last night for a secret rendezvous with a girl with dyed red dreadlocks and a full-length black dress. They stood kissing sloppily against a bar at a rock venue and then fucked standing up in a graffiti-covered women's toilet, toilet paper loose from the reel and tangled around their ankles. He drove her home afterwards and they sat kissing in the car outside her place, his fingers stroking her sopping wet cunt, her fingers wet with spit and sliding up and down his pointed cock. He crept home in the early hours of the morning and woke up with the scent of her cunt on his fingers and a huge smile on his face.

I stayed in the bath till seven and then called him. He sounded asleep when he picked up the phone. I wanted to scream at him at the top of my voice and then pulverise his face with my fists. I wanted to kill him. I accused him of fucking someone else and he told me to fuck off and hung up the phone. I tried calling back but the line was engaged. I was furious, I felt like I was going to explode. I picked up a chair and smashed it against the wall. Then I tried calling again. Then I sat down and tried to think clearly.

Why was the phone off the hook ...? I couldn't think why the phone was off the hook. He'd mentioned going to see Pasolini's film, *Salo*. I hurried to put shoes on, no socks, dragged on a pair of filthy jeans I found lying on the floor, pulled my black torn cardigan sleeve-first out of the dirty washing basket, filled my pockets with loose coins and ran out the door. I took the stairs four at a time, holding on to the banister. In no time I was out on the street. I took off in one direction, feet pounding the pavement, then stopped short, turned around, and ran back the way I'd come and around the corner and onto the main road. I kept running, past the row of art deco apartment buildings and on past the brothels, trendy restaurants, milk bars, supermarkets, laundries, international hotels, busy cafes, bars, Japanese noodle bars, Japanese supermarkets, chemists, antique shops, terrace houses, boarding houses, backpacker hostels, pizza bars, book shops, until I came to a newsagent. I stood panting in front of the daily papers, unable to decide which one to buy, unsure which one had the most comprehensive movie listing. I picked one up, hesitated, returned it to the top of the pile and then someone pushed in in front of me, a tall man in tracksuit pants and a checked flannel shirt, and took the paper from the top of the pile and I looked at him, hating him, and then told him to fuck off, my voice growling and deep. He walked away as if he didn't hear. I turned back to the piles of newspapers. Which one had the most comprehensive movie listing? One paper specialised in the big commercial cinemas in town, the other tended to list both small suburban cinemas and commercial cinemas but sometimes didn't give times on the large cinemas in town. I walked over to the counter. The pimple-faced youth eyed me suspiciously. I asked him which paper gave the most comprehensive movie listing and he stared at me, not answering me, and I wanted to slap him across the face and call him stupid but I spat at him instead and stormed out of the shop. I stood on the street while cramps racked my abdomen. I bent over double and the stench of urine, rubbish and vomit wafted into my face from the nearby gutter. I counted to ten, my eyes closed tight. I straightened up, the pain lessening, and started looking for another newsagent. I took a few steps and then bent over double again. 'Shit,' I hissed between clenched teeth. I took a few deep breaths then stood up, no longer sure what I was doing. I crossed the street and walked quickly past the shops and milk bars and brothels until I passed another newsagent. I backtracked but once inside I still wasn't sure, and I hovered in front of the counter pretending to look at the chocolate bars while I tried to remember what I was looking for. Another horrific cramp tore through my stomach and then I farted loudly. My face red, I left the newsagent nearly gagging on the rotten stench. My pants were wet against my backside and full of shit. I started running home but then looked around in desperation for a cab. I screamed hey and a cab pulled up and I climbed into the back seat, barking out my address and winding down the window. Even so the stench was unbearable, and furious I noticed the driver rudely wind his window down as well. The ride to my place seemed to take forever and as I handed over the money I considered giving the driver a tip but then decided not to, thinking about the window. He glared at me as I waddled up the stairs and into the building. Another fart tore through my pants and I started running up the stairs, liquid shit dribbling down the insides of my legs. I held my hand against my ass as still more farts rippled out. Inside my flat I ran straight into the bathroom and undressed, leaving my clothes in the bath and, wiping my legs with toilet paper, threw myself at the toilet as another fart ripped me open and what felt like my entire insides gushed out, filling the bowl. I collapsed back against the cistern, head lolling against the window sill, and blacked out.

I came to stretched out in the bath. The sound of my clothes spinning in the drier in the laundry next door kept me calm enough to think and I splashed tepid bathwater on my face and sighed. I dragged myself out of the bath, swaying a little on weak rubbery legs and stood wrapped in a musty towel in front of the steamy mirror. I reached up and wiped a clear circle in the glass. My face stared back at me, puffy-eyed and white. The last few hours were a total blank. I dialled Sade's number. It was engaged.

I opened the phone book and called up a few cinemas asking about the Pasolini film. It was showing at two suburban cinemas. I wrote all the sessions down in the spiral notebook next to the list of names and information. There were six sessions in all. I was starving but I didn't have time to eat so I dressed and ran downstairs and hailed a cab from the main road.

The traffic was moving slowly. I kept looking at my watch. I told the driver to step on it, I said that the way things were going I'd get there faster if I got out and walked. After that the driver drove like a lunatic. My stomach lurched every time we boldly overtook a car in the face of hostile oncoming traffic but I was grateful just the same. I asked the driver to drop me a few blocks away from the cinema. We skidded to a standstill and I thanked him and left him a generous tip. He smiled a gold-toothed smile and sped away. I crossed the road and sat down at a window table in a pub opposite the main doors. I desperately needed to go to the bathroom but I waited until the session had started before abandoning my lookout. After I'd emptied my bowels once more, but normally this time, I returned to the window, waited a few minutes, and then caught another cab to the other cinema. I repeated this for each of the six sessions. As the last of the six sessions began I caught a cab back to his place.

A few blocks from his apartment building I saw him crossing the street at a pedestrian crossing. I told the driver to pull over. He was carrying a small package in one hand and I wondered what it was, knowing it would explain where he'd been, considering he hadn't been to see the Pasolini film. Maybe he would take me to see it one day next week? I considered paying the driver and running after him but I didn't want to give him another chance to tell me to fuck off or close the door in my face so, sighing loudly, I directed the driver back to my place, paid the fare and, shoulders painfully slumped and neck aching, stomped upstairs.

I forced myself to eat an apple when I got in even though it tasted too dry and was nearly impossible to swallow. 'I'm not going to ring him,' I told my apartment. 'Painkillers, bathroom cabinet; painkillers, bathroom cabinet,' I chanted. I threw the apple away. I took a few swigs of mineral water from the fridge. My heart pounded in my chest. I don't want to eat, I felt like screaming this out. I am not hungry. I dialled Sade's number.

'Hello,' he said, happy.

'It's me,' I said, playing it cool.

'Yes,' he said, 'I know.'

'What have you been doing?' I had to know.

'Why?' he replied.

'Because,' I said, cool all gone and hating him.

'Why don't you give me a call when you've got a reason?' he said, hanging up on me.

I dialled him straight back but the engaged tone drilled into my ear.

'Fuck you, fuck you, you fucken asshole,' I screamed, picking up a book and throwing it across the room. The spine cracked open against the wall. Disgusted, I slammed the door and left.

I walked to the bottle shop and bought a bottle of wine. The streets were crammed with couples holding hands. Back home I opened the wine and poured myself a glass. I thought about dinner. I wasn't really hungry. I was full of wine. I switched on the TV. The phone rang. It was Sade wanting to know if I wanted to have dinner. I told him to fuck off and hung up. I drank more wine. I called him back to say yes but the phone was off the hook. I poured another glass of wine and looked at the telephone. White dots of dust clung to the grey buttons and brown curls of carpet fluff clung coiled between them. I gulped down the wine as tears plopped from the corners of my eyes. I picked the receiver up and slammed it hard down into its cradle. I held the phone to my ear. I could no longer hear a dial tone.

I went into the kitchen and started chopping up a carrot into thin strips for a salad. In between slices I gulped down more of the wine, slamming the glass down on the bench-top, surprised the stem didn't break. 'Fuck it,' I said, looking at the chopped carrot. I threw the knife across the kitchen, shielding my eyes with crossed arms as it bounced off the cupboards and walls. I threw it again and again. Finally the plastic handle cracked and came off. I held the heavy metal in my hands. I looked at my wrist and then moved the knife across the white flesh with the sharp edge until it drew blood. I did this all the way up my arm. I threw the knife axe-style into the bookcases, but it didn't stab into a book. I reached for the bottle of wine. There was a quarter of a glassful left in the bottom of the bottle. After another large swig I fell back on the floor crying and rolled my head around, moaning and rubbing my face with my hands. 'Oh God, oh God, oh God,' I moaned.

I sat up and made the room sway. I took another swig from the bottle. I picked up my keys and slammed the door closed behind me. The streets were quiet and I managed to stagger the few blocks to Sade's place without passing anyone. I looked up at the windows. The kitchen light was on. I pressed on his buzzer. There was no answer. I toyed with the idea of sneaking into the building and then climbing out the window in the fire escape and crawling around the ledge and breaking into his kitchen window. Inside his flat I'd take the large carving knife from the wooden knife stand and the long two-pronged fork and then creep on tiptoe through the small entrance hall and freeze outside the bedroom door, ear pressed to the cool polished wood. Then I'd peer in and if he was alone I'd leave exactly the way I'd come. But if there was someone with him—as I suspected there was—I'd calmly walk over to the bed and demand an introduction, the knife and fork hidden behind my back. I'd make her wait to shake my hand, her hand outstretched, her naked shoulders, her stupid dull eyes glazed from fucking and her ugly long dishevelled hair. Then instead of shaking her hand I'd grab it and holding it firmly, I'd slice it clean off at the wrist. Then, while she was howling with pain and while the blood poured from her wrist in streams, I'd ram the fork through her eyes, starting with the right eye, and twist it in circles. Finished, I'd smile at Sade and leave.

I rang Sade's buzzer one more time and then started off back home. I dug my hands into my pockets and looked down at the ground before me, dodging the cracks in the pavement and carefully avoiding treading on the scattered dead leaves. I decided to take the long way home. I cruised the cafes and restaurants looking for Sade without success.

Turning the corner into my street I saw something out of the corner of my eye. It was Sade. I waited for him to catch up, blood tearing through my rigid body, too much blood pumping too fast and almost forcing its way out through my eyes, my nose, my mouth, any opening it could find.

'What have you been doing?' I slurred, lurching in the dark and finally crashing into a brick wall.

'Are you all right?' Sade said, looking me up and down. 'You seem drunk.'

'I am,' I said, 'and I've been doing terrible things.'

He frowned at me and took a step backwards.

'I'd like to tie you up and leave you trapped for days starving and stinking in your own shit,' I whispered under my breath.

'I think I better get you home,' he said, taking me by the hand. I followed along, tears streaming down my face.

We reached my flat and I closed and deadlocked the door behind us and pocketed the keys. Snot was dribbling out my nose and hung from my face in long gooey strands that reached all the way to the floor. I wiped it on my sleeve. Sade stood in the middle of the room and surveyed the carnage around him. I told him he was fucking someone else and he turned around slowly. His eyes met mine. Dark, cold and ecstatic with hatred. He took a few steps towards the door, not noticing the absence of keys, and continued to glare at me. I repeated my accusation. He moved closer to the door, close enough to place one hand on the handle.

'You dirty rotten liar,' I growled, reaching an epiphany of disgust.

He turned the handle of the door but it didn't budge. His face went into a slow melt-down and something that looked a lot like surprise but was more likely to be outrage transformed his handsome features.

'You filthy fucken liar,' I repeated, this time at the top of my voice. Then I screamed, 'You're a total root-rat and you think I don't know,' pounding my thighs with my fists in time to the words.

His back to me, he struggled uselessly with the door.

'You liar, you creep,' I shouted, my fists pounding my stomach and moving up my body. 'You treat me like shit,' I concluded, pounding my breasts, and finally my head.

His eyes watched me, two enormous blue bubbles I wanted to stab with a pair of scissors, the lids peeled back onto the balls which popped out like fresh lychees ready to eat. He was absolutely livid although he didn't look the least bit threatened or disturbed or frightened or concerned. He just looked distant, very distant, as if what was happening had nothing to do with him.

'So what do you have to say for yourself?' I demanded in a low whispered growl, my fists clenched at my thighs.

I waited, holding my breath, blood pounding beneath my scalp, long enough for him to take full stock of the situation, long enough for him to realise how much danger he was in. It occurred to me that I should draw his attention to the knife over near the bookcase but I decided not to. I wanted unspecified terror. Still he stared at me with his hideous bubbling eyes. I was just about to start shouting again and pulling out my hair and banging my head against the wall just to let him know how angry I was when he shook his head and sighed. Then he walked over to my dining table, sat down, crossed his legs and lit a cigarette.

'Fuck you,' I hissed inaudibly and went into the kitchen and swallowed the remaining drops of wine.

Without turning around or returning to the other room I asked him again if he had anything to say for himself. He said nothing. I thought of killing him then and there and then ran for the door, unlocked it with the keys and leaving it open ran down the fire escape and out onto the street, skipping first and then breaking into a run. At the bottle shop I bought another bottle of wine. Back at my flat I found the door ajar and a note from Sade on the dining room table warning me that if I ever did anything like what I'd just done again then he'd leave me for good. I tore the note into tiny pieces and tossed them into the air. A gust of wind blowing in through the open windows made the pieces flutter and spin in miniature whirlwinds. I slammed the windows closed, opened the wine and turned off the lights. Then I played L. L. Cool Jay at full volume into headphones. At some point I woke up on the lounge-room floor tangled in speaker wire and the cord to the headphones and, still drunk, I eventually managed to free myself and crawl into bed, removing the phone from the receiver on my way.

Intense white light turned the insides of my eyelids a brutal bloody red. My bedroom blinds were open and outside the sun was high in the bright blue sky. Dried vomit was caked into the corners of my mouth and covered the pillowcase beside my head. Gagging, I ran to the bathroom. But when I kneeled heaving in front of the bowl and breathed deeply and heaved again my twisted insides betrayed me and knotted themselves tightly into a stubborn ball, indifferent to even my most desperate shuddering pleas. Giving in I returned to the bedroom and stripped the bed, rolling the blood-stained sheets into a ball, and threw the lot into the dirty washing basket. I carried this down to the laundry and put on a load of washing. Then I ran a bath, soaped myself from head to toe over and over again with pure vegetable soap, rinsed under fresh water, counted the bruises slowly appearing on my thighs, stomach and chest, roughly towelled myself dry, dressed and went to the kitchen and made myself a cup of tea. Then I sat down at my desk and stared at the note-book in front of me. Apart from Juliette I only had one name and surname so I circled this in red. Then I went to the phone book and looked up the address. I copied it onto a piece of paper and shoved it deep into the back pocket of my jeans. Just in time I covered my mouth with my hand as the vomit lurched from my stomach up the back of my throat. I ran for the bathroom but didn't make it to the toilet and sprayed the white tiles above the bath instead. Then I knelt beside the bath and emptied myself into the deep white bathtub. Afterwards I rinsed the tub and tiles, sprinkled them with powder cleanser, washed my face in the sink, cleaned my teeth, transferred the washing from the washing machine into the drier and hit the street. I hailed the

71

first cab I saw and gave the driver the address. It started to rain.

The cab pulled up in the narrow lane, tyres hissing in the wet, and I paid up and stood while the rain spat down on the top of my head and went dripping into my eyes, watching the cab back out to the main street. I turned to the row of free-standing wooden cottages and looked for numbers. I walked further down the lane until I found the number that matched the address on the piece of paper. I stood outside the small timber cottage in the light drizzle and listened at her window. I heard a woman giggling inside and someone else making low animal growling noises. I heard the thud of footsteps on bare floorboards as the inhabitants of the house went running around crashing into furniture. I walked away, not knowing what to do. After a few minutes' consideration I walked around to the back of the house and knocked on the back door. The door was unlocked and slightly ajar. Inside I saw Sade tucking in his shirt and picking up his leather briefcase. When he saw me he said hello in a loud voice as if me being there was the most natural thing in the world.

'We've just been to the pub,' he said, and kissed the woman, a skinny waitress from a cafe that he frequented, goodbye on the lips.

Out in the rain once more I asked Sade if he'd been fucking her. He gave me a withering look and then walked quickly away. I half-heartedly hurried after him and then gave up chasing him altogether. I reached the main street just in time to watch him climb into the front seat of a cab and drive away. I dug around in my pockets for some money but I didn't have enough for a cab home. I resigned myself to a long rainy walk unaccompanied but for the delirious presence of countless murderous fantasies. Miserable, I calculated that I'd spent a whole fortnight's worth of my grant on cab fares and wouldn't be able to pay my rent. Not only that but I now had a broken phone.

4

I RAN MY HANDS UP AND DOWN THE BRUISES ON MY THIGHS. There were huge lumps under the skin and the surface was red and faintly dark blue. The red marks and submerged blue were concentrated around the middle of each thigh. I looked at them some more and then covered them up. The black tights felt good on the disfigured flesh. It felt like they were holding me together.

I opened the book Sade had given me by the wealthy contemporary American novelist. I read the first chapter. The novel chronicled the daily lives of an incestuous group of Wall Street businessmen. Their identities were interchangeable. They were all misogynists. They lived and breathed the material world. Their conversations and observations read like dialogues from soap operas and advertising copy. They were obsessed by clothes and success. They were infinitely greedy. They were all in their early to mid twenties. They were so rich they lived above and beyond the law. They dressed and looked alike. They made fun of bums. Their opinions and behaviour were amusing but would be read as pure inexcusable provocation by feminists, humanists, Marxists, literary critics and moralists alike. They were so ugly they were funny. For this reason they were typical of everyone in a way, despite their wealth and power.

As I read I laughed out loud. I wanted to ring Sade and discuss the novel with him, but something held me back. Soon I was running through my flat to the bathroom, unbuttoning my fly and sitting moaning on the toilet. I couldn't shit. My abdomen was hugely distended but I couldn't even fart. I considered running away to America. Life was better there. I moaned and tried to force out the shit I could feel through my skin and flesh, the long hard tube that pressed against all the other organs making it difficult to breathe, but nothing came out. I pushed again, this time clenching my hands into fists and I heard a tiny plop and looked down into the bowl, hopeful to the bitter end. A small turd about the size of my little finger floated in the water. I walked into the kitchen. I swallowed a laxative and washed it down with a large glass of freshly squeezed grapefruit juice. I went back to my desk, pushed Sade's novel aside, opened my notebook and waited.

The new phone rang. It was Marcelle.

'How the fuck?' she wanted to know.

'The usual,' I told her. 'If there weren't any men in my life I wouldn't have any problems.'

'I thought so,' she chirped. 'So how's it going with Sade?'

'I don't really want to talk about it,' I muttered.

'Unsatisfactory is about the nicest word that comes to mind.'

'I gathered as much,' she was quick to say, 'because a friend of mine saw him out at dinner the other night with two girls and he had his tongue down one of their throats.'

I quizzed Marcelle for details and to my horror it wasn't the waitress. Uncomfortable, I changed the subject.

'What about you, Marcelle,' I said, 'are you still seeing that guy, what was his name? You know the architect, or was he a gym instructor?'

'No,' she said, anger creeping into her voice. 'He's history. This time,' she said, her voice gradually recovering its even tone, 'this time I've found myself a pretty boy, a teenager. He's perfect. It's very part-time, it has no future, it's exactly what I need. The occasional fuck, no expectations, no strings, no complications. Almost nothing.'

'Body?' I demanded, jealous.

'To die for,' she said. 'And he doesn't work out because he doesn't need to.'

I got off the phone and tried to calm down. I swallowed more of the laxative followed by more of the grapefruit juice. I still couldn't breathe so I went into the bathroom and swallowed a handful of pills. Normison, Sinutab, Panadol, pseudoephedrine, I wasn't sure what exactly. Still breathless and shaking I opened my notebook and skimmed a random page.

I was a planned baby. My mother and father had been married for a year and then they stopped using contraception.

76

When I was two we moved to a huge house with a garden full of camellias and fruit trees. I watered the garden with my watering can and ate snails and swam in a little inflatable pool and played with my dog. I used to wrap my arms around her neck, hanging off.

I flipped back and checked the cover of the notebook. It said, 'Thesis Notes', and I wondered when I'd become distracted and started writing my family history instead. I skipped a few paragraphs and read on.

From then on I was haunted by my dark side. Out of the blue I would explode in a violent rage, lashing out at whoever was nearest at hand. By the time I reached high school I learned to contain these outbursts to my room where I would close the door and howl and scream and beat and kick my lime-green beanbag to my heart's content. But I always felt there was a certain emptiness to this gesture. I knew I wasn't really angry with the beanbag.

A tingling sensation travelled up through my spine and I hurried to the end of the entry.

In the meantime my first relationship with a man erupted in violent physical abuse. I stared at the bruises for hours on end and stroked the contours of swollen flesh. As soon as I finished high school I left home, deeply estranged from my family. In vain I hoped that the problem wasn't mine, that it was his, and that it would go away. It didn't. I was deeply preoccupied by this.

I kept going over and over my family history. All I could come up with in terms of violence was my father's ex-wife's attack. She tried to kill my mother and unborn baby brother one day. I hadn't seen the attack because my father protected me by locking me in the house. Even so, it must have affected me...

Suddenly the laxative was working and leaping up I knocked the notebook to the floor. I ran to the toilet and collapsed explosively onto the plastic seat. 'Oh my God,' I chanted mindlessly, losing it, 'God, God, God.'

Out on the street it was warm and sunny and backpackers and tourists filled the outdoor cafes. Passing a public telephone I had a sudden urge to ring Bataille but there was an English backpacker inside and a queue of Japanese and Swedes stretched along the pavement all the way to the corner, all patiently waiting, credit cards at the ready. I hurried on. Half an hour later I ran into Simone, Marcelle's sister, who was wearing six-inch platform heels, a black lycra midriff top and a black wrap-around miniskirt. Her skin was lightly tanned and a pair of large black French-looking sunglasses hid her eyes and half of her face. She smiled when I told her how great she looked and then, her hand resting lightly on my arm, asked me if I was OK. 'You look pale and thin,' she said.

'I just don't have,' I mumbled, looking down at the ground, 'I just don't have any,' I hesitated, trying to find the right word, 'any appetite,' I concluded, pleased with myself.

'Why don't you come swimming with me one day?' she said, all sweet and nineteen and coy beneath her dark curls.

I told Simone I'd call her and continued on my way, my arms folded across my chest and hugging my ribs to myself.

The first shop I passed was a bookshop. Inside I went straight to the psychology section and stood in front of the rows of books, my eyes running across the spines, but I was unable to stand still long enough to read any. I checked over my shoulder to see if anyone was standing close by. I didn't want anyone to see what I was doing. I was looking for books on love and relationships. My eyes darted right and left. The coast was clear. I took a step towards the shelves. A row of twelve-step books leapt out at me. I moved a few shelves up. Dream analysis, horoscopes, the Linda Goodman section. I was getting closer. Soon I was standing in front of a shelf of what-is-wrong-with-me books and self-esteem guides. Finally the word 'anger' caught my eye. I pulled the book out and hurried towards the back of the shop.

I found a quiet step, well out of the way of the sales assistants and other customers, and sat down to read. After a while I tucked the book discreetly under my arm and moved out to the fiction section of the bookshop. Even though I wasn't particularly enjoying the book Sade had given me I bought another book by the same author and then, feeling brave and clever, moved towards the counter and pushed both books, the novel hiding the self-help book, towards the cashier. I waved my credit card in front of her face. She stared out the window at the cloudy skies mouthing the words to the song playing quietly on the stereo. I hurried home, not looking passers-by in the face but keeping my eyes glued to the pavement before me.

For dinner I prepared a simple frugal meal. Biscuits, cottage cheese and lettuce covered in salt, vinegar, ground pepper and olive oil. I fell asleep, face pressed into the anger book. A little after twelve a disturbance from the street below woke me up and I switched off the overhead light and peered out through the blinds.

A woman stood next to a beaten old car. She slammed her fists, wham wham wham, on the bonnet and screamed, 'Johnny, come back. Come back you fucken creep. Don't fucken leave me here on the fucken street.' She opened the car door and stood swaying, peering inside. She bumped her head on the roof leaning in and her hips slumped over to one side against the door. When she straightened up I saw she held a gold-covered tube of lipstick in her hand. Then she bent down again and, ass poking out into the middle of the street, she applied the lipstick in the cracked side mirror of the car. Finished, she threw the lipstick inside again. She rubbed her lips together and fluffed her hair in the mirror. Then, her hands on her hips, she walked out to the middle of the road, looked each way and then stomped back to the car. Wham wham wham, her fists thumped on the bonnet. 'Where are you Johnny, come back, come back you fucken creep, don't leave me here.' And then again but louder, 'Johnny, where are you, come back you stupid asshole, don't leave me here.' And then hysterical, screaming, 'Please come back, Johnny, please come back, where are you?'

A police wagon approached, slowly, blue light twirling, and stopped just behind the woman and the car. Leaving the wagon double-parked, two police walked over to the woman and one of them, a policewoman wearing trousers, started talking to her in a low voice, asking her what was wrong, pointing out that she seemed a little upset and asking what she could do to help. The woman stepped forward aggressively and spat a torrent of abuse at the woman cop. 'Just fuck off, just fucken leave me alone, I don't want to talk to you, you hear?' The policewoman took a few steps backwards and looked over her shoulder at her partner. He stood hands on hips and looked up and down the street.

'Are you looking for someone?' she said in a quiet voice, one hand on her holster. 'Maybe we can help you find them?'

Wham wham wham, went the woman's fist on the bonnet of the car, her back turned to the police. 'Fuck you, Johnny, don't leave me with this shit, come back you bastard, come back.' Finally she screamed as if she was being beaten and collapsed head first onto the bonnet of the car, sobbing loudly.

I closed the blinds, climbed back into bed and I immediately thought of Sade. An image of his hard cock floated behind my closed lids. Soon the woman was screaming again and I wrapped the pillow around my head. I desperately wanted to get to sleep but it was impossible while the woman continued screaming on the street below. Not that I had anything to do the next day, I just wanted to drag myself out of my lethargy. Finally it was quiet on the street. I peered between the blinds and both cars were gone. I climbed back into bed and examined the bruises on my thighs. I shook down the bedcovers, breathed the sweet smell of laundry detergent on my pillow cases and closed my eyes once more. Just before I fell asleep I imagined stabbing Sade in the stomach with a flick-knife and then twisting it around in circles.

My intercom went off. It was just after one. Fuck, I thought as it buzzed again. I staggered through the dark, tripping over something on the floor and grabbed the handset.

'Hello,' I said, sleepy.

'It's me,' Sade slurred. 'Do you mind if I come up?'

I stood in the dark listening to the clunk of the lift downstairs. My building was built in the fifties. While it was a perfect example of modernist aesthetics—the absence of ornamentation coupled with the pure functionality of the design—it conformed to a pre-post-modernist modernist aesthetic rather than to a post-post-modernist one. Typically, it was constructed from industrial-strength materials rather than their more contemporary simulacra. The building was incredibly solid and while the ceilings were low and the insulation atrocious, the walls and doors were thick and the windows incredibly large, letting in plenty of light and sun. The walls were painted with cream gloss paint. The lift was small and plain. The doors were the sort of doors you'd expect to find on a goods lift. The floor, walls and roof were covered in grey lino tiles. At each floor the lift opened onto a spacious tiled vestibule. Fabulous city views could be glimpsed from each of the vestibules by glancing through the glass doors which led out onto long, open-air corridors with more incredible breath-taking views. The other apartments in my building were rented by drug dealers, single-income families, unmarried homosexual and heterosexual couples, single men of all ages, young ethnics who worked in the catering industry and people who would be yuppies if they earned more money. The building had been renovated in the eighties. I heard the lift clunk on the other side of the vestibule and then the groan of the doors.

Sade was drunk. When I opened the door he stumbled into the room and tripped over a chair and landed flat on his back. He lay not moving in a swirling cloud of stale cigarette smoke and breathed champagne and brandy all over me when I knelt down beside him and asked him if he was OK. His face twitched and blinked, stupid and pathetically confused. I considered taking advantage of the situation by tying him up, gagging him and then maybe torturing him with kitchen utensils for a few hours, but his helplessness repulsed me so I dribbled stale-smelling spit onto his face instead. He reached up to wipe my spit from his eyes and cheeks but his hand failed to connect with his face and hovered in mid-air before flopping onto the carpet. Disgusted, I went to the door and locked us in. Then I hid the keys in the bottom of the refrigerator, closed the blinds and turned on all the lights. I moved my desk lamp over to the floor beside his collapsed form, plugged it in and then shone the light directly into his eyes. Not satisfied—his eyes squinted closed but that was all—I swapped the globe with the one in the kitchen which was brighter, and tried again. This time he moaned and tried to cover his eyes with his arm. He only succeeded in hitting his nose with his hand and then his arm slipped out of control onto his chest. I brought the lamp down even closer to his face, close enough for the heat from the brilliantly glowing

83

globe to burn his skin. Then, leaving him there I closed the bedroom door and climbed back into bed. I awoke a few hours later to loud shuddering sobs coming from the lounge room. I got out of bed and, without putting any clothes on, went to see what was happening with Sade. Sade was sitting cross-legged in the middle of the room, his face buried in his hands and crying. He'd unplugged the lamp from the wall and it lay knocked over and dark on the carpet beside him.

'I only wanted to make you happy,' he blubbered into his hands.

'You're a liar, Sade,' I told him, 'I don't believe a word you say.'

He turned towards me, eyes swimming in his face, lips trembling.

'I love you, Justine,' he slurred, drool stretching all the way to the carpet in thin silvery strands.

He struggled to bring his eyes into focus. Realising I was naked, he wiped his face on his sleeve and hurried towards me on all fours. I stood rigid, towering above him while he, reaching up unsteadily from his knees, grabbed handfuls of my ass, his lips slobbering across the top of my thighs in search of my cunt, his tongue probing amidst my thick honey-blonde pubic hair and sloppy on my clitoris. I laughed and, resting my foot on his shoulder, pushed him easily away and went into the bathroom and ran a bubble bath.

'Justine, Justine,' he called after me, 'I can't live without you.'

'Sure,' I shouted over the water. He watched me, swaying

84

in the doorway. 'You can't live without me and every other woman you meet.'

'No,' he started to say, walking towards me, 'it's not true.' But I cut him off and pushed him fully clothed into the bath.

He rolled over a couple of times and then lay still, face down in the water, the foam from the bubble bath pushed out of the water and sitting in piles on the edge of the bath, quietly popping. I counted to fifty and then watched as huge bubbles of air rose with a deep rumbling sound from Sade's mouth and burst through the surface of the water. His body shuddered a couple of times and then lay still. I counted to twenty before I rolled him over. Then I lifted his torso out of the water and, twisting him around, hung his arms over the edge of the bath, his face towards the floor. I pulled out the plug and went into the kitchen and found a bucket. Back in the bathroom I slapped him across the face hard and watched him vomit into the bucket. Clenching my jaws together to stifle my own nausea I opened the window. When Sade stopped vomiting I emptied the bucket into the toilet and flushed it. I was just rinsing the bucket at the sink when a loud clanking sound came from the drainpipe. I turned around and looked at the toilet. The orange-coloured vomit, now mixed with water, surged around the bowl in circles and was steadily rising to the top. I turned off the tap and watched, mesmerised, as vomit and water bubbled up and surged, dripping, over the rim and onto the floor, flowing in a stream towards the rug and then soaking into the rug and moving beneath it across the bathroom tiles until reaching the brass drain, where it dripped with a steady plopping sound down into the pipe below. I dropped the bucket to the floor and, trying not to panic, flushed the toilet a few times. Then I swept all my make-up and skin-care products off the top of the cistern onto the floor and lifted the heavy china and carefully placed it on the rug. I contemplated the mechanics of the flushing mechanism and was fiddling with the plastic ball which controlled the amount of water entering the cistern when suddenly, with a long hiss, the water and vomit started to subside and was slowly sucked from the bottom of the bowl leaving it orange and empty. I looked at Sade, who was shivering blue-lipped where I'd left him at the edge of the bath, and then at the carnage at my feet and I laughed.

'Take off all your clothes,' I told him.

With great difficulty he obeyed. I threw his clothes onto the rug, rolled it up with the clothes inside and deposited it in the laundry. I picked up all my cosmetics, discarding any that were even slightly soiled with vomit, replaced the cistern top and returned the bottles and tubes to the top of the cistern. Then I splashed the tiled floor and toilet bowl with buckets of water and disinfectant. Finally I ran a fresh bubble bath and climbed in opposite Sade.

'Sorry about the mess,' he mumbled, wrapping his legs around my neck and, eyes drawn into two tight slits, he pulled me towards him down the length of the bath.

'Would you marry me if I asked you to?' he said, releasing his hold on my neck.

'No,' I said, dead-pan and floating away.

'No, I guess you're right,' he agreed too quickly. 'But we do need some kind of contract, don't you think?'

'Persuade me,' I said seductively, stroking my breasts and slitting my eyes back at him.

'I could always adopt you,' he said, looking at me sideways and stroking his chin thoughtfully. 'An adoption contract's a much nicer contract than a marriage contract.'

'Adopt me as what?' I asked suspiciously, fingers poised over an erect nipple.

'As my daughter,' he said slowly, his hand wrapped around his chin.

'But I already have a father,' I protested.

'And I already have a daughter,' he informed me, sitting on the rim of the bath, no longer looking at me, his eyes darting around the room looking for something.

He went to get his cigarettes, ashtray and lighter and returned. We lit up our cigarettes and sat smoking together in silence. Sade was sitting on the rim with his legs spread. I lay full length beneath the bubbles, my eyes mesmerised by his cock. It was engorged with blood and hugely swollen, although not engorged enough to be hard, and hung loosely to one side of his balls along his glabrous inner thigh, lurking with intent.

'So are you going to tell me?' I asked, eyes glued to his cock.

'It was a long time ago, five years ago to be precise,' he began. 'We met at a party in Chelsea. It was a publishing party, I was doing PR in those days, and she was recently widowed. Her husband had been a pastry-chef, something of a gourmet, I believe. Anyway, I was leaving the next day for Paris for the weekend, I had to attend a book launch there, and when we left the party I suggested she come away with me to Paris. She accepted.'

Sade lit a second cigarette from the first and sat blowing smoke rings. His cock was getting harder with every word and now stood straight out in front of him. I tossed my butt into the toilet bowl and waited for him to continue.

'I don't remember leaving the hotel room all weekend,' he said, dragging heavily on his cigarette and blowing more rings. 'On Monday I arrived at the book launch drunk and late, stayed for half an hour and rushed back to the hotel in a taxi. It wasn't that I couldn't bear to be away from her. There was just something about her, something I couldn't leave alone. I can't explain,' he declared, exasperated, puffing at his cigarette again and then lighting a third from the dying butt of the second. I heard a hiss as the butt hit the water inside the toilet bowl.

'Anyway,' he went on, 'I think I must have hurt her or frightened her because after that weekend I didn't hear from her again. Then one day, a year later, I picked up the phone and there she was. She told me I was a father, that I had a daughter, and asked me whether I wanted to see her. I did. It was then, meeting my baby daughter for the first time, that I realised my feelings for her, the mother of my only child. Not only did I not want to be with her any more, I found her repulsive, hateful for what she had done.'

Sade finished the third cigarette and tossed the butt into the toilet bowl with the others. Then he reached over and flushed the chain. I shivered in the bath. The water was tepid, so I climbed out and had just begun rubbing myself with a towel when Sade grabbed me by the wrists, hurting me, and held me still.

'She wanted me to go to jail for what I'd done to her,' he hissed, a fine spray of spit hitting my face. 'She took me to court,' he rasped on, his eyes bulging, furious, 'and I was proven innocent. But she has stolen my child, she has stolen my child and there's nothing I can do.'

I looked down at his cock. It was now fully erect and staring right back at me with its single unseeing eye and my cunt melted between my legs. I collapsed against him. Soon he was inside me, the towel discarded beside us on the wet bathroom floor.

We fucked each other standing up in the bath. We fucked each other lying sweating in the bed. We slept and woke and fucked each other again.

'I miss you,' he said, his words erasing a thousand nightmares.

'Me too,' I echoed and lay clasped to his chest, his boozy breath damp on my face. For an instant I was in love with him again.

Just after six he woke and dressed and kissed me good-bye. I told him that the keys were in the bottom of the refrigerator, not wanting to get out of bed to let him out. After he left I lay in bed drifting in and out of sleep all day. Towards evening the phone rang and I struggled up, squinting as orange light from the setting sun streamed across the room.

'It's me,' my mother's voice boomed down the phone line.

'Hi,' I said, instantly wary.

'I don't know how to tell you this,' she said, her voice uneven.

'What is it?' I said, keeping calm.

'Your father's dying,' she said, her voice dissolving into quiet tears. 'It's cancer. He's been given between three and six months to live.'

In my mind I saw tumours proliferating wildly all through my father's body, multiple lumps popping up beneath the skin on his arms and legs, lumps bulging out of the sides of his neck.

'Can you come home?' she pleaded. 'Can you please just come home?'

'Sure,' I said, suddenly made of steel. 'I'll be there.' I advised her to be strong. It'll make it easier for him, I reasoned, while she continued to cry.

I hung up the phone and sat on the floor, my back to the wall and my legs pulled up. My father was dying. This was not a problem. I went through my wardrobe item by item deciding what to pack. It was always cold at this time of year at the coast and even though the large weatherboard house had oil heaters in every bedroom and a huge open fire to heat the lounge room, kitchen and dining room, I would still need warm things for long walks at dusk along the beach and for the chilly mornings before the fires were lit, for fetching wood and weeding the flowerbeds and the rose garden. Each day began with huge pots of tea brewed in the chipped yellow enamelled tin teapot and served in fine white bone china cups and saucers from a shiny painted wooden tray, the milk in a small matching china jug and the sugar in a blue china bowl with a tiny tarnished silver spoon. Gulls screamed outside the windows and the dewy morning air was heavy with the scent of sea spray and rose blossoms. After breakfast everyone climbed into the car and glided down the long circular gravel driveway and through the black ornate cast-iron gates. We drove into town and bought cases of wine, boxes of fruit and vegetables, and watched the butcher carve up a dead baby cow for our knuckle of veal. Then it was home for lunch and an afternoon spent reading in the garden or in the north-facing music room if it was cold. The late afternoon was spent preparing the fire, playing the piano, mowing the lawns, swimming in the freezing water or working in the garden. My father wheeling a wheelbarrow full of chopped firewood up the drive from the shed where it was stored to the back porch where it was kept until we used it. Long evenings that started early with a gin and tonic, a sherry or a scotch in front of the fire, that lingered over the polished mahogany dinner table where bottles of red and white wine endlessly found their way from crystal decanters into heavy glasses, and that concluded with drunken ventures into the garden under the stars and moon, or asleep on the couch while the video played on, rewinding at the end and starting back at the beginning and playing and rewinding over and over again well into the night.

I picked up the phone and started to dial Sade's number but I hung up before the number connected and stared at my desk chair, running my hands along its legs and squeezing the wooden spokes at the back. I had bought the chair ten years ago when I first moved out of home. Even then it was cheap, second-hand, in need of a coat of paint. Now it was more so. I reached for the phone and dialled again. No-one answered. I tried Bataille. This time the phone answered on the second ring. He told me to come over right away. I dressed in a clean pair of jeans, a cotton T-shirt and a black leather jacket and ran out the door. I climbed in the back of the first cab that drove by. The driver was young and fuckable. He was wearing a black skivvy, black Levi 501s and black riding boots. His hair was cropped close to his head except for a single straight long lock at the front which hung over his eyes. He couldn't have been twenty-one. His eyes were exactly the shade of cold sharp blue that made my mouth dry, my breath short, my hand go down the front of my jeans, finger probing the warm fleshy lips of my cunt in search of my clitoris, and my thoughts jolt about unpleasantly in my head. Our eyes met in the rear-view mirror. He smiled shyly and looked away. I sat back, staring out the window, waiting for him to do something. Outside Bataille's house I was reluctant to leave the cab. I paid the fare not getting out of the cab, the door open, talking about nothing, when he got off his shift, how he survived the long hours. Finally I ran out of small talk. How do I do this? And while I was sitting there wondering, trapped by my own indecision—should I ask him what time his shift finishes, should I get out and tell him I enjoyed meeting him and smile my regret as I wave good-bye?—he fished around in the back pocket of his jeans, his pelvis pushed up into the air and his ass off the seat and me staring at his groin making a hasty assessment, and pulled out a ragged black leather wallet which he opened out and from whose warm depths he produced a slightly bent white business card. He handed it to me and told me to give him a call sometime. The card said he was a photographer which turned me off a bit but not enough for me to get rid of the card, and thanking him, I slid the card into the back pocket of my jeans and smiled goodbye, one eyebrow provocatively cocked, my hands openly playing with my clit inside my jeans as he drove slowly away.

I ran my hands through my hair and straightened my jeans and rang Bataille's bell. As I waited for him to answer the door I found myself thinking about a guy I fucked a few years ago who had an irrepressible obsession with peepholes. I was still thinking about his shower when the door opened and Bataille stood before me wearing exactly the same clothes as he'd been wearing the last time I saw him and with fresh shaving cuts glistening up and down either side of his face. He told me to come in and led the way down the long winding corridor which divided the two huge front rooms, through the double living area and down to the back of the house.

This time we ended up in a study. It was separated from the bedroom by a corridor which led out onto a wide closed-in verandah. Both the bedroom and study had a door opening out onto the verandah and another door opening onto the living area which was full of expensive shiny black and chrome modern furniture and black matt European electronic equipment: video player, stereo system, TV set, CD player, video camera and tripod, telephone and answering machine. The study was empty except for a three-seater couch, an office chair and a desk with a portable computer. Bataille offered me the office chair and stood behind me looking over my shoulder as I read what was written on the screen. The file was titled 'Students I Have Slept With', and it consisted of a long list of students' names arranged in alphabetical order with the date he'd fucked them and a column of comments on the far right of the screen. I looked up my own name to see if it was on the list and it was. I read the comment. It said, 'Nice ass. Tits soft and pink, a little pointed and small but very responsive. Fabulous cunt: wet, deep and incredibly strong. Orgasm: very vocal, nice and quick, and unexpectedly exciting. Overall quite satisfying, if a little too straight for my taste.' Reading Bataille's assessment I felt a warm glow spread from my lower abdomen down to my cunt and then up my stomach over my chest, around my tits, along my neck and all over my face. Then I looked at the next entry below mine. It was dated two days before our fuck and then the next day and every successive day up until yesterday. I started to read the comments but had to stop after the first sentence which infuriated me and I felt my whole body, especially my anus, tense up in an ugly cocktail of jealousy, betrayal and anger. *Even Bataille preferred fucking someone else.* I contemplated leaving, just standing up and walking out, but I decided that that would make it too easy for Bataille. No doubt she was just a phone call away.

'What's this?' I demanded, pointing at the offensive comments.

'It's sort of a diary,' he said, quitting the file and turning the computer off.

I reached over and turned it back on but the computer was locked. There was no way of getting the file back on the screen.

'It's locked,' he said superfluously.

I refused to look at him and stared obstinately at the screen. I considered my options. I could quiz him about his other lovers, I could be unrelenting and unpick his character, thread by thread, I could amass accusations, or I could get straight to the point. I decided to get straight to the point and after a few moments' reflection, my resolve strengthened, I swivelled around in the chair and without another word slapped him hard across the face.

He hit me straight back even harder, taking me by surprise. Then he ran from the room. I was slow to take chase and by the time I reached the door leading out to the verandah it was locked. For a few seconds I threw myself at the door but it didn't budge, the wooden frame didn't even split, so I gave up and ran for the second door. But Bataille had already run down the corridor and we ended up crashing against the second door at roughly the same time. A struggle ensued. Bataille tried to close the door and thereby lock me in the room, and I struggled to get out of the room. Stronger than me, he reached through the closing gap and tried to pull my arms away from the door. His hand gripped my wrist and squeezed, hurting me, so I bit it until he let go. Finally he held my wrists so tightly I cried out and fell to the floor. The door slammed closed in my face.

I hammered on the door for a while with clenched fists. I started screaming abuse. I threw myself around the room, hitting my head against the walls and floor, butting the door with my forehead. Next I attacked myself, thumping my thighs with balled fists and pulling large clumps of hair from my head. Then I started to cry. 'I don't want any more, I don't want any more,' I moaned over and over. Exhausted, I let the tears continue in a steady stream down my face and snot run dripping from my nose. I wiped the snot on my sleeves until they were soaked and then I just used my hand, flinging the watery mucus onto the floor, the drops making puddles on the carpet and then I traced things with my fingers in the puddles.

I suspected I couldn't be seen or heard. Hours passed. I stopped crying. I was sick of this game. I had no idea of the time but I remembered I had things to do and I wanted to leave. Just when I'd given up on Bataille there was a knock on the door. A slender dark-haired girl with full deep red lips, fair freckled skin and long sinuous limbs stood in the doorway with a tray of tea. I thanked her and shook my head. Then I walked past her through the door and on into the lounge room. Bataille sat in one of the shiny chrome and black-painted wooden chairs listening to music through headphones with his eyes closed. A white cat with no ears and only one sky blue eye sat purring on his lap and the hand that was covered in the cat scratches gripped the cat's deformed tail, white-knuckled. I didn't bother to say goodbye and kept walking on through the house and out onto the street. I walked for a few blocks, sneezing every few steps and rubbing my eyes. I hailed a cab, climbed into the back seat and blacked out.

When I got home there was a note in my mailbox. It was handwritten and I thought I recognised the writing, although I couldn't be sure. It said, 'I want to beat you, fuck you dead, kill you, cook you and feed you to my dog.' Then it told me to call sometime and left a phone number. I puzzled over the note as I rode upstairs in the lift. No doubt it was from an old boyfriend of mine, a jilted lover, and I quickly dismissed it, crushing it in my hand and throwing it in the rubbish as soon as I got inside.

I made a cup of tea and sat down at my desk. I thought about eating but decided I preferred to read instead. I had no appetite. I selected the novel by the young American from the piles of books strewn across my desk, the notebook looking abandoned at my feet. Nothing horrible had happened yet but as I read on I became aware that the author was dropping a lot of clues designed to alert the reader to the fact that things were not what they seemed. For example, he kept making references to famous serial killers at inappropriate moments, and hinting that he was an evil psychopath. It wasn't until I'd read a third of the book that I realised the narrator wasn't joking. That he *was* an evil psychopath. I put the book down, goosebumps prickling my arms, and looked around my flat. It was nearly eight o'clock. It was dark outside. I hadn't eaten anything all day. I hadn't started packing or done anything about going to my parents' house at the coast. And my flat looked like a total pigsty.

I hauled out the vacuum cleaner and plugged it in. I

pushed the machine around the room, at the same time sweeping the carpet with the nozzle and brush. I hated vacuuming. Soon I was sneezing. Five, six, seven, ten times in a row. Then I was laughing, kneeling on the floor and laughing. I was just opening the windows to blow away some of the dust when the phone rang. I made a serious face and picked up the phone. It was Sade.

'Where are you?' he wanted to know.

'What do you mean?' I said, still laughing.

'It's nine o'clock. You were supposed to be here an hour ago,' he said, his voice a mixture of anger and despair. 'Don't you remember?'

'Sorry,' I said, 'I forgot.' As I hung up the phone I could hear Sade's voice calmly telling me not to bother, that he'd gone off the idea, that he was eating out. I hurried out the door.

The streets were deserted. The road and pavements relucent with rain. The frigid drizzling sky stung my eyes. I sneezed and crossed the street. I looked over my shoulder. On the other side of the road not far behind me I glimpsed a dark-clad figure as it passed beneath a street lamp and watched it dissolve once more into the murky shadows. I guessed it was a man, although I couldn't be sure and, teeth chattering, I quickened my pace into a slow run. When I reached Sade's I held my finger impatiently on his buzzer. There was no answer. I pressed again, anxiously looking over my shoulder. Still there was no answer. I tried one more time and then moved away from the door and stood waiting, back to the wall of the building, facing the street. The rain continued, the cars made delicious swishing sounds, my nose started to run, my eyes watered and finally I sneezed. I wiped my nose on my sleeve and took up my vigil once more.

Even so I didn't see Sade until, feeling a gentle tap on my shoulder, I turned around and there he was standing right by my side. He held a 1.5 litre bottle of Italian red wine and a loaf of crusty bread in the crook of his arm. I repressed a shudder. He glared at me and without a word turned on his heel and opened the huge brass security grille with his key. I followed him inside, my mind racing—Sade had followed me along the street, he'd written the note, he was trying to frighten me, he was succeeding—as the lift doors clanked shut and I stared at the lights flashing on and off as we passed each floor. The lift shuddered and stopped at the fifth floor. Sade opened the doors and nodded to me to get out. I did but I didn't want to walk down the long corridor knowing Sade was following unseen behind me, so I waited for him to close the doors and we walked to his apartment together.

His flat was warm with cooking smells and with the table set—complete with candles and a vase of white roses—seemed almost homely. He told me to sit down, and as I listened to him slice up the bread and open the wine I almost felt reassured enough to suspect someone else of following and harassing me. But I didn't quite relinquish my suspicions or let down my guard. And when the phone rang just as we were about to start on the salad—rocket, baby English spinach and vine-ripened tomatoes tossed in a lemon, rock salt, virgin olive oil and coarsely ground black pepper dressing—my anxiety about Sade increased exponentially.

'I'm not going to answer that,' he said, and then answered it.

I watched, salad leaves poised mid-air on the tip of my fork, as he picked up the phone and disappeared with it into the bedroom.

I finished my share of the salad and sipped at a glass of the cheap Italian wine. I considered leaving but curiosity got the better of me and I walked past the bedroom door to the kitchen, hoping the sound of my footsteps would encourage him to hang up. I started to make a cup of tea. Leaving the kettle to boil on the stove I tiptoed back and stood listening outside the bedroom door.

'Just because I fuck you sometimes doesn't mean I want to spend the rest of my goddamned life with you,' Sade shouted.

I pushed the door open and he cupped his hand over the receiver.

'I think you should hang up now,' I said.

He shrugged, told me to close the door behind me, and resumed his conversation.

I left and ran home, the streets, everything, a blur. I tried calling him, confused and upset, but the number was busy. When I finally got through there was no answer. I sat on the floor and let my head fall into my hands. 'Annihilation,' I chanted, 'annihilation.' I had to get out of the flat.

It had stopped raining outside and the wide street was sleek rather than shiny. I made my way back to Sade's apartment building, all the time looking over my shoulder in case someone was following me but I saw no-one and was absolutely alone on the street. Soon I stood gazing up into Sade's windows, but they were all dark and I saw nothing through their grimy glass. I made my way back home but at the last minute turned towards the shops and restaurants. I went walking among strangers keeping my face turned from theirs, hands in my pockets and my shoulders slumped forwards. At some stage I crashed head-on into a skinny young woman prostitute. As I apologised I glanced into her eyes. They were rust-brown and pinned and didn't quite focus. 'You are dead,' I told her in a whisper as I passed. Then involuntarily I stopped dead in my tracks and watched mesmerised as she wove her way—black leggings rolled up to the knee, black pumps, faded blue denim jacket, black camisole, calf muscles dotted with bruises—through the crowd. I realised I envied her and the chilly distance she maintained between herself and all that happened in the world. I turned away and hurried home.

Door locked, lights out, I sat cross-legged crying on the floor and dialled Sade's number every half hour. Finally, shortly after midday the following afternoon, he picked up the phone and I told him I was going to kill myself if he didn't come over.

Satisfied that I had his attention at last I turned on the TV and waited for him to arrive. I kicked off my shoes and changed into a T-shirt and a pair of shorts.

There was a knock at the door. I hesitated to open it—if it was Sade then how did he get in without using the intercom?—and asked who it was through the closed door.

'It's me,' he answered.

I opened the door and Sade pushed past me into the room and walked straight over to the window.

I asked him how he was and offered him a cup of tea but he didn't answer me and shook his head.

'Well, I'm going to have one anyway,' I continued, 'are you sure you don't want one too?'

His fists clenched and unclenched at his sides. He squinted up his eyes and pressed his temples with his forefingers. He wiped his brow on his sleeve. Then he exploded.

'Look,' he said, spinning around. 'I thought you were supposed to be committing suicide.'

I stood my ground. 'Do you want to talk about it?' I said, my hands on my hips.

'Why don't you just hurry up and get it over with?' he said, walking towards the door.

I ran across the room so I was standing in his path.

'Are you fucking her?' I demanded. 'Are you fucking the woman you visited the other day?' I stared him in the eye.

'I don't know what you're talking about,' he said, pushing me aside and running for the elevator. I went to follow him and paused in the doorway looking around for shoes but there wasn't time. I grabbed the keys and leapt into the lift just as the doors were closing. We glared at each other all the way down and then when the doors opened he pushed in front of me and strode out onto the street. I followed him. He looked back over his shoulder and seeing me, crossed to the other side. So did I.

I ran to catch up with him. Then I tugged at his sleeve.

'You treat me like shit,' I said, furious.

'Look, will you just fuck off?' he snarled, stopping and facing me. 'I don't want to talk to you.'

Despondent, I looked down at the ground. It was hot outside, a final burst of summer and the pavement was so hot it was sizzling my feet.

'Have you any idea how hot the pavement is?' I said, wanting to cry.

'Why don't you just go home?' Sade snapped. 'I don't want to talk to you.'

I considered going home but something crazy inside me clicked and it was impossible. When Sade walked away again I ran after him, screaming at him at the top of my voice. People on the street stopped and stared. He started to run but I ran too, glass entering my feet in long thin shards. I wailed for him to stop but he paid no attention to me. He turned into a little park and slowed down to a walk. I caught up with him at the bubbler. He held his mouth down ready to drink but nothing happened. I grabbed his sleeve and begged him to wait and he hit my hand away, shouting, 'Don't touch me.' He walked up the stairs into the belvedere and sat down. I sat opposite him. He would not look me in the eye. I sighed. From the corner of my eye I watched a young man and woman shoot smack in the bushes nearby. After they'd rolled down their sleeves they crawled out and he dragged her to her feet. They stood swaying, clasping each other. Her eyes were closed and her head so slumped her chin touched her chest. Catching me staring, the man smiled. He

103

half-carried, half-dragged the woman over to a bench and sat her down. Then he wove his way over to the belvedere and up the stairs and asked me for a cigarette. I shook my head and told the junkie to ask Sade. Sade lied and said he didn't have any.

'He's lying,' I told the junkie.

The junkie stood shaking his head for a while and then joined his friend on the bench. As soon as he was gone I started screaming at Sade, not really caring what I was saying, but demanding to know what was going on and accusing him of betraying me. Sade ignored me. I kicked him in the shins and he kicked me back. Then I punched him in the face. He swung back at me and missed. I laughed. I resumed glaring at him from my side of the belvedere. From the corner of my eye I saw the junkie walk over again.

'She's really beautiful,' the junkie told Sade. Sade raised his eyebrows. 'Really man,' his dry rasping voice croaked on, 'all I see's someone who's a very beautiful person and who's very very hurt. You two've got something really special. A real strong vibration, you should stop fighting.'

Sade and I stared off in different directions.

'Do you have any cigarettes?' the junkie asked, his voice soft and dry.

'Sure,' Sade said, offering him the packet.

'Thanks mate,' the junkie said, looking at me. 'Good luck, you two.'

We didn't say goodbye. When the junkie left I told Sade to get fucked. He told me to fuck off and I said,

'No, you fuck off.' He stood up and left. This time I didn't follow him. I closed my eyes. When I opened them again it was growing dark and I was alone in the park. I examined the undersides of my feet under a street lamp. Long white blisters covered the pads and deformed the underside of each foot, giving the shapely curves and delicate sweeps hideous new contours and monstrous proportions. The heels were speckled with glass.

I left the belvedere and crossed the street. The public phone booth on the corner was empty and I used it to call Sade. There was no-one home. My feet hurt though not as much as I expected. I didn't really know what I expected any more. I guess my feet didn't really hurt. I wandered the streets. I decided things were over with Sade and me. There wasn't any point in going on. I just wanted to tell him not to call me ever again. I really didn't want any more. There weren't many people around, or at least, I didn't see many. It took forever to get home. When I did, I noticed that an entire ethnic family were moving into the one-bedroom flat next door to me. Mother, father, baby and toddler. I closed the door behind me. There was still so much noise in my flat from the family that I had to cover my head with a pillow. I called Sade again. Again he wasn't there. I soaked my feet in the sink in warm water and disinfectant. I lay down across my bed and fell asleep. I woke up with an image of Sade smiling at me floating around in my head. I called him again. The family next door must have finished moving in and gone out because it was quiet in my flat again. I changed and went out. I reminded myself it was over with Sade. I felt pangs. I told myself to ignore them. I decided it was time to move to a new flat. Moving would help me get away from Sade. In any event I hadn't been paying my rent. No doubt I would find an eviction notice in my mailbox any day.

It was raining outside. I made my way to Sade's and circled his apartment building, walking around and around the block. I had to walk on the outsides of my feet because of the blisters and glass. This didn't feel strange, but I was moving very slowly. Tired, I sat on the bench opposite the doors to Sade's apartment building. I half expected to see him pull up in a cab with Juliette. After a while I limped over to the cafe and sat at the window table. The waiter smiled hello, remembering me. I ordered a cup of tea, then a glass of red wine, then another glass of red wine. There was no sign of Sade and I could feel my anger subside. I reminded myself I was angry. I asked the waiter to bring my bill. While I waited I flipped through a magazine. There was an interview with the young American writer inside. I read it and wished I was like him. Male, American, wealthy, successful, creative, famous. I went to the bathroom. As I washed my hands under the taps I planned how I'd go home, make myself something to eat, and spend a quiet evening at home reading the rest of the American novel.

I'd paid my bill and was on my way home when I saw him. Or at least I thought it was him. I abandoned my plan and went running after Sade. As I drew closer he turned around. It was him. He started running away from me but I was ready for him this time and sprinted after him, blisters momentarily forgotten. In no time I held him by the back of his coat. I stopped. The coat started to tear. He stopped and turned around to face me.

'What do you want?' he demanded, pulling at his coat.

'I want an explanation,' I said, not letting go.

'But I don't want to talk to you,' he said, tugging hard on the coat, the coat ripping in two.

'OK, Sade, have it your way,' I said, dropping the strip of coat to the ground. 'But before you scurry away I just want you to know that I think you're a lousy scumbag. You're a liar and a cheat and I don't want anything more to do with you. You're totally fucked. So just fuck off.'

I turned to leave but he grabbed me by the wrist and prevented me from moving. I noticed there were people watching us but when I looked at them they looked away. Sade twisted my wrist, hurting me. I gasped.

'You're the one who's fucked,' he growled. 'You're so fucked up you need a psychiatrist.'

Not wanting to hear any more I kicked him hard in the shins and when he loosened his grip, squealing with pain, I tore my wrists away from him and ran as fast as I could. He chased me for a while, I heard his footsteps thundering after mine, but I ran down a narrow lane and he didn't follow me. I soon found out why. The lane was a dead-end. Gasping for breath I retraced my steps, looking to my left and right for other lanes or walkways, Sade's final words echoing in my head. I came upon an alleyway that led past the steps of a church. I hurried along it. I could hear his footsteps chasing me again. It wouldn't be long before he turned down the alleyway. I had no idea where it led. To the left of the church steps was a stack of folded tables and chairs. They leant against the wall of the church. On hands and knees I crawled behind the stack of tables and chairs. My heart was beating so loud I was sure he'd hear it. His footsteps thundered past. I waited, too frightened to move. Soon it was quiet but I still didn't leave my hiding place. Hours passed. It grew colder. I sneezed and, panicking that someone might have heard, crept away from the stack of furniture. I hurried, feet clenched into balls of pain, back the way I'd come and slowly made my way home.

Two blocks from my building I stopped for a rest. I sat down on a damp cement step and closed my eyes. I didn't notice anything at first. A prickling sensation at the back of my neck, a change in the direction of the wind, a long break in the passing traffic. By the time I did notice that there was someone standing right beside me it was too late to get up and walk away. He was too close, so I pretended not to have noticed for a while and I wondered what to do. I couldn't think of anything. My mind was blank. I was so tired, so fed up with everything, that it almost came as a relief when he grabbed me by the wrist and twisted my arm behind my back. He twisted harder and lifted me to my feet. Then, his hand over my mouth he half-dragged, half-pushed me along a pathway that led between two blocks of apartment buildings. We passed beneath a walkway. He threw me against the wall. It was very dark, I couldn't see his face, I didn't really want to know. I considered asking him not to hurt me because I was pregnant but I couldn't be bothered. I just wanted it to be over so I could go home. He hit me across the face and then beat my head against the wall. It sounded like my skull was cracking. Then he threw me to the ground and dug around in my pockets for my wallet. I heard my wallet land on the ground beside me. Not thinking about what I was doing I started screaming, 'Help, police, help,' but he was gone.

The police arrived half an hour later. She hadn't moved. She lay face down at the top of a flight of stairs in a pool of blood. The police lifted her up, examined her injuries, called an ambulance, asked her what had happened and took down her personal details. They wanted to know how much money had been stolen from her wallet. She didn't know. They asked if she knew her assailant. She told them he seemed familiar, but it had been too dark for her to see his face. They helped her into the ambulance. They advised her to have photographs taken of her face and head, just in case anything turned up and she wanted to press charges. They also told her to go to the local police station and make a statement about the assault. She did neither.

Later that night, alone in her flat once more, she went through the yellow pages, looking under P for psychiatrist. She squinted, her blurred vision singling out the only familiar name before her. She copied the number into her diary. Finished, she let her bloodied head slide aching to the floor.

Ophelia

1

THE TRAFFIC INCHED ITS WAY DOWN THE NARROW ONE-WAY street, hemmed in on both sides by uneven asphalt footpaths seething with an inclement mob. Some held brown paper bags to their lips as they ambled along, others applied lipstick, standing still. Others stared, smiling hugely into shop windows, opening and closing their eyes, touching up their hair. A group of ten or more women wearing stilettos, short tight skirts and huge shoulder pads in their jackets clacked past, tripping up on the uneven surface, and bursting into shrill inexplicable showers of sharp giggles. A group of African-American sailors stood outside the twenty-four hour newsagent, blocking the streaming crowd and grabbing people as they squeezed past. Another fountain of laughter from the stilettoed women. Through a gap in the crowd the smeared faces of child-runaways stared out at the passers-by, watching for likely faces and then waving cardboard cups filled with loose change and mumbling about needing money for phone calls.

113

A barefoot teenage girl walked from car window to car window asking for cigarettes.

A man stood between two parked cars and vomited into the gutter. His friends formed a tight circle around him and continued smoking cigarettes, telling jokes and staring across the stagnant sea of cars at the women clacking down the other side of the road. Another man gripped the cold metal pole of a street sign, his knees wobbling beneath him, his eyes rolling back in his head, his free hand scratching his nose, ears and cheeks, his head slowly sinking back, then stopping and then sinking in the opposite direction, slowly falling forwards, then stopping again. Finally he collapsed onto his knees, one hand still holding onto the pole, forehead down against the pavement. He was only wearing one cowboy boot. A woman wearing knee-length black vinyl boots, sheer black stockings and suspender belt, a G-string and a leather vest stood on the corner bitching at the ogling suburbanites and smiling into the dark windows of the slowly passing cars.

Above the heads of the crowd and the slow stream of traffic, above the roofs of the huge Japanese-filled diesel-drinking tour buses, a network of neon signs laced the balconies and windows of what was formerly an elegant row of grandiose three- and four-storey terrace houses. Behind the fantastical twisting array—playground for semioticians and ethnologists, map and guidebook for pornologists and visitors from the jungles of the suburbs—the windows themselves were mostly sealed off. Either they were blocked in with cardboard, hung with rags, or if double-glazed, the cream-coloured undersides of heavy silk curtains made sure nothing within could be seen from outside and whatever took place behind the curtains remained there. Hidden, secret and utterly transparent at the same time.

Intoxicated, Justine sat in the back seat of a cab and watched the passing crowd. Beer, pool and cigarettes in the early hours of the evening had been followed by red wine, chips and joints, which had been followed by speed, vodka and dancing. She'd only been dancing for a few minutes when she'd bent over double—her short stretch velvet dress bunching up to reveal her black cotton stockinged ass, the centre seam buried deep inside the crack that ran between her cheeks and the lips of her pussy split in silhouette against the dance-floor—and had to make her way outside murmuring, fresh air, I need fresh air. After walking around the block a few times she'd finally slipped into the front garden of a dilapidated terrace house, removed her fur waistcoat and, pressed between the wrought iron fence and a dense row of privet, relieved her insides of some of the toxic waste that had accumulated within.

She looked across the seat at Ophelia. Ophelia smiled back, cocking her left eyebrow and nodding her head. Ophelia was very beautiful with her long loops of red-blonde hair, round blue staring eyes, fair freckled skin and boyish physique. Suddenly the car accelerated into a space in front and bumped through a ditch. Justine's breasts thumped against her chest, huge and sore. She gazed mournfully through the window. There was a corrugated-iron wall covered in posters and graffiti. One poster in particular caught her eye. It was a black-and-white photograph of a

115

woman, her hair tousled and her eyes underlined with dark circles. She held a clump of hair in her hand. Beneath the photo it said: FREE PREGNANCY COUNSELLING and gave a phone number. She felt sick again. She held her hand over her mouth as a fresh wave of nausea bubbled up. Being out of it didn't help. She took deep breaths until the nausea began to subside. She was exhausted.

'I've got to have an abortion tomorrow,' she said, chewing on the rough edge of an already bitten fingernail. 'I'm not supposed to have anything to eat or drink after twelve o'clock tonight.'

Ophelia stared at her, her eyes huge, her mouth opening and closing like a fish. Finally she said, 'Oh my God,' and took Justine's hand.

'This time I don't even know how or when it happened,' Justine complained, squeezing Ophelia's hand before freeing her own. 'With all my previous unplanned pregnancies I've always been able to pin-point a specific instance of negligence—you know, either it was a case of the diaphragm that didn't work because it stayed in the bathroom cupboard throughout intercourse, or it was a case of the it-couldn't-happen-to-me-again syndrome when it always does, or it was a case of the art of withdrawal that ends up a simultaneous orgasm, or, worst of all, it's the I-don't-give-a-fuck-any-more syndrome, or the dreaded let's-have-a-baby misunderstanding when it turns out he was only joking that day on the beach when you were stoned and eating ice-creams but you thought he was serious—I mean, I think I've just about done them all. But this time. Fuck only knows.

116

'For years doctors have been telling me that pre-come is as dangerous as ejaculation but I never believed them. But after this last instance of the unplanned pregnancy I'm afraid that I'm going to have to agree even pre-come can do it. I just feel so sorry for myself, seven abortions and I'm not even thirty yet. By the time I get around to having my mid-thirties baby I probably won't be able to hold onto the fucking foetus any more. And all because I won't take the fucken pill. And why won't I take the fucking pill? Because there's something about the fucking pill that really makes me mad. I mean domestic animals take hormones, athletes, women. I don't know, call me a feminist or something but no matter how many abortions I have I'm never going to put up with the fucking pill.

'But I guess it's not even the pill. It's just that I have real problems with contraception. Real problems. I can't take care of myself, something like that, the old passive woman routine or something like that. I keep expecting the man to take care, to care more about me than about his pleasure. I keep dreaming of the man who's just so understanding and responsible that he absolutely won't come near me without ten feet of protection, but I haven't met him yet.'

She stared miserably out the window at the row of posters. She counted eight FREE PREGNANCY COUNSELLING posters as the taxi inched agonisingly slowly down the crowded street. With a sickening thud a beer can full of vomit splashed against her half-open window. Pink vomit oozed down the other side of the glass. She dry-retched on the smell and turning away buried her face in Ophelia's black leather shoulder. The nausea began to subside. She wound up the window and looked through the thicket of cars for the assailant. A derelict old man sat wrapped in a blanket in a doorway screaming abuse and waving his fists around in the air. No-one listened to what he said. She suspected he was responsible for the beer can. She wondered if he had anywhere to go.

'Does Sade know you're pregnant?' Ophelia asked.

The stench of vomit trapped inside the sealed space made Justine's head spin. She wound down the window again and took huge gulps of the fetid, exhaust-filled air.

'He knows,' she said bitterly, running her hand over the dry scabs on the back of her head, the bumps still sore to touch. She considered taking out the small make-up mirror she carried with her wherever she went and checking that the layers of foundation covered her black eye. She was too tired. She counted the days since she'd seen him. She straightened her back, the bruised vertebra ached where it pressed against the seat.

'So where is he? Why isn't he taking care of you?' Ophelia demanded.

Justine shrugged her shoulders.

Ophelia shook her head and blew air angrily through her nose. 'Is he going with you tomorrow?' she asked. 'Because I'll come if you need me to.'

'That's OK,' Justine said, 'I can go on my own.'

'You can't go on your own.'

'I don't want to talk about it any more,' Justine snapped, closing her eyes and leaning back in the seat. She lifted her dress above her waist and gently massaged the soft roll of fat beneath her belly button.

'I hate seeing you so miserable,' Ophelia complained.

Justine smiled a wan smile.

'Just so long as you don't feel guilty because you're not having the child,' Ophelia persisted. 'Remember that it's society that makes women who don't surrender their lives to the labour of mothering feel like shit. Shaming women into becoming mothers is one way of making sure the social world reproduces itself. Anyway, there's plenty of other women out there queuing up for the privilege of reproducing the species, I mean really, you don't need it. Trust me. Become a mother when you want to and when it matters. Don't do what I did.'

The cab broke free of the traffic and they went speeding down the street, the driver making wild loops around cars reverse parking into tiny spaces. After the third loop the cab pulled up without warning, sending them forwards in their seats, and Justine crashing into the back of the front seat. *If only I could miscarry*. A sharp cramp went shooting through her abdomen. She was swept away by a tidal wave of self-pity. Nothing good ever happened to her. She couldn't even kill herself when she wanted to. She was an absolute loser. Her whole life was just one big abortion. Seven abortions proved it. You can't abort something that's already an abortion.

Preoccupied, hands draped across her abdomen, Justine followed Ophelia from the cab to the entrance of the nightclub. Soon she was pushing her way to the front of the crowd of teenage suburbanites and middle-aged lowlifes, brushing aside huge fronds of frizzy hair and scratching and clawing her way through a jungle of

119

trench coats and leather jackets. The air was rich with the sweet stench of hair-care products. She held her breath. Finally she reached the swinging double doors and stood clutching Ophelia by the arm, awaiting inspection by the Door.

The Door was tall and blond, his large-boned frame enhanced and enlarged with countless telltale gym-built muscles. His hair was styled à la *Triumph of the Will* and he spoke with an East End twang.

'Yeah, you two.'

He nodded his head and opened the door. When she looked up to smile her gratitude he was already checking out the new arrivals as they flocked around him, toothpick between his full orange-red lips, heads only reaching what was undoubtedly a hairless white chest.

Inside, Justine fought to keep up with Ophelia amidst the seething crowd. It took forever to get from the doorway to the bar, people were so tightly packed into the dark narrow space.

'Jesus,' she complained into Ophelia's ear, 'I don't know if I can stay here very long, I've seen about four ex-fucks already. It's a real Friday night crowd.'

Ophelia wriggled closer to the bar and joined the queue of people waiting to order a drink. Suddenly a man's face popped out of the tangled mass of bodies and two pink round smiling cheeks grinned at Ophelia.

'Ophelia,' he said.

'Oh hi, Masoch,' Ophelia shouted above the music. 'How're you?'

'I'm having the craziest time, I'm so stoned,' Masoch

shouted back as he was swept away by the wash of people.

'God,' Justine shouted, her lips searching for Ophelia's ear amidst the loops of fine hair. 'He's absolutely fucking gorgeous.'

'I met him on my last trip to Europe,' Ophelia shouted back. 'He's a famous performance artist. He's really into masochism. You know, he embroiders his own skin, that kind of thing.'

'I think Sade's a bit of a masochist,' Justine confessed.

'Is he really?' Ophelia exclaimed. 'Masoch's actually a really nice person.'

'So what's he doing in a dump like this?' Justine asked provocatively.

'He must be on tour,' Ophelia explained.

Masoch was close to the door. It looked like he was going to leave. At the last minute he turned around, smiling, and waved goodbye.

'I don't think they're here,' Ophelia shouted. 'Let's try the bar across the road.'

2

THE BAR WAS OVERCROWDED. THE BUMPS ON JUSTINE'S HEAD ached. She felt nauseous again. Everywhere she looked she saw a seething sea of bodies as the intoxicated hordes made their way up and down the length of the bar, sometimes plunging into the row of occupied barstools and sending the black-clothed patrons giggling to the tiled floor, at other times grinding to a halt when too many people tried to force their way between those leaning against the wall and those seated at the bar. With each new surge in the crowd she swished swarms of careless cigarettes away from her stockings. When the crush subsided again she quickly examined her attire.

Her black stretch velvet dress had wriggled up her thighs and gathered into clumps and folds around her hips and the low-cut bodice was twisted to one side leaving her breasts almost totally exposed. Her fur waistcoat had slipped back on her shoulders so that the V at the front pressed uncomfortably at her neck. Her G-string had insinuated itself deep between the cheeks of her buttocks and her black cotton tights were piled elephantine atop her ankles. She removed her make-up mirror from her bum bag and checked her eye. The purple bruise was hidden beneath layers of foundation. She was seized by a minor anxiety attack. *There were too many attractive young women at this nightclub.* She applied a fresh coat of lipstick. She twisted the mirror this way and that and studied her face reflected back in puny rectangular planes. Large blue eyes with short straight lashes and fine curved eyebrows, the skin beneath the eyes as fine as paper and lightly smudged with faint purple smears; high cheekbones and smooth cheeks of dazzling fair skin; full lips and a wide smiling mouth of small ivory teeth; delicate nostrils and a straight nose lightly dusted with freckles; oval forehead and temples blue-white and framed with soft wisps of white-blonde hair. Anxiety momentarily appeased, she zipped up her bum bag. She wrestled with her dress, waistcoat, G-string and stockings and took another sip of her drink. Stoli, lime and soda, tall glass, black straw. She took a puff of Simone's cigarette.

'I need drugs,' Justine whined, shaking her hair back from her face.

Simone nodded absently and continued staring at the crowd.

'This is crazy,' Justine exclaimed, 'I don't know what I'm doing here. Simone, do you know what I'm doing here, can you tell me what I'm doing in this dive?'

'Trying to get laid,' Simone answered, sounding bored.

Justine sighed, checked over her shoulder and saw that

THE RIVER OPHELIA

Ophelia and Marcelle were still deep in conversation, still leaning against the wall, and then let her eyes wander down into the smooth dark cavern between Simone's breasts, a place of deep shadows and steep descents. Simone's high, pointed, olive-skinned breasts were clad in a black body suit with a criss-cross lace-up front. Over this Simone wore a black silk voile shirt open to the waist. She looked up from Simone's breasts just in time to notice a businessman in a designer suit with a smooth suntanned face make eye-contact and Simone's flicker of recognition. She felt like giving up. Besides, she had a termination to go to tomorrow morning.

'I'm out of here,' she announced and emptied her glass in one gulp.

'Justine, don't go yet,' Simone said, looking away from a tall man with intense dark eyes, his black curls parted to the side and slicked back from his face, her attention only briefly focused on Justine, 'I haven't finished telling you about last Saturday night.'

Justine looked outside at the quiet street. *Despair.* 'OK, tell me about last Saturday night,' she said, resigned, 'but then I've got to go.'

'I bought a gun,' Simone began, her mouth pressed to her ear. 'I bought a gun a couple of weeks ago, you know, to feel safe. I have it with me now, here in the inside pocket of my jacket. And last Saturday night I raped a lawyer at gunpoint and then I shot him.'

'Are you serious?'

'He wanted me to,' Simone added, ignoring a good-looking man wearing a suit and tortoiseshell prescription

124

glasses who was trying to buy her a drink.

'I don't believe this,' Justine said, feeling inadequate, 'my best-friend's sister, a degenerate sex-offender.'

'You want to hear the whole thing?'

'Sure.'

'Well,' Simone said, her lips tickling Justine's ear, 'all through dinner I've got the gun in my handbag, loaded. Then after dinner we go back to his place and he tells me he really wants to fuck me and I ask what kind of sex he likes and he tells me that he'll do anything I want no matter how weird or kinky and at first I think, ooh, how creepy, but then I remember the gun in my handbag and I relax.

'Anyway, so then he asks me if I've ever been tied up by a man and I say no and ask him if he's ever been tied up by a woman and he says yes and I ask whether he liked it and he said he did but it wasn't his favourite thing to do, not by a long shot.'

'Let me guess,' Justine said, interrupting, 'he's into body parts and he opens the freezer and it's full of pieces of women's bodies.'

'Wait, I'll get to the body parts, don't rush me,' Simone said, turning her back, Justine noticed out of the corner of her eye, on a young guy dressed in black with piercing blue eyes who was staring meaningfully at Simone's breasts. 'So I ask him what his favourite thing is,' Simone continued, 'and he won't tell me, he goes all coy and smiles this little-boy smile and even though I'm totally freaked out by this guy I lean over and kiss him, you know, I can't help myself, and his lips are incredibly soft and loose and they smell like fish but he didn't have fish for dinner he had beef, and they sort of melt in my mouth and it's really weird like there's no muscle or flesh or whatever there normally is in lips, these lips are like two rubbery flaps of skin and I feel like I'm drinking them and when I bite them just a tiny little bit they bleed, but they don't just bleed a little bit like you'd expect, they bleed and bleed and I feel like I'm choking there's so much blood going down my throat so I stop kissing him and try to swallow it down but spit it out on the floor instead and wipe my mouth on his shirt.'

'Jesus, Simone, where'd you meet this guy?'

'Here, a couple of weeks ago,' Simone said defensively. 'I did warn you about coming here.'

'Yeah, yeah,' Justine said, desperate for another drink. 'So are you going to finish the story?'

'There's not much more to tell. Basically he turned out to be a total sicko blood-lusting degenerate, the kind of guy whose daily life makes the Marquis de Sade's one hundred and twenty days look like an amateur dress rehearsal, the kind of guy nice girls like us who go out looking for wild times should absolutely definitely keep well clear of but can't help getting mixed up with once they've started because they never back away from adventures even when they threaten to become terminal.

'Anyway, body parts. By the time I've finished with him he's not looking so great. I mean I might have shot him once but only after he'd ejaculated and when he asked me to. So yes, there were lots of body parts and they were his. In other words I don't expect to see him here again

126

tonight, at least, not in the flesh, if you know what I mean.'

'On top of everything else he was obviously a haemophiliac,' Justine said, looking at the crowd of people waiting to get in. *Simone was really wild.* The anxiety was back. She needed alcohol, she needed drugs and she needed them right away. She noticed a pretty brunette, early twenties, nice tits—large and high—perfect teeth, great body, expressive smile. The brunette held onto a tall youth, six-two, six-three, perfect pectorals, long blond dreadlocks, lightly tanned, designer clothes. She noticed them and she hated them. She watched, transfixed, as the doorman singled them out and, gently nudging the guy as he walked past, the brunette reaching up and kissing him, actually invited them into the club. The brunette pushed through the crowd, tits thrust out proudly before her and the youth followed behind, smiling at everyone as he passed. She came close, close enough to smell, and the mixture of perfume, smoke and sweat made Justine want to vomit. She dry-retched against Simone's shoulder.

'What about you,' Simone said, adjusting her skirt, 'how's Sade?'

'I haven't seen him for a while,' Justine said, recovering. 'He's got a bit of sorting out to do. He's experimenting with his sexuality. I think it's over.'

'And how's your night life going?' Simone said, reaching into her body-suit and rearranging her breasts. 'Any crazies, any wild times?'

'I felt four hard-ons last night,' Justine said, a cigarette stinging her thigh.

'Justine, you're giving women a bad name,' Simone quipped, smiling.

'I know,' she said, rubbing her leg. 'I mean, I'm not. I was drunk and I got squeezed by four guys.'

'So what were the guys like?' Simone asked, staring hard at a new arrival, handsome, thirty-ish, hard blue eyes, a black mole on his left cheek and a strong jaw line. 'Any possibilities?'

'Well, there was this really young one.'

'And?'

'He tongue-kissed me on the dance floor and pressed me against his hard-on,' Justine said, making a face.

Simone shook her head. 'And what was the ratio of free drinks to hard-ons like?'

'Pretty low, they were really cheap last night. So cheap that the last one actually stung me for his cab fare home, can you believe it?' Justine was livid.

'Who *are* these guys?'

'Not only that but he kept trying to kiss me and I kept having to clench my teeth and spit out his tongue,' Justine said, her cheeks red, her eyes staring straight ahead of her, not seeing.

'Where were you last night?' Simone asked, impressed.

'Here.' Justine was triumphant. 'And now I need alcohol.'

Justine stared into the bottom of her empty glass and then handed it to Simone. She rummaged inside her bum bag. Lipstick, make-up mirror, eye-liner, eye-shadow, keys, Swiss army knife, loose condoms, bank statement, loose coins, nail file, newspaper clipping and finally, so crumpled they felt like rags, a ball of notes. She handed a ten-dollar note to Simone. Simone laughed, accepted the bill, asked Justine if she wanted another Stoli, and strutted away. Looking up Justine noticed the pretty brunette and the tall youth leave. They didn't look back. *Places to go, people to see.* She clutched her fur waistcoat to her chest, out of place. She reached into the bum bag and took out the newspaper clipping.

The article was about a young woman who was brutally murdered and bashed by a man she knew from work and recognised at a nightclub. The night of her death she'd borrowed her father's car and gone out with two girl-friends. The man had recognised her and she'd danced with him at the nightclub before she told her friends she'd be right back and left the club with the man. A few hours later she was found dead in a pool of blood in the fire escape of a nearby hotel. Her head had been beaten against the rail and the stairs of the fire escape. The young woman was twenty-one when she died. She died from loss of blood, the result of severe blows to her face. Police believed the killer was sighted soon after the bashing when someone reported a possible victim of a stabbing. A man was seen standing covered in blood not far from the hotel, ten minutes after the attack. Next to the article was a photo of the young woman. She was pretty with a sweet smile, almond-shaped eyes, short shiny hair, large gold hoop earrings and dimples.

She held onto the article in a tightly clenched fist. She shivered. The hotel where the young woman was found was just around the corner from where she lived. She stared into the crowd. Her eyes, acting independently of the rest of her, singled out a perfect face. Twenty-four/twenty-five, black leather jacket with zips, goatee beard, crew cut, gold-framed glasses, single gold earring. She felt a smile creeping across her face, the half-dozen Stolis suddenly warm inside her. Everything became hazy and very slow: Simone paying for the drinks at the bar, the scantily clad African-American barman writing down his phone number on the back of a drink coaster and handing it to Simone with her change, the jazz/funk/rap fusion the DJ was playing, the surges in the crowd, all took place in an indistinct soft focus slow motion. She was still staring at the perfect face, incapable of making the first move or of acting in any way when Simone returned, handed her a drink and stood swaying in triplicate before her.

She felt a tap on her shoulder and spun around on her heel. Ophelia and Marcelle stood just behind her. Marcelle wanted to know if she needed another drink. Justine shook her head. Marcelle went to the bar. When Justine turned around to look for Simone she was gone. At her side Ophelia was staring blankly into the writhing sea of faces and puffing on a freshly lit cigarette. There were two dark, deeply-etched semi-circles beneath her eyes. She panicked. Who *was* Ophelia, anyway? She tried to recall the last time they'd met, a fragment of conversation, a time, a place, anything that had taken place before tonight, but she drew blanks. No meetings, no conversations, no times, no places. *Speak first and think later.* She crossed her fingers behind her back. Sweaty and trembling they wouldn't stay crossed. *Now, now.* But the moment passed. Had anyone noticed? Ophelia? The man with the square-

130

framed glasses and the strong jaw? No. No-one had noticed. And already she wasn't sure what had happened, if anything. She was upset, she was anxious, she was nauseous, she was having an abortion tomorrow. They were the facts. She let all the bottled up air out of her lungs. She turned to her friend. Ophelia looked tired. Justine smiled.

'I walked out,' Ophelia shouted. 'I snuck away and called a taxi from a public phone. Then I packed my bag and left, without even saying goodbye.'

Justine had no idea what Ophelia was talking about. Had she walked out of a marriage? Left home? Quit her job? What? She shook her head in confusion. She frowned. Then she frowned harder.

'I can't believe it either,' Ophelia agreed. 'I think he was just interested in me for sex.'

That narrowed it down. Justine nodded her head. So she'd left him, whoever he was. 'So now he's making harassment calls,' she ventured, shouting at the top of her voice.

'How did you know?' Ophelia asked defensively.

'And the police have told you there's nothing they can do,' she continued.

'Except change my number to a silent number and move to a different suburb,' Ophelia cried over the din. 'If I'd known it was going to turn out like this I never would have become involved from the beginning. I mean, everyone knows married men are dangerous, but he seemed so sweet and it all seemed so innocent, a weekend spent in his holiday house while his wife was overseas visiting her family, and we were friends, we've been friends for years. At the time I wondered if his invitation had sexual overtones but then I wondered if I wasn't reading too much into it, and I was, I admit, a little unsure, I didn't know if I wanted to fuck him. But I decided then and there that no matter what I wouldn't fuck him because he was a friend and because he was married.

'And so when I arrived and he didn't show me to my own room he showed me his room I told myself that was OK because we were going to share a bed, but it didn't necessarily mean we were going to fuck.'

'Fatal mistake.'

'Tell me about it,' Ophelia agreed. 'Anyway everything was fine until later that night when we started talking about sex.'

'I gather you were in his bed by this stage.'

'Well yes, but then he got really violent when I said I didn't want to sleep with him.'

'How long's his wife been away?'

Ophelia shrugged her shoulders. 'A few months I think.'

'Figures.'

'I just don't understand why he got so pissed off with me, why he had to spoil everything. I mean, I didn't say I was going to sleep with him and then change my mind, all I said was I didn't want to do it, I just didn't want to, I just couldn't explain. Anyway he pushed me out of the bed and then he wouldn't let me get back in and we had this fight and I got covered in bruises, you know, from wrestling all over the floor.'

'He hit you?'

'It was just a playful fight, you know, we ended up pulling the bedclothes off the bed and onto the floor. But in the middle of the fight he climbed on top of me, lying on me and then he started kissing me. So I said no again, I didn't want to. And then he got really indignant, you know, he said that he was really offended and that I'd rejected him and I said that I hadn't rejected him, I'd just rejected the idea of fucking him.'

'You rejected him.'

'Then he told me he thought I was sexually fucked up and that fucking someone was the best way to get over it and he thought that he was the person I should fuck.' A loop of hair fell into Ophelia's eyes and she brushed it angrily away.

'Of course there's nothing wrong with his sexuality,' Justine couldn't help pointing out. 'He's the one who's married and fucking around.'

'Well, that's why I didn't want to get involved in the first place,' Ophelia exclaimed, the hair back in her eyes. 'Anyway, we made up the bed again and climbed back in and I just wanted to go to sleep, you know, I was tired. Then right out of the blue he asked me to hold his cock because it was hard and when I said no he said that because of feminism men knew all about women and how to finger-fuck a woman and lick her out but women knew nothing about men and had no idea how to hold a cock or what felt nice.'

'Not that old trick,' Justine concluded damningly, enjoying herself. 'He sounds absolutely desperate.'

'I think he might have been,' Ophelia agreed, leaving the hair to dangle.

Justine cast her gaze out into the mass of bodies once more, her attention catching on the glimmer of an earring, the dazzling white of an intoxicated smile, a grey ringlet of smoke, a shiny dancer's brow.

'The thing is,' Ophelia said ominously, making her turn around, 'the thing about all this pain we go through, all this love that just hurts all the time, the thing about all this pain is that it's really exquisite. It's exquisite pain. That's what makes us keep going back for more.'

Justine nodded her assent. *Exquisite pain.* She was going to be sick. She reached inside her bum bag for the strip of Stemetil. She swallowed two dry. Marcelle appeared with fresh drinks. She grabbed Ophelia's and gulped it down. She wasn't going to make it. Abject, she gazed blankly into the crowd. From the other side of the room Sade's hard blue eyes stared back at her. Her eyes went rolling around her head. *Fuck.* She pushed the drink back at Ophelia, fell to the ground and crawled away on all fours, worming her way through the crowd on hands and knees. Marcelle and Ophelia watched speechlessly, mesmerised as the black cotton-clad cheeks of Justine's ass wobbled and shook and disappeared amidst the swaying coats and the thicket of legs.

3

SHE WENT RUNNING THROUGH THE CROWD. *SADE.* SHE WAS terrified. She crashed straight into a hugely pregnant woman. The woman complained. She didn't have time to apologise. The woman screamed after her. She pushed even harder against the stream of people who were heading for the door and fresh air. She heard Ophelia's voice over the din but she didn't stop. Soon she was swallowed by the swell of the crowd, just another body in a sea of black and leather and cigarettes and hats and fronds of denatured hair.

Simone stood leaning across the bar, waving a fifty-dollar bill at the African-American barman and smiling. Justine shouted hello and asked Simone to buy her a double vodka, straight up. Simone nodded and, smiling wider, waved the bill in the barman's face. He took Simone's order. He didn't look happy. Justine squeezed in next to Simone at the bar. Simone smiled at the man standing to her left. He smiled back.

'I know what you're going to think but I just have to tell you anyway,' the man told Simone. 'I don't normally go around doing this you understand, but I just have to tell you that you're an incredibly beautiful woman, I mean, movie star beautiful.'

A phone started ringing. The man reached inside his dinner jacket and pulled out a mobile phone. He placed the phone against his ear and covered his other ear with his hand.

'Yes it's me darling...' he shouted, 'sorry it's difficult to hear in here... it's difficult... no never mind... what?... breakfast tomorrow... OK, I'll pick you up at seven... a busy day, yes... I thought you were finished working Saturdays... what?... no, Saturdays... never mind... I said never mind... bye sweetheart... call me when you wake up... I love you too... I said, never mind.'

He folded up the aerial and put the phone back in the inside pocket of his coat. The drinks arrived. Simone handed the barman the money and he handed her the change. He didn't thank her for his tip. He danced to the other end of the bar, swinging his hips in his tight black leather pants. The man to Simone's left shook his head, huge Nazi-blue eyes bubbling out of his face, bow tie askew and bald head shining even in the dark of the smoky bar.

'Wow,' he said, acting amazed, 'you're really something. Are you sure you don't work in the movies? I mean, I don't understand why you don't. I'd love you to come do some work on my new film, just one day?'

'I'm too busy.'

'Do you have a boyfriend?' he persisted.

'Yes.'

'Well, where is he?' He looked from side to side.

Simone stared him dead in the eye. He looked down. 'He's away,' she said, sipping on her drink.

'Well, how can he go away and leave a beautiful woman like you?' the man wanted to know, not ready to give up. 'Isn't he afraid you'll be snatched up by sharks like me?'

Simone shrugged and picked up the drinks. The man leant very close and spoke into her ear.

'Do you know what,' he said in a stage whisper, 'I'd drop my girlfriend this very second if you'd agree to go out to dinner with me one night this week.'

Simone shook her head, ready to walk away.

'Look, you don't understand,' he explained, 'I know we've only just met but I've fallen hopelessly in love with you. I just think you're absolutely wonderful and I don't want you to go.'

'Oh well,' Simone said, feigning sympathy and walking away.

'Don't go,' he called after Simone, 'my girlfriend's a business consultant, she earns fifty grand a year, she's intelligent, attractive, maybe your boyfriend would like her, maybe we could line them up so we could go out together?'

'Look,' Simone said, deadly calm. 'I understand what you're going through. You're drunk, it's late, but I've got to tell you, I'm not madly in love with you, so that's that. Bye.'

Justine followed Simone as she forced a pathway

through the crowd. Suddenly someone grabbed her from behind by the arm and pulled her back. Almost tripping, she spun around. Sade stood holding her arm, his eyes staring playfully into hers, the corners of his mouth turned upwards in the beginnings of a smile. She stared back at him, abhorrent. *He was repugnant to her*. Gradually his eyes hardened and lost their glistening appeal. He buried his hands deep in his pockets and looked down at his feet. Nauseous again, she covered her mouth with one hand and wrapped the other across her abdomen. She bumped against Sade as the crowd surged around her. She bumped against him again and Sade reached out and steadied her, taking hold of her elbow.

'Don't you dare touch me,' she hissed from behind her hand. He let go, his arm flopping uselessly at his side.

'Justine, Justine, don't be like this,' he pleaded.

'What do you expect?' she spat.

'You look like you're going to throw up,' he said tenderly.

'I feel like I'm going to throw up,' she groaned.

'Look,' he said, matter-of-fact, 'I just want to say, I just want to tell you that I'm really sorry things worked out the way they did between us.'

'It's a bit late now.'

'I just want to apologise for what I did, for the way I treated you,' he continued, his voice soft, his eyes wet. 'I'm sorry I was such a creep. I was crazy, I still don't understand why I acted that way. But, and I know you're going to find this really hard to believe, I just want you to know that the way I acted didn't always reflect my feelings for you. Sometimes I was angry with you and I did things I regretted but it didn't mean I didn't love you. I just couldn't admit I loved you.'

'That's easy enough to say now,' she said, reminding herself of Juliette, the waitress, the foetus inside.

'Look, you can take what I've said however you like,' he said defensively, 'it's up to you.'

'Sure,' she said, stubborn.

'So can I buy you a drink?' he said, his head slightly bowed and tilted to one side, his eyebrows raised hopefully, his eyes sad and his mouth drawn into a pout.

'No.'

'Come on, what do you want, anything?' he went on. 'I want to buy you a drink.'

'That's OK,' she declined, 'I just don't want anything to drink.'

'Are you OK?' he asked, concerned.

'No,' she said, sighing.

'Not feeling well,' he prompted.

'I told you, I feel like I'm going to throw up,' she snapped. 'So how's it going at *Playboy*?' she asked, changing the subject.

'Actually I'm thinking of quitting,' he said, resigned.

'Again?' she asked, sounding bored.

'So you don't want a drink?' he said impatiently.

'No.'

'Will you wait here?' he told her. 'I'm just going to the bar.'

She shrugged. She waited until he was busy ordering his drink and then fell in with the crowd, letting it carry her away towards the front of the room. She hid from two other faces she recognised, faces without names, and suddenly she crashed head-on into Marcelle who was rushing in the opposite direction. Marcelle laughed and pulled her into a quiet backwater, tucked away to one side of the swirling stew.

Justine's teeth would not stop chattering. She scanned the room, watching the crowd come and go in waves. One wave would bring a whole wash of people seething and pushing to get in. Another wave would almost carry them outside. Marcelle held an almost full glass of Stoli in her hand. Justine pointed at it with her finger and Marcelle nodded. She gulped at the vodka. A fresh wave of people pushed past and bumped her arm. The vodka sloshed against her dress.

She swapped the vodka into her other hand and licked her wrist, sticky with the spilt drink. Droplets of vodka went running up her velvet sleeve. She held the glass in front of her as the next wave of people pushed their way out. The vodka slopped over the rim once more and spilled into her shoes, soaking into her stockings. *Oh fuck*. She moaned and fought her way through the crowd until she found a table and deposited the glass of Stoli. Marcelle tapped her on the shoulder.

'Are you OK?' Marcelle wanted to know, shouting into Justine's ear.

'No,' Justine said, her teeth chattering.

'I thought as much. It's Sade, isn't it, he's here,' Marcelle suggested, baiting her.

'How did you know?'

'You seem so unhappy,' Marcelle pointed out. 'Also, I've seen him.'

'Happy or sad,' Justine said, staring absently into her glass, 'they both have their downsides. Sadness because it's always accompanied by a sense that you're missing out on something, namely, being happy. Happiness because it never lasts. But yes, you're right, Sade *is* here.'

'He walked boldly up to us and introduced himself and he's busy sleazing onto Simone this very second. Ophelia and I made our excuses and split the scene, leaving Simone to hold the fort. I thought I'd come and find you and see if you wanted to leave.'

'I hope Simone knows what she's dealing with.'

'What's that supposed to mean?' Marcelle was all concern.

'He's a real creep. He's an absolute monster.'

'Maybe I should go and drag her away?' Marcelle said, panicking.

Was there any point? If Sade wanted to find Simone he had his ways. Then Justine remembered the gun inside Simone's jacket and breathed a sigh of relief. 'No,' she said slowly, 'Let's go see what they're up to instead.'

'Are you sure that's a good idea?' Marcelle asked, surprised. 'I mean, I didn't think you two were on speaking terms.'

'I don't really care any more,' Justine said, dispassionately. 'I'm not angry with Sade, I just feel really deflated. It's like, so what, I made a mistake, I made another mistake, I made another major mistake, so what, everybody makes mistakes. I made the old I-can-make-him-fall-in-love-with-me mistake, I made the old hoping-that-he'd-change mistake, I made the old love-

141

conquers-all mistake and then I made them over and over again. I've repeated the same mistakes a thousand times and you know what?'

'What's that?'

'I fucken hope to fuck that I never fucken make this stupid fucken asshole mistake again because I'm sick of this bullshit mistake and I'm ready to start making a new one now,' Justine announced and laughed.

She took Marcelle by the hand and joined the tail end of a wave of people heading down towards the toilets at the back of the bar. As she pushed she let herself be jostled, flotsam and jetsam, by the crowd. *Don't think*. She swallowed a fresh wave of nausea and a dribble of burps escaped from the corner of her mouth. The people she was following stopped moving. She was pressed up against a balding man wearing a black bow-tie. He smiled at her as they waited, wedged between a table and the bar and trapped from ahead and behind. She recognised him as Simone's friend from the bar.

'I hope you don't mind me telling you this,' he said, oblivious to who she was, 'but you're really beautiful, you're movie star beautiful, do you know that, has anyone ever told you?'

She looked around just in case he was talking to somebody else and then looked back at the balding man. His bright blue eyes bulged out of his head and his bow-tie was turned up to one side. He saw her looking around and asked her if she was crazy, of course he was talking to her. She smiled back at him, and thanked him for the compliment.

He folded his arms across his chest and his smile grew wider. His eyes ballooned out of their sockets, the whites grew fuller and she stared, her eyes succumbing to an irresistible pull, at the moist line of red skin which popped out from behind his eyelids. Nauseous again a burp bubbled up into a mouthful of vomit. She held her hand over her mouth and closed her eyes.

'Justine,' Marcelle was shouting into her ear. 'Justine.' She opened her eyes. Marcelle was pointing at something to her left. She looked over. Ophelia, Simone and Sade were standing talking in a group. Sade had his arm around Simone's shoulder. Justine nodded in response to Marcelle's worried frown and let herself be dragged through a tight knot of girls until she was standing at Simone's side.

'Hi,' Justine said, not looking at Sade.

Simone and Ophelia contemplated the bottoms of their glasses. Simone's slice of lime was chewed and bent over in two. Ophelia's slice of lime was buried in smooth lumps of ice. Simone picked out her slice of lime, sucked on it, dropped it back in her glass and pulled a face. Ophelia volunteered to buy another round of drinks. Sade handed her a fifty-dollar bill. Ophelia disappeared into the crowd.

Justine watched the flux of faces in the dark sea of bodies. She ran her fingers up and down her thighs. Her stockings were a mass of cigarette burns. She inserted her little finger into each hole. Miraculously her legs had escaped her recent exploits without incurring fresh singes. She looked at Simone sideways. Simone's cheeks were flushed bright red and her eyes darted about wildly.

Manic. It was hot in the cramped bar and Simone wore her tweed coat slung over her shoulder. Simone scratched her neck, itchy from the coarse wool, then rolled the jacket up inside-out and put it on the floor against the wall.

She looked at Simone and smiled. Simone smiled back and stared off into the teeming crowd. Gradually the smile changed its shape. She watched it fall at the corners and the top teeth come creeping over her bottom lip. She watched Simone's eyes open wide and stare unblinking into the swirling sea of bodies.

'What is it?' she wanted to know.

Simone shook her head and then bumped against Justine who looked across at Marcelle. Sade had his arm around Marcelle's waist and was talking into her ear. Simone squealed, and failed to repress a string of giggles. Justine glanced suspiciously at Sade. His free hand was now pressed up under Simone's black wrap-around suede miniskirt and buried between the cheeks of Simone's stockinged ass. Justine looked back at Marcelle but Marcelle ignored her and continued listening intently to whatever it was that Sade was saying. Justine struggled to catch his words.

'And tell me,' she heard him begin, but before he had a chance to complete his question Simone was shrieking and jumping up and down.

'Ouch,' Simone finally said, brushing at her thighs.

'Are you all right, Simone?' Marcelle called out from the other side of Sade.

'I'm OK,' she said, giggling. 'Someone just got me in the stockings with their cigarette.'

'Oh, no, so are your stockings ruined?'

'I think so,' Simone said, and then gasped. Simone bit her lip.

Justine watched Sade's hand go reaching into Simone's tights from behind. Then he slid his hand inside Simone's underpants. His fingers disappeared between her cheeks and reappeared as he moved them in and out. Simone's tongue languished between her moistened lips and her eyelids drooped.

Justine tore her eyes away and forced herself to pay attention to the conversation. Sade was staring at her.

'And how are you, Justine?' he said, smiling lasciviously.

She nodded, hating him.

He disentangled himself from Marcelle and, delicately, from Simone. He circled behind Simone to lean in front of her, and kissed her full on the lips. He watched for Justine's response. She didn't respond. He put one hand around Justine's waist and the other hand around Simone. She guessed from the wanton expression on Simone's face that he had re-inserted his hand between her legs.

'You're not still cranky with me, are you?' he teased.

She felt his hand slide down her back, caress the curve of her buttocks and go reaching for the hem of her velvet dress. The fingers hooked beneath the fabric and went creeping up her inner thigh. He then repeated what she'd just seen him do to Simone. Involuntarily her head tilted back, her eyes stared into a faraway void, her mouth hung open and her tongue poked out, spittle lacing the corners.

She realised there was nothing inside her cunt. Strange.

There's a vast emptiness between my legs. Big enough to fit the whole world inside. Sade's fingers pressed against the walls of her cunt and they gave way, uncovering an excess of space inside she never knew existed. Meanwhile, in spite of herself, she imagined he wanted her. The want she wanted him to want stretched out to infinity. It was a trap. *Damn.* She wanted him to want her. She'd become trapped by want. It was all her cunt's fault. From a distance the part of her that wasn't her cunt watched what was happening between herself and Sade with dismay.

Sade's fingers plunged inside her once more, deeper this time and pressing against something that hurt. Immobilised, she watched Sade staring at the outline of Simone's breast visible through the slinky bodysuit. The nipple stood out large and pointed even in the dark room.

'I just want to get laid,' she heard Simone shout in his ear.

He nodded, smiling, and meanwhile pushed his finger higher up inside Justine's cunt. She moaned, her lips against his neck.

Suddenly Ophelia appeared before her and handed her a drink.

'I've just spotted some talent,' Ophelia shouted.

Justine dragged herself out of the sweaty mire where the cunt ruled and concentrated all her attention on what Ophelia was saying.

'Where?' Justine slurred. Meanwhile Sade's fingers continued their assault on the walls of her cunt and his tongue came poking into her ear.

'Over there,' Ophelia shouted, pointing.

'With the ponytail?'

'Not the one with glasses, the other one.' Ophelia was desperate for her approval.

'Totally fuckable,' Justine opined.

'Do you think?' Ophelia still wasn't sure.

'Mmmm,' she groaned convincingly. 'He's an absolute fuck, Ophelia.'

'I want to fuck that guy,' Ophelia announced.

'Go for it.'

'Do you think I should?' Ophelia clearly still had doubts.

'Yes, go on, he's gorgeous.'

'Will you come with me? I don't want to go on my own,' Ophelia almost begged her.

Sade stopped licking Justine's ear and extracted his fingers from her cunt.

'Look girls,' he announced loud enough for all to hear, 'why don't we go ingest some of the fantastic cocaine I've been carrying around all night?'

Justine nodded her head up and down very quickly. It was a unanimous, wordless decision.

Ophelia led the way into the crowd, drink sloshing all over the floor in her haste, followed by Sade and Simone, Sade's hand no longer inside Simone's cunt but holding her ass from behind, and Marcelle. Justine followed last of all.

Finally they reached the cubicle. Simone, Marcelle and Ophelia stood pressed up against the walls, Sade sat back to front on the toilet seat and cut up five lines on the china top of the cistern and Justine cowered, squashed against the door. He offered Marcelle a fifty to roll into a tight tube.

Marcelle rolled the note and gave it to Ophelia to snort the first line.

Ophelia leant over between Sade, Marcelle and Simone and surveyed the five lines of coke. One was fat and slightly longer than the others. Three were equally short and fat and the fourth was short, bent and thin. Ophelia hesitated over the longest fattest line and then snorted one of the three short fat lines all in the one go. She handed the note back to Marcelle who gave it to Simone. Simone snorted up another short fat line without an instant's hesitation and handed the note back to Marcelle. Marcelle considered the three remaining lines and batted her long dark eyelashes furiously in front of her huge round green eyes and pretended to fiddle around with the note. Sade looked away as Marcelle lowered her face to the top of the cistern and sighed, careful not to send the fine white particles all over the wet blood, urine and dirt smeared floor. Checking again to make sure Sade *still* wasn't looking she snorted the first half of the longest fattest line in her left nostril and the second half in her right nostril, tapped the note on the porcelain to loosen any remaining powder and picked these up on a moistened finger tip. Sade looked at the remaining lines and lifted the largest of the two through the note in one long snort. Then he looked at Marcelle, trying to catch her eye but failing, opened the plastic satchel and cut out another line. Then he snorted it, handed Justine the note and put one arm around Simone's ass and the other arm around Marcelle's shoulders and played with Ophelia's hair.

Justine looked at the last line, the smallest of the six, and

148

held the note to her nose. She snorted it in one go. Tomorrow seemed a long way away. Somehow she'd have to deal with it. Tomorrow.

'Why don't we get the hell out of here?' he said while everybody took long greedy gulps of their drinks.

Ophelia and Marcelle hurried back to the bar for another round leaving Justine alone in the cubicle with Simone and Sade. She watched him insert his finger between Simone's legs again and push her, giggling, from behind into the crowd. She followed close behind him, hooking her finger through his belt-loop. She wasn't exactly angry with Sade any more but she still wasn't quite satisfied. She could have left him to Simone and her gun but she wanted something else. She wanted the final word. She tugged hard on the belt loop, bringing him to a standstill.

'I want to talk to you,' she shouted in his ear.

He smiled fearlessly over his shoulder. 'Oh, no!' he exclaimed sarcastically.

She watched him whisper into Simone's ear. She saw Simone shrug her shoulders and go dancing away. Justine grabbed Sade's hand and dragged him along behind her. 'Hey, hey,' he complained but she didn't let up. She fought her way between people dancing in ragged groups and talking in tight beer-swilling circles. She'd almost reached the door when he shook free of her hold and stopped.

'I want to talk outside,' she informed him.

He looked away, ignoring her.

'So you're not going to talk to me,' she told him.

He shrugged.

'I gather you have nothing to say,' she spat.

He glared at her. People were starting to stop what they were doing and stare.

'Well fuck you,' she screamed.

Sade ran away but he didn't get far in the crush and Justine caught up with him in no time, tearing his sleeve.

'You're an absolute fuckwit,' she screeched, losing it. 'I'm fucken pregnant with your filthy bloody child and you're standing there with your fucken hand inside my fucken girlfriend's fucken cunt. What the fuck do you have to say for yourself you fucken prick, surely I deserve some kind of fucken explanation after all the fucken shit you've put me through?'

He stood glowering at her, about to run away again.

She noticed people stepping aside, forming a ring and staring.

'You jerk,' she screamed at the top of her voice and threw herself at him, hitting him across the face with the palms of her hands and punching him in the stomach with clenched fists.

At first he merely turned away from her blows. Then he grabbed one of her wrists and twisted her arm behind her back until she screamed in pain, lashing about wildly with her free hand.

'Are you going to shut up and get the fuck out of here?' he growled into her ear.

'Let go of me, you fucken creep,' she shrieked, hysterical, 'let go of me.'

She grabbed a handful of his hair in her free hand and pulled on it hard. He twisted harder on her wrist and she squealed, over and over again. He let go of her and she dropped sobbing to the floor.

He stood back, his hands on his hips and his head ringing from the blows. A man stepped forward and told him to leave her alone.

'Tell her to leave *me* alone,' Sade said, shaking beads of sweat from his forehead. 'She went for me, I was just defending myself.'

Justine lay whimpering on the floor. She started pulling her hair out in huge clumps and banging her head on the painted cement. 'I don't want any more, I don't want any more,' she moaned inaudibly.

All of a sudden the music stopped playing and the lights came on. She blinked in the rude light. Out of the corner of her eye she saw Ophelia break through the ring and freeze, watching her anxiously. Then Sade stepped towards her and told her to get up.

'Pull yourself together,' he reasoned, 'it's not as bad as you think.'

Justine sat up, her hair matted into knots, and bawling buried her face in her hands. 'Why're you doing this to me?' she cried. 'Why're you doing this?'

'You're doing it to yourself, Justine,' he said, firm. 'Now pull yourself together.'

'You hate me, don't you?'

'No, I don't *hate* you,' he said placatingly, reaching for her hand.

She recoiled at his touch. 'Don't touch me,' she screamed.

Determined, he took her by the arm and said, 'Come on.'

She pulled away, screamed, 'How dare you touch me,' and punched him smack in the middle of his nose.

He hit her back, his fist collecting square with her jaw and she fell to the floor. Too winded to sob she lay absolutely still while blood trickled down her chin. She felt Ophelia's arms around her. Ophelia wanted to know if she was OK to sit up. Justine let herself be dragged into a sitting position. Sade was being restrained, a man holding each arm, but in a calm firm voice he pushed them away, telling them everything was under control. Ophelia lifted her to her feet and gently dabbed at the blood with a paper napkin. The circle dispersed. Leaning against Ophelia's shoulder Justine saw Sade, Marcelle and Simone huddled together in a group. The music came on and the lights went down.

'I want a drink,' Justine said, starting to cry.

Sade emptied his pockets and unravelled a handful of crumpled notes.

'Look, you two,' Ophelia said, handing Justine over to Sade, 'if you can stop fighting for a few minutes I'll buy the next round of Stoli's, how's that?'

Justine closed her eyes and dried her tears on Sade's shirt. Her breathing became calm. He rubbed her back. It hurt her bruised vertebra but she didn't complain. Her toes flooded with warmth and her teeth ached deep in their roots.

It was last weekend, or a few weekends ago, and she'd been standing on the terrace in the rain, huddled into her coat. The light from the street lamps glowed yellow and hung close to their iron stems. Rain hissed onto the footpath and the paving stones were glazed smooth and silver. Droplets slapped the surface of the harbour. Inside the gallery the song was playing again, the second or third time that evening. The last traces of acid came and went in gentle waves. Words collected in the back of her throat and piled up on top of each other trapped behind her tongue. Without moving she was dancing. Air gushed down her throat and filled her lungs. She looked in through the steamy panes of glass at her friends dancing. It occurred to her that they could go on dancing with each other forever without her ever returning. But that was OK because she could leave them if she wanted to and never come back. She smiled into her reflection in the pool at her feet. There was everything she needed in the rain and the dark and the harbour and the light. She'd been over-whelmed by a feeling of now. Breathless.

Justine lifted her face, greedy for his lips. Sade kissed her briefly and hugged her close, his breath warm on her cheek. Her lip stung and she tasted blood in the back of her throat. He guided her step by step to the bar and lifted her up so she was sitting on the edge. He spread her legs and drew her to his chest, his lips sucking her breasts through the velvet. Then pushing the dress aside with his nose she felt his tongue wet on her nipple. She gasped as he bit her too hard. She squeezed her knees around him. Her stockings were wet to her touch. She reached down and slid her hand inside his jeans. She felt the tip of his cock through his cotton briefs, engorged and hard. His hand slid inside her stockings and fingered her clit. She pulled him up beside her on the bar. He lay flat on his back and pulled her down on top of him. His lips clung to hers. She could feel him through his jeans. She undid his belt and unbuttoned his fly. She cupped his balls in one hand and slowly drew his cock—hugely swollen and purple and the veins all sticking out—into her mouth. Then she made a wet ring around his cock with her other hand and wrapped her lips around the head once more.

She vaguely sensed a change in the atmosphere when the lights came on and the music shut down. It wasn't until the tall thin DJ with the gold earring and pinned blue eyes lifted her off the bar that she realised where she was, what she was doing.

4

THE HULKING MUSCLE-BOUND JAMAICAN DOOR WARNED Sade that if he did one more thing he'd have to leave. Sade stood hands in pockets and looked at the floor. Justine imagined how his cock would feel in his pocket, small and soft. A worm turned out of a warm bed of black earth, wriggling and pink.

'It's just a question,' the Door lectured him, 'of where you're going to draw the line. I don't have any problems with what you two were doing, you have a little lover's quarrel, then you want to make up, what could be more natural? It's just that,' he said, pausing to look over his shoulder, 'it's just that the boss doesn't like it, and if the boss doesn't like it, I've gotta try and make sure it doesn't happen. Who knows, if I was in the boss's place I'd probably do the same thing, because when you're the boss you've gotta watch out for the owners, and the owners don't want to lose their customers, see?'

'Yeah, I know what you mean,' Sade said, humbly

staring at the cement floor.

Justine looked down at the floor in front of her. She counted six cigarette butts around her shoes. She counted them over again. She looked over at Sade. He looked restlessly at Simone and Marcelle, now talking to the African-American barman, and sitting on stools at the bar. Sade told the Door he'd be right back and joined Marcelle and Simone. He stood close to Simone and slid his fingers up inside her skirt. Justine looked around for Ophelia who was laughing with the tall DJ and then hurried after Sade. She squeezed between Marcelle and Simone. She sipped at Simone's drink.

'Anyway, sis,' Simone was saying, 'I ended up going to that Sex Party on Wednesday night.'

'How was it?'

'Actually,' Simone complained, ignoring Sade, 'I found the performances really boring.'

'Really?'

'There was this guy doing skin embroidery,' Simone recounted. 'Then someone told me he did it under anaesthetic, you know, I thought the whole point of it was for it to hurt so why did he have the anaesthetic?'

'I bet it hurt later,' Marcelle said, drolly.

'Anyway,' Simone continued, 'then he bound his dick and his balls together really tight, right down at the base, and stuck a pencil, you know, for writing, he stuck a pencil inside his penis all the way down.'

'I used to go out with someone who did that,' Marcelle said, sounding nostalgic. 'He said it didn't hurt, that it was only castration that hurt.'

'Really?' Simone was watching the African-American barman go bending down to restock the refrigerators, the black leather skin-tight along his thighs and buttocks.

'Yeah. He used to stick one of those metal rods used for rolling meat in his dick.' Marcelle smiled into her glass.

'Anyway,' Simone said, back to her story. 'Then he injected a needle into his balls.'

Marcelle raised her eyebrows. 'What did he hit up?'

'I don't know,' Simone said, savouring the barman's thighs once more, 'but after that he became incredibly sweaty.'

Sade bit the back of Simone's neck and moved his fingers slowly in and out of her cunt. He whispered into Simone's ear. Simone collapsed speechlessly against his chest. Marcelle ordered another round of drinks.

Justine watched Sade's hand play with Simone's nipple. His hand was square and the skin so tan it was almost golden. The fingers were short and stumpy. His hand clung to Simone's breast like a gold star plastered to a child's forehead. *I hate men with tanned square hands.* Justine shivered and looked away.

There was a newspaper on the seat beside Marcelle. She picked it up. It was open at an article about the President of the United States. In the article a woman claimed to have been sexually harassed by the President. According to the woman, he'd invited her up to his hotel room, kissed her, and then dropped his pants, demanding oral sex. It was difficult to believe what the woman said: the President of the United States, guilty of sexual harassment.

Sitting next to her at the bar but a few seats down was a

man staring sadly in front of him. Without altering his melancholy air he looked at her and sipped at his drink. He was beautiful in the classical sense, young, Greek-looking. His eyes were deep-set, widely spaced and of such a dark blue they appeared to be black. Glazed, they stared blindly, two holes on opposite sides of his face. His head was a mass of thick blond ringlets which he wore cut short, flat and brushed forwards so that his smooth oval forehead was framed with curls. His nose was large and straight. His upper lip parted in a wide V into smooth feline curves. His bottom lip was full and pouting, leaving the chin in shadow. His jaw was square, his cheeks round, his neck thickset, and his ears were small and hidden by his hair. She smiled at him and he stared remotely back, his eyes fixed on nothing, his face blank. She looked away and then she looked at him again.

She slid off the stool. Marcelle pushed a fresh Stoli at her. Sade and Simone had their tongues down each other's throats. She emptied her glass. Contagiously her lips imagined kissing the beautiful man beside her. *Crazy.* She rearranged her fur waistcoat. She wasn't herself. She walked along past the other stools to the door. His dark eyes followed hers in the mirror behind the bar. The glass door slammed behind her.

She stood leaning against a telegraph pole outside a twenty-four hour newsagency. The news sheet read: HAPPY FINAL HOURS, and showed a photo of the murdered woman in a nearby hotel with her two girlfriends. The picture was taken in a photo booth, hours before her death. She wanted to vomit. She held her head in her hands. The nausea passed. Looking up, her eyes became glued to the swinging door.

He sauntered down the pavement towards her and offered her a cigarette, his blond ringlets only slightly ruffled by the sharp gusts of wind blowing along the street. He smiled. *A regular Apollo.* She thanked him and shivered in her velvet and fur as she bent towards him for a light. *It was going to rain.* He suggested they go for a walk and put his arm around her waist. A stairway yawned open to their left and he pulled her after him, both of them stumbling down the gloomy stone stairs. She held onto his arm, digging her nails in, and he dropped his hand to her ass.

Four steps down, he pushed her up against the wall and she was peeling down her stockings and grabbing at his fly. He kissed her, his lips sliding all over hers. He dribbled spit onto his hand and felt between her legs. She wasn't wet but with the spit she was wet enough and he slid inside. All the air came shooting out of her mouth onto his face mixed up with a high-pitched squeal.

'Am I hurting you?' he wanted to know, pausing between thrusts.

'Yes.'

He kissed her and moved into her, languid. 'Do you want me to stop?'

'No.'

'But if I'm hurting you?' he insisted.

'I'm not sure.' Spinning.

'Either I'm hurting you or I'm not,' he reasoned, pulling out.

She hesitated. 'But I'm not sure whether I want you to

stop, and I won't know if I want you to stop unless you keep going.' The paradoxical truth.

He knelt down in front of her and pressed his face between her legs. The slight stubble on his chin burned her skin. She didn't complain. He fucked her again. *Sade hurting her, plunging inside her right up to the hilt. Her delight.* A little cough spluttered in the back of her throat. He slid out, small.

He offered her another cigarette. She smoked, her bare thighs blue on the dark stairs. *Don't leave me, Sade, please.* She pictured Sade's golden hand on Simone's breast. *Disturbing.* She tossed her butt and pulled up her stockings. She watched his cock grow hard again. She left. Soon she was walking along the street above him. He tucked in his shirt and buttoned up his jeans.

'Wait,' he called after her, smiling. 'Would you like to go for a drive in my car? We could drive to the beach.'

She stood smiling at her reflection in the swinging glass doors. She considered going back inside and seducing Sade, forcing Simone into the background, and convincing Sade to leave, to take her home, to fuck her again. She shivered in disgust.

'OK,' she said and followed him across the street. Up above the sky was an ominous mass of storm clouds. A powerful gust of wind shook the leaves from the trees while she waited for him to open the door. He drove a small white sports car with a black top. Still he didn't open the door. Instead he rapped his knuckles on the window. She didn't understand. He made signals. He rapped on the window. A strong wind lifted her fur waistcoat over her face. She wrestled it down. What did he want? She tried the handle. She lifted it. It was very stiff. It came up halfway and then became stuck. She couldn't budge it. She couldn't open the door. *Open, open.* He rapped his knuckles on the window. She looked in. He mimed opening the door. She read his lips. They said, up, up. She pointed for him to wind the window down. He shook his head violently. She struggled with the handle. She pulled it really hard. The silver metal snapped in her hand. Leaves swirled around her ankles. The handle lay broken in her palm. She started laughing. She heard his door slam. What was he saying? She'd have to go around to his side of the car. The wind started up so she had to hold her waistcoat down. She climbed in his side of the car and giggled when she ended up spread-eagled on the hand-brake. She slid into the passenger seat. He closed the door. He was talking about the car. Something about rust, something about money. He reached down near her feet. See, he was saying. He lifted the rubber mat. She looked at the floor of the car. She looked at the road below. She looked at the hole in the floor of the car.

'The Flintstones,' she cried, putting her feet through the hole, touching the ground. 'It's a Flintstones car.'

He nodded and replaced the mat. Then he showed her the handles. Where the handle for the window should have been there was only the end of a silver screw. The handle was in the glove box. He opened the glove box and showed her. Where the door handle should have been there was a hole in the lining of the door. He showed her his door. His door was without handles too. The only handle left was the handle on the outside of his door. He reached through the open window and showed her how to open the door. Then he pushed the window up, palms flat against the glass until the top reached the canvas roof. He switched on the engine. It started straight away with a tremendous roar. He told her to feel and placed her hand on the gear stick. The engine throbbed right up the stem and through the wooden head. Lights, windscreen wipers, down for first gear. The car lurched into the traffic. In no time at all they were at the other end of the street and around the corner. The steering wheel was made of polished wood. As they stopped at a pedestrian crossing, the rain suddenly came thundering down on the canvas roof.

Damn. She was an idiot. Everyone else was back at the bar and here she was driving around with a guy she couldn't even bear to fuck. She sighed. At least the nausea was gone. She was too irate to be nauseous. He turned on the tape. Dance music pounded through small round speakers, making them shiver. She watched the windscreen wipers. He handed her a chamois and asked her to wipe. She didn't understand and held the cloth in her lap. The window was so foggy she couldn't see the road. She wiped it with her hand. He told her not with her hand but with the chamois. She wiped the window. He grabbed the chamois out of her hand and wiped the window in front of him. The car swerved from one side of the road to the other. He shouted at her to hold the wheel. She couldn't make out what he was saying over the music. She pressed buttons on the stereo randomly. Soon there was no music and only a screeching, whirring sound. He pulled over.

Her head hit the headrest and hurt because of the bumps. The fresh bumps stung and the old bumps ached. He was angry. He pulled the cassette out and a string of shiny tape streamed behind. He fiddled until the tape was loose. He was angry because it was his favourite cassette but she was starting to get angry as well. This just wasn't what she wanted. *It never was.* He wound the tape back into the cassette with a pen. Then he replaced the cassette and pressed play. At first the rhythm was uneven and the instruments unclear but the rough spot passed and then everything was fine again. He re-entered the traffic.

Soon they were bouncing down the dark wet winding road that led to the beach. He drove faster. She gripped the seat. He flicked the lights up to high beam and then down. He flicked them again. He changed down for a sharp corner and accelerated so fast into the curve her head hit the headrest again. Blood dripped from her hand. She wiped it on the chamois. She had no idea what to do about her head. He made the final turn at top speed and then sped down to the beach. The car lurched to a standstill. The windscreen wipers groaned through a final semi-circle and stopped. The lights made two tunnels through the dark rain. Lightning flashed at the horizon. He counted out loud for the thunder. The waves crashed on the sand.

He said his name was Hamlet and started to tell her all about how hard it was being an unemployed film-maker and single dad in the big city and how he'd been waiting a long time to meet someone new.

'Someone just like you,' he said, placing his hand on her thigh and smiling.

She told him she wanted to go back. His smile changed into a frown.

'I just want you to know that I really like you, Justine. I think I could really fall in love with you, have children with you and spend the rest of my life with you,' he said in a solemn tone. 'I understand that you don't feel the same way about me. It's really OK,' he went on, switching back to his joking voice, 'this happens to me all the time.' He laughed.

Lightning flashed. The street lights went out. Hamlet switched the headlights to high beam. He drove faster. The tyres skidded all over the road.

They drove the rest of the way in silence, the rain easing up as they approached the city. As they sped past the newsagent she read the news-sheet out loud: HAPPY FINAL HOURS. Hamlet parked the car. He placed his arm along the back of her seat.

'I'm sorry about before,' he said, flashing a huge white smile. 'It's just that it's been a long time since I've met anyone who really cares.'

'That's OK,' she said, reaching for the door handle. Not finding it, she turned around to look at the door before she remembered. 'Can you let me out now?' she said, swallowing hard on the rising panic.

He laughed and shook his head. 'Can I let you out?' he chuckled. 'That's a good one. Sure.' He pressed his palms against his window and dragged at the glass. It didn't budge. He wriggled the tips of his fingers between the top of the window and the roof and pulled hard, his fingernails white, and still nothing happened. He pulled again, inching his fingers further between the glass and canvas. Nothing.

'Damn,' he grunted, finally all joked out. He reached across her knees into the glove box for the handle for the window. He wound it onto the protruding screw and tried to unwind the window. The handle just went around and around on the worn thread. 'Shit, shit, shit, shit,' he mumbled. He turned to her, his face twisted with concern. She wanted to laugh at his ridiculous face.

'Try your window,' he snapped. 'If you can get your window open we can climb out that way.'

Just like a film, her hands were going in slow motion. The tips wriggled between the glass and the canvas. The muscles tightened. The wrists took the strain. The window didn't budge. She took the handle. Twisted the handle on the screw. The handle went around on the thread. She turned back to Hamlet. She shook her head. They were quiet, listening to the rat-tat-tat of the rain.

'I hope you don't mind getting wet,' he said, reaching up for the metal clasps that secured the canvas roof to the frame of the car. The first of the clasps came undone easily. The second clasp was harder. He paused. If this clasp broke, they were really stuck. He gently jiggled the clasp. His hand started to shake so badly he had to stop.

She glanced over at the news-sheet. The faces of the dead girl and her two friends smiled eerily across the street. *Sade's fist on her jaw, his cock in her mouth, the blood from her head. Exquisite pain.* She shivered as a fresh downpour began.

He jiggled the clasp. *Hamlet's sensitive fingers were all thumbs.* He swore. He jiggled again. The clasp snapped in two, but not before it had loosened its hold. He handed her the broken clasp. She threw it in the glove box with the rest of the broken parts.

'OK,' he said authoritatively, 'are you ready?'

She nodded.

He threw the roof back and rain poured into the car. She turned around in her seat, climbed into the back and slid down the boot of the car. She landed on her ass in the gutter. Her head hit the side of the car. There was a smear of blood but the rain washed it away. Then he was pulling her hand, he was dragging her to her feet, he was lifting her up, he had his arm around her waist. She reached the awning outside the bar and he let her go. She stood shaking herself. She looked up. She met his eye. Everything was OK. She was free of him at last. She laughed.

5

JUSTINE WATCHED HAMLET SLIDE HIS HAND UP THE BACK OF Ophelia's short denim dress and start playing with her G-string. She was impatient. The lane was ill-lit, narrow and deserted. It was taking forever. Sade, Simone and Marcelle stood at the beginning of the queue, just outside the entrance to the nightclub. Simone was beating her fists on the graffiti-covered door. Every so often she stopped, waited and started beating again. Finally a woman dressed like a trapeze artist stepped outside. She threw her arms around Simone's neck and thrust her tongue down Simone's throat. Then she asked Simone for her phone number. Simone wrote something down on a white card and handed it back to the Door. No-one had to pay.

The dance floor was raised up like a stage. It was crowded with two types of dancers. One type consisted of men dressed head-to-toe in skin-tight shiny black leather. The other type consisted of women in black suits and white T-shirts with short slicked-back hair. Justine was hungry. Her stomach gurgled and bubbled noisily. Sade stood close by with his tongue down Simone's throat. Justine waved to a group of women she recognised from university. They were dressed like men or like strippers or like mistresses and had their arms around each other. The next thing she knew Sade had pulled her towards him and was kissing her, his other hand still inside Simone's skirt. The women from university watched, smiles frozen on their faces. Justine struggled free of Sade and joined Ophelia and Hamlet at the foot of the stairs. Someone had just handed Ophelia a tab of acid. Ophelia offered her the tab of acid to bite. She shook her head. Ophelia swallowed half of the tab and gave the rest to Hamlet. Justine followed them upstairs.

She found herself in a room full of women playing pool. The women were either bare-chested or topless beneath their leather waistcoats. Sade and Simone appeared. Marcelle came with a round of drinks a few minutes later. When the acid started to kick in Ophelia and Hamlet went back downstairs to dance. Ophelia reappeared with a huge bunch of irises and handed them to Marcelle. Ophelia left, laughing. Marcelle buried her face in the purple, blue and yellow blooms. She held the shot-glass to her lips. Bottoms up. It was taking forever to get a game.

Sade walked over to the nearest pool table. He swallowed the shot of vodka in a single gulp. He took note of the state of play. One team only needed to sink one more ball before they were on the black. He dug into his coat pocket and pulled out a handful of coins. He held them out in the palm of his hand and stared at them. He couldn't tell one coin from another. He walked towards Justine, holding the coins out for her to see in the palm of his hand. She struggled against the way all the coins bled into each other and collected into a pool in the middle of his palm. Moving in slow motion she selected a small gold coin and held it in her hand. He smiled, took the coin and walked back towards Marcelle and Simone. His eyes wavered between the green eyes of the brunette, Simone's smooth olive-skinned cleavage and the dancing purple-blue faces of the flowers with their yellow and white flecked eyes. Justine looked back at the table. The game was over. She called out to Sade. He dawdled over to the table and inserted the coin. The balls rumbled down the wooden slats. He racked the balls. He wanted to play with Simone, he explained. She felt like leaving but she went downstairs and bought a round of drinks instead.

When Justine returned it was Simone's turn to shoot. She passed around the shots of vodka. She watched the game. Simone placed her feet side by side and bobbed down to shooting height by bending her knees. Her firm round ass poked out proudly beneath her short suede wrap-around skirt, and her black crisscross lace-up sleeveless bodysuit let her tits hang out, swinging behind the cue. She squinted across the green table, tongue hanging out to one side and then swishing over her lips, and moved the cue backwards and forwards across her fingers.

The cue gently tapped the white and the ball slowly made its way down the length of the table before connecting with the small yellow and nudging it into the corner pocket. Simone walked around the table, cue held out before her, eyes already lining up the next shot. She leaned over and gently tapped the white again. The ball trickled across the table and poked the black into the centre left pocket. The game over, Simone looked up and smiled. Then a frown twitched over her perfect features. Justine followed the direction of Simone's gaze.

Marcelle and Sade were kissing at the other end of the table, Marcelle's ass pressed up against the edge, his hand up her skirt and his hips lunging between her spread legs.

'Come on,' he urged between fierce kisses, 'let's get up on the table.'

Marcelle dropped the irises to the painted cement floor. Justine watched, speechless, as they crawled up on the table, Marcelle inching along on her back, Sade on hands and knees. When Marcelle's head reached the cushion she lay down, dark curls spilling over the side of the table, and set her drink on the green baize. He put his knee between her legs and squeezed her breast. Marcelle reached up and pulled him down on top of her, knocking the shot-glass on its side and spilling vodka onto the smooth green felt. He thrust against Marcelle on the table. Their heads moved together and apart as they kissed between giggles.

Simone placed her glass on the table and climbed up. She squatted behind Sade and reached around to the front of his pants for his cock. Her glass sloshed onto the table and went rolling into the far corner as Sade pushed Marcelle's hands from his face and turned around to kiss Simone. Marcelle sat up and pulled Sade away from Simone. Simone suggested everybody go back to Marcelle's place. Nobody disagreed.

6

'HANG ON,' MARCELLE CROAKED FROM HER BURGUNDY three-seater couch, 'there's a tampon in there.'

Justine slumped further down in Marcelle's brown velvet armchair and watched through slitted eyes. Sade bit on the end of the damp string and pulled the tampon out with his teeth, tossing the sodden wad of cotton doggy-style onto the floor. It landed with a thud, just missing the ragged bunch of irises. His fingers fumbled with his black button-fly jeans. He undid his belt. Sade started fucking Marcelle. Marcelle was moaning. Justine closed her eyes and looked at the inside of her mind.

Inside she saw Simone flamenco dancing across the middle of the dance floor, her black suede wrap-around miniskirt held up above her waist, her dark brown eyes glowering, her pupils swollen hugely, her blood-red lips smiling sweetly, like red roses, and then the thrusts from her hips and Simone taking off the black silk shirt and swinging it around her head and throwing it on the dance floor and

171

then strutting across the front and shaking her tits at the crowd in her black crisscross lace-up bodysuit. She saw Simone stroking the middle-aged man's sharp grey beard. She saw Simone in the men's toilet listening outside one of the cubicles as someone got laid on the other side of the door. She saw Marcelle and Simone standing amidst a sea of irises between two mirrored walls painting their lips with a bright red pencil and watching their tongues poke back at them in a blue and red echo chamber, reflections of reflections of reflections to forever. She saw Marcelle and Simone making their way across the dance floor to Sade and his coke. Finally she saw Sade and Simone and Marcelle lying in the spilled vodka on the pool table—Simone's tongue in Sade's ear, Sade's mouth on Marcelle's neck, and Simone asking Sade if he wanted to have a threesome and Sade agreeing, kissing them both at once, and Marcelle and Simone both grabbing at his cock hard in his jeans and trying to send him crazy by sucking and biting him all over.

Exquisite pain, exquisite pain, Ophelia's words echoed uncomfortably inside her head. Meanwhile Marcelle's grunted, 'K-Y, in the bathroom, in the cupboard, can you?' brought her back to the present. Justine watched Sade pull up his boxer shorts and button up his jeans through half-closed lids. She listened to Sade's feet pad unevenly down the carpeted hallway. Soon she noticed that Marcelle, her G-string twisted around her knees, had passed out on the couch. Justine succumbed to the gentle pull of a deep drugged sleep.

The phone rang over a dozen times before it woke her up and even then, long after she'd heard it, it kept on ringing and ringing while she lay there with her throat so dry and sore she wasn't sure if she could speak. Finally she reached down and picked up the receiver. Holding it to her face, she made inarticulate croaking noises in the back of her throat. Eventually the person on the other end hung up on her. Loose in her grasp the receiver slid onto the floor and skittered across the bare floorboards. The radio alarm clock said it was 6.08. Marcelle was sound asleep.

She reached up beneath her velvet dress and slid her singed stockings down her legs and over the ends of her feet. The lycra and cotton felt wonderful moving across her weary flesh. She felt between her legs and separated the gluey strands of hair and inserted her middle finger. First she poked into the soft flesh inside the mouth. Then she thrust in deeper right up to the end. She spread her legs and stroked the lips of her cunt. *Delicious.* She inserted her finger again and pulled out strands of clear sticky jelly. She pushed her dress off her shoulder and pressed her mouth into the creased flesh of her underarm. She picked up a biro, held it in her hand and inserted it inside her cunt. In and out. Then she ran the biro lightly over the lips. *Squeezed very soft skin inside thighs together.* She slid her tongue out and licked the crease of her underarm. *Nose probed perfumed flesh.* She slid the pen in again, slowly, light, then faster and harder to finish. She couldn't come. She needed to go to the toilet. She walked down the corridor to the bathroom, glancing into the bedroom as she passed. She saw Simone, ass-up, sucking Sade's cock and rubbing her cunt on his big toe.

She had to wait for a while on the toilet before she could pee. *He likes fucking Simone more than he likes fucking me.* Her nausea and aching head forgotten in sharp spears of panic. The piss came out in a slow steady stream. Afterwards the toilet paper was bright yellow. Her fingernails were covered in discharge which smelt like egg under her nose. She checked her eye in the mirror. The bruise was hidden although the foundation had hardened and was crisscrossed with fine cracks.

She walked into Marcelle's bedroom. Simone was sitting on Sade's face and sucking his cock. His tongue was stretched full-length to reach the lips of her cunt. She watched Simone's cunt pulling away in quick, jerking movements. She stalked across the room and joined them on the bed, face to Simone's ass. She watched as her fingers entered Simone, who moaned and jerked her ass and cunt away. She dangled her breasts close to Sade's face, her tongue hanging out, searching. He leant upwards, grabbed her tits in his mouth and sucked at her nipples. She gasped as his teeth sank into her flesh. Simone turned around. Justine covered his mouth with hers. Simone wrapped her lips around his cock. His head was thrashing from side to side. He opened his mouth wide. His tongue came hanging out. She licked his tongue, Simone licked his cock. She watched Simone grip his cock in her fist and insert the tip into her mouth. Simone masturbated her cunt on his leg. Simone took him all the way in, way down the back of her throat before pulling him out and

174

looping her fingers around the tip and moving them up and down very loose and very slow. Then Simone held his cock absolutely still. He moaned. She ran her hand teasingly up and down his huge glistening cock very slow, very long, then short and fast. His cock started to twitch, the tip gigantically swollen, purplish red and fanning out. He went into a total body convulsion, his head doubling forwards and squashing his chin. Simone's cunt was spread wide over his leg, the knee disappeared inside the butterfly-shaped lips. He held his breath. Then he let it all come sighing out, his cock spurting straight up in the air. Justine sucked him into her mouth, swallowing the sperm. He growled deep in his throat. He whimpered.

When she opened her eyes Simone was tying Sade's arms and legs to the bed frame with her black silk stockings. He lifted his head.

'What happened to your last victim?' he asked, his voice slow and slurring.

'He's in the freezer,' Simone giggled, tightening the knots at his wrists and feet. 'You're just like a cake,' she said, stroking his stomach with her nose and lips.

His cock grew hard again.

'What're you doing?' Justine wanted to know.

'What does it look like I'm doing?' Simone said, and went rummaging in Marcelle's drawers. She pulled out a black silk scarf and tied it over his eyes.

Sade moved his pelvis from side to side. 'Just don't try and put anything other than Stoli in my mouth or coke up my nose, OK,' he instructed them happily.

Simone licked the inside of his thighs and the tip of his

175

cock the way a cat licks up milk. Wet, Simone sat on top of him, ass to his unseeing face, and rubbed her pussy against the soft hair on his chest. Simone wrapped her hand around the base of his cock and held it away from his body so that it stood out like an obelisk. Sitting on top of him, Simone rubbed her cunt, the wet part open, against the tip of his cock. Then Simone pulled herself away.

'Do you want me to fuck you?' Simone whispered seductively in his ear.

He writhed beneath her on the bed. 'Fuck me, just fuck me,' he moaned.

'But what if I don't want to fuck you?' Simone teased.

'Just fuck me anyway,' he pleaded, 'even if you don't want to, just give me your cunt.'

Simone slid on top of him and then lifted herself off, then she lowered herself on him hard, and then moved up and down on the swollen tip very fast. Just as he was about to come she stopped. He thrust up beneath her but she held herself away. She licked his lips. He struggled against the stockings. She lowered her cunt down on his cock, only letting the tip inside. Then she held her cunt over his face. His tongue came up towards her. She let him nibble her clit and then pushed down onto his tongue. She started to come and then sat on his cock again, her hand tickling his balls. She threw herself down onto his chest and ran her tongue over his neck moaning, her body going stiff and her hands holding herself against his hips. He was moaning too and finally Simone rolled off him and he came, the sperm shooting up into the air and onto his chest.

Justine caught the last drops of sperm inside her

mouth and then lay still, overwhelmed and exhausted. A faint line of grey light crept through the blinds. All she wanted was the oblivion of sleep. She buried her head into the pillow. The sound of the toilet flushing in the next flat, the whine and hiss of the cistern, sounded like rain, and, listening to its sweet cadence, she fell asleep.

There was a knock at the door. She opened her eyes. The knock knocked again. Simone and Sade hadn't stirred so she tiptoed across the carpet, wondering where her bag with the Stemetil was as a terrible wave of nausea rose up inside, and opened the door. It was Ophelia, bedraggled and acid-laced. Justine held her hand over her mouth. Ophelia smiled a weak smile. She told Ophelia she'd be right back and went madly running around Marcelle's flat, trying not to wake people, trying to find her clothes. She had to prise her underpants out of Simone's clenched fist. As she did so she noticed there was blood all over the pillow where she'd slept. Where was her bum bag? She checked the time in the lounge room as she rushed to the kitchen sink to dry-retch over Marcelle's unwashed dishes. She had to be at the clinic in just under an hour. Her mouth tasted foul. She rinsed it out with water and was just about to swallow some orange juice from the fridge when she remembered she wasn't supposed to eat or drink. *Damn.* Her bum bag was on the floor beside the velvet armchair and she swallowed two Stemetil dry, hoping they wouldn't kill her later on. Back in the bedroom she wrestled with her fur waistcoat where it was caught up in Simone's silk stockings and contemplated whispering a warning about Simone in Sade's ear. She decided not to.

Accessory to murder. She liked the idea. Heaving, she ran for the bathroom and vomited green bile and the two Stemetil into the toilet. She washed her face in cold water, mascara smudging the puffy skin beneath her eyes, and ran out the door.

Ophelia threw her arms around Justine's neck. 'I came back to get you, I came back to get you,' she chanted mechanically into her ear.

Justine hailed a cab and collapsed along the back seat and rested her head in Ophelia's lap. They pulled up a block away from the clinic. As Justine slid out the back door of the cab she noticed a little park with a fountain. She walked over to a wooden bench and sat down. Ophelia joined her. The fountain was shaped like a sea-anemone and covered in spines. At the end of each spine was a light. She imagined how at night drops of water spurting out the end of each spine would look like fireflies. On the other side of the fountain people were sleeping on benches, swigging booze out of paper bags and shooting up in the bushes. A group of runaways stood pissing on the grass. Behind the fountain the traffic crawled up and down the street.

Nauseous, she looked down at the paving stones at her feet. No doubt the cigarette butts were crawling around like ants from Ophelia's point of view. Dizzy, thoughts came very slowly and were difficult to pin down. They dazzled psychedelically; it was as if there was a kaleidoscope inside her mind and her thoughts buzzed around like glass beads. She looked at the ground, her gaze spiralling out in ever-widening circles until she spied an uneven brown mass. Unrecognisable at first it soon assumed a strange and halting significance. *Fuck*. She pointed it out to Ophelia.

'See that?' Justine said.

'Yeah.'

'See that pile of shit matted into hair, cardboard and dead leaves?' She had to be absolutely sure Ophelia was looking at the right one.

'Yeah,' Ophelia said at last. 'Do you think it's human or dog?'

'I don't know,' Justine said impatiently. 'But do you know what it reminds me of?'

'What?'

'Me.'

'No it doesn't.' Ophelia was horrified.

'Yes it does, it even looks like me,' Justine said poisonously.

'It does not,' Ophelia protested.

Justine nodded, intractable.

'OK then,' Ophelia said defiantly. 'See this?'

'See what?'

'Well it's inside my head so you'll have to close your eyes,' Ophelia explained.

'Close my eyes?' Justine didn't understand.

'Close your eyes,' Ophelia commanded.

'OK,' Justine said, closing her eyes.

'I can see a field of flowers and bleached grass and kittens playing in the sun,' Ophelia told her.

'That's beautiful,' Justine agreed, not seeing.

'Thank you.'

They opened their eyes to flashing lights as a police van made its rounds.

'I've got to go,' Justine said, standing up.

'Think I should go with you?' Ophelia offered.

'Well it doesn't look like Sade's going to make it,' Justine pointed out superfluously.

'What time's the termination?' Ophelia was suddenly businesslike.

'Soon,' Justine said, stifling a wave of nausea.

'Do you want me to stay with you?' Ophelia asked, frown lines crisscrossing her forehead.

'It's up to you,' Justine called over her shoulder. She almost ran down the street. She had so many things to do. She had to have the abortion and then she had to go home and pack and hurry to visit her father before he died. She had to call university and cancel all her classes and she had to give notice on her flat before she was evicted.

7

SIX LANES OF TRAFFIC, THREE EACH WAY, SPED CRAZILY IN
and out of the city. The lanes leading out of town were driving directly into the face of a huge yellow moon. Tail-
lights wriggled on the ends of cars, red and wet, and the
road flowed like a river, the tarmac dark and smooth over
the invisible tug of a strong current. Headlights twisted
and turned like spotlights, seeing nothing, and everywhere the light went dancing about as if the stars above were
being reflected on coloured stones or bouncing off the
smooth surface of a river made uneven by movement.

The road turned a corner and the moon was left hanging
behind the shop fronts. Cold damp air nibbled with sharp
fishy teeth around shirt collars and bit into the eyes and ears
of passers-by. The wide pavements were brilliantly lit by
coloured lights streaming out of the row of shop windows, allowing crowds of people to flood up and down both
sides of the street. Winter was not far away.

Justine watched it all through a hazy blur. She vaguely

understood that she wasn't going home, that Ophelia was taking her back to her place. The cab was driving in the direction of the city. She observed the flow of the crowd—the amblers stopping every few paces to gaze at the window displays, the professionals climbing quickly in and out of cars, the curious dashing into pubs, shops and restaurants, long overcoats swishing about their ankles.

'I'm never going to have kids,' she drawled miserably.

Ophelia stroked her hand and sighed.

'What would happen to my work?' Justine wanted to know.

'There's always child-care,' Ophelia suggested.

Justine opened her window. 'That's not what I mean. I mean I'm never going to get married, start a family and settle down. I'm never going to buy a house or a dog and do the whole suburban nightmare.'

'I'm not having any more kids unless I'm married,' Ophelia said defensively. 'Then when my husband and I stop liking each other we'll just get divorced and live separately. That way I'll have a nice house and a few kids and alimony and my independence. Not like now, trying to bring up a family on my own in a one-bedroom flat at the back of a brothel.'

Ophelia asked the driver to pull over to the side while she bought a mixed bouquet at a florist.

'Who're these for?' Justine asked when Ophelia returned and deposited the flowers in her lap.

'They're for you,' Ophelia explained patiently. 'You had an abortion today, remember?'

Justine was quiet, a white rose pressed to her lips as

the cab fought with the traffic. Soon they turned off the main road and went speeding down narrow streets lined with terrace houses. Ophelia told the driver to pull up outside a four-storey terrace with a huge dark blue door. Justine paid the fare and hobbled, doubled over in pain, feeling the blood starting to trickle, from the cab to the door. The door was made of metal and was so flat and fitted so tightly into its metal frame that it looked like the door to a safe.

'Is this it?' Justine asked, looking uneasily from side to side.

'This is it.' Ophelia searched her black leather backpack for her keys.

'It doesn't look like a brothel,' Justine pointed out, trying to be polite.

'I could've made lots of money last night if I'd wanted to work,' Ophelia said, turning the key in the lock.

'Are you saying you work sometimes?'

Ophelia laughed. 'No, I've never done that sort of work. All I'm saying is that if I want it, it's there and there's plenty of it.'

Ophelia opened the door. The parlour was empty. Justine looked around the room and took in the details of the scene. The large cane chair, the ornate light fittings, the hanging beads, the desk lamp with the red globe, the screen, the curtained doorways, the green light of the answering machine. She followed Ophelia up the dark narrow stairs to a landing, their footsteps loud on the painted wooden floorboards. Ophelia opened the door to their left with another key. The door to the front bed-

183

room was closed. A phone rang unanswered downstairs. The message on the answer machine began with Marilyn Monroe singing 'I Wanna Be Loved By You'.

'That's one of the working rooms,' Ophelia said, nodding in the direction of the front room and closing her bedroom door. Monroe's whispering pout faded into the background. 'You can hold a glass up to the wall and listen if you want,' Ophelia said, offering her the bed.

Justine gave the flowers back to Ophelia and climbed between the smooth silk-satin sheets. She shivered with a sigh so deep it made her teeth rattle in her head. An old brown oil heater stood covered by a towel in the middle of the room. Ophelia straddled it and sat down. She offered Justine a cigarette. She declined. Ophelia sat smoking on the heater. Justine listened for noises from the front room. She heard nothing.

'I'm just going to get a vase,' Ophelia said, leaving the room.

Justine's eyes wandered. The floorboards were painted black. A single bed stretched all the way across one wall of the room under two narrow windows. Each window was made up of four small rectangular panes of glass set in wood. The wall opposite the bed was lined with shelves of clothing, everything neatly folded into piles; tops and jumpers in one pile; tights in another; and coats hanging on hooks on the side. Between the bed and the shelves was a rickety old cane chair covered in dirty washing and opposite the chair next to the foot of the bed was a deep-set mantelpiece covered in white candles, snapshots of children, and black-and-white photos of Ophelia with her arms around the necks of a number of different men. The fourth wall was covered with a poster-sized reproduction of a painting. The painting depicted a fair-skinned woman wearing a white wedding dress floating on her back, drowned in a river. She held a chain of flowers in her deadly pale hands. The river was lined with bushes and lilies. In the foreground there was a bed of bright green moss. Ophelia returned with a vase and stood arranging the flowers.

'Tell me about the painting,' Justine said.

'It's by a painter called Millais and it hangs in the Tate Gallery in London. It's called *Ophelia*,' she said, her back to her friend.

'And where are your kids?' Justine asked, inquisitively.

'They live with my mother,' Ophelia said, turning around.

There was a bottle of cognac on the bedside table and Ophelia poured them both a glass. Justine gulped down the cognac and straightaway held her glass out for a refill.

'You're probably still in shock,' Ophelia said, handing her back her glass. The liquid sloshed around amber in the candle light.

Justine lay back on the soft pillows and studied Ophelia's face. Ophelia wore her red-blonde hair up in a bun and loops fell down each side of her round pink cheeks. Her teeth were chalk white when she smiled and her lips were full and a deep cherry red. Her gaze swept over Ophelia's face, thighs and breasts. *So vibrant.* Suddenly she smiled and shook her head. She took a deep breath, about to speak, but Ophelia held a finger to her lips and told her to shush.

Justine heard voices on the landing outside and then footsteps stomping down the stairs.

'You should read this,' Ophelia said when the footsteps had faded away, handing her a heavy book.

She read the cover. The book was called *Justine* and it was written by the Marquis de Sade.

'You've probably read it before,' Ophelia guessed.

'I'm familiar with his work,' Justine said in a serious voice.

'Oh well, if you've already read it,' Ophelia prattled, pouring out another two glasses of cognac. 'I just thought it might cheer you up.'

Justine nodded thoughtfully and felt the book go sliding down the bedclothes and come to rest somewhere around her knee. She couldn't move. Her eyes started to close.

'God I'm pissed,' Ophelia said, climbing up on the bed. 'Am I disturbing you if I lie down for a while?'

She shook her head and inched closer to the wall. Ophelia moaned high-pitched little-girl moans and went into a deep sleep. The book was hard against her knee.

She stared at Ophelia's red-blonde hair. She considered pulling out the tie and sending the long tousled curls dancing down her back. She pushed the book further down the bed and moved a little closer to Ophelia. She stared at her cherry-red lips.

She pictured the seduction scene. She would dress up like a man—hair slicked back and wearing a suit—and knock at Ophelia's door. Ophelia would open the door and stand back, inviting her inside. Then she'd take Ophelia in her arms, she'd kiss Ophelia on the lips and pull her clothes away from her shoulders and bury her face in Ophelia's neck. Then Ophelia would undress her, Ophelia would mess up the slicked-back hair and she'd giggle and turn her head away. Then naked she'd tumble onto the bed and Ophelia would tumble in too and she'd lie with Ophelia under a white cotton sheet and pull the sheet over Ophelia's head and she'd swim in Ophelia's arms and cover her with kisses.

Ophelia seemed to be smiling while she slept and Justine couldn't help leaning down and kissing her on the lips. She put her tongue inside but Ophelia just moaned and turned her head away. She moved down the bed and unbuttoned Ophelia's black denim shirt and flared denim pants. Then she pulled down Ophelia's underpants and stared at her hairy blonde cunt. She slipped her pinky inside and Ophelia moaned. She pushed back the hair and exposed the tiny red clit. Then she licked it very very gently. Ophelia lay perfectly still. Was she raping her friend? The words didn't make any sense amidst the general fog. Everything was Sade's fault. She inserted her finger once more. *Damn, she doesn't want to fuck me either.* She prodded Ophelia in the stomach.

'Ophelia, Ophelia,' she called, 'wake up.'

'I'm too tired,' Ophelia slurred and turned over, away from Justine.

One by one the candles flickered and blew out as a cold draught came rushing in under the heavy painted door.

Careful not to wake her up, Justine left Ophelia snoring lightly and went to the bathroom. She peed, wiped herself, flushed the toilet and then stood bent over the sink, staring down the drain.

'Is my little baby down there?' she asked the sink. 'Is Sade's and my baby alive down there? Little foetus, can you hear me?' There were matted strands of hair tangled in the stainless steel mouth and she scraped them out with her fingernails. 'Goodbye little darling,' she said. 'Even though I had you killed it doesn't mean I don't love you.'

Back in Ophelia's room she sat staring out the window and smoking Ophelia's cigarettes well into the night. The candles were dead and the moon high in the sky. Outside a streetlamp illuminated the narrow garbage-strewn lane.

Just after two the phone rang. In her hurry to pick it up she knocked the ashtray clattering to the floor. Ophelia stopped snoring and then moaned and started up again.

'Justine, it's me. Sade.'

She slid to the floor amidst the ash and scattered butts.

'What do you want?' she hissed into the receiver.

'Look, I just bumped into Marcelle,' he lied.

Sure. 'Sade, it's a quarter past two in the morning.'

'OK, I didn't bump into her, I called her,' he almost apologised.

'I see, so now you're harassing my friends.' Annoyed.

'I wasn't harassing her,' he explained. 'I'm just looking for Simone and I asked Marcelle and Marcelle said she might be with you.'

'Why do you want to talk to Simone?' Very suspicious.

'I just want to talk to her,' he whined.

'But why?' Angry and suspicious.

'None of your business why,' he protested.

'Then I can't help you find her,' she snapped.

'That's fine,' he said, barely maintaining his cool. 'Look, if you see Simone and you change your mind just ask her to pretty please ring me, OK?'

She quietly slammed down the phone. *Fuck him.* She watched the moon through the window until it moved out of sight. She smoked more cigarettes. She picked up the book and started to read, laughing under her breath. Finally she undressed and lay down next to Ophelia. She slept.

Justine opened her eyes as the first rays of light came creeping through the glass pane. Outside the window the laneway was deserted except for a drunk lying sprawled against a garage door and a group of pigeons pecking at refuse in the gutters. High above, a thin grey cloud cast everything below in a soft still light, colours washed out, edges blurred. The grey sky made her nervous. It was a scene from a thriller just before an innocent bystander is killed. She went to the bathroom. She sat listening on the toilet not switching on the light. Making her way back across the landing on tiptoe she heard someone knock at the door downstairs. *Sade!* She wasn't at all surprised. She wanted to climb out the bedroom window, down the drainpipe and escape along the sordid little lane. She ignored this impulse. First she would go downstairs and make sure.

She went to Ophelia's bedroom and dressed in her

soiled clothes. She secured a fresh sanitary napkin in her G-string. She smoothed her hair in the mirror. She wiped the sleep from her eyes. Ophelia was still asleep. She crept across the black floorboards and out onto the landing and then tiptoed down the narrow stairs. The knock came again. She crept towards the lace curtains. A floorboard creaked. She stopped. Her breath screamed back at her in the quiet room. She heard movements upstairs. She would have to hurry. She cleared the distance between herself and the window in two large steps. She stood trembling, nose itchy with dust from the curtains. She leant close to the window. The synthetic white lace tickled her hair. She held her breath. She leant closer and closer until she could see. *It was only Hamlet.* She leant backwards and let her breath out in a long sigh. Above, footsteps thundered on the wooden stairs. *Damn.* She opened the door and smiled hello. Just then the sun broke through the clouds and for a moment the street was saturated and bright with its warm brilliance. The door sparkled with fine specks of gold glitter and the dark blue paint became five shades lighter, bright enough to swallow the whole sky like the sea in the late afternoon.

He mumbled hello and stood awkwardly before her, smiling an apologetic smile. She smiled absently back, waiting for the owners of the footsteps to appear. Two women dressed in black, hair streaming behind them and both wearing high platform heels glided across the room, barely registering her presence. She heard giggles as they locked the door behind them. He asked her if she'd eaten any breakfast. She shook her head. Had she led him on somehow, given him false hopes? *Something was wrong.* She racked her brains but the only image that came to mind was one of Hamlet kissing Ophelia under a streetlamp outside the club.

'I don't think that's a very good idea,' she said. 'Do you?'

He looked even more confused. *Damn.*

'Unless,' she ventured, cautiously, 'unless we take Ophelia along.'

His face brightened at the mention of Ophelia's name. *So that's it. Thank God.* Outside the sun had disappeared again and through the window the street was colourless, diffuse and drab beneath a web of cloud.

'Let's go upstairs,' she said, relieved, repressing an urge to laugh out loud.

He followed her up to Ophelia's room. Ophelia was standing in front of the mirror. She noticed Ophelia smiling at him in the glass.

'He's taking us both to breakfast,' Justine announced, throwing herself onto the bed. She raised her arms above her head and let them flop up onto the pillow. She sighed. She turned her attention back to the mirror. She saw Ophelia staring angrily at Hamlet and Hamlet's apologetic shrug. When they noticed Justine looking Ophelia smiled a fake smile and Hamlet looked away. Justine frowned at Ophelia but Ophelia was staring at herself in the mirror, picking at her chin. Meanwhile Hamlet was busy rummaging around in his pockets. He pulled out a tube of lipstick and joined Ophelia at the mantelpiece.

'Here,' he said awkwardly, 'you left this in my car.'

He handed Ophelia the tube.

'Thank you,' Ophelia said, blushing bright red, her voice barely a whisper.

He placed his hand on Ophelia's shoulder. Ophelia's eyes burned into his.

'So where are we going to go for breakfast?' Justine wanted to know. No-one answered her.

A sharp cramp went through her abdomen. She leapt to her feet. She winced. She noticed Hamlet had his arm around Ophelia's waist. She hurried from the room and stood trembling at the top of the stairs. She could hear his muffled words through the door.

'Oh shit,' he began, the words coming out fast, 'this is so hard for me to say so I'm just going to say it, and well, I think that's all I can do. I'm not here to have breakfast, I'm here because I wanted to see you. I haven't been able to get you out of my mind and I've been thinking some really crazy things—that I want to share my life with you, that I want to have children with you, that I want to put your children and my children under the same roof and call it a family, that you're everything to me and when we fuck I feel everything. What I feel when I fuck is everything and I feel everything when I fuck you. What I mean is the idea of living without you is just unbearable to me.'

Silence from the room. She stared down the stairs into the darkness below. *They were taking a long time.* She needed a drink, or food. She heard muffled tears.

'You just feel sorry for me,' he was saying in a deep soothing voice, 'you feel sorry for me because you know I'll be totally fucked up without you.'

192

'I don't feel sorry for you,' Ophelia said. 'It's just that that's the most beautiful thing anybody's ever said to me. I think you're so beautiful.'

Justine heard them laugh together loudly, then the squeaks of their kisses. *Sade*. The stairway opened before her like a dark void. *Sade and Simone*. Closing her eyes she let herself fall forwards in silence. There was nobody waiting when she landed with a crash at the foot of the stairs.

The phone was ringing. Her back ached. The answer machine clicked on. 'I Wanna Be Loved By You', sang the tuneless husky voice.

'Are you OK?' Ophelia's voice shouted down the stairs.

Justine sat up. She'd taken the skin off her left elbow, her back felt like it had been snapped in two and the sores on the back of her head were open and bleeding.

'I'm fine,' she called out.

An engaged tone shrilled from the answer machine. Whoever had called hadn't left a message. The machine clicked and rewound. She heard them talking together upstairs. Ophelia's high-pitched laugh. *What an idiot.* Her face was crimson. Blood trickled down the back of her neck. She grabbed a towel draped over the back of a chair and held it to the back of her head. She wiped at the blood. She struggled to her feet. Looked at the towel. Bright red blood. Shit. She wiped her head once more, pressing down hard and squeezing out the blood, and then threw the towel across the room. It landed behind the couch, hidden from view. The parlour. She collapsed in the large cane chair, her eyes held prisoner by the newspaper

193

headline: SERIAL KILLER DEATH HUNT HEADS NORTH. She considered reading the article. She thought nostalgically of Sade. She listened to their footsteps, thumping on the stairs. She tore her eyes away. The red light shivered with each step. Ophelia knelt at her side. She rubbed her hand.

'Did you fall?' Ophelia wanted to know, 'Did you hurt yourself?'

Justine shook her head. She looked up as Hamlet entered the parlour. He didn't meet her eye.

'I don't want to have breakfast any more, I just want to go home,' Justine said, sulking.

'We'll drop you off on the way,' Hamlet said, a little too fast.

Ophelia gave him a hard stare.

'Let's go,' Justine said, struggling to her feet.

Soon she was outside—the grey sky up above, sharp pains shooting up her spine—and then they all went speeding down roads writhing with early morning traffic. She was sitting pretty in the back—despite Ophelia's noisy protests—and she made Hamlet drive with the roof down. Tears went streaming from her eyes as the cold air clutched at her face. And she only half-listened to their conversation about how robots would replace real people as marriage partners, his idea and a stupid one at that and she wasn't sure what sort of pills Ophelia had handed her once they'd piled into the car but whatever they were they were fantastic and soon her back didn't hurt at all and when the car pulled up at a red light in front of a FREE PREG-NANCY COUNSELLING poster she actually laughed instead of cried and thinking about Sade made her want to go on a

long holiday instead of killing herself and she was just
about to ask Ophelia for some more pills and interrupt
what Hamlet was saying when she found herself listening
involuntarily to their conversation.

'Robots will be for all those public occasions,' Hamlet
was saying, 'for your family and friends and you'll be
able to update them every few years or so. You'll just go in
and buy a new face or a new body—no more divorce. But
the really great thing about robots is that you'll never
really be able to lie in bed with one and imagine that
you're not alone, that you don't live and die alone. Lying in
bed with a robot you'll just know you're alone, you won't
feel like there's anyone there to depend on, it'll be like
sleeping with a computer wrapped up in a pillow.'

'Will anybody fuck their robots?' Ophelia was smiling,
her hair blowing all over the place.

'No, no-one will really *fuck* their robots,' Hamlet
explained, enjoying himself, 'I mean it will be possible to
fuck robots but nobody will really want to. You might
fuck a robot once a week or once a month. No, when
people really want to fuck each other, they'll fuck people
they work with. Working and fucking and socialising will all
be one and the same. You'll only get jobs depending on
whether or not the employers want to fuck you and
whether you want to fuck them. If you don't want to fuck
them then you won't accept the job. Your employability and
your fuckability will be the same thing. So you'll have
love affairs with and fall in love with people at work but
you'll change lovers and jobs as you like, no-one will be tied
to each other beyond how much fun they have, and

there'll be no way a fuck can become a robot. There'll just be robots and fucks and no getting confused.'

'So would I be a robot or a fuck?' Ophelia asked, already knowing the answer.

'You're definitely a fuck.' Hamlet placed his hand on her knee.

'And you?'

'I'm a fuck too.' He smiled confidently.

'So we'd never even think of living together?' Ophelia was looking worried.

'No.' He shook his head.

'Or being with each other for the rest of our lives?' Ophelia whined.

'God no,' Hamlet replied, not catching on.

'We'd just fuck for as long as we wanted to and then move on?' Ophelia was sullen and her mouth drooped down at the corners.

'We'd fuck while we still wanted to fuck and then we'd stop,' Hamlet said, turning to face her. 'Sweetheart, what's wrong?'

Suddenly Justine couldn't take it any more. The car was stopped at another red light. So she hopped out the back and, feeling no pain, ran as fast as she could in the opposite direction, not looking back. In case they came looking for her she caught a cab home and bolted the door behind her, took the phone off the hook and switched the intercom off. She went into the bathroom and took the mirror down from the back of the door, carried it into her bedroom and hung it on a screw in the wall opposite her bed. The remaining foundation came away in crumbly lumps. The bruise was the same colour as her purple dress. She peeled off the stretch velvet dress and stockings. She lay flexing the muscles on her thighs in the mirror. First she lifted one leg up high into the air, pointing the toe. Once the leg was as high as it would go, she stretched it hard and watched the muscles pop out, running her hands along the lines, feeling the caverns and ridges her contractions produced. Then she let the leg go loose, then she tensed it again, stroked it, let it go loose, then she tensed again, stroked and released.

She turned around so that her toes touched the smooth glass of the mirror and her buttocks were resting on the edge of the bed. Then she raised her legs in the air like a dog itching for a scratch. She peered down across her belly and stared at the long line of her cunt, floppy pink flaps pushed out to the sides and the shiny gelatinous lips dripping wet and the tiny purplish tongue poking out. She ran one finger along the line of her cunt and then held it beneath her nose. She looked down at her finger. It was dripping with blood. Sade's cock waving in the air beneath her as Simone held herself poised above him flashed into her mind. She regarded her bloodied finger with suspicion. There were lumps of Sade's dried sperm on her neck.

She pushed more and more fingers inside and each time she forced them in her cunt made a delicious squelching noise. She scratched the walls with her fingernails, trying to puncture the skin. *Infertile*. She didn't care. Her cunt spurted blood onto the sheets and down onto the floor and her breath came in faster and faster gasps as she shoved her hand in and out with more and more force. On the brink of orgasm she rammed her feet out in front of her, soles crashing against the heavy glass. As her body surrendered to the long ferocious spasms and her fingers kept going pushing the peak higher and higher, the mirror went swinging on its thin chain and finally loosened the screw in the plaster, slid down the wall with a crash, and split in two as a deep spidery crack opened the smooth surface of the rectangle to the diagonal, splitting the perfect plane into two jagged-edged triangular slabs.

Her legs twitched once, then twice before she fell into a light dreamy daze, the blood mingling with a clear sticky jelly, running down her legs and dripping down onto the mirror cracked at her feet.

Hamlet

1

SLUMPED IN OPHELIA'S RICKETY CANE CHAIR JUSTINE LET her gaze drift aimlessly across the dark glass floor where a thin film of dust dulled the otherwise sleek surface. She closed her eyes. Images floated behind the red lids like jellyfish. She opened them again. Dazzling, a myriad of twirling points of light. Soporific, she watched countless fine particles of dust go dancing in circles in the early morning sunlight as it came streaming in through the domed windows up above, warming the room. Winter was already becoming spring.

She gazed over at the bed. Hamlet was still asleep. Naked, his body drew a diagonal line across the white cotton sheets. He rolled over onto his stomach. Traffic roared on the street below. He squeezed the middle of his half-hard cock and opened his eyes. When he saw that she was watching him he looked away. He climbed unsteadily to his feet. The floor was scattered with piles of clothes. He went through the contents of the nearest pile with his left foot, big toe working like a shovel, until he found a clean pair of boxer shorts and a white T-shirt. Dressed, he ran his hands through his hair. His hair was greasy and damp.

She followed him downstairs to the kitchen where he drank a tall glass of water from the tap. Then he filled the glass again and emptied it, then he filled it and emptied it once more. He offered her a glass of water. She shook her head. Dirty glasses were piled up around the sink, empty bottles lined the bench-top. A green garbage bag stood against the cupboard and garbage spewed out onto the large white square tiles. He picked up the loose garbage in his hands and put it back in the bag. He gathered the top of the bag together and forced the contents deeper into the bag. He moaned and held his head in his hands. The traffic sounded a constant hum as cars accelerated down the busy one-way street.

He lifted and carried the bag of garbage out the front door, across the communal walkway and headed down the fire stairs to the garbage chute. She filled her arms with empty bottles and hurried after him, taking the stairs two at a time, her bare feet warm against the smooth cool cement. He had to put the bag on the ground in order to open the door to the chute. Giggling, he held his nose. She moved closer to the chute. The smell of the bags that littered the floor inside nearly sent her dizzy to her knees. He picked up the bag and swung it hard. She watched it crash against the other rotting garbage strewn on the floor below.

The clatter of an empty tin.

She placed the empty bottles in the black plastic recycling

box and stood at the foot of the stairs waiting for him to come, but he remained standing in the doorway of the garbage chute, as if he couldn't walk away. Nearly gagging on the stench she retraced her steps to the chute. She looked down at the cement floor. It was splattered with what looked like blood. So was his foot. Her eyes moved up his leg. Halfway up the calf muscle blood oozed from a deep, wet gash. It looked exactly like an eye.

He looked down at his leg. As soon as he saw the cut he covered it with his hand—simultaneously letting go of the door to the chute which closed with a slam—and went limping wildly back up the stairs of the fire escape, scattering drops of blood in spurts with each step. He stopped on the landing and bent his head down to see. Bright orange-red blood oozed from the deep slit and dribbled down his leg in a steady stream. He stopped the blood with his hand and then wiped his hand on his shorts.

'Can you believe this?' he exclaimed. 'Have you ever seen anything like it?'

She ran ahead of him while he half-hopped, half-ran up the last flight of stairs, across the communal area and back inside. She rummaged through the drawers beneath the bathroom sink but there weren't any bandages inside. He held his leg under the cold water tap in the bath. The blood turned pink and disappeared down the plug hole, spotted with tiny dark clots. He laughed quietly to himself, unable to look away.

'There are no bandages and bandaids will be useless with a cut this size and with this amount of blood,' she said, peering closely at the bloody gash.

She searched the cupboards below the sink. She handed him a box of Kleenex. He turned off the tap and dried his leg with a handful of tissues. They quickly dissolved into a soggy orange mass that stuck to his fingers. He threw the tissues down the toilet and rinsed his hands under warm water. He dried them with a towel. He watched as blood made its way from his leg onto the small white oblong tiles and flowed in a stream along the plaster between the tiles and disappeared through the stainless steel drainage hole in the bathroom floor.

'It's tickling my leg,' he said, laughing. He grabbed another handful of tissues and wiped up the blood until they were sodden and bright and then he threw them into the toilet. He flushed. Grabbing another handful he held them to his leg and hopped into the kitchen.

'There isn't even any disinfectant,' she called out, slamming the cupboards closed again before joining him at the kitchen sink.

He filled a glass with water and emptied it in one gulp. He hopped upstairs. She checked in the cupboards under the kitchen sink. The closest thing to disinfectant was a bottle of household-grade bleach. On her way upstairs she noticed that the slate floor of the lounge room, the bathroom tiles, and the kitchen floor were dotted with dark red pools of blood. He stood at the top of the stairs gazing at his leg. In his hand the tissues were soiled and red. She went back to the bathroom and picked up the box of Kleenex. She also poured a glass of water and picked up a packet of painkillers. She made her way upstairs.

He lay across the white cotton sheets staring at his leg.

She placed the box of tissues at his elbow and offered him the painkillers. He ignored her. She swallowed two pills and washed them down with the water.

'I have the worst hangover,' she said. She collapsed with a sigh in the old cane chair.

As soon as each handful of tissues was dark with blood he threw it onto the smooth glass floor and held another handful against the wound. Soon there was an untidy orange pile. When finally the box was empty and he'd thrown the last handful of tissues onto the pile, he looked down at the cut once more. The flow of blood had slowed somewhat but the parted flesh still oozed a wet puddle of bright orange-red blood.

'Who would have thought,' he cried, 'that a cut like this could produce so much blood? It was so fast and it didn't even hurt, I didn't feel a thing, it was entirely painless and it still doesn't hurt. I've absolutely never seen anything like it. I've never had a cut like this before.'

She stared into its deepest slice and it winked back at her like a cut open eye. 'It's just like an eye,' she observed, 'a hideous blind eye. It looks without seeing and yet it makes you look at it and then you can't look away.' She shuddered, unable to take her eyes away from the brimming red slit.

The afternoon passed. She dozed. She heard the front door slam. She gazed down through the one-way glass floor and watched the kids go stampeding through the house, strip off and start running a bath. Ophelia went around after them picking up their towels and dirty clothes from the floor and throwing them into the laundry.

Ophelia took off her shoes and shook out the sand in the kitchen sink. Then she came upstairs.

'What happened?' Ophelia wanted to know, sitting down on the bed. Hamlet smiled a weak smile. Ophelia pushed the sodden tissues aside and examined the cut, her fingers expertly holding the skin apart and separating the two flaps of flesh. The cut had almost stopped bleeding but continued to ooze blood from the wet puddle between the strips of flesh.

'But sweetheart,' Ophelia complained, 'I don't understand why you didn't go to a doctor, you should have had stitches with a cut like that.'

Hamlet sat up. Ophelia wore her long fine red-blonde hair in a French plait and tied with knotted black elastic. He moved closer. She sighed. He reached up and gently massaged the back of her neck. She held herself stiff in his hands. Blood started to trickle slowly down his leg. He slapped his free hand against his leg and held it there to stop the flow.

'I'm sorry, sweetheart,' Hamlet explained, 'I don't really know why I didn't call a doctor, I just didn't think of it. I guess the shock must have confused me, I'm very tired. I've just been lying up here half-asleep laughing and daydreaming all day.'

Ophelia arched her neck away from him and stood up. She went pacing up and down in front of the bed wringing her hands. Hamlet closed his eyes and sighed.

'Have you made any plans for dinner, Ophelia?' he said abruptly. 'I was thinking of ordering some takeaway pizza. What do you think?'

Ophelia didn't answer and when Hamlet opened his eyes she was standing with her back to him.

'Pizza sounds great to me,' Justine said.

'How did you do it?' Ophelia persisted. 'I just don't understand how you could cut yourself like that and then just lie around and do nothing about it.'

'I was taking out the garbage and I must have cut myself on a piece of broken glass,' Hamlet whined.

'Well you should have a tetanus injection,' Ophelia berated him.

Ophelia turned around, picked up the pile of red tissues and went downstairs. Justine could feel the floor tremble beneath each heavy step.

'I'll order pizza by phone and pick it up on my way back from the doctor,' Hamlet called out, rolling his eyes and climbing unsteadily to his feet.

Keeping his hand cupped against his leg Hamlet changed into a pair of khaki shorts and put on a pair of sandshoes. He wiped his bloodied hand on a dirty T-shirt on the floor and stood up. The blood was still trickling down his leg but he paid no attention to it and, after calling up the pizza bar, he hurried dripping downstairs and out the front door.

Justine was exhausted. She scrutinised the TV room directly below where she slept on a sofa-bed. It would be hours before the room was hers again and she could go back to sleep.

2

SHE OPENED HER EYES. ONE OF OPHELIA'S CHILDREN, A little girl, sat in front of the TV while cartoons blared from the screen. She checked the time. It was just after seven o'clock. She struggled out of the sofa bed and into a black cotton dress. She put on a pair of black socks and black lace-up shoes. Yawning loudly she padded into the kitchen and made three cups of tea. She placed the cups on a painted wooden tray and carried them upstairs. They were still fast asleep. Leaving the tray on Ophelia's desk she left a cup of tea on the floor beside each sleeper's head. Hamlet opened his eyes and held his finger to his lips.

'She was up working late,' he whispered.

His thick blond ringlets were plastered to his temples with sweat and frizzy on top and his cheeks were creased with indentations left by the crumpled cotton pillowcase.

She eased herself into the cane chair. The strips of cane creaked noisily. She sipped her tea.

All of a sudden Ophelia sat bolt upright in bed, her

208

long red-blonde hair swinging in loose uneven hoops around her wide large-boned face. Eyes of the palest grey-blue stared out blankly, focused on invisible particles of air suspended in the middle of the room, the whites slightly pink and framed by thick brown eyebrows standing out at odd angles from her brow. Her face, neck and shoulders were golden brown and covered with sand coloured freckles and small dark moles. Her mouth was slightly open, her lips were pressed forwards so that her tongue protruded between them and rested on her bottom front teeth. The bedclothes, clasped close to her neck in a tight fist, fell away as she began to run her fingers along the strong lines of her chin. Her large milky breasts hung full and round and pink-nippled from her chest, rarely seen by the sun's blind red staring eye. Blue veins meandered beneath the creamy curves. Beads of sweat slipped down between her breasts and filled her bellybutton.

Hamlet sat up in bed beside Ophelia, gazing admiringly at the puddle of sweat oozing from the scoop of her bellybutton as it glistened and ballooned in the early morning light. He touched it with the tip of his finger and it was gone. His attention shifted to her face. He hovered around her, brushing hair away from her eyes and mouth and kissing her forehead. He stared into her cool grey-blue eyes. She continued to stare obliviously into the middle distance. Sitting back he watched her fingers move backwards and forwards, sliding like socks on a polished wooden floor along the groove between her neck and chin. He looked at her mouth, at the tongue poised as if ready to speak, at the frozen lips. Frowning, his gaze began a slow measured descent and, finding the blonde of her pubes, stayed there.

'How's my pretty little darling?' Hamlet chirped.

Ophelia turned to stare at him, irritation clouding her features, her lips stretched thin and her mouth turned down at the corners.

Frowning, he lay back down on the pillows. He clasped his hands together in his lap, apparently deep in thought. Then in an instant his expression changed. Severe consternation metamorphosed into dazzling insight. He turned over on his side and, propping himself up on his elbow, he placed his other hand on her arm, fingers fidgeting up and down, brushing the hairs different ways against her skin.

'I'm sorry, Ophelia,' he apologised, 'I know I shouldn't call you "pretty little", that it's sexist and diminutive.'

'And.'

'I'm sorry about the darling bit as well, I really am,' he added, humbled. 'In theory they seem like harmless little words, sorry, there I go again, they seem like mere words in theory but in practice they trivialise and marginalise whatever painful meaningful experience it is that you're going through. I'll keep trying.'

Justine almost spat out her tea but succeeded in choking it down. She muffled the coughs against her shoulder. She writhed miserably in the cane chair. It creaked again. Nobody noticed. She wanted to leave but Ophelia was staring straight at her even though her expression was devoid of even the most minimal flicker of recognition. She waited and slumped down even further in the chair.

Hamlet bent his head close to Ophelia's chest and sucked one of her nipples, drawing it deep inside his mouth. Then with a pop he let it go. It stuck up red and swollen. He blew cool air against it and watched the tiny hairs rise. He kissed around the circle of her nipple.

'If I keep trying, if we all keep trying,' Hamlet continued, adopting a lecturing tone, 'then perhaps we can make this world a better place, a more equitable place to live and work, a more productive place to be. Because discrimination on the basis of gender begins at home. And difference is inscribed in language, in the way we speak and think.'

He covered Ophelia's throat and chest with kisses and slowly moved down her body. Kneeling at her feet he pulled the bedclothes away from her stomach and thighs until she was sitting naked before him, propped up by a feather pillow, legs bent at the knees and spread wide. He punctuated his words with kisses planted upon the hairy lips of her cunt—hesitant kisses, light, his warm tongue pushed forwards, wet and tangled in the long strands of her pubic hair.

'It's only—by changing the way—we—speak and think that—we—can—hope to check—and—reverse—the terrible injustices—suffered by women—forced to live—in pain and misery—in patriarchal—societies.'

Hamlet moaned loudly and looked down at his groin and at his swollen cock. He looked up and met Ophelia's grey-blue eyes with his round deep blue eyes. But she soon looked away and then, tears running down each cheek, she started to cry.

'You don't love me,' Ophelia moaned.

He knelt over her, his cock inches from her face, his hands wiping away her tears.

'Have I done something to upset you?' he fussed. 'Was it something I said, sweetheart, was it something I haven't said? Please darling, don't be upset, please just try to be a tiny little bit happy to be with me on this rainy Sunday morning, all cosy and wrapped up in bed and the children playing quietly downstairs.'

He studied her face, now turned hard and fierce and wet with tears. He lowered his lips onto hers, kissed her gently and moaned, the breath escaping his mouth in a fast warm rush.

'Darling, my sweet darling,' he gushed.

He covered her chest with heavy wet kisses. He moaned and rubbed his cock between her breasts, holding them together with the palms of his hands.

'I can't help it darling but look what you've done to me,' he cried, 'you've aroused me.'

He brought his cock up to her lips.

'Oh God Ophelia, will you please suck my cock,' he begged, poised trembling above her, cock pressed to her lips.

Ophelia sniffled quietly, her lips loose enough to allow the swollen tip of Hamlet's penis inside. Instantly his body started to spasm as the thick white ejaculate spurted all over her face. Moaning loudly, he collapsed beside her on the bed.

'I'm sorry,' he apologised, 'but I think I just must have really wanted to fuck you.'

Hamlet lay where he had fallen, eyes rolled back in his head, one hand holding his penis and the other twirling his hair. Thick white globs of sperm soaked into Ophelia's hair, hung dripping from her eyebrows, ran streaming down her cheeks, dribbled from her chin and oozed from the corners of her mouth. Beneath the dewy emission her face wore a puzzled frown and she stroked her nipples erect with the tips of her fingers.

After some time had passed he knelt in front of her and began mopping her face with a tissue.

Justine emptied her cup of tea. Here was her chance. She waited until Ophelia's gaze was obscured by Hamlet's dabbing handful of tissues. She slowly eased herself out of the chair. She took two steps towards the stairs and then froze. *Damn.* Ophelia's eyes met hers in a steely stare. Embarrassed, she smiled. Ophelia patted the bed beside her. Justine looked at the stairs. *Five more steps.* She sat down at the foot of the bed.

'You know Justine, I've been thinking,' Ophelia began ominously.

'Yes,' Justine chimed obediently.

'I was swimming at the pool yesterday afternoon while the kids were in day care,' Ophelia announced.

'Yes.'

'Well, I was thinking about my swimming and wondering why I've been an obsessive lap-swimmer my whole life,' Ophelia continued.

'Yes.'

'And I realised that it's all to do with escape,' Ophelia said.

'Escape?' Justine didn't understand.

'Well, we live on this huge island,' Ophelia reasoned.

THE RIVER OPHELIA

'Continent,' Justine corrected, 'yes.'

'And the only way to leave is by sea or air.'

'Yes.'

'So my swimming is to do with leaving,' Ophelia explained. 'All my life I've been swimming laps, up and down the pool, and it's all about escaping from this country. All the time in the back of my mind has been the idea that I'll escape from this blasted country one day, even if I have to swim my way out.'

'You mean you want to swim away from me,' Hamlet complained, licking his fingers so they were covered in spit and then rubbing at the white clusters of membranes tangled in Ophelia's eyebrows.

'No,' Ophelia snapped, 'just away from here.'

Hamlet pinched his fingers together and drew them down the length of each eyebrow hair and then wiped his fingers on the sheets. Patches where he had already wiped Ophelia's cheeks and lips were covered in a white dry skin which peeled off as he scratched at it with his finger-nails. He looked at her hair and prodded at the solid clumps but made no attempt to untangle them. He inserted his little finger inside her nose, one nostril at a time and dug out sticky clumps of half-dry sperm. He wet his fingers again and rubbed at her chin. He threw the tissue to the floor and took out a new one. He wiped his penis, starting at the tip and then, dribbling spit down into his lap, he pulled and scratched at the sperm which clung stubbornly to his thick blond pubic hair.

Justine averted her eyes. 'It would be an incredibly long swim.'

214

'It could take forever and it still wouldn't stop me from trying,' Ophelia sulked.

'You would have to swim in a cage,' Justine teased.

'A whole pack of sharks could go into a feeding frenzy up and down the walls of the cage and I'd still keep swimming,' Ophelia insisted.

'I thought you were frightened of sharks,' Hamlet reminded her, wiping his pubic hair and throwing the soiled tissue to the floor.

'I am,' she admitted, 'even swimming laps I have to keep looking over my shoulder just in case there's a fin following me.'

He took a fresh tissue from the box. He squeezed out the last remaining drops of sperm from the tip of his penis and spotted them with the tissue.

'Anyway,' Ophelia announced, 'I've decided that I have to face my fears and leave. I have to just pack up a bag and go and live somewhere else for a few years, or indefinitely.'

Panic clouded Hamlet's eyes. 'We'll be filming on location in New Zealand next month,' he said, an edge of desperation creeping into his voice. 'Why don't you come along, we could leave the kids with your parents for a couple of weeks?'

'No, I don't think that's a good idea, do you?' Ophelia almost snarled. 'Remember New York last month, and Barcelona before that? You're always impossible when you're shooting. Besides, I want to live overseas, not just go for a visit.'

'Well, where will you go?' he cried.

'I haven't decided yet,' she snapped.

Hamlet looked away from his penis, tissue in hand. He looked at Ophelia's breasts, the nipples no longer a hard throbbing red but a soft and pointed dark pink. She held her hand out for the tissue, intercepting his line of vision. He crushed the tissue inside his fist.

'What if I don't want you to go?' Utterly forlorn.

'I feel trapped here, I feel crazy, I have to go,' she said, an air of indifference creeping into her voice.

'But we've only been living together for three months.'

'So what?'

Justine stood up to leave—*this is so ugly*—but Ophelia leapt up—sending the bedclothes skidding across the floor—and grabbed hold of her hand. Ophelia wanted Justine to help pack. Not wanting to, Justine agreed. She held the empty backpack open for Ophelia to fill. In the meantime she watched Hamlet. The white sheets were stained different shades of red, burgundy and brown with dry and wet blood from his leg. Alone in the bed he reached down between the two folds of sliced flesh. He picked off the hard crust of dried blood and hair. He reached for the tissues and dabbed at his leg. Then, glaring at Ophelia, he crawled along the bed on hands and knees and reached across the floor for the covers and pulled them up. Kneeling at the head of the bed he shook them out, splattering blood in tiny squirts from his leg onto the sheets. He lay down. He held the covers up to his chin and scowled at Ophelia over the white cotton edge.

Ignoring Hamlet's performance, Ophelia peered down

through the dark layer of glass beneath her feet and into the lounge room below.

'I wonder what the kids are up to,' she asked, changing the subject.

The master bedroom comprised the entire top floor of the large inner-city townhouse. Ophelia's desk, the ravaged cane chair and the king-size futon were the only pieces of furniture. The roof was made of panes of glass shaped into a magnificent dome. The floor was made entirely of one-way glass which allowed those above to observe everything that happened below unobserved. The bed sat exactly in the middle of the room. The corresponding space on the bottom floor directly below the bed was sealed off. A dark silent rectangular prism filled with stale still air.

The rest of the bottom floor was divided into four rooms, each in the shape of an isosceles triangle but with the top chopped off. The walls extended diagonally from each corner of the sealed-off space. The children slept in one room, ate in the second room, watched television and played games in the third room and bathed and defecated in the fourth room. The whole townhouse was designed so that those upstairs could keep an eye on everything that happened in the house and everything those downstairs did without having to leave their bed. A flight of stairs made of a heavy dark glass descended from the foot of the bed, right through the middle of the lounge room where the kids played and watched TV, to the front door below. Ophelia's desk was located directly above the room in which the children slept. The cane chair was located

217

above the television room. The house had belonged to Hamlet's father. Now it belonged to Hamlet.

Downstairs the children were playing in the lounge room. They were playing their favourite game, strip dictionary, and were in various stages of undress, some even nude.

Ophelia rushed around picking up clothes from the floor and shoving them screwed up into tight balls into a black leather backpack. Justine had to hold on tightly to the bag. Once the backpack was full, Ophelia swung it up onto her shoulder and set off down the dark glass stairs.

'Haven't you forgotten something?' Hamlet called after her.

Ophelia followed the direction of Hamlet's gaze which was moving steadily down her body. Finally, realising she wasn't wearing any clothes, she opened the backpack and pulled out a crumpled floral dress and a pair of under-pants. Downstairs the children each removed an item of clothing, giggling and screaming and grabbing each others' private parts.

'Oh,' Ophelia exclaimed from the bottom of the stairs while she attended to her hair, 'that reminds me. While I'm away, Hamlet, I want you to do something about the children playing that horrible game.' Then she pulled her uncombed hair back from her face, smoothed it between her hands, twisted the elastic around the bunched hair and let go.

'Fuck you you stupid fucken asshole piece of floor,' Hamlet muttered as he threw himself out of the bed, almost falling over on the slippery floor.

'Goodbye,' Ophelia called in a singsong voice and waved, one hand on the door.

'Will you just wait?' Hamlet whined, sighing and rolling his eyes. He kicked at the piles of clothes that littered the floor until he uncovered a pair of shorts. When he picked them up he saw that they were the same pair of shorts he'd been wearing when he cut his leg. Dirty and stained with blood he slipped them on. He ran his hands through his greasy curls.

Ophelia was still standing in the open doorway when he got downstairs. At first he didn't look at her face. Then, his fingers twitching at his sides, he looked into her eyes. She stared back at him, her eyes a cold grey-blue and filled with tears.

He couldn't win. 'You'll call me, won't you, as soon as you're ready?'

She shrugged.

'I don't want you to go,' he pleaded.

'But you understand,' she sniffled.

'No,' he said shaking his head, 'I don't understand why you're leaving me.'

'Look,' she said, starting to cry, 'I'll see you later.'

'Darling, sweetheart, please,' he begged, tugging at her sleeve.

'Don't call me that,' she chided, pushing his hand away, and left without looking back.

He stood frozen in the doorway, watching her climb into the back seat of a cab, blood streaming steadily down his calf, across his foot and onto the slate floor. He dug his nails into the palms of his hands.

Justine hurried down the stairs and into the kitchen. *Escape.* Hamlet turned back from the door and hung his head in despair. He plodded up the stairs, one blood-splattered step at a time. She heard the sigh of the bed as he lay down, and then his quiet sobs. She wrung her hands.

She went and sat down on the sofa in the TV room where the children were playing strip dictionary. They were so deeply engrossed in their game that they didn't even look up when she came in. Strip dictionary had the following rules: one person would think of a word and everyone else had to guess the meaning. If no-one guessed the meaning then everyone had to remove one item of clothing. Then the person who was thinking of the word chose another word and everyone tried to guess the meaning. If someone guessed the meaning of the word then the person who's word it was had to remove an article of clothing. Then it became the turn of whoever had guessed the meaning of the word.

She dozed on the couch. Hours passed. The children screamed and giggled intermittently. It started to rain. The rain thundered against the glass dome up above. Finally, holding his head in his hands, Hamlet came hobbling downstairs, a handful of bright red tissues held to his leg, and told the children that they had to stop playing strip dictionary and that it was time to get dressed. Justine pretended to be asleep. He herded the children into their bedroom and waited for them to get dressed.

'I don't know, kids,' Justine heard Hamlet say, 'I love Ophelia, and I really respect her but I still have trouble with my own feelings of abandonment. I just feel so incredibly abandoned whenever she leaves me like this.'

'Not again,' Ophelia's little boy whined.

'I'm afraid so,' Hamlet complained.

'Will she come back?' Ophelia's son wanted to know.

'I guess so,' Hamlet admitted reluctantly, 'and then it will be champagne and pizza every night and Ophelia and I will have wild sex and I'll be so glad to see her, but in the meantime,' he whined, on the verge of tears again, 'I just don't know how I'm going to get through the next few days. I'm going to need your support, I mean I just feel so down.'

'Oh Hamlet,' Ophelia's six-year-old daughter advised, 'don't be too hard on yourself. Why don't you go visit a friend? We could have the baby-sitter and you could go out and get drunk. That might help.'

'But I just want to be with Ophelia,' Hamlet moaned, bursting into tears. 'I just want to fall asleep in her arms and there's no-one else in the world for that.'

Hamlet's son, also called Hamlet, had the following advice: 'Maybe you two should split up. I wouldn't mind, I think separate houses are cool.'

'Yippee,' Ophelia's daughter screamed, 'I want to have two houses.'

'My life would be meaningless without her,' Hamlet said, obstinately disaffected.

'Hamlet, don't cry,' Ophelia's son pleaded.

'It's important for me to cry, kids,' Hamlet said, blowing his nose. 'I've got to feel that I'm free to express my feelings.'

'But don't you think it's about time you got over this abandonment stuff?' Hamlet's son chipped in. 'Maybe you should go back to psychoanalysis?'

'But I don't want to be cured,' Hamlet said defensively. 'I love Ophelia and I don't want to fall in love with a psychiatrist.'

'Well, you've got to do something, Hamlet,' Ophelia's daughter insisted.

'I think I'll just go upstairs and go to bed,' Hamlet moped.

'Don't you have any work to do?' Ophelia's daughter said, trying to be helpful.

'I can't work when I'm in this state,' Hamlet snapped.

'But that's such a defeatist attitude,' Ophelia's daughter pointed out.

'I just feel so down,' Hamlet complained. 'I don't want to be distracted from my sense of loss.'

'Well, no wonder she leaves you, Dad,' Hamlet's son said. 'You're unbearable when you're like this.'

'Come on, Hamlet,' Ophelia's little boy said, 'come and have some chocolate milk and biscuits.'

'OK,' Hamlet sniffed pathetically. 'You win.'

The children all started screaming and shouting and ran into the kitchen. Hamlet followed sheepishly behind them, sniffling and blowing his nose.

'OK,' he said, lining up the mugs along the bench-top, 'four biscuits each at the max, and for the chocolate milk, put two spoonfuls of chocolate in each cup, then stir in a spoon of hot water, then add a little honey and then when it's runny and dark brown, pour in the milk.'

Justine heard cupboard doors slamming and the squeal of stools as the children took turns fetching things from the shelves and climbing up and down the stepladder in the huge walk-in pantry. Hamlet appeared in the doorway. She continued pretending to be asleep. He moped over to the stereo and looked through the CDs. He found a re-release of dance hits from the seventies and fast-forwarded the disc to Ophelia's favourite song. He sang along to the first few lines and then listened to the rest in silence, staring at the floor, not noticing the dark pool of blood forming at his feet.

Justine yawned loudly and went into a stretch.

'Oh sorry,' Hamlet shouted over the music, 'did I wake you?'

She shook her head and smiled. He frowned and made his way aimlessly back to the kitchen. Caught out, she followed lamely behind. She froze in the doorway, confronted by the scene.

The children were dancing wildly around the kitchen, pulling faces and pulling down their pants and swinging their hips to the music. They mimed singing into microphones and playing air-synthesizers and guitars and sang along to the chorus in four-part harmony. They rammed their naked ass-cheeks together in time to the beat and grabbed their crutches and fingered their chests where their breasts would be if they had any. They incorporated making the cups of chocolate milk into their dance routine and went about mixing and adding the ingredients in time to the song.

By the time the song ended Hamlet was crying again.

'You kids are fantastic,' he said, admiring the tidy row of brimming cups of chocolate milk through tear-stained eyes and dripping blood all over the floor, 'you know that? I don't know what I'd do without you.' Still sobbing he laughed into a Kleenex, and then blew his nose and wiped his eyes.

'Sure, Dad,' his son said sarcastically, 'we've heard it all before.'

'Here, Hamlet,' Ophelia's daughter said, handing him the box of tissues, 'have this for your leg.'

Hamlet held the tissues to his calf. They offered him a cup of chocolate milk and they all climbed up onto the stools.

'So what's it going to be this time, Dad,' the young Hamlet teased, 'the baby-sitter for us and a binge for you?'

'I thought we might call up some of Ophelia's friends and go out and get something to eat,' he said, addressing Justine for the first time and squeezing her hand. 'You kids don't mind spending a night at home with Simone, do you?'

The kids all screamed and jumped in the air and ran into the bathroom and started running a huge bubble-bath.

3

THE CHILDREN SAT STRUMMING OUT-OF-TUNE GUITARS IN front of the television. Justine yawned. She recognised the lyrics to 'Nowhere Man'. She picked up the newspaper she'd been reading and returned to the article about Healing Relationships. According to the journalist, and the psychologists and mystics quoted in the article, a healing relationship was a brief sexual encounter that restored the participant's self-esteem. Healing relationships were the first step in repairing emotional and physical damage incurred during previous and familial relationships.

Justine curled her lip in distaste. *Healing relationships. Sure.* She preferred to call a spade a spade and a fuck a fuck. *Still.* She looked at Hamlet as he knotted a strip of white rag around his leg. There was a lot to be said for hot sex.

She heard a key in the front door. Suddenly Simone was waltzing into the kitchen wearing a pair of sheer black stockings, short black silk shorts, black Cuban heeled riding boots, a black singlet top and a black leather jacket. Uncomfortable, Justine wandered upstairs. She stared up through the glass dome. The clouds were clearing and the sun hung low in the sky. *Damn. Simone made tough competition.* When she came back downstairs she paused at the foot of the stairs and listened to their conversation.

'The thing I hate about being a student,' Simone was saying, 'is having to spend time with other students. I can't stand the way they complain about being poor all the time. It's such a cliché,' Simone complained, 'it's like worse than my worst nightmares about living in suburbia with a mortgage and three kids and all anyone talks about is real estate and work and children.'

Justine peered around the corner. Hamlet held a match to the end of the joint. 'So you're never going to get married?'

'Well, that's a boring question,' Simone said, leaning towards him on her stool, her breasts almost falling out of her top.

Justine ducked back behind the corner.

'Well, I'm as good as married,' Hamlet said, provoking her, 'what do you expect?'

'That's no excuse.' Simone giggled.

'Yes it is,' he said, dragging on the joint.

'You're fishing for compliments,' she teased.

He exhaled loudly. 'What if I am?'

'I see,' she said, giggling again. 'So you ask me if I'm ever going to get married because you want to know if I think you're boring?'

'Well, am I?'

226

'No, not boring,' she hedged. 'Bored maybe, but not boring.'

'There's a difference?' He sounded offended.

'Well, yes,' she said, hesitantly.

'I don't see it,' he snapped.

She took a drag of the joint. 'No?'

Justine peered around the corner once more. Hamlet had his hand on Simone's thigh and was sliding his tongue in and out her lips. He reached into her shorts and stroked the wet rubbery softness of her cunt.

Justine ducked back and then retraced her steps, coughed loudly and then entered the kitchen.

'Ready to go?' Hamlet asked amiably, crushing the joint under his shoe, his hand still resting on Simone's thigh.

Justine nodded, careful not to stare at his hand.

'Simone,' he said business-like, 'will you wait up for me?'

Simone straightened her shorts. 'OK, but don't be too late.'

Simone leaned over and kissed Hamlet hard. Justine noticed his hand wriggling around deep in the front pocket of his jeans. The back of her neck prickled in irritation.

4

THE PIZZA BAR WAS NOISY AND CROWDED WHEN THEY arrived. Marcelle was waiting at a table inside. Justine had to push past a man and a woman and their three blond children to get to the table. She kissed Marcelle hello. She sat down.

'How are you?' Marcelle wanted to know, pouring the wine into the still-wet duralex glasses.

Hamlet remained standing next to the table wearing a sheepish grin.

Marcelle told him to sit down and handed him a glass of wine. She made a toast. They clinked glasses. Marcelle ordered two large pizzas and sat looking from one to the other and gulping down her wine.

'So Justine,' Marcelle asked, 'how the fuck?'

Justine sipped nervously from the side of her glass. 'Well,' she said hesitantly, 'I'm still seeing Juliette once a week and that's OK. It's great getting out of my flat and living with Hamlet and Ophelia and the kids. But I'm still really depressed, I don't know what to do with my life. And I wake up crying every day.'

'You know what you need, Justine,' Marcelle said boisterously.

'No,' Justine said.

'You need a man,' Marcelle said and laughed.

Justine smiled. 'Sure.'

'I mean it,' Marcelle went on, playfully.

'OK,' Justine said, entering into the spirit of things, 'what kind of man do you think I should go for?'

She leaned forward on the edge of her chair and looked at Marcelle, her eyebrows raised, daring her to reply. Her black cotton dress was hitched up high exposing her thighs and her ass-cheeks poking out from her underpants stuck to the shiny plastic seat. Pressed up against the table and with three buttons undone, her breasts were clearly visible in outline between the soft folds of her light summer dress.

In the meantime she noticed that Hamlet wasn't listening. Out of the corner of her eye she watched him run his hand along his leg. It had stopped bleeding again. He started pulling at the dried clotted lumps of blood and hair.

'Well,' Marcelle began, gulping down her glass of wine and her heavy black leather jacket squeaking as the stiff sleeve rubbed against the front zippered panel, 'I think he'll be called Bill and he'll be very big and very laid-back, he'll be so laid-back he'll make everyone nervous.'

'OK, Marcelle,' Justine agreed, 'I'll go for a Bill, and he'll be incredibly handsome.'

'He'll have big blue eyes and dark long lashes,' Marcelle decided.

'He'll wear very thick glasses but beneath the glasses his eyes'll be beautiful and round and just like lollies,' Justine said.

'He'll be myopic,' Marcelle exclaimed, 'that's what'll make everyone nervous.'

Justine laughed. 'He'll make everyone nervous because he's so smart but totally un-neurotic, very spacey.'

'He'll be a nuclear physicist and he'll be rolling in dough and money just won't be a question.'

'He'll be American and he'll wear really yuppie clothes, he'll wear baggy khaki trousers from Paris and linen shirts.'

'And he'll be a little fat,' Marcelle said between laughs.

'And he'll have a *huge* personality.'

'But he'll be very quiet.'

'And he'll love drugs.'

'And he'll be incredibly generous.' Marcelle said, gulping at her wine.

'And he'll have a huge cock,' Justine said, laughing again. 'He'll have to have a huge cock and be into really wacko sex, and because he's so scientific he'll be into mystical sex, into magic and animals.'

Marcelle couldn't stop laughing. 'All he'll think about is sex and science.'

'But he'll be good with food. He'll be very regular and he'll make sure I get fed.'

'He'll have a *big* appetite.'

'But what else, Marcelle,' Justine said, leaning back in

her seat, 'I mean I'm not really sold on Bill the nuclear physicist.'

'You mean what's his weakness?' Marcelle teased.

'It's not that so much as I want someone really *big*,' Justine said, thoughtfully. 'What about an actor?'

'An actor's perfect,' Marcelle cried. 'No-one can argue with an actor.'

'No-one can pretend to understand him because he'll always be playing a role.'

'And it'll just be obvious with an actor. It'll just be obvious that it's *all cock*.' Marcelle was deadly serious.

'He'll have to be smart,' Justine insisted.

'OK, let's think of someone.'

'Maybe someone up and coming?'

'No, he's got to be huge, someone you can't argue with,' Marcelle said. 'Someone to shut everybody up.' She refilled the glasses. 'What do you think, Hamlet?' she said. 'What do you think he'll be like?'

Hamlet looked up, still tugging at his leg. 'Who?'

'The guy I marry,' Justine said impatiently. 'Going on my recent past, what do you think he'll be like?'

'I don't know,' he said, avoiding the issue.

Marcelle looked Hamlet dead in the eye. 'Will he be a tall, dark, handsome, nuclear physicist?'

'Or an up and coming star?' Justine said, leaning forward in her chair again. 'Or a big name?'

Hamlet shook his head and sat back in his chair. 'I don't know,' he said again and shrugged his shoulders. He held his glass in his left hand. Justine watched him run the fingers on his other hand between the rag and his sliced open skin. She noticed how red wine had stained the corners of his mouth.

'I know, Justine,' Marcelle said excitedly, 'he'll work in publishing, he'll be an editor.'

'Yes, Marcelle, of course,' Justine exclaimed, 'he'll work for an international publishing firm, he'll publish best-selling works of fiction.'

'No, he won't be in fiction,' Marcelle disagreed, 'he'll be in history or politics, something very respectable. And he'll be English or French rather than American.'

'But there's nothing that shuts people up like an American,' Justine pointed out.

'Americans shut people up at the time but afterwards they're very easily dismissed as Americans,' Marcelle claimed. 'You know, loud and brash.'

Justine remained unconvinced but conceded the point. 'I see, so an intellectual.'

'A totally eccentric publisher with wild red curly hair, very tall, who wears safety pins in dress shirts instead of buttons and his shirts are always, you know, really crushed and hanging out of his trousers,' Marcelle said enthusiastically.

'Someone very rich.'

'People in publishing are always very rich.'

'But he'll hate his family so we'll live in America.'

'OK, Justine, but his name'll be William if he's English and Jacques if he's French.'

'He'll still be big although he'll be on the long-legged skinny side rather than the olive-skinned big side.'

'He sounds wonderful,' Marcelle said, satisfied.

'Yes, now I know what I'm looking for I just can't wait to meet him,' Justine joked.

She watched Hamlet pull away a piece of dried blood, loosening the rag so that it flopped to the floor. A fresh stream started down his leg, garish against his pallid skin.

'Don't fall in love,' Hamlet whined, his eyes shiny as two raw fish fillets.

'Hamlet,' Marcelle fussed, 'I hate to see you so depressed. Aren't you a little bit happy for Justine now that she's worked out her future?'

'He misses his Ophelia,' Justine needled.

'Do you miss her that bad?' Marcelle wanted to know.

'I can't think, I can't eat,' Hamlet whinged. 'The kids have been great but there's nothing worse than climbing into an empty bed at night. I'm just dreading going home.'

'You know, Hamlet, do you know what I think you should do,' Marcelle advised.

'No,' Hamlet whined.

'I think you need to work at becoming a little more emotionally independent in the relationship,' she said bluntly. 'You need to learn to be a bit more independent.'

'Well, now I know what you think,' he said sarcastically.

'Yes, but you know what I mean, don't you?' she insisted.

'But I am independent,' he said defensively. 'My career is really taking off, I fly around all the time making award-winning documentaries. You really think I'm too *dependent*?'

'Well it's no good you falling apart every time Ophelia and you are separated for a little while,' she advised.

'But I love her,' he confided.

'But then everything's all right so what's the problem?' she said, losing her patience.

'I just can't stand being abandoned like this,' he said, angry.

'You sound like a love-struck teenager obsessing over a pop star,' she said, bored.

Justine watched the blood soak into his sock. 'You know what's funny, Hamlet?' she said.

'No,' Hamlet said dismissively. 'Tell me what's funny, Justine.'

'What's funny is that Ophelia says that when she's around you hardly pay any attention to her at all,' she said, dead-pan.

He went into a total panic. 'Is that what she says? God, I mean.' He fell into a despondent silence. 'Well,' he lied, 'what she probably means is that I'm a little boring, always tired from work, never opening my heart to her enough or exposing my feelings.' He shook his head in mock disbelief. 'Is that really what she said?'

Justine shrugged her shoulders and Marcelle filled their glasses from the bottle and gulped the wine, her jacket squeaking at the elbow. Justine went into seduction mode. *Act now while he's feeling weak.* She would have to move fast if she wanted to wrestle him away from Simone. She rubbed her knee against his. Worried about getting smeared with blood she shifted in her seat so that their legs were no longer touching. Hamlet made no response to her advance other than to pick up his napkin, slide it down into his lap and then hold it against his leg. He wiped up and down his calf and gently dabbed around the edges of the sliced flesh. *She would have to try again.*

Just then she felt a tap on her shoulder. A man sitting at the next table pointed across the restaurant and outside. She looked across the crowded pizza bar, through the floor-to-ceiling sliding glass doors and out onto the dark street. A man and woman stood with their arms linked. The man had thick dark curly hair, a strong jawline, a prominent nose, a broad forehead, full pouting lips and hard blue eyes. She gasped. The man wasn't looking at the woman whose arm he held. Instead he was staring in through the floor-to-ceiling sliding glass doors and across the crowded pizza bar at her. *Fuck.* She recognised Sade and the French woman from his office.

Justine stared at Sade, and Sade stared at Justine. She recognised his look, and like a familiar well-trodden path she knew exactly where it would lead. It was dark, intense and brooding, it went on for too long and it was alto-gether too blind to everything else going on around it to be mistaken for anything else. She took deep breaths. They didn't help. She emptied her glass of wine. She craved sleeping pills.

He looked, she reflected, like he wanted to eat her but he didn't quite know where to start. His look was predatory, although in his case he was the kind of predator who needed guidance from his prey, dangerous and needy at the same time. She felt her knees go weak as she reached up to cover her mouth with her hand. She was a predator too, staring back into the eyes of her adversary, only she was cold as a snake on the outside and a surrealist performance piece on the inside. She knew exactly how it felt to be devoured by and to devour those lips.

Between her fingers the first wave of nausea dribbled out, burning the back of her throat, sour in the back of her mouth. Like a snake shedding its skin, what was outside folded in upon itself and what was inside bubbled out through the breach. She turned away from the table and, half-closing her eyes, vomited a dark pink stream across the white tiled floor.

The sickly smell of vomit snaked its way up through the spicy fatty pizza bar air and suddenly Marcelle was telling Hamlet that she wanted to pay up and leave. Hamlet took Justine's hand and led her to the tiny upstairs bathroom. Halfway up the stairs she vomited again, this time the stream was blood-red thrown up in a single giant splash on the white wall, shiny with grease.

5

SHE WAS ALMOST ASLEEP, STRETCHED OUT ON THE RUG ON THE floor at Marcelle's place, her head resting on a pile of newspapers spread out on the floor. Marcelle and Hamlet sat watching a video, a pirated copy of Pasolini's *Salo*, drinking more wine and eating chocolate. His cut was freshly bound in the white rag. He ran his hands through his hair. His forehead was damp with sweat.

When the video was finished Marcelle woke her with a cup of green-leaf tea. Hamlet went upstairs to call Simone.

'I think I should go home soon,' Justine sighed.

'Are you sure you're feeling OK?' Marcelle inquired.

Justine nodded and took a deep breath. 'I don't know, Marcelle,' she began, taking in Marcelle's black, button-fly jeans, black skivvy, black lace-up shoes, black leather jacket, pale blue-white skin and the dark waves of curls. She gazed into Marcelle's dark brown eyes. 'Do you ever feel like you'll just go absolutely crazy if you don't get a boyfriend soon?'

Marcelle shook her head vehemently. 'Not at all. I'm just really enjoying my own company at the moment.'

'But don't you ever get lonely?' Justine persisted. 'Don't you hate getting into an empty bed?'

'I like sleeping on my own,' Marcelle reflected, sipping her cup of tea. 'I really like to stretch out and take over the whole bed.'

'Really?' Justine said, puzzled. 'Because I feel crazy lying in my bed alone at night. Sometimes I stroke my body and I feel like the whole world's fucked because here I am all soft and warm and nice to touch and alone and it just seems so unfair and I just desperately want someone to touch me and then I can't sleep, I really can't sleep at all at the moment. I try reading but I can't concentrate on the book and then I try drinking tea but it always goes cold because I forget about it as soon as I've made it, so you know what I do? I go out, often at one or two in the morning, and I walk the streets, sometimes just crying and crying, other times I talk to myself out loud and wring my hands, I just feel so rotten that I'm alone, I think it's because I'm unlovable because there can't be any other reason. I know it's indulgent but I can't help it, I'm just crazy with it all, and after I've talked it all out of my system, how I'm not like normal people, how I can't be close to anybody, how I can't have relationships, I sometimes feel a little better. Then I go into a bar, really hoping that I'll see someone I know but then hoping I don't because I realise how strange I must look, and then I drink a few drinks but that really sends me into a panic and I have to go back to Hamlet and Ophelia's. Then I sit up and go through my photo album wondering why I don't have any photos of myself in the last few years until I realise it's because I haven't had a boyfriend and I don't have a camera and then I look through my address book and think of who I can ring up because I feel desperate and it's by now five or six in the morning. Sometimes people say, look anytime, just call, ex-lovers, girlfriends, but then I imagine that when I call they'll be in bed with someone else so I don't call.'

Justine sipped at the tea but really wanted wine so she held her wine glass out and Marcelle topped it up. 'And the worst thing is I've felt like this for so long now I can't imagine anything ever changing, I can't imagine anything getting any better.'

'God, Justine, I had no idea, you always seem so cool,' Marcelle exclaimed. 'I mean, I know exactly how you feel, I went through something like that a few years ago, but I sort of got over it, I really had to force myself but in the end I did it. One day I just woke up and I didn't care any more. And it was like, where did this idea I just want a boyfriend come from in the first place? It wasn't my idea. Then I realised that deep down I'd always been quite content to be me, and ever since then I've devoted myself to becoming more of myself. Now I really can't imagine just wanting someone else for the sake of it, just needing a boyfriend to be me. It really dawned on me, no wonder I'd always ended up with such ridiculous people, when I was trying to believe I needed a boyfriend when I didn't really even want one.'

Justine was on the verge of tears. 'I can't imagine being like that, happy.' She excused herself and hurried upstairs to the bathroom. She sat down in the dark room breathing deep breaths. 'I need a lover, I need a lover,' she chanted as her piss tinkled into the china bowl. She closed her eyes and ran her hands through her hair. She was exhausted. She was alone. She heard a voice. In the next room she could faintly hear Hamlet talking on the phone. *Hamlet.* She dressed and, not flushing the chain, crept out into the corridor.

'Of course I want to fuck you,' Hamlet was saying. Then, 'Whatever you say, Simone, I'm only thinking how nice it would be to see you, it's been so long, but I guess if you're too tired, you're too tired.'

She closed the bathroom door. She switched on the light. In the mirror her face was pinched and small. She had no money. Her possessions were in storage. Everyone was fucking Simone. She did not cry. She heard him walk downstairs. She switched off the light. She needed another glass of red wine. Downstairs the bottle was empty. She followed Marcelle into the kitchen.

She stood at the sink rinsing out the mugs and glasses while Marcelle went through the cupboards looking for more wine. Marcelle's doves woke up. They started cooing and pecking each other in the cage built into the window. Justine walked over to the cage and they grew silent. They froze except for their eyes which darted about looking at her. Marcelle told her there wasn't any more wine. Justine shrugged. One of the doves laughed a harsh sneering laugh. She glared at the doves. The doves were still on their perches. Marcelle put the kettle on. Justine followed her out to the lounge room. The dove laughed again.

240

Marcelle stretched out on the rug and lit a cigarette. Hamlet finished the last of the chocolate. The kettle boiled. Justine stood up. She wanted to make the tea. Back in Marcelle's kitchen she went through the cupboards looking for tea. The doves were asleep. She closed the door to the cupboard. One of the doves started cooing. She counted while it repeated the same phrase six times. Where was the tea? The laughing dove snickered. *The tea!* The different packets were stored in glass jars and lined up and down the bench top. *Idiot.* The dove snickered again. This time she snickered back, mimicking its rhythm and cadence and waited. The dove laughed again. She tried to work out which one of the doves was the laughing one. She gave up.

She filled the teapot with fresh tea and then lifted the kettle off the stove. It was nearly empty, all the water had boiled off while she was looking for the tea and laughing at the doves. She went to put more water in the kettle but she couldn't fit the kettle under the tap with all the dirty glasses and plates in there. Fuck that. She went to put the kettle down so that she could clear the plates from the sink but ended up putting the kettle on the dish rack on its side and then all the just-boiled water poured out. She looked at the kettle, at the water pouring out the spout. *Damn.* Water was pouring out of the kettle faster than she could get it in. In the cage the doves cooed softly. She waited for the snickering laugh but nothing happened.

She filled the kettle and waited for it to boil. It seemed to take forever. She stared at the stove. *Filthy.* Marcelle didn't even have time to clean the stove. She found a scourer under the sink and sprinkled it with powder cleanser. She took the knobs off and scrubbed at the dark grease until the metal was white and clean. Then she wiped the top of the stove and she was just about to open the oven door when she stopped. *Ridiculous*. Then she started scrubbing again like a maniac. The water started to boil but she'd only just started cleaning the oven. In a panic she reached up and took the kettle off the stove. Not looking she poured boiling water all over the edge of the teapot and onto her hand. She swore and kicked the doors of the cupboard. The back of her hand screamed hot pink red. It hurt. It stung when she put her hand under the cold water tap. She was not going to cry. Tough, she listened for the harsh snickering laugh but the doves were quiet again, back on their perches and still. Then she walked over to the cage and laughed back at the doves, mimicking the snickering laugh. The doves looked up, their heads darting from side to side but they didn't make a sound.

She abandoned the tea and filled a bowl with ice cubes and water. She took the bottle of Stoli from the freezer and carried it and the bowl out to the lounge room. She sat on the floor with her hand in a bowl of icy water. She poured three Stoli's into coffee cups.

Marcelle and Hamlet were arguing about feminism. Marcelle insisted that feminism was going nowhere until men started to liberate themselves as well. Hamlet suggested eliminating the nuclear family if it was motherhood which caused women to be oppressed.

Bored, Justine lifted her hand out of the icy water. The

skin glowed back, a radioactive red. The entire back of her hand was burnt. Not enough to blister, just enough to throb. She was reminded of the novel Sade had given her about the Wall Street yuppie who sat in his office doing deals and flirting with his secretary by day and killed and tortured people by night. The psychopathic yuppie was a liberated man, a kind of feminist. He wasn't going to be confined to the traditional masculine roles. She wanted to laugh. She slid her hand back in the icy water.

'The thing is,' Marcelle was saying, 'that unless men become a little more liberated then there's no point in women getting more and more politicised because they just fall back into what they're trying to escape every time they get involved with a man.'

Suddenly Marcelle broke off abruptly and gasped, covering her mouth with her hand. 'Hamlet,' she cried, 'what in fuck's name have you done to your leg?'

Hamlet slapped his hand over the cut and shrugged his shoulders. 'I think there's something wrong with me,' he said, guiltily. 'It just doesn't seem to want to stop bleeding.'

'I think you might be bleeding on the rug,' Marcelle said evenly.

Hamlet followed Marcelle upstairs to the bathroom. Justine carried her bowl to the kitchen and emptied the water into the sink. Her hand felt almost normal again. Not a sound from the doves. She was ready to go home. She climbed the stairs, her feet like lead, a sigh caught in her throat. In the bathroom she sat on the side of the bath while Marcelle dug around in the cupboard behind the mirror and pulled out a packet of bandaids and a sanitary

243

napkin. Marcelle placed the sanitary napkin on Hamlet's leg while she fiddled with the bandaids.

'I'm not wearing that,' he said, pushing the sanitary napkin onto the floor.

'You'll do as you're told,' she said, pretending to scold him, retrieving the sanitary napkin from the floor and sticking it to his leg with the bandaids absorbent side down. 'They're super-absorbent, but you need to change them every two to three hours. They're called Stay-free and you can buy them just about anywhere if you know where to look.'

Hamlet smiled happily at Marcelle and then distantly at Justine. His dark eyes gazed blankly into hers. She searched their empty pools and looked away.

'I've really got to go,' Justine said.

'Me too,' Hamlet echoed.

Their eyes met. Justine blushed. *Maybe it wasn't going to be impossible to seduce Hamlet after all?*

Out on the street she studied his hands, which he held clasped against his chest. His fingers were small, of the fairest blue-white skin and tapered at the tips. Such beautiful hands. She found herself staring at them too long and without really wanting to. Beneath her black cardigan and cotton dress she started to sweat. Rivulets trickled down from her underarms tickling the soft sensitive skin at her sides. *She wanted to hold his hand*. She reached the corner of Marcelle's street and stopped automatically at the kerb. She folded her arms across her chest. Listening rather than looking for traffic she crossed the street and turned into a wide tree-lined avenue lined with terrace houses. Sweat ran down the back of her knees.

Across the water to her left was a brightly lit maze of glass and concrete, steel and light. The wall of towers drained her of conversation, and apart from the shuffling sound of Hamlet's rubber-soled footsteps it was deadly quiet on the empty street. She kept bumping into him as she walked. *He wants to fuck me.* She avoided looking at him. She wanted to get close but she wanted him to make the first move. She bumped against him again. He apologised and took hold of her arm. *Damn.* He only wanted to know if she was all right so she shook her head briskly and said yes, she was all right. She was wrong. He didn't want to fuck her after all. The silence stretched out between them. She changed her mind again. It was worse than she thought. He hadn't even thought about fucking her. She snuck him a sideways glance. A cloud of misery descended upon her in a fine damp mist. Oblivious to the beautiful wide street and the dazzling glow of the city towers she struggled beneath the sorry cloud. Could she make him want her? She gazed intently at the pavement in front of her, her head a rubber room.

Turning away from the towers, she encountered a row of renovated terrace houses. The terraces were three and four storeys high. Some were subdivided into apartments. Small windows insured privacy but meant many of the rooms were dark. High ceilings lent the rooms a sense of spaciousness but were expensive to heat. Huge double living areas looked good but lacked the intimacy of the kitchen or small TV room. Bricked in courtyards were pretty to look at but tended to become breeding grounds for mosquitoes in summer and wind tunnels in the winter. Marble mantelpieces were perfect for vases of flowers but open fires proved ineffective sources of heat and covered everything in black soot. Playgrounds for yuppies, terrace houses disguised a lifestyle of dizzily excessive austerity and utter depravity with expensive fixtures and charm. Architecture of the emotional void. She shuddered. She thought of taking off her cardigan but the idea of carrying it was worse than the sweat that kept pouring down her middle and legs. She could smell her cunt wafting up through her clothes.

Despondent, she walked the deserted streets in silence. Soon she stood waiting for Hamlet to unlock the door.

'Do you want to have a coffee somewhere?' she asked.

He hesitated, the keys in his hand. 'I don't know, Justine,' he equivocated, 'I really should be getting back to Simone.'

She shrugged, disappointed but not surprised.

'It isn't that I don't want to have a coffee, it's just that baby-sitters are so expensive,' he complained.

She looked the other way and nodded her head.

'I mean,' he hedged, 'I guess it would be OK as long as we were quick.' She looked around in time to catch his way-ward glance down the front of her unbuttoned dress. 'Oh, who cares,' he exclaimed, 'it's only money.'

She smiled.

Most of the cafes they passed were closed and the street was empty. She stood outside the dark window of her favourite cafe. He ran his hands through his hair again and told her how tired he was. She didn't believe him. She was thinking of Simone sitting at the bench in the kitchen drinking scotch, her thighs wrapped around his face and him kneeling on the floor and licking out her cunt. He looked at his watch. He looked indifferently up and down the street. He scrutinised her face. She realised he was staring at her. She frowned, her hands in her pockets, chewing on her bottom lip. She started to walk away, slowly, aimlessly. She didn't want to go home to the empty sofa-bed. She didn't want him to fuck Simone. Not tonight. Tonight she wanted him to be with her.

'Hey,' she called, standing beneath a street lamp, her face in shadow but her hair a curtain of silken strands. 'I know where we can go.'

He shrugged his shoulders. Undeterred she hailed a passing cab. She gave the driver directions and climbed into the back seat. He sat in the front. She opened her window. She tried to think of things to say. She couldn't. Soon a brightly illuminated window came into view. She asked the driver to stop the cab. She paid the fare and he followed her, shuffling his feet, into the tiny crowded cafe.

She chose a table and sat down. He sat at the opposite side of the table. She leant towards him. Her knees rubbed against his under the small table. He stared at the smeared laminex table-top. He seemed sad. He ordered two coffees.

'Have you any idea,' he began, but then paused when their coffees arrived. 'Have you any idea,' he continued, leaning across the table, whispering in her ear, 'what it was like to become a father?'

She gulped and shook her head. *This was the last thing she wanted to hear.*

He sat back in his chair, sugared his coffee and stirred it with a spoon. 'It was an absolutely mind-blowing experience.' He sucked on the spoon and placed it on the saucer. He leant closer. 'I wasn't there for the birth, I was on location in Manhattan, shooting a documentary about cocaine. Crack hadn't hit the streets yet and the cocaine trade was still a fairly glamorous affair. The shooting was mostly over and we were doing a mock-up of free-basing when the call came through.' He sipped at his coffee. He leant even closer, his lips touching her ear. 'Her voice was a whisper,' he whispered, 'she could barely speak after all the screaming she'd done. I started laughing and crying just at the sound of her voice.' He shook his head, amazed. 'But later, coming down on valium, as I cried alone in bed in my hotel room, I cried for us. I cried for her because I thought she had died and I cried for myself because I thought I was to blame. I know it sounds crazy now but at the time I was terrified I'd killed her.'

She stood up, the chair screeching across the floor, and went running through the jumble of tables and disappeared outside. She collapsed against the window and slid her hand inside her dress. She massaged her stomach. Sharp cramps formed a tight band around her abdomen. She gasped at the onslaught of each aching contraction. Warm air, only slightly cooler than the air inside, swept across her cheeks. She listened to the faint hum of a radio playing through the open door of a terrace further down the street. *Don't panic.* Don't panic because you're not a

248

mother. She swallowed hard, the back of her throat choking and sore.

She watched him through the window. Morose, he gazed at the bottom of his coffee cup. Suddenly he grabbed the waitress by the sleeve as she rushed past. She stopped dead in her tracks, raised her eyebrows and mouthed, yes? He smiled, face positively beaming. Then he was talking excitedly, his hands gesturing wildly, and looking over at the cake stand. The waitress rearranged the cups and saucers against her hips. She recited the different cakes. He interrupted, nodding his head. He held up two fingers. The waitress nodded, freed herself from his grasp and was gone. Swallowing hard, Justine straightened her dress and wandered back inside.

A woman brushed past her and said hello. Justine shrugged her off irritably, recognising her but not wanting to talk to her, and sat back down.

Hamlet was anxious. 'Who was that?'

Justine frowned into her empty cup and shook her head. She couldn't even remember the woman's name. On top of everything the pain was back. She winced as cramp after cramp wrapped itself malignantly around her stomach. *The ghosts of her foetus.* His eyes were glued to the waitress as she went running about the room, zigzagging between tables, disappearing into and emerging from the kitchen. Finally the waitress returned his gaze and nodded. He smiled confidently. He glanced vaguely at Justine. She raised her eyebrows as if to say, yes. He shook his head and began fiddling with his teaspoon. *Forget it. He was too fucked up to fuck.* She gazed miserably down into her lap, convinced that she'd be going home to an empty fold-out bed.

A plate clattered onto the table followed by two glasses of cognac. *Lemon meringue pie!* In an instant the pain disappeared and was replaced with sheer terror. She stared intently at the varnish-coloured liquid as it went sloshing around inside the round bulb of glass. She ground her teeth. She had to force herself to look at the cake. She dragged her gaze from the cognac across the greasy laminex table-top to the cake. She commanded her eyes to focus. She held her breath. She considered each detail in quick succession—height of the whipped whites, texture of the lemon goo, dryness of the crumbly crust, colour of the burnt tips. It was an excellent piece of pie. She snatched a brief glance in his direction. He was still staring into the bottom of his coffee cup. She tried to keep calm. She hated lemon meringue pie.

He handed her a fork and a spoon. She acquiesced.

'Lemon meringue pie's my favourite pie,' he declared solemnly, 'have you ever tasted it before?'

She nodded and lifted the spoon to her mouth. 'I love lemon meringue pie,' she lied and smiled a wan smile. He sighed and took a large slurp of cognac. He asked the waitress for a cigar. They didn't have any.

She toyed with a second spoonful of pie. She felt sick. The sticky white meringue clung to the back of her throat, the sweet lemon goo was so sweet it made her head ache, and the thick shortbread crust swilled around inside her stomach, the fat bubbling up in a stream of silent sickly burps. She concentrated on his small feminine hands, and imagined putting them in her mouth instead of the pie. *Disgusting*. She choked on another stream of burps.

The woman whose name she couldn't remember sat down uninvited and smiling at their table. 'I loved Dublin,' the woman said zealously. 'People there are so polite, they're interested in talking about books, about films and about travel. It's so different, here no-one wants to talk about books, or films, or travel.'

'Do you think so?' Justine countered. 'I find that that's all people want to talk about here.'

The woman became defensive. 'You sound like you don't like talking about literature, the opera, the movies, or telling travel stories?'

'I detest British colonial culture,' Justine announced.

Why wouldn't she fuck off? She rolled her eyes at Hamlet who raised his eyebrows and looked away.

'Surely you're not serious?' the woman asked politely.

She leant across the table. 'I can't help thinking about my father,' she explained, gesturing furiously with her hands. 'He was born in an Eastern European country during the time of the Nazi Occupation. As a child he brewed a kind of home-made vodka made from potatoes which he sold to German troops so that his mother had money for food. That was after the German police had taken his father away to Auschwitz. He's never forgotten the German beer-drinking songs he listened to as a child. Or the High German he had to learn in school, which was the official language, until the Germans blew up the school, that is. It's a little bit like that. And I think the way he felt about German culture is a little bit like the way I feel about

British colonial culture here in this country.'

A huge self-satisfied grin spread all over the woman's face. She sat back in her chair and regarded Justine coolly. 'No, the British aren't like the Germans,' she pronounced slowly, carefully considering each word. 'At least the Anglo-Irish aren't. Have you see John Huston's *The Dead*?'

Justine pounded the top of the table with her fist. 'Exactly,' she hissed. 'Based on Joyce's critique of a ubiquitous and repressive British culture from a local point of view.'

'I disagree,' the woman argued. 'It's such a celebration of British culture and of the arts of conversation and dance.'

Justine felt her face turn a brilliant red. She stared down at the smeared laminex table-top, her shoulders slumped forwards and her lips quizzically turned up at the corners. She almost slid off her chair and then hesitated, poised above the floor. Then she was sliding gracefully up to her feet. Her face twitched with hatred as she goose-stepped up and down between the tables in the tiny cafe, shouting out the melody of a boisterous German beer-drinking song in a make-believe German-sounding language. The room became hushed and all eyes silently followed her convulsive shouting and kicking as she went about the room.

Ach nan zal zupp
Ich niner zupp
Huss nik der zinerman
Huss nik der zinerman

Ach nan zal zupp
Ich niner zupp
Huss nik der zinerman
Huss nik der zupp.

She sat back down at the table. Applause thundered from the other customers. She stood up briefly to bow and sit down once more. She glanced at the woman, triumphant. The woman's face was white with anger and her jaw trembled unchecked.

'I'll have you know, young lady, that I lost five members of my family in the concentration camps,' the woman snapped bitterly.

'So it's a competition or something,' Justine said, flippant.

The woman was furious. 'My father was the only member of his family to survive.'

'My grandfather went to Auschwitz,' she said, scowling.

'You're not Jewish so what would you know?' the woman chided. 'Anyway, I don't think the concentration camps are very funny.'

Justine was growing bored. 'I think you might have missed the point.'

'I don't think the Nazis and the British have much in common,' the woman persisted.

'So you're calling me a Nazi.'

'You seem to think the whole thing's a big joke.'

'It's true,' Justine said, off-hand, 'I have trouble taking historical accounts of World War Two seriously. I have a lot of trouble with history.'

'You're just ignorant of history,' the woman said accusingly. 'If you knew anything about history, if you knew the historical facts, you'd understand that there were varied local reasons which enabled the Nazis to single the Jews out and to gain popular support for what they were doing.'

'History seems to me to have little to do with events and the way they take place,' Justine said arrogantly. 'History sees everything in terms of causes and effects, and once you can isolate the cause from the complexity of events, then the effect is inevitable, destined.'

'But I believe in destiny, in fate,' the woman exclaimed.

'And once history becomes destiny then there's no possibility for anything new to take place,' Justine lectured. 'No matter how specific the circumstances, history will always find the same in each new occurrence. The countries of Eastern Europe deserved the Nazi occupation, they'd lived as Germans for years, or so the historicist argument goes.'

'That's true,' the woman cried.

'And that reminds me of the way the law always proves, despite all evidence to the contrary, that women who get raped by men ask for it,' Justine snarled. 'History.'

She felt someone tap her on the shoulder. She turned around. A man holding a half-empty bottle of red wine in one hand stood smiling at her. She glanced up at him, her face icy and calm.

'I was wondering if you knew any Marlene Dietrich,' he asked in a heavy European accent and pointing to a woman wearing wire-framed glasses whose sunken lips concealed the absence of both teeth and dentures. 'I have my sick mother over there, she very much enjoyed your song, and she remembers Dietrich from when I was just a tiny baby.'

The woman sent her chair screeching across the floor and stood towering over Justine. Justine cowered. 'You've got a lot to learn, young lady,' the woman hissed, covering her face with spit. 'I only hope you live to see your own children making such jokes about your parents' lives and their personal tragedies.'

'I think,' Hamlet said, climbing to his feet and pulling her with him. 'I think we'd better be getting back home.'

6

THEY LAY STRETCHED OUT SIDE BY SIDE ON THE BLOOD-stained futon drinking a bottle of brandy. Hamlet was complaining bitterly about fatherhood, comparing children to hostile aliens whose mission is to deprive a father of his identity. Justine was in the grip of a major anxiety attack and drank glass after glass of brandy, only half-listening to what he was saying. Her only defence was the contents of the bathroom medicine cabinet. 'Medication time, medication time,' she chanted quietly, and stared grim-faced into the bottom of her glass.

She must have fallen asleep because the next thing she knew Hamlet was shaking her awake.

'What about you, Justine?' he was saying. 'Are you ever going to have children?'

She gasped. *Children?* What was he talking about? 'I'm not going to have children until—' *What was she saying?* She blundered on, 'Until I can offer them a life free of abuse.

'You see,' she continued, swallowing hard on her rising panic, 'my father's family were terrorised by Nazis, my mother's family were terrorised by my grandfather, and my family was terrorised by my father's ex-wife. I won't have children unless I can offer them something else.'

Resisting an urge to flee she climbed unsteadily to her feet and took deep breaths. *She needed pills.* She watched for Hamlet's response. His blank wet eyes stared expressionlessly into hers from the tangled sheets.

'I have to go to the toilet,' she lied, 'and then I think I'll go to bed. I'm tired.'

She kissed him goodnight and crept away. The stairs creaked as she tiptoed down. *Simone could have him for all she cared.*

She paused outside the kitchen door and peered through the crack. Simone sat on a stool smoking a cigarette and drinking scotch from the bottle. Between sips and puffs she wrote in her notebook. Her other hand disappeared down the front of her skirt.

Justine went to the bathroom, closed the door, switched on the light and opened the cabinet drawers. She found some Normison and swallowed two, washing them down with water from the tap. She picked up the bottle of pills and switched off the light. She went to the kitchen for a glass of water. Simone was no longer sitting at the stool. She pictured Simone's hand wrapped around Hamlet's cock. Her tongue licking up his cock. Justine's heart began to race. She swallowed two more Normison with the scotch. She collapsed onto the stool. She read Simone's notebook.

257

He was lying in bed asleep when the phone rang. It was his lover and she was calling from a public phone a few streets away. She told him she just wanted to come over and fuck him, she just wanted to climb on top of his huge fucken cock, she wanted his cock deep inside her cunt from behind, she wanted his fingers wedged inside her ass, she wanted her nipples pulled so hard she screamed, she wanted to sink her teeth into the back of his neck and chew his cock as if she was going to take the head off. She wanted her knees on his shoulders pinning his arms to the bed. She told him all of this and by the time she got to the end of it all he was awake and he instantly wanted to fuck her but he was too tired. He told her he was asleep and that she should call him back later. She persisted, don't you want to fuck me any more? She pleaded with him and then she got angry. She told him to get fucked and hung up on him. Now he was awake, angry, his head bursting with things he wanted to scream back. He went out to the kitchen and drank some orange juice. He went to the toilet. Then he tried to call her, idiotically, to see if she was home. She wasn't. He didn't leave a message on her answering machine.

She imagined Hamlet picking Simone up and carrying her to his bed. When he put her down she clung to him. He opened his fly and pulled out his cock. He pulled up her skirt and peeled her underpants to one side and then plunged inside her, her pussy sucking him in. He only moved in and out three or four times before she was coming. He came inside, she was still coming, and she kept moving on his cock after he stopped. They both lay still, Simone's cunt throbbing around Hamlet's cock, which was already getting small. She lay passed out beneath him. He shivered awake, stood up and, wiping his penis with a tissue and tucking himself in, zipped up his jeans. Justine sipped at the scotch and turned back to Simone's notes.

He threw the phone against the wall and started to cry. He was crazy about her only she made him feel too crazy to be with her. He wiped his face on his T-shirt. His T-shirt hung wet against his skin. He thought of fucking her. He saw himself pressed up against a wall and her lunging against him, holding herself above him and then sliding down, falling onto his cock, his breath getting knocked out of his lungs. He shivered, goose bumps running up and down his arms.

He threw his T-shirt on the floor and ran a hot shower. He lathered the soap in his hands. He ran his hand up and down the length of his cock. There was a knock at the door. He let go and wrapped himself in his towel. He answered the door. He hoped it was his lover. It was his lover. He let her in. She walked past him down the hall and looked around the lounge room. He followed her, dripping—had he been secretly waiting for this to happen, had he only pretended to forget all about her in the shower? He dried himself with the towel and walked into the bedroom. She followed him. He chose a shirt and slipped it on. She stared at the poster on the wall. He started to do up the buttons. She turned around and stepped across the room. Suddenly she was pressed against him, kissing him, her mouth swallowing his and him smiling behind his tongue.

She took another swig of the scotch, emptying it. Then she took the pen and, checking over her shoulder to make sure no-one was watching, she inserted it inside her cunt top-end-first, twirling it around and then pulling it out. Slippery and wide, she wanted something bigger. She thought of a hairbrush and looked in the bathroom. She couldn't find one. She went into the kitchen and opened the frig. She took out a carrot but inside it felt too cold. She went back to the bench and looked at the empty bottle of scotch. She heard a door close. Guilty, she straightened her dress and wiped the pen. She turned around. Simone stood swaying in the doorway. Then she lunged at a stool.

'Did you have a nice time at dinner?' Simone wanted to know.

Justine nodded. She remembered Simone fucking Sade. The blood went shooting to her head. *Why wasn't the Normison working?* She made her hands into two tight fists. She was reckless. 'Do you still see Sade?' she asked, and looked down at the tiled floor.

'No,' Simone said and laughed. 'One day I came home and found him in bed with my boyfriend. I haven't seen him since then.' She shrugged. 'Do you keep in contact?'

'No,' Justine said, the Normison finally kicking in, edges becoming fuzzy. 'Anyway, goodnight,' she said, her tongue thick, and slid off the stool. She made her way into the lounge room. She collapsed on the couch. She examined her hands in the light from the hall. She turned each hand from side to side, held them far away and then looked at them right up close. She thought of Hamlet's hands, imagined them touching her, how lithe they would be, how strong. The way he grabbed her hand in the cafe. She tried to remember his cock, his hands were pale and small and tapered at the tip. She curled her hands into soft balls and clasped them under her chin. She slept.

Just after three Hamlet shook her awake. 'I want to show you something,' he hissed.

She sat up, blinking, not understanding. She stood up. The floor writhed beneath her. He caught her as she fell. Was she all right? She said she was, although she had no idea. He wanted her to hurry up. She stumbled after him on jelly blubber legs. He held his fingers to his lips. His face contorted into a scowl. He pushed her close to the bathroom door. He pointed through the keyhole. It was difficult to focus. She struggled with the keyhole. Everything that had happened so far came spilling back in a blur—Ophelia leaving, Simone arriving, bumping into Sade, scalding herself at Marcelle's, the woman at the cafe, the conversation with Hamlet, and Simone's notebook—and on top of this she could barely stand straight or still enough to see what was on the other side of the door and the light was on inside which hurt her eyes and the painted surface of the door kept getting in the way so she held onto the wall which helped things a little and then Hamlet wanted to know what she thought only she didn't know because she couldn't see. She shrugged her shoulders. She pressed her face to the door once more. She listened instead.

'When I was a child growing up in the seventies I used to enact everything I saw on TV,' a voice which she recognised as Simone's was saying, 'I used to enact *The Box* and *Number 96*. Then when it became necessary to fuck I used to dress up as a boy and seduce my best friend. We used to tell each other that when we grew up we'd be just like prostitutes only we'd fuck for free. When I played dolls, all my dolls were on the pill and all anyone ever did in my games was fuck. I thought Bugs Bunny was absolutely the sexiest thing I'd ever seen.

'It was the seventies. We were the sex generation. Where the sixties talked about love, the seventies talked about sex. For as long as I can remember my favourite fantasy consisted of getting everyone I've ever fucked into the same room and then standing in the middle with music blaring and stripping off all my clothes. Even when we get careers all we do is complain that we don't get enough sex or that we don't like the sex we get or we gloat about how great we feel about getting laid. We're obsessed with sex. We never say no, we can't ever get enough.'

Justine stood back a little. She squinted up her eyes. She needed a coffee. She couldn't concentrate. Gradually the forms started to take on definite shapes. Simone and Hamlet's teenage son lay naked on the bathroom rug. Her eyes were closed although she wasn't asleep. Her smooth-skinned leg was sandwiched between the teenager's dark, hirsute, muscle-bound thighs. Justine watched Simone press her knee up between his legs and nudge the flabby sack of his balls and his shrivelled penis. She watched as Simone smeared her sperm drenched cunt along his lower thigh and tickled his balls with her fingers.

The teenager moaned, planted a warm heavy kiss on Simone's lips and ran his sad eyes whimsically over her body. 'So when am I going to see you again, Simone?' he wanted to know.

Simone's eyes refused to meet his. 'Well, I guess I'll give you a call,' she said, fobbing him off and pulling her cunt away from his leg.

The teenager stared mournfully at Simone's perfect breasts. His lower lip drooped. 'You're not just saying that,' he sulked, 'are you?'

Simone disentangled herself. 'Look,' she said, matter-of-fact, 'I'll call you, OK?'

Hamlet hissed unintelligibly in Justine's ear. She staggered after him into the kitchen. He went to the pantry and took out an unopened bottle of scotch. He slapped two glasses on the bench-top. He cracked the lid. The scotch slurped into the glasses. He slammed the bottle on the bench-top.

He was furious. 'Now what,' he cried, 'am I supposed to do about *that*?'

She wasn't sure what he meant. What could he do? What could anybody do? She needed coffee in her scotch. She filled the kettle with water and switched it on. She was sinking deeper and deeper. The ground was soft. She was warm and sleepy. She wanted to fall back and slide down. She jerked herself awake. Hamlet was raving, foaming at the mouth, and the kettle was boiling. She dug around in the cupboards looking for the coffee plunger. She found it dirty in the dishwasher. She washed it under warm water. She went to the fridge and took out the coffee. She emptied four scoops into the plunger and poured on the boiling water. The back of her hand hurt because of the steam. She wasn't listening to what he was saying. He leant his face close to hers, confronting her. She blinked and shook herself awake.

'Are you even listening to me?' he cried, incensed.

'Shhh,' she said, hearing something.

He closed his eyes. 'What have I done to deserve *this*?' he moaned.

'Really,' Simone was saying from somewhere out in the hall, 'you saw me on TV, on that vox populi show? I still haven't seen it, what did I say?'

'Well,' the teenager began, his voice squeaky, 'they shoved a microphone in your face and asked you about sex. They wanted to know if the missionary position was your favourite sexual position and you said that your favourite position was the inverted missionary position,' he said and then paused to deepen his voice. 'Anyway, I had no idea what you meant by the inverted missionary position but I thought it sounded pretty cool. You were beautiful too and I just wanted to fuck you.'

Justine heard a noisy kissing sound. She poured the coffee into the glass of scotch. She cricked her neck. She gulped the coffee and scotch. The coffee wasn't working. She emptied the glass and added more scotch and coffee. She drank again. Hamlet came into view. He sat slumped across the bench, his hair sticking up at the back and his shoulders shaking in quiet sobs. She swallowed more scotch and coffee. The stimulants were taking effect.

'So what is the inverted missionary position anyway?' the teenager was squeaking, his voice louder as he came closer to the kitchen.

'I guess the inverted missionary position is the missionary position back to front,' Simone said vaguely, 'but I don't really know what it means. It's just that I felt trapped by the TV camera and then I had to say something.'

Justine heard the sloppy kissing sound again. This time it was accompanied by a quiet moan. Awake enough to realise what was going on she wanted to crawl back to bed and hide under the covers. She desperately wanted to avoid the impending scene. No doubt Simone's coat pockets were filled with dangerous objects and kinky sex aids. She didn't want to find out what Simone had inside her coat pockets tonight. Hamlet moaned that he couldn't cope and she knew exactly how he felt.

'Actually,' Simone reflected, from the other side of the kitchen door, 'the way those TV cameras work is really interesting. They're the priests on wheels of the new church, roaming the streets collecting confessions. I was just incredibly obedient about confessing, but then I've always been very obedient about confessing things.'

Justine slid off her stool and peered around the door. There was no chance of escape without detection. Simone and the teenager were standing just on the other side. She watched Simone scratch her head and run her hands through her hair like a comb. Then Simone took another step forward. Justine cowered from view.

'Not only have roving TV cameras replaced going to church but confessions have been given a new use,' Simone lectured. 'No longer limited to private individual instruction, the TV camera confession is the plaything of the new ever-hypocritical bourgeois mass audience. The TV

265

confession allows them to keep playing their hypocritical games, moral outrage as mass banality, as banal diversion.'

Why don't they just turn around and go back to the bathroom? Her head clearer, she returned to her stool. Hamlet lay snoring on the bench-top. She felt her face slowy break into a smile. *Perfect.* Simone preferred fucking Hamlet's son to fucking Hamlet. Perhaps she could seduce Hamlet on the rebound from Simone? She took his hand and squeezed the fingers. He moaned, but didn't stir. She rolled her eyes at him and blew air impatiently through her nose. *Damn.* She peered around the door once more. Simone let her jacket fall from her shoulders. The teenager pushed her against the wall. He slid the singlet strap off her shoulder. He leaned over and sucked gently at her nipple. Simone closed her eyes. The nipple stood up red and alert.

'Simone,' the teenager squeaked, 'you know in that novel you're writing, do you ever write anything about us?'

She stroked the other nipple through the black cotton with the tip of her fingers and slowly opened her eyes.

'Actually,' she said, going into a rave, 'the novel's full of confessions, it's nothing but one great big long confession. The contemporary novel's just another Church. I do my studies badly, then I run around fucking people when I shouldn't, then I put all the guilt I have about not doing what I'm supposed to be doing into my novels. No wonder I've never been attracted to psychoanalysis—who needs it when your whole life's already a confession?'

She stared blankly ahead, her fingers frozen over the erect cotton-covered nipple.

He leant forward to suck the naked nipple again. He let go of the nipple with a loud smacking sound. 'But do you ever write about us?' he persisted.

'You're not listening,' she complained, her voice starting to rise, 'all my writing's a confession, don't you see? I go to uni and everything but I don't really bother with what's going on there, I just go to my tutorials and then I go home and write. I sit at a computer and I write down all my exploits.

'They put me in an institution once when I was young because they all thought I was crazy but I didn't really think I was crazy, it's just that I didn't have any control over my life. So I started writing, but I don't mean anything by what I write. They told me to write so I obeyed them and in obeying I'm also absolutely free. So free sometimes that I become physically sick, anything to tie me back down. Sometimes I get sick for months on end, but it's only because I sometimes become too free and I have to ground my voice in something very mechanical, such as my body. And if I'm not sick then I'm masturbating all the time. At home I have the computer right next to the bed so that I can masturbate as often as I want. That's the other thing about writing, so much time on your hands.'

Her finger started moving around her nipple again. Then she put her finger in her mouth, sucked on it and then once it was wet she slid her finger inside the singlet and stroked the pointy bubble hard again. Her breasts were large and full, the nipples dark pink and the skin was the smoothest pale olive.

Help. Justine tugged Hamlet's sleeve. Why wouldn't he wake up? She poured him a cup of coffee and nudged him in the ribs. He opened his eyes and then closed them again. Fucking him had never seemed so impossible.

Outside the teenager was busy taking off Simone's singlet. 'So you're saying,' he said between moans, 'that your writing's all about confessing things and that it doesn't matter what you confess just as long as you do?'

Simone pulled her singlet down, annoyed. 'Well what did you think I was saying?'

He unzipped her zipper and slid his hand inside her shorts. 'I don't know Simone,' he said, 'I guess I just really want to fuck you.'

'Try telling me something I don't know for a change,' she snapped, 'this's getting really boring.'

The teenager removed his hand and held her hips. 'OK, Simone,' he began, acting tough. 'The real reason you don't have to have psychoanalysis isn't because you write everything down, it's because there's nothing wrong with you. Your only problem is that you're fucking my father and all you have to do to solve that problem is to stop fucking him.'

She glared at him. She pushed his hands away. 'Trust you to say the first reductive and simplistic thought to come into your head,' she snapped. Then she zipped up her fly and started rubbing her cunt through her shorts.

'Anyway, Simone,' he went on, his voice quiet, deep and honeyed, 'Hamlet's the one who really needs psychoanalysis, not you. He's so desperate to confess, he even confesses to us. Everything. This morning when he and Ophelia broke up again and she stormed off in a huff, he came running in to tell us how it made him feel and we just told him to go out and get pissed or to go fuck someone else or go back to psychoanalysis or to call you up for us.'

Justine turned around on her stool. At the mention of his name Hamlet was sitting bolt upright. His face was twisted into a murderous scowl. His fingers were clenched into fists at his hips that were so tight his fingers had turned white.

'What makes you think, Dr Freud,' Simone was saying, her voice heavy with sarcasm, 'that I'd keep on fucking you if I stopped fucking Hamlet? How do you know I'm not just fucking you to get back at him?'

Hamlet looked down into his lap and shrugged miserably. Justine reached for his hand. He pushed her away. *Fuck*. She told herself not to panic.

'Don't you want to fuck me any more?' the teenager whined.

'Not really,' Simone informed him.

Justine heard the teenager start to cry. Hamlet leapt to his feet and started pacing up and down the kitchen. She pointed to the ground and held her fingers to her lips. He stopped. He stood in the doorway, just behind the door. She crept across the kitchen tiles so she was standing behind Hamlet. She could see everything that happened.

'Why're you saying we can't see each other any more?' the teenager cried in a high thin wail.

Simone lifted his face by his chin. 'You're too young.'

He screwed up his face. 'But Simone,' he sobbed, 'I don't care about the age difference, and you said you didn't either. And if we don't care, then who cares what other people think?'

She stared at his down-coated chest. 'It's not just our age.'

Hamlet reached for the door. Justine grabbed his hand and held it in hers. He glared at her. She shook her head violently. She mouthed, wait. He could barely contain his agitation.

'There are some things it's just better not to know,' Simone said melodramatically.

The teenager clenched his fists and started to walk away. After three steps he turned around and glared at her, his chin jutting out defiantly. His forehead was shiny with sweat.

'Tell me why, Simone,' he growled.

She shook her head. 'No.'

'I'll do something,' he said threateningly, 'I'll do something horrible.'

His eyes narrowed. She wouldn't look him in the eye.

'No you won't,' she mocked.

'I won't if you don't make me,' he said.

'Do what you like, Hamlet, I'm not scared,' she snarled, getting ready to grab her jacket and run.

Simone reached for her jacket but the teenager fell upon her, ripping her clothes off her body and throwing them in shreds all over the floor. She hit him across the head, her fist smacking against his ear, bruising her fingers and leaving his face red. Hamlet wrenched his hand free and hurled himself at his son, trying to tear him away

from Simone. Justine leapt into the hall and grabbed
Simone's jacket. She went through the pockets and
pulled out the gun. Hamlet twisted the teenager's arm
behind his back. He gripped him under the chin, choking
him. The teenager's face went bright red, unable to
breathe. Justine waved the gun around wildly. *Everything was crazy.* Simone grabbed her jacket and ran for the
door. The teenager's eyes were popping out of his head. Justine pointed the gun at Hamlet and told him to let go. He
didn't notice. She pressed the gun to Hamlet's head. She
shouted at him to let go. He looked at her and, terrified,
dropped the teenager to the floor.

Justine collapsed against the wall, turning the gun over
and over in her hands. Hamlet looked up at her, blankly. The
teenager went running after Simone. Justine let her eyes roll
back in her head and started to cry.

'I'm sorry,' Hamlet apologised.

'I thought you were going to kill him,' she moaned.

He stood up and offered her his hand. She let him drag
her to her feet. She didn't know what to do with Simone's
gun. He bundled the shredded clothes together, making
them into a pile on the floor.

'Just go to bed,' he told her. 'I'll clean this up. Don't you
worry about a thing.'

She nodded. She saw Simone's nipple standing out
from her breast, red and erect. In a daze she made her
way up the blood splattered stairs and collapsed on the
stained white sheets. She undressed and wrapped the gun in
her cardigan. It was hers. She didn't ever want to see
Simone again. She covered herself with the sheet. She

271

moved over to the side and peered down through the glass floor over the edge.

She watched Hamlet go into the kitchen and take a swig from the bottle of scotch sitting on the bench. Then he went into the bathroom and pissed noisily into the toilet. Finally he crept into the bedroom and circled each bed in turn, rearranging covers and stroking heads of curly blond hair. When he reached the last bed which was empty he froze. Standing up straight, he lowered his head back until he was staring up at the underside of the thick glass floor. His whole body began to tremble, his face twitching as if shrinking from invisible blows. He sank to his knees and his head slumped towards the floor. Minutes passed. Very slowly he rose to his feet and made his way through the bedroom and climbed the wide glass stairs.

He stood at the foot of the bed. 'Here you are.'

She willed him to join her on the bed. He crossed the floor and sat down beside her. She stared up at him and then rolled onto her back and flopped her arms above her head. He didn't move.

'You can kiss me if you want,' she said.

He lowered his face until it was just above hers. He placed his hands, one hand at a time, over her wrists and kissed her. *Not bad.* Mid-kiss she heard a creak from the stairs. Looking up she discovered the teenager watching them from the top of the stairs, naked except for a pair of black Cuban-heeled cowboy boots, one hand behind his back. She froze.

'I want you to go to bed now,' Hamlet commanded in a deep, even voice and without turning around.

The teenager poked his tongue out and pulled at the end of his cock until it was erect. His cock was long and thin and curved upwards in the shape of a banana.

'I'm waiting,' Hamlet growled. 'Downstairs.'

The teenager pulled out the gun, cocked it, swung it above his head and fired it. The gun had not been loaded. Then he turned around, bent over, pulled the cheeks of his ass apart, farted loudly and left, waving the gun around his head.

'Leave that with me,' Hamlet said.

The gun thudded onto the glass floor. The teenager stomped all the way downstairs in his cowboy boots and without taking them off, crawled into bed.

Hamlet let go of her wrists and sat up. He pressed his palms together, forefingers pointing through the floor into the children's bedroom. A frown clouded his face then passed with a sigh. He looked tired. He slumped his shoulders and became sad.

She rubbed his back. 'Are you OK?'

A tear collected in the corner of his eye. 'Yes,' he said, swallowing hard. 'I just wish I wasn't so very, very unhappy.' He looked at her between his tears. 'I'm sorry,' he sniffed. 'I don't think I can ...'

'That's OK,' she interrupted. 'I understand.'

'You do?' he croaked, surprised.

She nodded and pecked him on the cheek. *Damn, damn, damn.* She climbed out of bed and collected her clothes. She picked up the gun, shot him one last look of regret, and made her way downstairs to the sofa-bed.

Without removing her clothes she stretched out on the

couch. She slid the gun between the cushions. She imagined Hamlet lying alone in bed upstairs. She wanted to be upstairs with him. Her head started to spin. She had to find somewhere to live, she had to write her thesis for university, she had to visit her father before he died, she had to talk to Ophelia and make sure that she was OK, and she had to look after Ophelia's children, now asleep in their beds, sheets and covers kicked to the floor, with their over-sized heads and tiny curled flower-petal hands. She was just about to fall asleep again but something kept her awake. *She had to try one last time*. She crept up the stairs. She paused at the top of the stairs. The room was dark and she could hear Hamlet's quiet snores. She tiptoed across the dark glass floor and sat down next to the bed.

She hated her life. After all, she had lived so many lives already, what was so special about the one she was living now? It would, no doubt, go the way of all the others. Marcelle was there, while they were still acquaintances, standing in the shade with an acoustic guitar slung over her shoulder, wearing an Indian dress without any shoes on the front lawn at university. She handed in a blank videotape for her first assignment but instead of failing her on the spot the lecturer had just laughed and taken her out for a drink. She awoke in bed one morning to find her father sitting beside her with a cup of tea while she sniffled and coughed with the flu. Her mother smiled knowingly, catching her running out the door late for school with money stolen from her father's wallet. She watched the school secretary read a note she'd forged on her mother's behalf which explained to the school principal why she was excused from scripture classes for the entire course of primary school. Her brother walked in on her with her arm in a tourniquet and a needle full of junk in her hand. After crashing through security at university and handing in a late essay she came back to the car to find her friend bailed up against the wall by a security guard with a gun to her head. Ophelia crying all night on the phone the first night she'd ever made love, convinced she'd have to have an abortion because the condom her lover'd been carrying around inside his wallet for a year or so had broken while he was inside her. She sat screaming, crouched into a corner of the room while Leopold smashed up all her furniture and far in the distance she could hear the faint wailing sirens of the approaching police cars. She stood in the middle of Hudson Street at four o'clock in the morning on the minus twenty degrees wind chill factor New Year's Day and stared downtown at the twin towers of the World Trade Centre while copious amounts of coke and booze surged through her veins. She held Sade in her arms and buried her face in his thick dark curly hair, breathing in his smell, in love.

She inched closer to the bed. Hamlet was breathing heavily, drawing long even pockets of air deep inside him and expelling them in abrupt puffs. She could just make out his fair curly hair against the white pillow in the dark. She drew back the covers and moved closer to him until she felt jets of warm stale air against her skin. She breathed it in, knees aching on the glass floor. She waited, watching him while he slept. Before her eyes the blood started to flow again, coursing in a fine stream between the hairs on his legs.

She ran her fingertips lightly across his white T-shirt. She felt the smooth skin of his thighs. She drew back her hand. He sighed a high tone in the back of his nose. He licked his lips and ground his teeth together. She froze beside him. She ran her hand from his body to the edge of the bed. She took off her shoes and socks. She unbuttoned her cardigan and pushed the sleeves from her arms, carefully rolling it up again and placing it on the floor. The buttons clacked against the glass. She paused, listening. He held his breath, sighed and turned over so his back was facing her. She slipped her dress over her head. Wearing only her underwear she climbed into bed and pressed her chest against his back, her back on the edge of the bed. She ran her toes up and down the soles of his feet. She linked her arm through his and pressed her hand against his breast. She kissed the back of his neck. And she closed her eyes, her breath coming in fast gulps and her heart pounding in her chest. She held him. Tears ran down her cheeks and she dried her face against his T-shirt.

'I want you,' she whispered into his hair.

He took her hand. Tears continued to run down her cheeks. She rubbed her face into the back of his neck. She kissed his neck, her mouth closed over his ear and she gently chewed the soft lobe.

'Please hold me,' she whispered.

Awake, he turned around and took her in his arms while the tears continued to fall. He wiped her hair away where it lay plastered to her forehead and stroked her cheek. He kissed her, he kissed her face. He wrapped his arms around her head and pressed her against his chest.

'I think you should go,' he said, holding her head in his arms, not letting go.

'Don't make me go,' she whined, 'I want to stay here with you.'

'Don't you have to work on your thesis tomorrow?'

'I want to stay,' she demanded, 'I don't care about my work.'

'I know what you mean,' he said, yawning, 'I hate my work too. Day after day I keep going through the motions and all the time I'm numb with despair.'

'Are you going to do anything about it?'

'Well,' he said sleepily, 'I'm not sure, I haven't made up my mind.'

'And Ophelia?'

'I don't know. Something isn't quite right and I've been thinking about asking Ophelia to move out and find a place to live in on her own. I just feel suffocated with her here, I feel numb and even if I feel terrible about her moving out at least I'll be feeling again, and that's the most important thing, that I allow myself to feel, even if feeling means guilt and feeling means feeling terrible. I want to be loyal to the way I feel and I'm feeling like I want her to move out. What I'm trying to say is that I'm thinking of splitting up with Ophelia when she gets back.'

She held herself away from him. 'That's great,' she said, disappointed.

'You sound disappointed,' he said.

'Well that's because I am,' she complained. 'What about me?'

'I think you should go back downstairs,' he said, pushing her away.

'But I don't want to go downstairs, I want to stay with you, I want to sleep next to you in your bed, I want to wake up in your arms.'

'But I don't know if I want you to stay,' he said. She started crying again. 'Look,' he said tenderly, 'what I'm trying to say is that I think I might want to be with you one day, but I'm just not ready now,' he insisted.

'You wanted to be with me before,' she reminded him.

'Well, I've changed my mind,' he said, wearily.

'But what if I want to be with you right now?'

'Well, I'd prefer it if you left but if you insist on staying then that's OK too,' he said, turning away from her in the bed again.

'I'm going to go,' she said, angry.

'Will you have breakfast with me?' he asked sweetly, turning around once more.

She didn't want to answer him. She climbed out of bed and started putting on her clothes. He watched her in the dark, propped up on one elbow, his head in his hand. She walked towards the stairs, her cardigan slung over her arm, her shoelaces undone. She stopped.

'Sure,' she said, sarcastically. *Thanks for nothing.*

She stormed off, angrily stomping down the stairs and out the front door. All she could think of was Sade and how he never would have turned her away like that. She sauntered over to Hamlet's sportscar and sat on the bonnet. She tried the door on the driver's side. It was open. She climbed inside. She sat staring at the icon glued onto the middle of the polished wooden steering wheel. She put her cardigan on and laced up her shoes. She looked out the window and across the road and saw that Hamlet had switched the light back on. The glass dome glowed yellow against the pink beginnings of the dawn. The front door opened and Hamlet stepped outside. He was wearing a white robe and smoking a cigarette.

'I just wanted to say I'm sorry for asking you to leave like that,' he said, opening the car door from the driver's side.

'That's OK,' she said. She held her hand out for a cigarette. He offered her the packet. 'I just really wanted you to know how much I want to be with you,' she said, puffing on the cigarette.

'Well, now I know,' he said, his eyes staring and dark.

'Now you know,' she said, drained.

He offered her his hand. 'You look tired.'

She let him help her out of the car.

'Why don't you lie down in my bed?' he suggested. 'I don't think I'll be able to sleep. That is,' he added, laughing, 'if you'll excuse all the blood.' Then in mock falsetto and lisping, 'Don't you just hate it when your tampon slips out during the night and you end up menstruating all over the sheets?'

She smiled. 'It takes more than a little blood on a sheet to make my stomach queasy.'

'Why don't you let me change them?' he said, grinding the butt of his cigarette beneath his slippered heel.

'Forget it,' she said, too tired to care.

'Come on,' he joked, 'what about liberating me from my traditional role as a man?'

She tossed her butt in the gutter. 'Liberate yourself.'

She followed him inside. He stood at the top of the stairs surrounded by light. Through the dome up above the sky was faintly pink. Bird calls filled her ears. She watched him bend over to examine his cut. He pressed his finger deep into the gash on his leg and then, placing the finger into his mouth, sang in falsetto, his voice weaving intricate variations around the familiar tune,

> *You make me feel*
> *You make me feel*
> *You make me feel*
> *Like a natural woman.*

She undressed and climbed into the bed. He collapsed heavily in the cane chair and lit another cigarette. She closed her eyes but had too much on her mind to sleep. She still wanted him to touch her, to climb in beside her, to kiss her once more. She heard the creak as he stood up. He tiptoed downstairs. She watched over the side of the bed as he crept into the bedroom, checking that the children were still asleep in their beds. He climbed the stairs, humming the words of the song under his breath. He stood at the top of the stairs and looked down through the glass floor at the sleeping children. He lay down on the floor and pressed his face to the glass. The glass fogged with his warm breath. Muttering to himself, he climbed slowly to his feet.

He glanced over at the bed and she quickly closed her eyes. He started walking towards the bed but he'd only taken a few steps when he changed his mind and swivelled around. She watched as the floor went sliding away beneath him and the glass floor shuddered beneath his back. He lay still, not breathing. Tears streamed from the corners of his eyes. Her heart raced. She debated what to do. He gasped loudly and struggled to his feet. He stood swaying, catching his breath. He looked down at his leg and the bandage had come loose and the sanitary napkin was stained a brilliant red and hung down secured to his leg by a single remaining bandaid. A puddle of blood collected at his feet. Blood was smeared all over the glass where he had slipped and fallen down. Beneath him the sleeping children were partly obscured by the pool and smears of blood.

'Now there's an idea,' she heard him say in a hoarse whisper. She watched him go creeping back down the stairs and into the kitchen. He opened the cupboard beneath the sink and lifted out a stack of litre-sized tins of house paint. He opened each tin in turn. The white was nearly empty, the blue was half-full but the third tin contained a brilliant vermilion and was almost full. He closed the lid and shook the can hard. He took a brush from the bottom drawer and went back upstairs. He picked up the piles of clothes and dumped them on the bed. He checked to see if she was still asleep. She closed her eyes. He started to paint the floor. He slopped the paint about carelessly, humming a little under his breath. She noticed that the paint didn't cover very well. It would need more than just a single coat. When the tin was empty he sat up and looked around. There was still so much to do. He heard stirrings from below. His eyes went darting about, this way and that, trying to see through the painted red floor. He frowned. She peered over the side. She could see nothing beneath the shiny red lines and curls, an impenetrable red sea. She could no longer see what was going on downstairs from where she was sitting in bed. She sighed, and drifted into a deep, dreamless sleep.

Juliette

1

IT WAS DARK INSIDE. LOCATED ON THE WRONG SIDE OF THE
block, on the southern side, heavy leadlight windows filtered
out most of the available light as it bounced, a hot
midday glare, against the blond brick wall of the adjacent
building. Justine lay recumbent on the Moroccan rug,
eyes fixed on the peeling white ceiling, palms and bare
feet flat against the coarse woven surface.

The rug was dirty and old. Coloured a deep burgundy red
and patterned with sections of yellow, blue and white, it was
faded in patches, ragged at the edges, stained with
splashes of red wine and coffee, and spotted with dark
black cigarette burns. It stank of mould and dust. She
turned her head slightly to one side and looked out
through the red and blue coloured glass of the leadlight bay
window. She closed her eyes. The surface of her skin tickled
where it rubbed against the rug and all around her it felt as
if tiny pins were binding her to the heavy weave, just
piercing the outer layer of her skin and clothing and tacking

her down, nailing her figure flat to the floor. She imagined there were two bigger, longer pins penetrating her head at either side of her nose, passing directly through the holes in the cartilage that allowed her to breathe and probing deep into the rug, burrowing right through to the wooden floorboards. Pinned down, screwed to the wooden floor, she could barely turn her head from side to side.

The phone rang. She tried to move her hand while she counted the rings. She counted to fifteen and the ringing stopped. She struggled with her hand, inching it towards her mouth. She blew on her fingers. They tingled with pins and needles. The phone started ringing again. She picked it up.

'I just want to come over and fuck you.'

It was Sade. 'I'm busy, I can't fuck you right now,' she said, annoyed.

'What about later this evening?' His voice was warm, deep, honeyed.

'I have work to do,' she reminded him, 'you know I have work I should be doing and boxes to unpack.'

'But surely you're not going to be working and playing house all night,' he insisted.

She rapidly lost patience. 'I don't know, I don't know what I'm doing yet.'

She listened to him breathing down the phone. Her eyes were two narrow slits and her mouth was twisted up to one side.

'Justine, are you OK?' he asked, sounding concerned. 'Really, you sound a little unhinged.'

286

She couldn't help smiling. 'I'm always a little unhinged.'

'Yes, but are you pleasantly or unpleasantly unhinged?' he teased.

Cautious. 'I'm not unpleasantly unhinged.'

'Then can I be not unpleasantly unhinged with you later tonight?' he suggested, triumph creeping into his voice.

She twirled loose strands of soft blonde hair around her finger. She chewed her bottom lip. 'Where?'

'My place.'

'It'll have to be late late,' she hedged. 'I have an appointment with Juliette early on.'

'See you later then,' he said and hung up.

The engaged signal honked rudely inside her head. The blood rushed pounding to her head. Suddenly, she was furious. *That's the last time, Sade.* She threw the receiver across the room. 'Who the fuck do you think you are?' she shouted.

She kicked the phone, sending it scuttling across the rug and bloodying her big toe. She grabbed at the cord. She wound it around her hand twice and then yanked at it hard, but the cord remained firmly tacked down to the wooden skirting boards. *Damn.* She sighed and rolled over onto her back and stared out through the coloured glass. She felt her feet go cold and stiff and an icy rod go shooting up the back of her legs and spine and wrap itself around her forehead. Her jaws locked together. She ground her teeth. She reached for the phone and dialled Sade's number. The engaged signal drilled into her brain like a pneumatic drill through the walls of a safe, setting off all the alarms. She slammed the phone down in its cradle and grabbed wildly at the cord. Slowly and on bended knees, she followed the cord around the room, pulling the tacks out one by one until she reached the tall wooden bookcase. She pulled at the cord again and this time the bookcase crashed to the floor. She screamed, Fuck you, Sade, at the bookcase and threw the phone against the peeling scarlet wallpapered wall. She sat down where the phone had landed and pelted its face with her fists. She stopped pelting the phone. She sat kneeling on the floor surrounded by books and, puffing, stared at the broken phone. She tried putting the pieces back together. She plugged the cord back into the wall and held the receiver to her ear. She got a dial tone and dialled Sade's number. As the clear plastic cover was missing, most likely buried somewhere under the books, she had to rest her fingers in the curved scoops and count out the ridges for each digit. When she finally got through the number was still engaged. She pictured Sade sitting in his office, someone's face buried in his lap, smiling deliriously. *The phone off the hook*.

Running her eyes across the confusion of jackets and spines she spotted a ragged paperback volume. She spread the book open and, holding it in each hand by its front and back covers, she tore it down the middle of its spine. Then she tore it again and again, each time emitting a half-strangled growl from the back of her throat, until the pile of books became a pile of pages. Spying the title page she stopped. She picked it up and read Sade's dedication.

Throwing the page over her shoulder she started to cry.

Minutes passed. She slowly picked up the torn pages and placed them carefully back into numerical order, her cheeks wet with tears and loud sobs yelping up through her throat. She organised the books into piles. She picked up a novel and stared listlessly at the cover for a while but her bleary-eyed attention was soon swept away and captivated by the long thin slice of clear plastic cover that had been lying beneath the unread novel. She put the book down and picked up the plastic. She rolled up her left shirt sleeve and looked at the smooth pale white skin. Then she started jabbing the plastic into the underside of her arm, beginning at her wrist and working all the way up her arm. She stared at the angry red welts and bloody pools. *I hate you.* She pressed her lips close to the bleeding skin. Then she wiped the plastic on her jeans and licked down the length of her arm, savoring the taste of blood on the tip of her tongue. She threw the slice of plastic across the room.

She looked at the piles of books. *I can salvage something from this.* She lifted the bookcase and stood it back up against the wall. She walked over to the stereo and played a tape. Work would have to wait until tomorrow. She stacked up the rest of the books. Tired, she left the books and bookcase for later and lay down on the rug on the floor and stared up at the ceiling. She rubbed her bare feet backwards and forwards on the coarse woven surface making them tingle and the skin turn red. She reached inside her jeans and moaned. She pictured Sade's cock and chewed on her bottom lip. She unzipped her fly.

2

SHE WATCHED THE WHITE MIDDAY GLARE MOVE ACROSS THE
blond brick wall next door until, just like time-lapse pho-
tography, the glaring light became a faint burnt orange
glow. She pressed her face to the glass and contemplated the
sea which lay to the east of the peninsula. Steel-grey
clouds sat glowering on the distant horizon. She made a cup
of coffee and took it to her desk where she sat mindlessly
staring at the book spread open before her. She stared at the
first page of the introduction. She read the first few
words. She stopped reading. *She was fucked.* Unable to
concentrate on the book, she pushed it aside and chewed the
rough edge of a bitten fingernail. She looked at the computer
pressed up against the wall and squeezed between piles of
unread books at the back of the desk. She spat a crescent of
fingernail into the air.

She pulled the computer towards her, its little plastic
feet scraping the unpolished wood. She clicked on the
screen and opened a folder filled with letters to Sade. She

started rereading the latest one. Like all the other letters she'd written to Sade, it was a letter that would never be sent.

Dear Sade. Why can't we be together? Why won't you stop fucking other women so you can be with me? I've spent most of the day hoping that you'd call, even though we're officially not talking at the moment. I keep fantasising that you'll ring me up and tell me you just want to come over and fuck me and that you're through with all the other women.

She stared at the white painted wall. Her mind whirled. She couldn't concentrate on the letter at all. Sade and his pathetic sex addiction. She choked down a mouthful of coffee, now too sweet at the bottom and cold. Irritable, she spat the coffee onto the floor next to her desk. It was immediately absorbed by the thick layer of dust which coated the dark wooden floorboards. She wiped her mouth on her sleeve. She stared at the screen. She read a few more words. She shook her head. She read them again and then stopped. She didn't understand. She couldn't remember writing the rest of the letter at all. Frowning, she sat staring at the wet patch on the floor, all that was left of the coffee, and chewed her fingernails, tearing viciously at the cuticles until they started to bleed. She read the passage again.

I hate you. One day I'm going to get a gun and come after you and kill you. I'll wait, I'll wait years if I have to and I'll stalk you, I'll follow you and one night when you're alone and you've forgotten that I even exist, I'll kill you. Then I'll kill myself.

She scratched the top of her head and then went back to chewing her fingernails, sucking at the sore tears in the soggy lumps of skin. Her screen-saver came on and she watched fish move across the black screen in short, even bursts. A deep shudder began to shake her from her core, gripping her at the base of her spine and shaking her ferociously from side to side. She closed the file and clicked back to the desktop. A death threat. That was the last thing she needed. She took out a pen and piece of paper and divided the page into two columns. In one column she made a list of people with motives. In the other column she listed possible assailants. She rolled the piece of paper into a ball and threw it across the room. The list included everyone she knew. *Paranoid*. She was acting like an absolute idiot. She tried deep breathing, she tried to relax. Obviously she had written the passage herself and saved it to the wrong file by mistake. Undoubtedly it was a section from an angry letter to Sade and she'd been so incensed at the time that she'd forgotten all about it. All she had to do was wait and everything would come flooding back to her in a few days.

She closed down the computer and stared out the window. The wall next door was a dark brown smudge. She checked the time. It was time to start getting ready for her appointment with Juliette. She looked back at the computer screen, dark grey and covered in fluff. *And if she was wrong?* Her flat was easy enough to break into—up through the manhole in the stairwell, in through the manhole in the bathroom. Anyone could have broken in, opened the folder and written the passage one day when she wasn't home.

292

3

'MY GRANDFATHER,' JUSTINE BEGAN NERVOUSLY, 'MY mother's father, was a huge man, over six feet tall, broad shouldered and muscular. His huge fat stomach hung over his trousers and his fingers were as thick as sausages.' She waited for Juliette to respond but Juliette's pale grey eyes stared coldly into hers. She shifted on the couch.

She surveyed her surroundings. Juliette's office was in the front room of a wide three-storey terrace house. The office was sparsely furnished. Two three-seater couches arranged at right angles in front of a marble fireplace, a filing cabinet, a desk and chair and a coffee table with a box of Kleenex and a vase of flowers. The couches were covered in a rich cream cotton twill and separated by a fine woollen steel blue carpet. She held a duralex glass half-filled with purified water in one hand. She sipped at the water.

'My grandmother was a small woman with deep-set blue eyes, of a melancholy disposition and incredibly feminine,' she continued, staring transfixed by a patch of carpet and starting to rave. 'As a child my mother hardly ever slept in her parents' house. At nights she used to lie awake in bed listening, ears picking up every sound, waiting for the dreaded thud of her father's drunken boots on the doorstep. And when she heard that sound her eyes would open wide, she would sit up in bed and her heart would start pounding in her chest. Was tonight going to be one of those nights, she would wonder?' She glanced at Juliette. Juliette's eyes met hers in a cool grey stare.

'Then it would start,' she resumed, her eyes glued to the carpet. 'My grandfather's voice would rise and he would begin to bellow. He would berate and abuse my grandmother and then everything would start crashing around. Later, when everything was quiet again and still, my mother would listen to my grandmother sobbing long into the night.' She stared down into her lap. She ran her fingers along a bitten nail. She chewed the nail. A slice came off in her mouth. She chewed and swallowed it. Her fingernail ached where the nail had been ripped from the sensitive skin. She bit the uneven edge. She took a deep breath.

'When my mother was five years old she started sneaking the large carving knife with her to bed,' she confided. 'One night as the crashing reached a crescendo, my mother reached under the bed, grabbed hold of the knife and stood breathlessly behind the closed bedroom door. At the next sound of breaking glass she opened the door and ran into the room pointing the knife at her father. "You leave my mother alone," she screamed, "you're hurting my mother." "You little traitor," he shouted, turning upon

294

her. He grabbed the knife out of her hands and dragged her screaming to the front door. Then he opened it and threw her outside and slammed the door in her face. "You stay out there till you learn how to behave yourself, young lady," he shouted, turning his attention back towards his wife. "So now you're turning my own children against me, are you, you evil bloody witch," he bellowed and hit her across the face once more. "No, darling, I didn't," she whimpered, "I didn't do anything of the sort, of course I wouldn't try to turn the children against you."

'Outside in the cold clear mountain air my mother choked on her sobs and waited on the doorstep to be let in. She waited sobbing all night,' she said, pausing for dramatic effect. She bit her nail once more and put it bleeding in her lap. She looked up at Juliette again. Juliette's hard eyes softened with sympathy.

'Your mother had a very difficult childhood,' Juliette said, her eyes moist at the edges.

'Yes,' Justine said, anxiously tearing at a new nail. 'But why didn't my grandmother leave my grandfather?' She leaned forwards in the couch and awaited Juliette's reply.

'Good question,' Juliette said.

Justine swallowed a strip of nail. She hurried to fill the silence. 'My mother said it was because she had so many children that she was economically dependent on her husband, but I can't help wondering if this was just an excuse, just a sign of the times. After all, my grandfather didn't offer much in the way of economic security, given that he'd gambled and lost both his inheritance and the family home at drunken poker games.' She looked up at

Juliette again. Juliette nodded. 'My mother decided not to press charges against my father's ex-wife. When I asked why she said she'd let it slip out of consideration for her children. Sometimes I thought this was just an excuse too. It seemed that for women like my mother and grandmother any behaviour was excusable if the security of children was in question. But how could children feel secure growing up in a house poisoned by physical and emotional abuse?'

Juliette raised her eyebrows and nodded her head.

'When I first started going to a shrink,' Justine said, changing the subject, 'when I was seventeen, I asked him what he thought I should do about my asocial behaviour. I think we talked about this once, my stripping in public?'

'You mentioned it,' Juliette agreed.

'It was funny because I started the analysis as a stripper and after a few months I'd changed from a stripper into a shoplifter. Now I just scream, smash things, shoplift, self-mutilate and hit people,' Justine rambled, staring at a patch of carpet. 'Anyway,' she resumed, 'so I was thinking of quitting the analysis and I asked him what he thought I should do. And he said that it was important to follow my impulses.'

'So you stopped going?'

'And I quit music,' Justine pointed out.

Juliette waited to catch her eye. 'We have to finish here,' she said, her voice firm.

Justine nodded and resumed staring at the carpet. Her mind wandered. Juliette offered her more water. She shook her head. She bit another nail down to the quick. It started to bleed. She savoured the blood. Juliette shifted in the other couch.

'If you have time, I'd like you to come and look at my books,' Juliette said.

Justine stared at Juliette and nodded. She was too frightened to go home. She was terrified of seeing Sade. Panic choked her throat. She swallowed hard. 'I think someone's just made a threat to my life,' she said, her voice hoarse.

'You think someone has, or someone has?' Juliette looked alarmed.

Justine hesitated. 'I think.'

Juliette tilted her head to one side. She rubbed her chin with her hand. 'And how does that make you feel?' she asked.

Justine was mortified. 'What kind of stupid question's that?'

'Not as stupid as it appears,' Juliette said enigmatically. 'Come on,' she urged standing up, 'I want to show you my books.'

Juliette held out her hand. Justine continued to stare into the bottom of her glass. Juliette took her hand. 'Come on.'

Justine followed Juliette up the wide staircase, her hand lightly grazing the surface of the smooth polished wooden banisters. When she reached the top, Juliette left her to wait on the landing and disappeared behind a large heavy door. The door was made of dark panelled wood, the highly buffed surface silken beneath her fingertips. The handle was made of white china and painted with pink flowers. The outer rim was finished with a circle of gold. She could hear Juliette moving things around inside.

'OK,' Juliette announced, opening the door.

Justine entered a large, bare room. A four-poster bed and an antique cupboard were its only contents. Two pairs of French doors looked out onto a wide balcony. The street below and neighbouring houses were concealed from view behind a row of densely leaved trees. In the centre of the room, a wooden ladder reached up to the high ceiling where a trapdoor hung down, open. She followed Juliette up the creaking ladder.

The attic spanned the full breadth of the house, like the office and bedroom below, although it was much larger given that it was also as deep as the house itself. Of the four walls, the two longest were the side walls, and these were lined with wooden framed glass cabinets with shiny brass knobs. The shorter wall at the back was lined with bookcases. At the front, the roof slanted down in the direction of the street below. Two skylights looked out onto mounds of dark shiny leaves. Somewhere downstairs the phone rang.

'Make yourself at home,' Juliette said, 'I'll be right back.'

Justine heard the ladder creaking and then Juliette's voice answer the phone. She walked towards the back of the attic where bookshelves lined the wall from top to bottom. She read the bindings along the nearest shelf. She recognised Shakespeare's *Hamlet*, and *Story of the Eye* by Georges Bataille. She came across a volume by the Marquis de Sade and pulled it out. The heavy leather bound edition fell open to a page roughly near the middle of the book.

She found herself looking at all the words on the page at once. Gradually the words and the white page blurred together into a shimmering grey until she no longer saw the printed words at all. Instead she stared at the slit where the two pages met along the binding. The leaves of white paper were separated by a thin dark line. At first black, she soon noticed that it was much less a black black and much more a very dark red. As she continued to stare the line started to blur away from itself at the middle. It took on a curvaceous shape, rounded out towards the middle and narrow at each end. Dark red liquid slowly oozed out from the middle of the slit invisibly soaking into the page. The slit of blood stared up at her blindly like an unseeing eye. Juliette's hand gripped her shoulder.

'What do you think?' Juliette wanted to know.

Justine shivered. 'I've never seen anything like it.'

Juliette held her hand out for the book. 'Kind of special, aren't they?'

Justine regarded the book with grim fascination. 'I mean, is it real blood?'

Juliette didn't answer. Justine's skin prickled at the back of her neck.

'I want to show you something,' Juliette said. 'Come over here.'

Justine followed Juliette over to one of the glass cabinets. Inside, mounted on a wooden stand, was a volume of Sigmund Freud's *On Metapsychology*. The book was open at the first page of the essay, 'Beyond the Pleasure Principle'. Blood and clotted tissues poured out from the centre of the binding and spilled over into a tiny stainless steel drain below.

'Incurable texts are of considerable scientific value,' Juliette pointed out.

Goose bumps went running up and down Justine's arms. 'They're part of an experiment?'

'The Freud's my personal favourite, but no, it's not an experiment,' Juliette said in a faraway voice. 'I'm going to sell my collection to an art gallery. Cologne, I think.'

Justine didn't understand. 'Are you the artist?'

'Artist, scientist, whatever. It took years to work out the relation between writing and the flow of blood,' Juliette said conclusively.

'So the blood is real?' Justine's teeth started to chatter. She clenched her jaws to stop them.

'It's not real or metaphorical, it's criticism,' Juliette explained.

Fascinated, Justine continued to watch the incurable text bleed, her teeth chattering noisily in her mouth. *Where did Juliette get all the blood?* Cold, she crossed her arms against her chest.

Juliette touched her sleeve. 'That's it for today.'

Justine followed Juliette down the creaking attic stairs. Her legs felt weak beneath her.

4

THE PHONE RANG CLOSE BY, WAKING HER UP AND ERASING HER dreams. Glancing over at the electric clock Justine noted that she'd overslept. For an instant she wasn't sure where she was, what day it was, she couldn't remember anything before waking up. When last night finally did come back it was with a jolt. A lonely and anxious cab ride home in the early hours of the morning the conclusion to an uncomfortable evening spent at Sade's drinking vodka and fucking compulsively. The night of the incurable texts. She reached down next to the bed and answered the phone. It was Sade.

'I just want to come over and fuck you.'

She opened her eyes and sat up. She looked at her legs. Both thighs were covered in bruises. 'I'm asleep.'

She pictured Sade sitting at his desk with his hand down the front of his jeans. 'I'd like to come over and suck your huge sloppy cunt.'

Not quite awake. 'I've got work to do.'

She listened to the rustling sound of paper sliding against paper as Sade started rummaging around on his desk. 'Oh no, can I call you back?' he asked, sounding apologetic.

Suspicious. 'What is it?'

'Look, I've gotta go,' he whined.

Furious. 'Your next fuck turn up, or what?'

'Justine, I'll call you back,' he said and hung up.

'Don't bother,' she said into the dial tone.

She checked the time once more. She had an appointment with her co-supervisor in ten minutes. She dragged on her clothes from last night, collected her notebook and went running out the door.

5

Bataille's study was a sparsely furnished room with two doors, situated towards the back of his long labyrinthine terrace house. One door led from the study to a wide glassed-in verandah. The other door led into a huge double living area. A small window looked out onto a narrow cement passage which was overlooked by a small shabby block of flats—dirty windows with ragged bed-sheets instead of curtains. The verandah looked out onto a mosquito-infested cement and bamboo yard.

The study was illuminated by a single dangling light bulb. A small fan was the only source of ventilation. Dusty air moved across her damp skin. She sneezed. Bataille continued to flip through manila folders in his filing cabinet. He was looking through the fourth and final drawer. He closed the drawer.

'I probably threw it out with last week's newspapers,' he joked.

She didn't laugh.

Abandoning the filing cabinet, he went around the office pulling books and folders out from bookcases and digging around in the stacks of cardboard boxes that littered the polished wooden floor.

'Would you like a cup of coffee?' he wanted to know, kneeling on the floor, one hand ruffling through his fine black hair.

'I'd like it more if you could find my thesis,' she said.

He shrugged, nonchalant. 'Let's have a cup of coffee. Maybe it'll turn up.'

She followed Bataille through the lounge room to the kitchen. The kitchen was dominated by a square bright yellow table. Bataille filled the kettle from the tap and tried to find the coffee plunger amidst the piles of dishes which covered both sides of the sink and the laminex bench-tops. He told her to sit down but when she pulled out one of the chairs it was piled up with old newspapers and manuscripts. *Fuck*. She attempted to lift the pile up onto the table but lost most of it as the papers slipped between her fingers and landed on the grimy floor. Bataille turned round, plunger in one hand.

'Now there's an idea,' Bataille exclaimed, kneeling down on the dirty floorboards and sifting through the newspapers and manila folders. He sighed. He pulled out a heavy folder and plopped it on top of the yellow table. Justine laughed, her voice cold and shrill.

Back in the study, she sat at Bataille's desk and sipped strong black coffee from a chipped black cup. Bataille leafed through her thesis. The fan whirred. The light bulb dangled above.

304

'I find your work absolutely fascinating,' he began, scratching the scabs on his chin and making them bleed, 'and I think you write very well. My only criticism is that the subject matter's a bit relentless.'

Suspicious. 'What do you mean, "relentless"?'

'Well it's a bit hard on the reader for one,' he complained. 'It's not exactly what you'd call a reader-friendly piece of writing.'

'But I explain that in the introduction,' she exclaimed, 'in the section titled, "Why This Thesis Is Written Precisely the Way it Is".'

'The introduction, what introduction? I don't have an introduction,' he said, flipping through the pages and smearing them with blood. 'I can't find any section titled "Why This Book's Written Precisely the Way it Is". You didn't give me an introduction.'

She was adamant. 'Well, I did give you an introduction.'

'Did you?' he said vaguely, scratching his cheek. 'I don't remember there being any introduction.'

'In the introduction I explain why the thesis is written the way I've written it and why there's simply no other way of saying what I wanted to say other than the way I've said it,' she declared.

'Even so, it's a little off-putting for the reader,' he insisted. 'The subject matter is very confronting—all the detailed descriptions of the bodies, the murders, the weapons, the execution of the crimes. It's very brutal, it's very hard on the reader—all the violence directed towards women.'

'Women aren't the only victims,' she interjected.

'All the same, it's very unpleasant,' he protested. 'I can't help wondering why it's necessary to go to such extremes of violence.'

'But you're missing the whole point entirely,' she cried, 'or you're missing the point. It's meant to be like that.'

'But I'm just a little worried,' he continued, unprovoked. 'I mean, when you're dealing with such extreme and brutal levels of violence, you might need to make some concessions, otherwise you risk losing the reader's interest.'

Indignant. 'Are you saying my analysis is boring?'

He looked at her, his wet brown eyes small behind the thick round lenses. 'Well,' he started to say and then broke off to wipe blood from his face. He cleared his throat. 'Well,' he began again, 'the material itself is extremely repetitive and abrasive and difficult to read.'

She stood up and grabbed the thesis. 'So what are you saying?'

'Look, will you just calm down?' He stood up as well and held his hand out for the thesis. She shook her head. 'Now Justine, I want you to give me your thesis and take a few deep breaths and *calm down*.'

'Patronise me one more time you lousy creep and I'll ram this fucken thesis right up your tight sick-fuck bourgeois hypocrite's ass,' she threatened, trembling from head to toe.

Bataille removed his glasses and polished them with his handkerchief. 'OK,' he said, shaking his head, 'that's enough for today.'

Justine glared at him hatefully, the thesis clasped to her breast. 'Oh, what a shame, I'm so heartbroken and disappointed,' she said sarcastically.

He returned the handkerchief to his trousers pocket and his spectacles to the bridge of his nose. 'For the last time, Justine,' he pleaded, 'I'm asking you to calm down, to sit down.'

She watched blood run down his cheeks in streams. Her stomach flip-flopped inside.

'If you can just do what I say,' he continued, 'then I can make a few suggestions and then we can forget about the thesis, OK? That is, if you're at all interested in anything I have to say.'

'OK. Yes,' she snapped, not sitting down, 'I would like to hear what you have to say. I've been waiting for nearly six months to hear what you have to say. So say it.'

'OK,' he said reaching over for the thesis. She let the manuscript slip through her fingers. He flipped to the end where he'd written a page of comments. 'Now,' he began, in a stern voice, 'I think you need to incorporate a feminist argument, a critique of the excessive violence. As it stands, the thesis reads as a celebration of violence against women and that's going to make it very difficult for the examiners.'

'But that goes against precisely what I set out to do in this thesis,' she cried. 'As I explained in the introduction, I want to take the author's position regarding violence very seriously. It's up to the reader to judge whether the author's use of violence is warranted, not me. If I tried to do what you suggest I'd have to write a completely different thesis, and a thesis that I have absolutely no interest whatsoever in writing.'

'Look,' he sighed, handing her back the thesis, 'I suppose what I'm asking for is a rewrite.'

'Well,' she sulked, 'I really don't think you're taking my work seriously. You're asking me to write something I have no interest in writing.'

He shrugged. He walked around the square yellow table until he was standing behind her. He pressed his lips against the back of her neck and nibbled the warm furry tip of her ear. He blew on the back of her neck. She didn't respond and continued to stare pensively at the thesis she held in her hands. He wrapped his hands around her waist and pulled her against him from behind. He kissed the back of her neck. She shifted her weight from one leg to the other.

'I want cunt now,' he whispered into her ear.

'Sorry,' she said, feigning regret. She turned around so they were facing each other. He reached for her jeans.

'Do you want me to suck you first?' he inquired superfluously.

She pushed him down to his knees. Head bent, he slowly unzipped her fly.

6

SHE PRESSED HER FACE AGAINST THE BEDROOM WINDOW AND stared east, directly into the early morning sun. Across the road the slate roofs of a row of terrace houses glowed warm and black. She watched washing blowing in the breeze on a clothesline strung across the roof of a block of flats. She traced the erratic path of drainpipes down red brick walls. She watched a young Asian man smoke a cigarette, legs hanging over the wall around the top of the roof, face squinting into the sun. Silver air-conditioning vents glared blindingly. Tin vents atop chimneys twirled in the breeze.

She went to the kitchen and made a cup of coffee. Sade's call had come earlier than usual, she wasn't usually awake this early in the morning. She carried the small glass of black coffee back to her desk and sat down. She wondered what to do. She regarded the computer suspiciously and pushed it towards the back of her desk. She took a sip of the hot sweet coffee, opened an exercise book and, holding a ballpoint pen awkwardly in her grasp, started writing.

I was a planned baby. My mother and father had been married for a year and then they stopped using contraception. She ran her hands through her hair, it was greasy. Even in her white boxer shorts and T-shirt she was still hot. Sweat ran down the back of her legs. She looked out the window, she looked back at the page. *God I hate the suburbs.* There wasn't a high-rise apartment that was high-rise enough—there wasn't a high-density suburb that was high-density enough. *My mother wanted a girl first and a boy second and when I was born I was a girl, just like she wanted, just like she'd planned.* She began writing again, the pen awkwardly clasped in her hand.

My father was so excited about me being born, that he got a speeding ticket rushing to the hospital to meet me. And there we were, my mother, me, my father and my grandmother, drinking champagne. Everybody was so happy they were crying except me, I was just crying.

My mother named me Justine after the heroine of the Marquis de Sade's novel. My mother never read Sade but she knew of his books and liked the name. I wouldn't read him until I was twenty-seven.

My father wanted to name me after one of his childhood sweethearts back in Czechoslovakia but my mother didn't want me to have a name that would make me a victim at school, that might lead other kids to tease me about having a refugee father.

My parents were in love when they married. You can tell just by looking at the photos taken on their wedding day. It's

310

obvious they really loved fucking each other.

In the photos they look incredibly beautiful. My father had worked as a model, among other things, and my mother was the real English rose type. Light blue eyes and freckles and the sweetest smile.

We lived in a huge house with a garden full of camellias and fruit trees. Everything was peaceful and quiet at this time. I watered the garden with my watering can and ate snails and swam in a little inflatable pool and played with my dog. I used to wrap my arms around her neck, hanging off. And I was smart too. And gorgeous.

Things changed when my brother Julian was born. Overnight I turned into a monster. I was seized by an uncontrollable jealousy and terrorised the entire family with my extremely violent fits of rage. The first time this ever happened was when my mother took me to preschool. Being left behind and watching her take another baby home in my place triggered the attack. My mother panicked, seeing me crying and screaming and ripping my hair out and beating myself with my tiny clenched fists in the middle of the playground, and returned to comfort me only to leave again a few minutes later, sending me crazy again.

From then on things weren't so rosy for me or for my family. I was haunted by my dark side and the fits of rage didn't stop nor did the tears and clenched fists. Much later at high school I learned to contain these outbursts to my room where I would close the door and howl and scream and beat and kick my lime-green beanbag to my heart's content. But I always felt there was a certain *emptiness to this gesture. I knew I wasn't really angry with the beanbag.*

Indeed Julian's birth may well have upstaged me entirely. Six months into her pregnancy my mother was violently assaulted by my father's ex-wife. She tried to kill my mother and unborn baby brother by beating my mother on the stomach, breasts and head with tightly clenched fists as she lay helpless on the footpath with her leg in plaster. For six weeks it was touch and go whether he would survive. Finally after six weeks of drugs to prevent my mother's contractions, he was born six weeks premature.

While Julian overcame his birth he later developed a mysterious incurable, untreatable and rare syndrome. At the age of seven, at exactly the same time of year as when the assault had originally taken place, he came down with the flu and vomited. But it didn't stop there. He vomited all night and all the next day and so regularly you could tell the time by his gruff barking sounds. He couldn't keep anything down, not even a few drops of water, and rapidly lost weight. On the third day, his eyes deeply sunken in his ravaged face, he told us what we all already knew: 'I'm dying,' he said, and then vomited again.

We rushed him to hospital and the doctors injected him with every drug they could think of but nothing worked. He was seventy per cent dehydrated and his veins were on the point of collapsing and it took hours for them to put him on a drip. If they hadn't been able to get him on the drip it seems likely he would have died. Finally, exhausted, he inexplicably stopped vomiting. He had been vomiting for nearly five days. Brain scans, all kinds of medical tests showed nothing, the syndrome was held to be linked to the assault and the events surrounding his premature birth. It was psychosomatic. It returned every year at the same time until he left home at seventeen. Julian attributed his cure to his discovery of psychedelic drugs which coincided with his new freedom. I hardly saw him after that.

In the meantime my own problems had taken on a new and terrifying life of their own. My first relationship with a man exploded in violent physical abuse. Shortly after this I left home, deeply estranged from my family. In vain I hoped that the problem wasn't mine, that it was my boyfriend's, and that it would go away. It didn't. From the age of seventeen I was deeply preoccupied by this.

I went over and over my family history. There was no violence at home. No-one was beaten. Julian was damaged when he was still in the womb and my mother was badly beaten up but I wasn't hurt by my father's ex-wife's attack. I'd been protected, my father'd made sure I was safely inside the house as soon as he learned what was going on. No, I was just a monster, an insanely jealous and resentful monster and I learned to blame my mother, Frankenstein to my Frankenstein's monster, the person who I was closest to in the whole world, I blamed my mother for my monstrousness. After all, I rationalised, she was the carrier of domestic violence. Throughout her childhood her father had routinely beaten her mother in fits of violent drunken rage. Somehow she must have taught me everything she knew about violence without hitting me.

Punching her in the face at the age of seventeen in the midst of my first violent relationship was my ultimate gesture of rebellion. It was all her fault and I truly and deeply hated her for what she'd done to me.

From seventeen I lived in a series of caves. Small inexpensive run-down bachelor or one-bedroom apartments. I went through long periods where I kept myself away from people and tried to hide my monstrousness in my loneliness and my cleverness. Occasionally I would forget that I was a monster and would imagine that I was just lonely and clever and a woman and then I would try and live with someone. Inevitably everything would end up smashed and destroyed and I would find myself another cave and return to the comfortable familiarity of my hideousness.

Then when I was twenty-seven everything changed. I didn't really want it to, but I had no control over what happened. And then I wanted something else. I started to want more than a cave. And somehow I had to crawl out. Or at least that's how it felt. Like crawling out, starved and crazy with visions, fantasies, memories and dreams, covered in bleeding wounds that I knew would never ever completely heal, and in this state I had to stand up and ask for more, for much much more than I ever dreamed could be mine. I had to ask for my life as if I believed it was something I deserved. This was the hardest thing I'd ever had to

The intercom howled into the quiet room, making her jump. She walked over to the headpiece and spoke into the microphone. A woman's voice boomed into the room. She was collecting money for Greenpeace.

Juliette

'Fuck off you fucken Christians,' she shouted, 'you fucken moralistic old hag, get fucked, do you hear me? I'm trying to work in here.'

She slammed down the receiver. She was foaming at the mouth. *Fucken Christians.* Just when the rest of the world has finally given up on saving souls, you guys want to start saving trees. Just get fucked, just fuck off. She walked around in circles in the small dark hallway holding her head in her hands and wiping sweat from her brow.

She walked into the kitchen and ran cold water from the tap. The water was warm, the pipes exposed to the sun. She filled her mouth with water and then spat it all over the kitchen tiles and window. The outside of the window was covered in black dirt and spotted after the rain. The weather oscillated between thunderstorms and heatwaves. She looked west, out over the shops and across the roofs of flats and terraces at the city skyline. *The city towers were a long way away.* She wanted to be closer, she wanted to be right up close, she wanted to hear the sound of horns and the hum of huge electric generators. She wanted to look out her windows at night and see miles and miles of brilliantly lit offices and apartments. She wanted to touch their touch-telephones as they sold off the world. She wanted to be right in there.

The phone rang. She ran to answer it and sat down at her desk. It was Simone. She closed the notebook.

'So tell me, Simone, how's the insanity going?' she asked cheerfully.

'I think I'm in trouble,' Simone whispered.

'Someone finally catch you fucking your lecturers?' Justine teased.

'You've got to help me,' Simone wailed.

'Well, I was planning on working until five or six.'

'It's an emergency,' Simone hissed, 'I'll see you in five minutes.'

'OK,' Justine said reluctantly.

She put down the phone. She opened the notebook. She read over what she'd just written. She picked up the notebook and tore it in two down the spine. *Her father.* Then she went into the bedroom and sat on the floor, back to the wall, and looked at her reflection in the wall mirror. She described herself to herself as she looked. Her face, her hair, her clothes, the cuts on her arm from yesterday. *As soon as Simone left, she would telephone her parents.*

The intercom buzzed and she pressed the brown button. She opened the door and then sat down again in front of the mirror. She listened to the door slam and to Simone's steps down the hall.

'I've done something terrible,' Simone said, sitting down beside her, a black leather satchel clattering suspiciously on the floor.

Justine looked at Simone reflected in the mirror across the room. 'So're you going to tell me,' she said, jolly, 'or are we going to sit here like this all day?'

Simone smiled at her in the mirror. Justine looked Simone in the eye, from one eye to the other and back. Because of all the combinations of looking and being looked at she felt as though she was part of a multitude of people.

'I've just killed someone, a man,' Simone said, trying not to

316

cry. 'I was driving along in the car, I didn't see, he just stepped out in front and I crashed straight into him. He bounced up off the bonnet and shattered the window. Then I slammed on the brakes and he landed on the road. His jeans were ripped at the knee and his head was split open, dark blood knotted through his short brown curly hair.'

'You ran someone over in your car and now they're dead?' Justine asked, in shock.

'I just didn't see him,' Simone wailed. 'So I parked the car in the garage, I'll have to get rid of it somehow, then I called you and came straight over here in a cab.'

'Are you OK?'

'Not a scratch,' Simone sniffled.

Justine needed to know the facts. 'What were you doing driving around, why weren't you at university?'

'I had an appointment, I had an appointment with a lecturer,' Simone began.

'I knew it,' Justine interjected, 'you're fucking one of your lecturers.'

'I'm not fucking him,' Simone countered. 'We had a coffee to discuss my essay and I was driving back to uni and that's when it happened.'

Justine looked at Simone in the mirror. She started thinking about Sade. Sade's cock inside Simone's mouth. Sade fucking Simone in Marcelle's bed. 'Have you really stopped seeing Sade?' she asked, surprised that she still wanted to know.

'No,' Simone said, guilty.

Justine's stomach sliced open with broken glass. 'Do you still fuck him?'

Simone looked at the floor and nodded her head twice slowly.

'But you told me you'd stopped seeing him,' Justine said, needing to hear it again.

'I just wanted you to think I had,' Simone confessed. 'I'm sorry.'

Panic flooded Justine's system. Simone was a liar. Simone was a killer. Simone was staring straight at her. *Intently.* She stared back at Simone in silence. She debated whether Simone's story about killing the pedestrian was true. She didn't know what to believe. It seemed that Sade had lied to her as well. She reminded herself of the passage on her computer file. Did Simone plan to kill her? Her head reeled as the panic proliferated wildly inside her body, up through her stomach to her chest and around her throat in tight coils. Her breath came in little gasps. Her eyes started to roll back in her head. She tried to think straight.

'What about the car?' Justine asked. 'What if somebody witnessed the crash and wrote down the number plate?'

Simone's eyes clouded over, not sure what Justine was talking about. 'The car?'

Justine tried to be more specific. 'How does the car look?'

'Well it looks OK to me,' Simone said, finally catching on, 'but a detective's bound to be able to find something there.'

'Well if they catch you,' she pointed out, 'they'll send you to jail.'

'I could always say I wasn't driving the car.'

Stubborn. 'They might have a description.'

318

'I could report the car stolen, and get somebody to steal it,' Simone countered.

'And then if they catch you, it's hit and run and, you know, perverting the course of justice,' Justine pointed out.

Simone shook her head. 'No-one's going to find out about the car theft.'

Cautious. 'Do you know somebody?'

'Yes,' Simone said, 'a friend of mine.'

'How're you going to get them to do it?' Justine said, anxious. 'What're you going to say?'

'I'm going to say it's an insurance job and I'm going to pay them the going rate,' Simone said, cool.

'You sound like you've done this before.'

Before Simone had a chance to answer the phone rang. Justine ran to her desk and picked up the receiver. It was Sade.

'Justine, I love you, I can't live without you,' he said.

His words brought tears to her eyes. Large round pools overflowing. Heart pounding, she wiped her smeared wet cheeks. Sade'd never said anything like that to her before. She didn't know what to say.

'I'm coming over,' he said, his breath loud in her ear. 'I want to take you to New York with me.'

The engaged signal honked through the plastic receiver. She turned around. Simone handed her a black leather satchel.

'Can I leave this with you?' Simone asked. 'They'll never think to look here. They'll never think any of this has anything to do with you.'

Simone reached into her jacket pocket and took out a pair of dark sunglasses. She polished them against her black miniskirt and put them on. Looking at Simone Justine saw only her own eyes reflected back at her in the dark glass.

'I'm leaving,' Simone whispered. 'I'm going to deal with the car and then I'm going to disappear.'

Justine shook her head.

'No,' Simone said, 'you don't understand. I wanted to kill him. I mean, I didn't want to kill him specifically, but I wanted to kill someone, anyone would do. It wasn't an accident. It's just that I accidentally killed the wrong person.'

'But who did you want to kill?' Justine asked, determined to get it straight.

But before Simone had a chance to answer the intercom howled into the room.

'Quick,' she said, 'it's Sade. You'd better go. Use the fire-escape and the door at the back of the building, just in case he sees you.'

Simone threw her arms around Justine's neck and ran out the door.

The intercom howled into the room once more. Justine pressed the brown button and hurried to hide Simone's satchel under the futon in her bedroom. She heard a knock at the door. Sade calling her name. She ran to the door. She ran her hands through her hair. She straightened her shorts. She opened the heavy door. Sade bounded into the room and swept her up in his arms. She stared at him, hiding her eyes and her mouth drawn into a tight sneer. He lowered her to the floor.

'Aren't you happy for me?' he wanted to know.

She was confused. 'You haven't told me what's happened yet.'

'Well,' he began, taking her hand and leading her into the bedroom, 'Juliette put me onto an art critic who's a really good friend of hers.'

'You're fucking her,' she interjected.

'Are you going to let me finish?' he said, pulling her down on the bed. 'Or are you going to keep on interrupting me?'

'Hurry up then,' she sulked.

He took off his coat and jeans and slipped between the sheets. She lay beside him on top of the sheets. 'Aren't you going to get in?'

She moaned and slipped out of her shorts and lay down beside him. He smiled.

'Anyway,' he resumed, 'Juliette's friend put me in contact with a professor at NYU and after looking at my work NYU have offered me a job in their Australian Studies department.' He leaned over and kissed her, his lips squealing like little birds. He moaned and moved closer. 'And,' he said, in between kisses, 'I was wondering if you wanted to come to New York with me.'

She inched away from him. He frowned. 'Is there something wrong?' he asked, petulant.

'You're fucking Simone, aren't you?' It was an accusation, rather than a question.

'They're taking care of the visa and everything,' he said, ignoring her. 'I start work in two weeks.' He reached over and took a cigarette and his lighter from his jacket pocket. 'I know it's a little sudden,' he said, puffing on his cigarette, 'but I thought I could go over first and get things set up, find an apartment, that kind of thing, and you could follow later.'

She felt poisonous. 'So are you taking Simone as well?' Suddenly suspicious, she wondered where Simone was going to disappear to. What better place than New York?

'Anyway,' he said, 'I'm faxing my acceptance first thing next week.'

'So this art critic,' she said, bitterly, 'did you fuck her?'

'She's a he.'

'You fucked him.'

'Must you constantly reduce everything to sex?' Sade protested.

'You're the one who fucks everything that walks into your office and I'm the one who reduces everything to sex,' Justine said, triumphant.

'It's absolutely none of your fucking business who I fuck, in my office, in the backs of cars, in parks, in elevators, in beds, against refrigerators or in toilet cubicles,' he said defensively.

'Well that just about covers everything,' she said, flippant.

'You're so fucking self-righteous,' he said, raising his voice, 'do you know that?'

She turned her head to face the wall. He stood up and stormed into the bathroom. She heard the key turn in the lock and then water running in the bath. She looked at herself in the mirror. Her eyes stared back at her wildly, the whites huge and the irises floating, deep blue pools inside the milky whites. She stood up and went into the next room. She sat down at her desk. Her chest hurt and a tight ring of anxiety choked her throat.

She stared at the torn pages. She tried to come to terms with what had happened. She couldn't think. She scratched her face. Her chin was covered in tiny white lumps. She scratched the heads off until they started to bleed. She made herself stop scratching her face and chewed her fingernails instead, swallowing thin semi-circles of nail down the back of her throat, but it wasn't long before her fingers started to bleed and ache where she'd torn the sensitive skin and her face was stinging where she'd scratched herself so she picked up a nail file and started filing her nails but the torn nails were too soft to file and the nails just bent and tore so she threw the nail file away and picked up a toothpick and started to pick her teeth and soon her gums were bleeding and there was a pile of broken toothpicks beside her on the desk and she realised she'd totally run out of things to do seeing she couldn't think and when she looked out the window the sun was shining and the only thing she could think of doing to break the spell was walk. Her life was in danger. It was just a matter of working out where the threat lay.

She heard the bathroom door creak open and Sade walk out into the lounge room. She heard the sigh of the couch as he collapsed onto the rusty springs and the hiss as he switched on the TV. She had to try to think straight, she had to go over things methodically, slowly, logically in her mind. This was very difficult to do.

She grabbed some money from her desk drawer and walked through the house without a word. As she left he called out after her, asking her where she was going. She didn't answer and slammed the door.

She wandered the streets, drank coffee, and finally went shopping in a supermarket. She pushed the trolley up and down the aisles, idly filling it with things she didn't know when she'd use. Finding herself standing in front of a shelf of vitamins she slipped a large jar of vitamin B complex into her coat pocket. When it came time to pay, no-one noticed the stolen bottle of vitamins in her coat pocket. Or no-one cared. I'm stealing, she wanted to say. I'm stealing back what's rightfully mine. Supermarkets owe their customers free vitamins because the food they sell is totally robbed of nutritional value. It's not really even a case of theft, so much as a case of taking back what consumer capitalism has already robbed from food. The girl at the checkout handed her her change and told her to have a nice day.

She crossed to the other side of the mall and stood in front of the butcher's window. She counted out her change and folded the notes and put them in the front left pocket of her jeans. She looked at the meat. Even for meat it was shit. Eye fillet steak was what she wanted, that is, if they even had any. She dug into her pocket and counted the notes. She was halfway through the butcher's swing door when she felt a tap on her shoulder. Expecting to see someone she knew but didn't want to see she turned around with a ready-made excuse at hand. She stared into the brown eyes of a totally unfamiliar face. The woman smiled at her. Justine smiled back.

'Hi, I'm with Security and I'm sorry but I'm going to

have to ask you to empty out your coat pockets,' the woman said.

Justine did as she was told and the woman looked at the bottle of vitamins.

'Do you have your receipt?' the woman asked.

Justine reached down into the plastic bag and moved things around inside. She couldn't find her receipt. 'I'm sorry,' she lied, 'I can't seem to find it but I'm sure I put it in with the shopping, or at least that's what I usually do.'

Justine knelt down on the floor and slowly emptied the bag out one item at a time. She got to the bottom of the bag but the receipt still wasn't there.

'How about in your pockets?' the woman suggested.

Justine put everything back in the shopping bag and stood up. Giddy, she suddenly needed to lie down. She couldn't talk or open her eyes and blindly and in slow motion she turned her pockets inside out.

'I'm dizzy,' she complained, 'I need to sit down.'

Although as soon as she closed her mouth she wasn't sure if she'd said anything or not because the woman was telling her, one hand on her gun the other hand on her hip, to come along with her as if she hadn't said anything at all. She followed the woman back through the turnstiles and into a corner of the supermarket where all the empty cardboard boxes were stored. The walk made her feel a little better. Then the woman started talking and her head started to spin.

'I could call up the cops right this very minute and have you charged for doing something like this,' the woman threatened. 'Shoplifting's a serious offence.'

325

Justine thought about telling the woman that she only stole because she felt guilty about being fucked-up and having to go to a psychiatrist. How she started shoplifting as soon as she realised she was fucked-up. She stole because she was fucked-up. She stole because she was seeing a shrink. It wasn't stealing that was bad, it was feeling guilty about it later. She wouldn't feel guilty.

'It's people like you that make it bad for everyone else,' the woman lectured. 'Security systems cost money and that has to be paid for somewhere down the line. Ultimately the books have got to balance. That means the money comes out of the consumer's purse.'

It wasn't fucking Sade that was bad, it was feeling guilty about it that was bad. Just because Sade was fucking Simone didn't mean that Sade didn't care for her. Just because Sade didn't really behave the way he was supposed to behave didn't mean there was anything wrong with anything Sade was doing. It was just her feelings about it that made things bad. She loved Sade but she just got so confused because she knew she shouldn't really be fucking him because he was fucking someone else.

'And if it doesn't come out of the consumer's purse then it comes out of personnel,' the woman raved on. 'Which means more staff cutbacks and more unemployment. It's people like you who get people like me fired.'

But she only fucked Sade because she loved fucking Sade and something that felt so good couldn't really be that bad could it? She didn't think it could.

Justine pressed her hands deep inside her pockets. She looked at the woman. The woman was staring at her. It was obviously her turn to speak. She smiled sweetly and shook her head and frowned and smiled with bemused regret.

'I don't know why I did it,' Justine explained, 'I don't normally steal things. I mean it's just that I didn't have the money on me and instead of going to the bank, getting more money and then coming back here and queuing up again, I just put the vitamins in my pocket with the idea that I'd come back and pay for them after I went to the bank. I mean, I paid for all the other things, it's not like I planned to do it, actually I'm a little embarrassed. This has never happened to me before and I don't know what to say except I'm really sorry and I really appreciate you for being so understanding and I'm only too happy to pay you for the vitamins. Do you take Visa?'

'Do you want to go down to the station with the police and get charged?' the woman said, getting angry. 'Because if you do I'm perfectly within my rights to call them up and get them up here. But if you don't,' the woman said, calming down, 'then I suggest you go up to the cashier and pay for the goods you've stolen and I don't ever want to see you back in this store again.'

Shaking the woman's hand Justine smiled and thanked her profusely. She was overwhelmed. She was insanely grateful.

'I can't thank you enough, really,' she blabbed, 'I feel so terrible about this. You've really given me the hugest break. Thank you.'

Standing in the queue again she blushed bright red, unable to stop smiling and shaking her head. The girl at the checkout didn't look at her as she swiped her card or when she told her to have a nice day.

Making her way back home she pictured Sade curled up listlessly in front of the TV. She thought about Simone killing the pedestrian. She thought about Sade fucking Simone. Passing by a public phone booth she thought of calling her parents. She twirled the shopping in her hand. She half-opened the door and then turned away. She felt crushed, breathless. The feeling intensified as she approached her flat and she found herself turning down a side street and walking across the peninsula towards the sea. She stood at the top of the cliffs and watched the waves crash on the rocks below.

Turning back the way she had come she found herself standing outside the phone booth once more. Holding the shopping in one hand she pushed open the glass door. Inside the booth smelled of urine, vinegar and cigarettes. She dialled her parents' number. The phone rang six or seven times unanswered and she hung up. A large black fly buzzed noisily around inside the booth. She followed it with her eyes and whenever she occasionally lost sight of it, her ears monitored its haphazard frenzied flight inside the smeared glass walls. The fly landed on the rim of an empty drink can and rubbed its legs together. She remembered reading somewhere that flies vomit on their food before they eat it. She imagined the fly vomiting on the sticky spilt drink and then sucking it up. She picked up the receiver and listened to the dial tone. She inserted the coins and dialled her parents' number again. This time she hung up before any connection was made.

The fly had taken flight once more and zoomed up and down the walls of glass. It threw itself against the rubber-lined corner, one moment coming up against the door, the next moment coming up against the wall. She opened the door but the fly moved away to the back of the booth and buzzed persistently around her ears. She let the door slam shut and watched the fly crawl across the top of the phone and then resume its assault against the walls of glass. She thought of ringing Sade. *I'll just ring him and make up a lie, tell him that there's been a family emergency, that I have to leave immediately, that I called home on an impulse while I was shopping and that my father's in hospital this very minute dying.* She picked up the receiver and dialled the number but it was engaged. She wondered who Sade was talking to. She hated to think.

She watched the fly as it circled around her feet. She reached into the bag of shopping and tipped the carrots out of the smaller clear plastic bag and into the larger white plastic carry bag. She slid her hand into the empty bag and watched the fly. It was slowly crawling across the glass. She bent down so that her face was level with the fly. She brought her hand close to the fly and held it still, frozen inches above the glass. She pressed her hand down on the fly, crushing it beneath the palm of her hand. The glass shivered, its shadowed frame moving backwards and forwards on the cement floor. She pinned the fly between her thumb and forefinger, felt its tiny form crunch under the intense pressure of her grasp. Holding the fly in one hand, she peeled back the plastic bag over her wrist with the other hand, only letting go of the fly once she held it trapped inside the bag. Its wings shook slightly. She smashed her hands together, squashing the fly between them and bursting the bag. The fly fell out, flattened, and landed on the cement floor. The palm of one hand was moist and she held it beneath her nose. It didn't smell but even so she wiped her hand against her black jeans. She screwed the plastic bag into a ball and left it on the shelf of the phone booth next to the empty can. She knew the fly wasn't her father or her mother. Was it possible, she debated, that the fly was simply a fly?

Before opening the door she stood outside listening, wondering what Sade might be doing, who Sade might have been talking to on the phone while she was away. It was suspiciously quiet inside. No droning TV, no voice on the telephone. She unlocked the door and walked down the hallway glancing into rooms as she passed. The last room she came to was her study. The door was half-open. She peered around the door and looked into the room. Sade was sitting at her computer, frowning intently at the screen, sunglasses lowered, resting on the tip of his nose, and fingers poised above the keys. She stood watching Sade for a few minutes, unable to speak or leave. After some time she drew in a deep breath and dragged herself away.

'Is that you?' Sade called after her.

Justine walked all the way back down the hallway to the kitchen. She dropped the bag of groceries onto the floor and stood in front of the stove, the gas turned on but without striking a match. She turned the gas off and slid down the wall until she was crouching on her haunches. She wrapped her arms around her knees and closed her eyes. *I'm having an attack. All I have to do is sit quietly here and it will go away.*

She lay down on the cool lino floor. Sade appeared behind her in the doorway. He held a book open and pressed up underneath his face. He breathed in deeply and sighed.

'I've just started a diary,' he announced. 'I'm going to get all the students to write diaries about what books they've been reading and hand them in at the end of semester. Don't you think that's a good idea?'

She stood up. Paced backwards and forwards in front of the cupboards and benches. She fondled fruit in the fruit bowl. She lifted the shopping bag up onto the bench. She took the groceries out of the bag one by one.

'A diary, that's a good idea,' she said. 'The only thing that bothers me, that I find fundamentally difficult to accept, is that you used my computer without asking.'

Justine stared at Sade but his face was hidden in shadow.

'Is that all you have to say?' he said, indignant.

'I don't want to talk to you any more,' she informed him.

She continued to stare at him and he continued to stand in the doorway.

'You don't want to talk to me.'

'No.'

'Well fuck you,' Sade said. 'Jealous bitch.'

Justine picked up a can of tomatoes and threw it hard at the wall beside the doorway. The can split open and red juice splashed over the wall, door frame and floor. Sade retreated further into the shadowed hallway and stood statuesque, silent, watching.

'Aren't you going to stop me, tell me to calm down, tell me I'm just having one of my attacks?' she screamed.

He ignored her. She picked up a can of tuna and threw it against the wall. The can burst open, leaving oil and pieces of pink meat splattered on top of the tomato juice. Then she picked up another can of tomatoes and threw it. Then a glass bottle of tomato juice.

'You know what you are, Justine?' Sade said, his voice icy and precise. 'You're a rude, belligerent child. You're a rude belligerent child having a temper tantrum. And it's really boring.'

A carton of milk exploded against the wall. Justine stopped what she was doing and looked up.

'All right then, are you ready?' she demanded, rude.

'Where are we going?' he asked, confused.

'Just get your things together while I phone a cab,' she announced, picking up the phone.

7

HARDLY ANYONE VISITED THE ISLAND ANY MORE. AS THE ferry pulled in Justine noticed that the long beach was deserted. The row of waterfront houses behind the dunes looked vacant. Walking up the beach to her parents' house there wasn't a single footprint in sight. Everywhere she looked the hills and troughs of sand were smooth and rippled by the wind. She went striding up the dunes. Sade followed behind. The house came into view. She waved to her mother who was leaning on the railing. Her mother waved back.

Full of dread she plodded up the wooden stairs to the deck above. The table was laid out for dinner. Her mother, Ophelia, Hamlet and Juliette were gathered around the table. Her heart sank. Blood pounded through her head. *Pain-killers, bathroom cabinet, pain-killers, bathroom cabinet.* Who invited Juliette? She imagined Juliette's mouth wrapped around Sade's cock. She shuddered. She decided Sade must have invited Juliette.

The deck looked out across the front lawn, over the dunes, across the sand, and across the bay towards the mainland. A boat was moored to the ferry wharf. To the left of the house the lagoon at the mouth of the river looked cool and still. She took a deep breath and sat down at the table between Sade and Juliette. Her mother disappeared inside the house and returned with an unopened bottle of red wine which she placed down in front of Sade. Sade opened the wine and filled the glasses. Ophelia handed Juliette a novel she'd just finished reading. Juliette flipped through the pages.

'Justine tells me you're a collector,' her mother said, addressing Juliette, 'and that you have an attic at home filled with rare and unusual books.'

Juliette looked up from the novel and gazed briefly into Justine's mother's round light blue eyes. Her eyes met Juliette's. Juliette looked away and returned to the book. She shrugged her shoulders and frowned.

'I'm trying to sell them at the moment,' Juliette said, uninterested.

'Are they very valuable?'

'They're proving very difficult to sell.'

'Why's that?'

'Well, no-one here will buy them,' Juliette claimed, 'so I have to try to attract interest overseas.'

'When you say people won't buy them here,' Justine's mother persisted, 'does that mean they're not interested in your collection, or is it too expensive and people don't have the money?'

'I'm not altogether sure why I can't sell them here,'

Juliette said, her voice measured and even. 'Perhaps it's money, perhaps it's the kind of books, I don't know.'

Sade lit a cigarette and passed the packet around the table. 'Well, I'm not surprised,' he said.

Everybody looked at Sade, waiting for him to explain.

'It's obviously the kind of books,' he asserted pompously. 'There just isn't the market in Australia for the kind of books Juliette's trying to sell.'

'That's just cultural cringe,' Ophelia chipped in.

'And all that's changing now, Sade,' Justine's mother added. 'People spoke like that about Australia years ago, but since then, I mean, things have changed.'

'Anyway,' Juliette said, 'I think I've got a buyer in Cologne.'

Justine's mother nodded, impressed. Sade puffed hard on his cigarette. Justine watched the tide slide away down the sand like a long weary sigh. Ophelia emptied her glass and looked hard at Hamlet. Hamlet continued to stare across at the waves.

'You know what I find incredible about Australia,' Ophelia said, changing the subject. 'I find it incredible that Australian men won't wear condoms. You have an affair with anyone else and it's condoms all the way. But Australian men. You mention wearing a condom and STDs and they start talking about how unlikely it is for them to catch anything, and how they don't care if they're exposed to anything anyway because it's so unlikely for them to get anything in the first place. It's like, to them their dicks are immune, they're not the most sensitive parts of their bodies but the toughest. They think of their dicks as indestructible. Sure,

335

they say, it's a well-known statistical fact that in normal heterosexual sex the woman is exposed to a much greater risk of AIDS than the man. I mean it's the same old story, the vagina is a wound, it's already sick. The penis is erect, visible, and as a result easier to protect.'

A hush fell over the table. Ophelia watched Juliette flipping through the pages of the novel.

'That's what I really like about that book,' Ophelia said.

Juliette looked up, her eyes an icy steel grey. 'This book,' Juliette said, almost snarling.

'Well, it's really interesting. The main character, he's not a hero,' Ophelia explained, 'he's just an everyday guy. He has an everyday job, and a conventional marriage, and then he falls for this woman who's very cynical, sophisticated, not his type at all. A divorced woman with a career and a small son. Even though he's tempted to fuck her, his feelings for her are more complicated than that. Even though he's attracted to the new woman, he manages in his eyes to honour both his wife and the divorcee. He's a sensitive guy. The writer turns a fairly mundane cliché—the love triangle—into a subtle and complex story.' She paused for dramatic effect, then leant across the table and stared hard at Juliette. 'And I think it's great,' Ophelia resumed, 'to see sensitive men in fiction.'

Juliette opened the book at the beginning and started to read it page by page, pinching the tip of her chin between the thumb and forefinger of her right hand. Juliette's eyes skipped over the text, pausing here and there to read small fragments in full before rushing on. Juliette's face

336

changed colour with excitement. Sade nudged Juliette
with his elbow but Juliette didn't respond. Sade held a
cigarette in front of the page. Juliette shook her head
energetically and returned to the open book on her lap.
Ophelia watched her every move. The waves crashed on the
beach below.

'I'm not sure, Ophelia, that I agree with you,' Juliette
opined. 'What's more I don't find this character sensitive at
all. His inability to act may be tragic but its hardly a sign of
exceptional sensitivity.'

'But what about the way the relationships between the
man and the two women are presented?' Ophelia countered.
'Don't you think they're sensitively portrayed?'

Justine agreed with Juliette. Furthermore, the man and his
wife reminded her of Hamlet and Ophelia. Hamlet was a
coward who couldn't live up to his desires and Ophelia let
Hamlet drive her insane rather than ask for more. *Poor
Ophelia*. She looked from Ophelia to Juliette and back
again. Ophelia's heavy features were drawn into two verti-
cal lines running up and down either side of her nose.
The corners of Ophelia's mouth followed the lines down-
wards in displeasure. Juliette gazed back coolly, slowly
grinding her teeth from side to side.

'You were reading this novel down on the pier when we
arrived,' Juliette said aggressively.

'I only finished reading it today,' Ophelia said, huffy.

Juliette slitted her eyes. 'Do you often sit down on the pier
and read?'

'Why do you ask?' Ophelia said, offended.

'You were sitting so close to the edge I wonder that

you're not afraid of falling in,' Juliette pointed out malevolently. 'If you fell in you'd be carried in the fast current out towards the headland. You might hit your head on the rocks and drown.'

'But that's silly,' Ophelia said, laughing.

Her mother started quizzing Sade about New York, but Justine was unable to concentrate on what they were saying because of Juliette. Juliette was gazing intently at the open pages of the book and running her finger up and down the inside of the binding. *The blood.* She held the book up to her face, breathed deeply and sighed. *Where did Juliette get the blood?* Suddenly Juliette stood up and looked at Ophelia.

'I think you and your book, Ophelia, are absolutely full of shit,' Juliette said calmly, and then turned to Justine's mother and said goodbye. Justine's mother pleaded with Juliette to stay to dinner but Juliette was adamant. 'I really ought to be getting back,' Juliette said. Then she kissed Sade a warm goodbye and left.

Ophelia was next to leave. Tears in her eyes, she leapt to her feet, sending her chair scuttling across the wooden deck.

'Please stay to dinner,' Justine's mother insisted, but Ophelia, wringing her hands, shook her head. Sobbing, she stormed off towards the water.

Hamlet excused himself. 'I really should make sure she's all right,' he said as he left.

Justine leapt to her feet. 'I'll come with you,' she called after him.

Hamlet ran down to the edge of the water and hesitated, looking up and down the beach. To his left was the mouth of the river, a dark line cutting through the fine white sand. To his right was the headland and the rocks. Justine ran to catch up. Cold air came rushing into her face, making her eyes water. Hamlet took a few steps towards the river and then stopped. When Justine reached him his cheeks were dotted with tears. Without a word they sat down in the sand. The waves crashed at their feet.

'Juliette's right, of course,' he began. 'The book is appalling, it's unmitigated misogyny from beginning to end. He's awful but the women are no better, they're absolutely pathetic, real guilt-trippers. The man only seems sensitive because he's not as bad as the unlikeable women. He's just another Hamlet,' he said, smiling with regret. 'I mean fuck Hamlet and his ambiguous feelings.'

'You've read it too?' she asked, not quite following.

'Ophelia gave it to me to read,' he explained and sighed. 'She said that the main character reminded her of me. I don't think I'm exactly her favourite person at the moment.'

'Were you ever?'

'I think so,' he said, holding his head in his hands.

'So the condom speech was for your benefit?'

Rubbing his head. 'I guess so.'

He looked up and gazed towards the headland. A small moon appeared above. The sand slippery below. She watched his eyes.

'Why didn't you come to bed?' she asked. 'You remember, before Ophelia came back.'

He shrugged his shoulders. 'I think I wanted to.'

'So what happened?'

'I don't know,' he said, looking away towards the river. 'Anyway, what does it matter now? I'm back with Ophelia and you're back with Sade and neither of us are particularly happy but that's how it is.'

She followed the direction of his gaze. For a moment she thought she saw a figure down at the water's edge. Then it was gone.

'Do you like me now?' she said, smiling. He raised his eyebrows for an answer. She kissed him on the lips, then knelt down in front of him and pressed her face between his legs, biting through his jeans. She undid the buttons and pulled them down over his hips. She licked beneath the elastic rim of his underwear and stroked the length of his cock with her tongue. She heard a far-off cry. *Ophelia*. She stopped licking Hamlet and they both listened. They heard nothing, just the wind.

Suddenly Hamlet jumped up and rearranged his jeans. He ran his hand through his hair and then took off, running all over the place in the dry sand, and faded into the night against the dark mound of the headland.

She turned in the opposite direction, towards the river mouth, walking directly into the wind. Her eyes started to run. She was cold in her T-shirt and jeans. She climbed the dunes and ran down the other side. The lagoon. The wind dropped. She could make out logs and branches scattered on the white sand. Her sandshoes squeaked on the sand. She stumbled across the remains of a camp fire. She bent closer to see. She heard something. She heard footsteps in the sand. They were up river. She strained her eyes.

The squeaking stopped. *Ophelia?* She started running in the direction of the squeaking sand. She ran faster. She came across the prints in the sand just around the first bend. They came down over the bank from the road and headed down to the river's edge. They followed along beside the river. Then the footprints became unclear. The sand was stained dark brown. She peered into the water. It was muddied from yesterday's thunderstorm. The footprints headed upstream. She followed them up to a pier where they disappeared onto the road.

8

'I THINK I'M SICK,' JUSTINE PANTED, STAGGERING ONTO THE deck. Sade and her mother had eaten dinner and had just opened another bottle of wine. The waves crashed on the beach below. She stood swaying on the deck. It was difficult to keep her eyes open.

'Take some aspirin and go to bed,' Justine's mother advised.

'What's wrong?' Sade wanted to know.

'I feel like all my bones are broken,' Justine whispered, 'it hurts to do anything, I think I have a temperature, I'm covered in sweat.'

Her mother swayed in front of her. She followed her into the spare bedroom. She climbed into bed.

'I wonder what's made you sick,' her mother fretted.

'I think I need to lie down,' she whispered. 'My teeth won't stop chattering.'

Her mother handed her two Panadol and a glass of water and closed the door and switched off the light. In her

342

dream she and Sade were kissing each other, lying side by side on the couch in his office. They were holding each other in their arms and gently stroking each other's skin. It felt like having sex for the first time. They kissed with soft, wet, little mouths, and tongues held in reserve. She played with his nipples and he ran his hand up and down her back. Her leg between his, she pressed herself against him. But when he went to fuck her, when he opened his fly, he found that he had no dick. He was a girl. They were two girls lying side by side on the couch kissing. Suddenly Sade's hands gripped her neck and he was trying to strangle her. She woke up covered in sweat. Her mother was sitting at the head of the bed.

'Where am I?' she asked, not sure.

'You're with us, at the beach house,' her mother explained, stroking her forehead. 'It's raining. You've been sick.'

'I've been having the most incredible dreams.'

'You were screaming,' her mother said, 'you were thrashing about in your sleep.'

Something was wrong. She couldn't remember what. 'Is everything OK?'

'Everything's fine,' her mother chimed, 'we lost the roof of the shed in the storm.'

'There was a storm?' she asked, confused.

'You couldn't see the beach it was blowing rain so hard.'

'And Sade?'

'Sade's gone to New York,' her mother said, sounding disappointed.

'Gone.' Her head started to spin.

'You know, we've been very worried about you, your father especially. He's been asking after you. Finally I called Ophelia and she said you'd moved out but she didn't have your new phone number.

'Anyway you're here now, that's the main thing. Your father's in hospital. You'll be able to visit him when you go back to the city.'

'My father?' She didn't really want to know.

'I've never told you this before,' her mother began, 'but when you were just a little girl, your father and I nearly split up,' her mother reminisced, her hands folded in her lap. 'Your father actually packed his bags and left a number of times. It was terrible for me and one day I just snapped and left you alone in the house and hopped on an overnight bus. I could hear you screaming inside the house as I climbed into the taxi, crying and alone, but it was like I was on remote control. I didn't feel anything, I was just numb. Your father left you with his parents and came looking for me and so I came back home but nothing was the same. I don't think I ever forgave him for leaving me those times.

'And do you know how you used to react when your father left us? You used to hit yourself with your fists, you used to have bruises up and down the insides of your arms. You would pull out your hair and scream and scream and scream. And sometimes I'd come inside after arguing with your father as he walked out the door and I'd find you holding something, anything, some sharp object in your hands. And you'd be trying to hurt yourself. And I'd take whatever it was out of your hand, and I'd smack you and say naughty, naughty girl. You were such a bad girl, making all that mess. And I'd be very angry with you,' her mother said, shaking her head.

'Do you remember, sweetheart,' her mother entreated, running her finger gently along the inside of her arm, 'do you remember when you were just a baby?'

She frowned. Nothing made any sense.

'And see,' her mother said, pointing to the underside of her wrist, 'you still have the scars.'

Her mother fixed her with a stare. 'You saw her attacking me, didn't you?'

'Saw who attacking you?' Justine asked.

'You saw her beat my head and try to kill your brother. I know you saw, Justine,' she said ominously, 'because I looked up for help and I saw you watching from the steps.'

She was beyond all feeling, although she knew what her mother said was the truth. *She hadn't been protected.* She closed her eyes and smiled. 'You know, Mum,' she said, 'I like the walls in here.'

'Do you? We were thinking of doing the whole house but it was hard work, it was too much to do,' her mother fretted anxiously.

'It's like finger painting,' she said, singsong.

'I suppose it is,' her mother agreed. 'You don't use your hands though, you use strips of cardboard.'

'I wonder what the painted walls would tell us if they could talk?'

Her mother bent towards her and felt her head. 'Do

you still have a temperature?' her mother fussed.

Her mother's fingers running through her hair. She slept.

When she awoke she switched on the TV with the remote control. Bored, she gazed out the window and down to the water. The storm was over and it was sunny outside. She saw Juliette. She was walking along the beach towards the mouth of the river. She stood still. She peered intently at the sand. She kneeled down and started digging. She climbed to her feet and started running towards the river and out of sight.

Justine wandered out to the kitchen and made a cup of tea. Hamlet was sitting on the deck reading a novel. She decided not to say hello. No doubt he was totally engrossed in another of Ophelia's noxious novels where a so-called sensitive man selfishly and self-consciously pontificates about infidelities that never even take place. More contemporary Hamlets and every bit as cruel in their self-obsession as Shakespeare's original. To be or not to be and who gives a damn once he denies Ophelia anyway? She sighed. To all the men who've ever fobbed off a woman with a bullshit story like that, the paralysing effects of the vicissitudes of being, get fucked. And yes, you better believe it, it is as if all the love were gone from the world. Sorry, Ophelia. Too bad about all those tears streaming down your face, and all those crazy words spurting out like a river of spew.

The water boiled. She poured a cup of tea and went

back to the spare bedroom. She looked out the window. Juliette was nowhere in sight. What had happened to Ophelia? What was Juliette doing walking along the beach? Where was Sade? She had no answers. She switched off the TV and stared at the ceiling. Hours passed. She slept, she woke. She turned on the TV. Days passed. Her mother brought in a bowl of chicken broth and told her Ophelia had left Hamlet again. She watched the news. A story about a serial killer. Then a story about a missing psychiatrist the media had dubbed Dr Blood. It was alleged that Dr Blood complemented a private practice with part-time counselling at a hospice. Police believed Blood was responsible for the disappearance of hundreds of donated organs and that he/she both drank human blood and used it in bizarre and gruesome experiments. The camera cut to Juliette's attic. A reporter stood in front of one of the glass cabinets. The camera cut to a close-up of one of the incurable texts. The story cut back to the newsreader. The police were investigating Blood's disappearance in conjunction with the recent disappearance of two young women. The chicken broth sprayed across the bedclothes. She turned up the volume and dropped the bowl of soup onto the floor. Too late. A story on abortion rights. She ran out of the room, out of the house, and into the blinding light.

She ran straight down to the river but the footprints were gone and the sand was quite quite smooth. She ran all along the beach looking for Juliette. The beach was deserted, the sand smooth and rippled by the wind. She ran back the other way, towards the river mouth and lagoon.

She climbed the bank of sand dunes. The water of the lagoon was still and as blue as the sky. Low tide. She ran to the water's edge. The bottom was sandy and lightly dusted brown with silt. She slowly walked around the edge of the lagoon. She reached the beginning of the river. Huge logs littered the entrance to the lagoon. The water splashed as a stingray scurried away along the bottom. She took off her sandshoes. The water was warm. She paddled out to the nearest log. Something glimmered from one of the small branches. The water came up to her knees. A few more steps. *A lock of hair.* Shivers up and down her spine. She grabbed it and turned quickly. It came away in her hand. Eyes watching the water, she hurried to the shore. The sand was warm beneath her feet. She gazed at the strand of hair. It glistened in the sun. She walked along the river up to the pier. The river was faster here. A shelf of rocks lined the bank. She dropped the hair into the river. Hands in pockets, she walked slowly back the way she'd come. She passed the spot where she'd seen the footprints. She looked anxiously towards the road. She walked on, gazing across the lagoon. She rinsed her feet and sat drying them on the nearest dune. She laced up her sandshoes. A hawk circled the lagoon, swooping closer and closer to the water. *There was something floating in the lagoon.* She stood up to see. There was something white floating just beneath the surface. She wiped her fingers against her jeans. The fingers soiled by the hair. She ran around the lagoon to see. From the shore it looked like a dead body. She fled.

She approached the house from the road. The front

door was open and a white car was parked in the driveway. Inside her mother was sitting in the living room with two men. The men were wearing Hawaiian shirts and dark sunglasses. They both had beards and were drinking beer straight from the bottle. Her mother stood up without a word and left. She sat down. She knew why they were here. The fatter of the two offered her a swig from his bottle of beer. She declined.

'We were hoping you could answer some questions,' the fatter detective said.

'Who're you?' she wanted to know.

'We're conducting an investigation into the alleged disappearance of Dr Juliette Lorsange,' the thinner detective replied.

'Fire away,' she said.

The fatter of the two asked her her name. She wrote it down on a piece of paper.

'When was the last time you saw Dr Lorsange?' the fatter detective inquired.

She shrugged. 'I don't know.'

'Have long have you been seeing Dr Lorsange?' the fatter detective persisted.

'A few years,' she said vaguely, 'actually a matter of months really. It just feels like forever.' She laughed.

'And you saw her last week, last month,' the fatter detective pressed on.

She frowned. 'Last week.'

'Did her behaviour seem odd in any way?'

'Yes,' she said. 'She always was a very highly strung type of person, you know, neurotic. She had very peculiar taste in books. The last time I saw her she mentioned something about selling her book collection to Cologne. She was incredibly frustrated, however. No-one was interested in buying her collection here.'

'Where's "here"?' the thinner detective interjected.

'Around,' she said. 'The people she showed it to.'

'Can you tell us anything about her private life?' the fatter detective asked, changing the subject.

'Juliette's private life was Juliette's private life,' she said, thinking of Sade. 'She did mention someone once, I can't think of his name, but it all went disastrously wrong. I think it had something to do with Juliette's method of contraception.'

The thinner detective made a note. 'Condoms?'

'Willpower,' she said enigmatically. 'Anyway, at the conclusion of our most recent session I watched her climb out her office window and walk quickly to her car and speed off the wrong way down a one-way street.'

'Did you suspect that she might be going through some kind of crisis?' the fatter detective asked.

'Hey, "crisis", I like that,' she joked. 'Ever think of going into the psychoanalysis game?'

'No,' the fatter detective replied, flattered. 'You think I'd be any good at it?'

' "Crisis" isn't bad for a beginner,' she teased.

'Been in the force a long time now,' the fatter detective said, adjusting his belt.

'Good for you,' she exclaimed.

'What about multiple personalities,' the thinner detective said, joining in. 'Was Juliette a multiple?'

'You think she might have been a multiple,' she said, thoughtful. 'She always was a very odd woman, rather enigmatic. But no, she wasn't a multiple. She wasn't even a neurotic having a crisis. Nothing that cathartic. Even her feminine gaze was working OK. She was just a bit frustrated. It's not easy doing what she's trying to do in a place like this. She wanted to make people's faces light up, explode with joy, intensity, affect. When they didn't it was as if everything she'd ever done was for nothing. Nothing. Nobody. No time.'

'Well that's just about it,' the fatter detective said, wrapping it up. 'Although if you have time for one more question?'

'I have all the time in the world,' she quipped. 'Do I look busy?'

'Was there anything in Dr Lorsange's psychical make-up that led you to suspect that she may have been capable of committing murder?'

She paused, carefully choosing her words. 'Juliette dealt violently with violence. She had a habit of picking up the phone and throwing it against the wall should it ring and interrupt a session, though she never properly destroyed a phone. Bits would fall off, and she had a cupboard full of spares. She hated and adored the telephone. But she would never destroy one. I never saw a phone that she'd dealt with that couldn't be put back together.'

'But no murder,' he clarified.

She shook her head.

'Just one final question,' the thinner detective requested. 'Were you acquainted with either of these women?' He handed her two photographs. One of Simone and one of Ophelia.

She nodded.

'When was the last time you saw them?' the fatter detective wanted to know.

'A few days ago,' she said, her head clouding. 'I'm not sure, I've been sick.'

'You are aware of their disappearance?' the fatter detective wanted to know.

She nodded.

'And Juliette knew of your friendship with these women?' the detective persisted.

She nodded and burst into tears. 'There's something you should see,' she said. 'Down at the lagoon.'

The detectives exchanged meaningful glances and thanked her for her help. Between sobs she directed them to the lagoon. She watched their bright shirts through the trees.

9

SHE SAT ON THE EDGE OF THE PIER LOOKING BACK TOWARDS her parents' house. The beach as usual was deserted. In ten minutes a ferry would come and take her back to the mainland. She thought about her flat, pictured her bed, her computer and her books. *The death threat.* She wasn't ready to go home. She would go to a hotel instead. Her hair whipped around her face in the chilly breeze. She looked at her feet. She thought of Ophelia. Was that Ophelia's voice, snapping with anger and protesting the patriarchy? She laughed. It was only the wind whining in her ears. She watched the ferry come chugging across the bay, its wide smooth bow making a slapping sound as it crashed against the persistent, white-tipped waves.

10

SHE RETURNED TO HER HOTEL ROOM, OPENED A STUBBIE OF beer and switched on the news. Another story about the psychiatrist, Dr Blood. She watched a medical expert handling a fresh liver. Of all the organs the liver had the most blood, he said, which may explain why it was Blood's preferred organ. The camera cut to the rows of glass cabinets in Juliette's attic and then to a small room which looked a lot like a science laboratory and was said to be concealed by false walls behind Juliette's kitchen. Dr Blood, the newsreader said, concluding the story, was still being hunted by police. Two more women had also disappeared. She turned the TV off and lay down on the bed in the dark room. *Ophelia's body, floating in the river, with her stomach cut open and her intestines hanging out.* She missed Ophelia. She'd first noticed Ophelia during her days as an undergraduate English student. Justine had had to write an essay about Shakespeare's *Hamlet* but all she'd wanted to write about was Ophelia. Hamlet, thwarted desire, the vicissitudes of being and all the rest were just alibis. She'd ended up failing the essay but she and Ophelia became allies. She closed her eyes and tried to summon an image of Ophelia to her mind. Instead she saw Sade's face. I love you, he whispered tenderly, his cheek soft against her ear, I love you Justine because of the way you smell. It was a deceptively simple remark. Transparent and opaque at the same time. It had haunted her ever since he'd said it. Would it continue to haunt her, she wondered, when she was dead?

She rolled over and lay on her side, eyes staring open and gazing at the clean cream wall. *Smell is more intimate than memory.* In her mind his words played over and over, one word running into another, the words becoming a constant stream; Ophelia's streaming tears, streaming like a long winding river, a river rushing on to meet the sea, and, in the quiet of dusk on a summer's night, the river cutting into the sand, making a dark incision in the white sand—the river a sea of blood, a bloody gash, the sand a dazzling ephemeral skin—and everything wet before the police photographer's lens, the flash exploding into a brilliant sky filled with stars, light bouncing away from Ophelia's teeth which gleam sparkling white, captured in the brief passage of an intensely bright light, in the instant of her abject cry, and reproduced to infinity. Justine couldn't cry.

The phone rang. It was her mother. Her father was dying. She had to come to the hospital immediately. She hung up the phone. She stretched out on the bed and finished her beer. She dozed. She opened her eyes. *I am awake.* I pack my bag and leave, pay the cashier and hurry out onto the street below. Simone's gun makes my jacket heavy on one side. It thumps around in the inside pocket and hurts my chest. I look back up at my hotel room, the last in a row of six narrow windows on the top floor. The flicker of the TV screen is just visible behind the white venetian blinds. I fondle the gun and press it against my breast. I'm not sure why I'm still carrying it around. All around me the trees are full of birds, their shrill voices louder than the muffled roar of traffic as it crawls up and down the busy, elegant street. In the distance the sky turns purple and the city towers are draped in a purple and burnt orange mist. And then all at once the birds are gone.

I walk straight out into the silence left in the wake of the hundreds of shrill crying voices and cross the street, head automatically darting from side to side monitoring the traffic, ears ever alert for the swish of tyres and the whine of accelerating engines. I run my hands through my hair. I hail a cab. I direct the driver to Sade's place. I ask the driver to wait and leave the meter running. I buzz the buzzer and look up and down the street once in each direction. Sade doesn't answer even though his lights are on. I wait for someone else to unlock the heavy glass and brass door. Then I'm inside, standing in the dark foyer next to an occasional table with a vase of eucalyptus branches and the door slamming closed behind me, remembering that Sade doesn't live here any more.

Justine

1

I'M STANDING LOOKING OUT THE WINDOW. IT'S LATE AT night and my father lies dying in the bed against the wall. I turn away from the window and sit down beside him. He's leafing through the diary he started writing when the doctors told him he didn't have long to live. I peer at the typewritten pages. He shuffles them around until he's back to the beginning. He explains each section to me, where it fits in—the string of unfamiliar names, Prague, Klatovy, Sudetenland and Auschwitz, interspersed with apologies for the poverty of his English and for the inexactitude of his memory—all pronounced in a strange dry halting voice peppered with a high rasping cough which I associate with his daily use of morphine, steroids and other drugs.

As I watch more than listen I have the sensation of holding my breath. When he's finished I nod and encourage him to write more when he gets better. I hold the manuscript in my hand and look down at the floor. It is too much of a strain for me to say any more. I look up at the dresser covered in syringes, vials and bottles of morphine, a host of drugs in tablet and soluble form, and repress a shudder.

'Justine,' he rasps as I stare into his pinned grey-blue eyes. 'I just want you to know that I'm very happy. I'm not unhappy about this experience. I'm really happy, please don't think of me as unhappy. I'm grateful that we have all had this time together. We've had a very close time. I just don't want you to think I'm unhappy. I've had a good life, so I'm happy, and I want you to be happy for me, please don't be unhappy on my account. Are you happy?'

For a few seconds I struggle with the desire to vomit and then with an inability to speak. But soon the words come, just in the nick of time, and like an actor stumbling through an unfamiliar script I manage to squeak out a few words and then a few more words and soon I am done.

'I haven't given up on you, Dad,' I say, forcing my face into a calm smooth sheet, letting my eyes wander slowly over his wasted body, taking in the science fiction of his head and neck, and down the bed and along the two sticks that are his legs, 'and I'm glad you're happy.' At the same time I see the whole thing from the other side of a TV screen, I see it all as a teenager watching a made-for-TV cancer psychodrama and I wish I could cry as freely now as I had cried then.

My mother and Sade stand talking outside the door which means it's time to go. Inside the cab I tell Sade about our conversation and he says, that's good that your father's happy.

I rest my head on Sade's shoulder. I don't know what I'm feeling. I'm probably angry or sad, but I can't be sure. *I didn't tell him.* I didn't tell him how sad I am that he's dying. I close my eyes. Exhausted.

Sade drops me home in the cab. I'm too tired to fuck. I crawl straight into my bed and when I wake up I get dressed and catch a cab to the hospital. I sit next to his bed and he's mostly asleep. The morphine doesn't touch the pain. He hasn't eaten for a long time. Every so often he winces and doubles over, his knees to his chest in jerky spasms.

'Please, Justine,' he says, 'please ask them to help me, ask them to give me some more.'

I rush outside looking for the nurse and then ask for another shot. The nurse refuses and tells me he has to wait for his next shot, or at least give this shot a chance to work. Then I go back to my father and he's still crying out in pain. So I go outside again and find the nurse.

'He needs more,' I say, 'he's really in a lot of pain. He needs help, please, I can't bear to see him in agony like this.'

The nurse goes to find the doctor. I stand in the corridor and wait for the doctor. Then I explain to the doctor that my father's in a great deal of pain and that he needs another shot, something stronger. The doctor replies that if he increases the dose there's a chance my father will die.

'What do you want to do?' he asks.

'Give him another shot,' I say.

The doctor nods his head.

Inside the room my father is still doubled over in pain in the bed. Unpronounceable words choke in my throat. I watch his legs flop loose onto the white sheets. Somewhere inside that shrivelled body bumpy with lumps of cancer, somewhere behind that ravaged, almost unrecognisable face—he looks like something the Allies might have found when they went through the death camps after the war—somewhere beneath the person who no longer answers when I call his name, somewhere behind the twisted features, the tightly closed eyes, the mouth wide open, the teeth pressed outwards, the tongue uselessly pointed, somewhere behind the person reduced to the scream is my father. One of my best friends.

The doctor speaks too loud in his ear. 'Are you in a lot of pain?' he asks.

My father's legs bounce up under his chin and he blows his putrid rotten breath in the doctor's face.

'There's a risk you might choke if I give you more morphine,' the doctor says. 'Do you want me to give you more?'

The spasm makes his legs collapse, two sticks, onto the bed.

The doctor stands up and I follow him outside. He tells me how much morphine he's going to give him and mentions another drug. I nod. The doctor takes me by the arm.

'You're doing a great job taking care of your father,' he says. 'It's a great help, thanks.' He looks into my eyes. I nod.

My mother arrives. In her hand she holds a letter from Czechoslovakia. It's from my father's ex-lover and he's been waiting for it all week.

'It's here,' she whispers into his ear. His eyebrows

twitch. 'The letter from Czechoslovakia, it's here,' she says, louder this time. His eyelids flutter but don't open.

'I'll just put it here for later,' she says in a normal voice again and puts the letter on the bedside table. 'We'll have to send it to his cousin to get it translated,' she tells me. 'What a shame it's too late.'

He is in constant spasms of pain and can't speak or cry out any more. The scream and his face have become one. I ask the nurses to do something and they tie his legs to the bed.

'I can't stand to see him in this pain,' I say, 'we've got to do something.' They go to get more morphine.

I sit next to his bed, his putrid breath filling my nostrils, and take hold of his hand. His hand is warm and very soft.

'Take deep breaths,' I tell him, 'take deep breaths.' I know he can hear me. For a few seconds his breathing becomes deeper, slower, then comes in gasps again. 'Imagine you're floating down a river,' I say, 'imagine you're floating down a river and out to sea.' His eyebrows twitch up. His legs jolt against the straps.

My mother and I are at the head of the bed, Julian sits at the foot. I go to find the nurses again.

'We can't stand it any more,' I say, 'please do something. He's in pain, isn't there anything you can do?'

The nurse gives me a knowing look. 'All right sweetie,' he says, 'just give me a few minutes and I'll be in with a nice cocktail.'

I go back to the bed. I take his hand. My mother strokes his poor bony head. When the nurse arrives we all stand around outside the room and wait for him to finish.

Inside again his breaths are shallow and there's a long time in between. Julian wanders off in one direction and I in another. I sit in front of a television and watch a game of basketball. After a while I make my way back to the room.

'He's close,' my mother says, and goes to find Julian.

I take his hand in mine. It's cold. The fingertips are blue. So are his lips. His face is calm. I count to sixty between breaths. He gasps. I count to seventy-five.

'That's it,' I tell him, squeezing his hand, 'you're nearly there.'

He moans, an awful hollow sound and gasps again.

My mother stands behind him and kisses his prickled head. She strokes the back where they cut his head open. Then she kisses him once more. He gasps.

'Goodbye my love,' she says.

Julian sits at the foot of the bed. I can hear him sniffling down his tears. We wait. I count to seventy and then count no more. My mother kisses his head. A single tear rolls out of one eye and trickles down his grey face.

This isn't real, I think, this utterly escapes me. I press my face against his chest as water flows from my eyes and nose in a stream, leaving a wet patch on his striped flannel pyjamas.

2

I START CRYING JUST AFTER SADE HITS ME, A HARD WHACK across my left cheek that nicks the corner of my eye. I cry for seven hours. My sheets, pillows and T-shirt are wet with tears and snot. It feels like it's drizzling rain inside my head. Outside the window, garbage trucks roar as they squash and shred packaging and other discarded shit into smaller pieces of packaging and discarded shit. I think of calling him but I don't know the name of the hotel he's staying in. I consider what I want to say. I realise there's nothing left to say. We've both been sorry too many times before. I go into the bathroom and rinse my face.

I look at my eye in the mirror. *A black eye*. A purple-red line follows the down sweep of a dark circle and a darker line darts out from the corner in the shape of Egyptian eye make-up. Damn. I dry my face and stand there dabbing on foundation but then fresh tears spurt from my eyes and I slide down the wall and sob into my lap. There are fingernail scratches all over my back and chest and along the

365

underside of my arm. There are bruises all over my legs.

I think of *Thelma and Louise* and what a depressing film it is. All the women can do is run away but it doesn't do them any good. It launches them on a crazy suicidal mission towards destruction.

Why don't I leave him? How can I still love him? What's wrong with me? Why don't I see this for what it is? Why don't I do what Juliette tells me and protect myself? I cry even harder. Nothing can help me. Not feminism, not psychoanalysis. I'm never going to be happy. I'm never going to believe I can be happy. I'm never going to be in control of my life.

I sit at my round dining table and flick through the newspaper. I read an article about a woman and her two small children who were found dead in their own home by police. Violent videos hired in the father/husband's name from a local video shop were also found in the house. The article ends with a censorship debate. I am amazed when I think of the way people conveniently blame violence depicted in the media, films, videos and novels for abusive behaviour. If a man walks into a shopping mall and shoots ten people dead and has copies of *Body Double* or *American Psycho* in his flat then the books or videos must be responsible. In my opinion it's a case of the chicken or the egg—the representation of violent abuse or the practice of violent abuse? To blame the media is also to mystify the media.

I go to the kitchen and find some ice cubes in the freezer. I wrap them in a facecloth and hold them to my bruised eye. I stand at the window and watch people walking up and down the street. Music blares from my stereo. *I am trapped.* I flash back to the last year of high school—wearing long-sleeved shirts and stockings during heatwaves to hide the bruises, holding the towel in a special way coming out of the bathroom so my parents wouldn't see, not going to sport, waking up each morning and rushing to the mirror to see if the bruises had gone yet, monitoring the changing colours, and once, the first time, staring at the bruises on the inner upper arms where my boyfriend had grabbed me, feeling huge swollen lumps under there and wondering if I needed to go to hospital.

I think about my father. He's dead, he's dead, I chant. *Dead men tell no tales.* My father who told me I didn't see my mother attacked when I did. I don't know what's true any more. All I know is it feels like my father lied to me. So maybe he did.

I put my father out of my mind until I see my new therapist again. I drop the ice cubes in the sink and go into my bedroom and dress. I'm still hoping Sade will call from his hotel, apologising and wanting to see me before he flies back to New York. I wear clothes that are skin-tight and brief. I wear shoes with a heel. Then I go to the bathroom and start dabbing on the foundation. I apply a layer and wait for it to dry, then I apply a second layer. I look at my face under the light from all angles. I can still detect a blue tinge behind the foundation. I apply a third layer. Now it looks like I've got three layers of foundation under one eye and nothing but dark circles under the other. I dab foundation beneath the other eye. Then I put on eye make-up and bright red lipstick. I fill a shoulder bag with foundation and make-up. I decide I look OK and, gazing at my telephone one last time with regret, walk out into the warm summer dusk. On the way to catch the bus I think about Juliette and Simone and wonder where they are. The last I heard of Juliette, police suspected her of moving interstate. With Simone, I have no idea. I wonder whether Simone's novel will ever be published. I remind myself to call Hamlet. I smile nervously into my reflection as I pass shiny shop windows.

I wait for the bus. I take a window seat. I plan how much money I'm going to spend, how many drinks. I almost miss my stop. I hurry to the party. I smile at my friends. I worry about my eye. I gulp down two vodkas. When my friend looks at my eye I turn away. I escape to the dance floor where it's dark. After a while I start to sweat and start worrying about my eye again. I leave my friends on the dance floor and hurry to the bathroom. Luckily the room with the mirrors and sinks is empty. I get really close and look at my eye. The heavy make-up is a few shades browner than my white face and looks lumpy and dry instead of smooth, slightly dark and damp with sweat like everyone else's. I wonder for the hundredth time whether anyone's noticed something funny about my eye and hope that they're all too drunk, that my bright red lips keep distracting their gaze from my eyes to my mouth.

I apply a fresh coat of lipstick, piss noisily into the bowl, and make my way back out, this time to the bar where I run into one of my friends and then move awkwardly around her so the bruised eye is furthest from her and hopefully hidden behind my nose.

I tell my friend that it's my birthday soon and that I'm thinking of having a party this year. She thinks having a party is a great idea so I invite her to come and we plan a venue.

The evening passes and I go home to my empty bed. I leave the foundation on overnight.

3

THERE IS A NOTE ON MY DESK. I READ IT. IT SAYS:

*Daddy, Everything makes sense now that I finally
know the truth. I know I watched that woman try and
kill my mother and my brother. And I saw her live on
unpunished. My life has been haunted by that day. You, your
ex-wife and your unprotected family reappear in all my
relationships with men.*

*Your ex-wife, the 'other woman', reappears now in
Juliette and in me. You reappear in Sade, the man
accused. A younger me who stopped trusting you reappears in an older me who can't trust men.*

*Daddy, do you realise your distance cost me ten years,
cost me every man I ever loved?*

*The secrets and lies couldn't save me, didn't protect
me, it was already too late. Daddy, I know you meant
well but I also know protecting me was protecting yourself.
We all paid for this protection but I paid more. Daddy, I
loved you and I wanted to trust you. But your baby girl*

370

stopped loving you, couldn't love a daddy she couldn't trust. She's sad now and it's too late. She's no longer a victim, she's had her revenge, and now she wants to forget.

It is written in my handwriting. I vaguely remember writing it. I realise I don't really want to remember writing it.

I go to the bathroom and look in the mirror. The lines around my bruised eye are very dark but seem to be shrinking. I hope they disappear in time for my birthday. I start crying, desperately wanting Sade to ring. I feel guilty for wanting him to ring. I feel so bad I lie down on my bed.

I make an assessment of my financial situation. I decide that not having enough money to eat let alone to amuse, clothe or maintain myself, contributes to my current state of chronic self-pity and depression *Another trap*. Not having enough money to eat makes it impossible for me to get a job which makes it impossible to earn money which means I don't have enough money to eat. I live, I realise, one rung above utter dereliction.

When the phone rings I nearly fall out of bed.

'Would you like to see me tonight?' Sade says, his deep voice warm and honeyed. 'I thought we could buy some seafood, some wine, some fruit and some bread and go eat it on the beach,' he continues while I'm in shock, trying to recover. 'I'm flying back to New York tomorrow,' he explains.

He waits for me to speak but the first thing I do is laugh. 'I was wondering when you were going to call,' I say.

He offers to pick me up. I'm smiling when I hang up the

phone. I get dressed. I go through the foundation and make-up ritual. I decide not to tell him about the black eye unless he notices. I hear the taxi through the window and lean out to see. Sade is standing beneath my window. He waves. I run around my flat, almost tripping on a fold in the Moroccan rug, and then leave. I get halfway downstairs before I realise I've forgotten my wallet. I run back upstairs. The door is open. I tell myself to calm down but my hand holding my wallet is shaking so much the wallet drops to the floor and it takes a long time to get the key inside the door. Finally the door's locked and I start down the stairs again. My heart's pounding. My knees are shaking. When I see Sade I want to cry I'm so relieved but I smile coyly instead. I slide in beside him along the smooth warm soft back seat and lean my head on his shoulder.

Sade directs the driver to the shops and tells him to keep the meter running. I choose the food and let him pay. All the time he's smiling a quizzical smile. I know by the smile that he's thinking how I can make it up to him later. I climb back in the cab and sit close to Sade while the cab goes speeding towards the beach. The driver pulls up near the stairs and I climb out, careful not to tilt the trays of oysters.

Sade spreads the hotel blanket out over the sand. I sit down and open the bottle of chilled dry white wine. Above me the sky is filled with storm clouds and lighter patches of sky are illuminated yellow, orange and purple, a cocktail of sunset and smog. I want to kiss him as soon as he sits down but he leans away from me and doesn't look me in the eye. I drink the wine and gobble down my tray of oysters.

'So what's happening with you and Hamlet?' he asks suspiciously, casting me a furtive sideways glance.

'Nothing,' I say, 'nothing from my point of view. I don't want to fuck him, if that's what you mean.'

'But you seem to be seeing a lot of him,' Sade was saying, but I stopped listening and started laying out the mud crab instead.

'I mean he's after you, Justine,' he was saying. 'Am I right?'

'Not from my point of view,' I said. I considered telling Sade how lonely I've been since he's moved to New York and that going out anywhere with anyone is better than sitting alone in my flat but I decide not to. I look at Sade and he's distant and cold but I still want him to hug me. *I can't let go.* I think about going home. I offer Sade the mud crab. He shakes his head. I eat my half, listening to the waves and the wind, watching the fading light and emptying the bottle of wine. Sade picks at his but mostly just drinks the wine. I clear the food away. The wine has made Sade's face soft. I lie down beside him and pull the blanket over myself. Sade lies down, too. The cool sea spray. It's dark on the beach now and everywhere around us the white sand is spotted with dark forms. I open the bag of cherries. Sade eats the cherries. He pisses in the sand and buries it. He lies down again and kisses me and I sigh into his mouth that it's taken such a long time. He reaches inside my jeans for my cunt which is very wet and smooth. He takes my hand and holds it to his cock. I wriggle down beneath the blanket until my head is near his cock and I start sucking him off. There are people around, it's hard to forget where I am. I suck harder. He's about to come in my mouth when I stop. I spread open the lips of my cunt and move up so my cunt is near his cock. I slide onto the tip of his cock and rub his penis up and down the lips of my cunt. I'm coming and it takes a long time. When I'm finished I squeeze him between my thighs. He moves in and out until he comes. I fill my mouth with cherries.

I look out over the water wondering why I want him to love me. *Pathetic*. Maybe someone else will. I sigh.

4

'HI JUSTINE,' MY THERAPIST SAYS, OFFERING ME A CHAIR. 'Come in.'

'Thanks,' I say and sit in the chair I always sit in.

'So how are you today?' she asks, making eye contact. I struggle not to let my eyes sink into the dark void of hers.

'I'm very anxious about my birthday tomorrow,' I begin, staring off into a corner of the room. 'I mean, I'm trying to do something about it, I've always had such a lousy time, I've always felt shitty, so this year it's going to be different. This year I'm having a birthday dinner with my family the day before and then on my birthday I'm having drinks with my friends at a club.' I glance at my therapist. She looks impressed. I'm really excited about my birthday drinks, this'll be the first time I've ever done anything like this. I hope it'll make me feel less like nothing.

'I'm glad you said "my birthday",' my therapist says, smiling.

I smile back but it feels like I'm faking it. I'm not sure. I can't be sure whether I said 'my birthday' because it is my birthday or whether saying 'my birthday' is just another defence.

My therapist shuffles her notes. 'Last session,' she says, 'you were talking about your father and the assault. You've always been told you hadn't seen your mother assaulted, but now you're convinced you were a witness. What did you see?'

'Well,' I begin, staring mesmerised by the carpet, 'I was two and a half. We were at my father's ex-wife's house. I was near the front door but my father was busy with the other children inside. I heard raised voices. I lunged inside, towards my mother, on my short, bowed legs. I knew she was in trouble. Then pausing at the top of the stairs to take hold of the rail—"Be careful on the stairs, darling," she'd told me so many times—then standing carefully holding on at the top of the stairs I saw. I saw her bashing Mummy, I saw her beating Mummy's face with her fists, I saw her beating Mummy's huge swollen stomach. "I'm going to kill your baby, I'm going to kill your baby," she shouted. Mummy's arms waved around in the air above her head. "Stop, don't hit me, you're hurting me," she screamed, and "Help, *help*," at the top of her voice,' I say then pause. I glance at my therapist. She meets my eye. 'Just like a stuck pig,' I say and stop. My therapist nods. I look back down at the carpet. 'Heavy footfalls in the hallway behind me,' I say, 'I turned around and looked up into his face. I looked to know. I looked to see. "Daddy," I cried, "Daddy ..."

'... Strong arms tearing me up from the ground, hurting me ...

' "... Daddy, *Daddy* ..."

' "... I want you inside, Justine," he said, his voice barking and impatient. Had I done something wrong? "No, Daddy, no," I screamed, but he wasn't listening to me and I screamed louder and struggled in his arms to get down to get away and he pushed me inside the door. I landed with a crash, my head slamming against the wall. High above me the door slammed closed. The light disappearing through the crack. The dark long hallway. I couldn't stay here. Here I simply ceased to be, and I cried and cried and cried, but it didn't do any good.

'I had to find Daddy and cry louder until I *was* again. So wiping the tears from my eyes I stood up ...'

'You felt,' my therapist says, 'annihilated.'

I nod.

'Can you think of anything that makes you feel the same way?' she probes.

'Doors,' I say. 'It's always a door slamming shut in my face. The door closing annihilates me. Sade slamming the door in my face. It isn't ever a simple matter of someone leaving. This implies their return, a temporary interruption to events. No. The closed door overwhelms me. When it closes it closes on me. I wasn't anything but his recognition at the time. I needed to go with him. If I wasn't *with him* then I *was not*.'

I am in a blur for the rest of the session. I walk home, my mind completely blank. The sun is very bright. There is a message on my answering machine. It's from my mother reminding me that my birthday dinner's tonight. I set the alarm clock so I have time to dress, and crawl into bed. The windows are open and there is a pleasant breeze. I doze. I sleep.

I wake up to the alarm. I'm drenched in sweat. I'm haunted by a dream. The dream starts with Sade living in a terrace house with three women. During this part of the dream it pours with rain. I keep trying to reach him on the phone but the different women keep giving me different messages. Finally I learn that he's spent the day with one of them and that they've gone out. Why isn't Sade at work? I wonder, imagining what he might have been doing with the girl.

Then Sade is in a terrible accident, a chemical spill, and he's sent to hospital. He wakes up next to a famous novelist. He's totally fucked up and he rings my parents and they ring me and the whole family goes in to visit him and Sade is an unconscious mess beneath the bandages. Then I see that the woman, the woman he lives with, is there too, standing in the background, and I realise that she's been with Sade all along. So I go up to my parents, although I tell them nothing, and we leave.

Soon after Sade and the famous novelist are taken hostage and held in a ten-storey apartment block. The media are all assembled outside the building. My mother and brother stand talking to the reporters and Dad and I go inside to see if we can find Sade. It turns out that there's a stairway which no-one will go anywhere near because it's too dangerous and that Sade's being held in a makeshift hospital ward on the roof.

Dad smiles and waves goodbye and I go looking for the stairway. When I find it I run up rows of carpeted white steps. Then the stairway becomes strange. The stairs become so narrow and winding I have to go on all fours. I come to a floor where the only way up is by climbing huge stuffed toys. I see the woman again in front of me. She keeps losing her grip on the animal's nose and falling onto me so I push her fat ass and scream, 'Go, go, go,' and push her up. Then I'm in the hospital ward and the head terrorist takes me to a bed but it's the novelist's bed. I feel absolutely torn, that I'll never see Sade again. A sense of desperation overwhelms me. I run up to the head terrorist and grab him by the sleeve.

'Please,' I say, crying, 'please show me where he is.'

The terrorist takes me to a stepladder leading up to the roof. 'He's up there,' he says.

I climb up the stepladder and come to a panel of bubbling glass. I knock on the glass. Six heads peer over the edge and look down at me. All the heads wear sunglasses and hold shot glasses in their hands. I knock again and they move the glass and let me in.

'Sade,' I cry, following him over to a cluster of director's chairs where we sit down. He sips at his scotch and smiles.

'How are you?' he asks.

'OK,' I say, 'you're OK?'

'Yes,' he says, and shows me his wrist which opens into deep slits in three places and then closes again. I am impressed.

The sun is brilliant above us and the air warm and clean. The city lies sprawled all around.

Four girls sit sipping glasses of scotch while another

guy tells them stories, making them laugh. Soon Sade joins in and he and the other guy take it in turns to tell funny stories and jokes and make the girls laugh. My eyes fill with tears.

'Sade,' I say, holding his arm.

'What, Justine?' he says and looks at me.

The way he says my name makes me smile. 'Nothing,' I say, and look up. One of the girls is watching us closely. Sade looks over and meets her eye. They stare intently at each other for a few seconds and she looks away down into her drink and smiles. Then Sade tells another joke and all the girls laugh.

I shiver. *It's dead up here.* Sade offers me a drink from the fridge and asks me to stay awhile but I shake my head. *I have to leave, I have to get away as soon as possible. I have to leave Sade. This is dead for me, this is Sade's life and these are Sade's friends and there is no place here for me.*

I crawl out of bed and into a shower. I dress and go through the foundation ritual. I check the time. *Sade's flight back to New York left three hours ago. He didn't call to say goodbye.* I put on a pair of sunglasses and a hat and leave. I walk to the restaurant. They're already there when I arrive. I pull my hat further down on my head and adjust my sunglasses.

'So are you in disguise?' Julian asks, kissing me hello.

I blurt out an excuse about the sun and the brightness of the summer light and he nods. I sit down, pushing the chair back from the table and smile hello.

'Happy birthday,' Mum says, pouring the champagne.

We clink glasses. I feel like the smile on my face is the

same as the one I'd drawn on in the mirror. It makes me want to laugh.

All through the meal I peer at them over the edge of my glasses. The sunglasses hide the make-up I'd put on to hide the bruises. Soon however the light starts to fade. I lean back in my chair, anxiety chokes my throat. *What will I do if they notice?* I rush to the bathroom and take off my glasses. I peer at my face. I bend the brim of the hat down so that it hangs over the disfigured side of my face. *Good.* The strange-looking eye is hidden in shadow.

Sitting back down at the table without my glasses it is a real effort to look anyone in the eye. This is typical, I go to all this trouble to arrange my birthday so it's on my terms, and I can't look anyone in the eye or take off my hat because I have a black eye to hide. I push bits of fish around the plate and toy with the idea of telling them. I laugh. Sure. I picture the uproar over dessert and coffee, the promises I would make to leave Sade for good, but then what? *I would become invisible again.* In the end it would be too difficult for them to appreciate that something could have been done and that something very sad had happened to me all those years ago.

I lean back in my chair and look my mother straight in the eye. 'Thanks for the wonderful dinner,' I say.

She smiles back and for a few seconds her eyes frown at the bruised eye. Then she takes another sip of her champagne and places her hand on my leg.

'You're looking very pale,' she says, 'you've got to look after yourself, Justine. No-one else is going to do it for you, you know.'

I go straight home after dinner and crawl into bed. I count the hours until Sade arrives in New York. Some time tomorrow afternoon. I can't sleep. I am awake all night. Sade's cock and Simone's lips, Simone's cunt and Sade's mouth. I am still awake when the garbage trucks start. Then I fall asleep for a few hours. I wake with a start and check the time. It's early in the afternoon and no-one has called for my birthday. Especially not Sade. I have a fever. I wait for him to ring. I decide he is with Simone. I can't let go.

I sit sipping tea and looking out the window. I think about going to have a coffee with my friends. I do not cry. On my way to my friend's house I rehearse what I'll say to Sade when he rings. How I'll tell him I never want to speak to him again, how I never want to see him again. But inside I'm desperate for him to ring and say happy birthday.

When I get back Hamlet calls and asks me out.

'Can you afford Bollinger?' I tease.

'Yes,' he says, laughing.

'Well,' I say, 'call me next week.'

'Really,' he says, still laughing.

There's a longish pause.

'Well,' he says, sounding hurt, 'you've got my number, so any time, just give me a call.'

I hang up and feel anxious. I consider ringing Hamlet back and telling him I was only joking, that I'd love to have a drink with him, and then I get angry again and I don't. I open a book and start reading. Sade still doesn't call. I check the venue for the party. Everything's OK.

I look at the time and it's seven. I decide to call Sade in

New York. I don't really expect anyone to answer. I tell the operator the number, my name and say that the call is for Sade. The phone rings and a woman answers. The operator asks for Sade and the woman asks who it is. The operator says it's a long distance call for Sade and then the woman says Sade's not taking any calls.

I hang up a little stunned. Sade promised he'd tell me if he was fucking anybody else in New York. I try calling again, hoping that if Sade's there he'll pick up the phone but she answers again and I tell the operator to forget it.

I sit at my desk staring out the window at the beautiful day and try not to panic. I refuse to cry. I decide to call again tomorrow. I get ready for my birthday drinks. I swallow four painkillers and smother my face in make-up. The evening passes in a blur of vodka and cocaine. I go to bed at some point but can't sleep. I take sleeping pills. I call Sade again as soon as I wake up. This time Sade talks to the operator and refuses my call. I walk around my flat wanting to smash things but I don't. Tears go pouring down my face. I ring Marcelle and tell her about Sade. Marcelle tells me to stop ringing him. I blow my nose. I eat stir-fry vegetables and go to bed. The phone rings. It's six in the morning. It's Sade. No, she's not his new girlfriend. She's just a friend. He tells me he'll call me in a couple of weeks once things settle down. I tell him not to bother unless he wants to clear things up. He says an icy goodbye.

I am sick. I spend days on end in bed. Sade calls again. I'm very calm and detached as I say hello and ask him how he is, how things are going in New York.

'Fine,' he says, 'you should think of getting over here

some time for a visit.' My stomach heaves. I want to ask him about Simone. I ask. He says he saw her the other day. I tell him to say hello from me and hang up the phone.

I don't cry, I drink a cup of tea instead and feel mad. I'm so angry I stand up and start pacing around the room. After a little while I stand at the window, the wind blowing in from the ocean making me sneeze. And for an instant I understand why I can't ever be happy with Sade, it's just like it was in my dream. Sade on the rooftop taking turns with another man to make four women laugh but the women don't tell any jokes. The most the woman Sade likes best can do is return his dark stare. *Sade's world is a world I experience as death.*

I go into my bedroom and lie down. Soon I'm running my hands over my ass and hips and thinking of Sade. Images of us fucking crowd my head and I think of calling him one last time but I don't and I masturbate instead. I'm my own lover now, I tell the empty room in a soft voice. I have to be me and my lover for a while.

I start reading a book but everything that happens reminds me of Sade and I can't concentrate and keep going off into long silent stares out the leadlight window and at the blond brick wall outside. *I hate this.* I try the book again. *Everything's going to be all right.*

I sleep. Days pass. I get better. Then late one night I'm woken up by the phone ringing. I check the time. It's after two. I guess that it's Sade on the other end of the line. I think about not answering the phone. I pick it up.

'Hello,' he slurs.

'It's late, Sade,' I say, 'what do you want?' I see his

head in my lap and me stroking his temples. I repress an urge to run out the door and leap into a taxi and then onto a plane so I can see him. I lean out the window and look onto the street, half-expecting to see him standing below my window.

'Do you miss me?' he slurs.

Things are going to be different this time. 'Look, Sade,' I say in a traitorous voice, 'what do you want?'

There is a longish pause. I look down at the street. The street below is wide and straight and it runs along the top of a ridge. It's lined with maple trees and the houses are either large two, three and four storey terraces or modern apartment blocks. My favourite bar is just up the street and most of my friends live a few blocks' walk away. It's often noisy on the street, car alarms, emergency vehicles and drunk suburbanites are the main offenders. On hot still summer nights I can smell the sea, the harbour is only a few blocks away. I like it here, on the peninsula, it's the only place I can stand to live in this country.

'Come and visit me,' he pleads. 'I'll send you the air fare.'

'Why?' I ask.

'Don't you want to see me?' he wants to know.

I take a deep breath and close my eyes tight, ready for the pain. 'No,' I say. 'I don't want to see you any more so please don't call me again.'

As I hang up the phone I think about all the times I've said this before and changed my mind some time further down the track. I become anxious. I almost call him back. I can't decide what to do. Part of me wants to be free of Sade and another part wants everything to stay the same. I'm torn, numb in the midst of this. I stand my ground. I switch on the TV. I decide to turn on the answer machine in case he rings back.

The next day my new supervisor calls. We talk about my thesis. I work out a deadline. I get to work.

Then I wait. I wait two weeks and then one morning when I'm lying in bed sleeping in, a rainy Saturday morning, the answer machine goes off. I'm pretty sure it's Sade ringing. Sure enough he leaves a drunken unintelligible message. Half an hour later the machine goes off again and the same thing happens. I bury my head under the covers and try to go back to sleep but I end up tossing and turning and pulling a muscle in my neck. I feel guilty doing this to Sade. I also feel anxious because part of me really wants to pick up the phone, just to hear his voice and to be reassured that he still wants me, but I don't. Even though I cry myself to sleep thinking about Sade and feeling sorry for myself I know it's pointless to answer the phone. Some people never change. I become very sad. I can't love Sade any more.

I get out of bed. *Why am I doing this?* I make a cup of tea. *You're doing this, Justine, because if you answer the phone you'll lose your peace of mind and you won't be able to do any work today.* I am very stern. I am absolutely firm.

I start to feel safe. The death threat seems less urgent. I am healthy and unharmed. I admit I probably constructed the threat myself. I sit at my desk and open my books but it's very hard to concentrate. I stare out the window and think of Sade. I try reading but the words swim on the page. After a while I get an idea and push the books aside. I decide to go swimming instead.

At the pool I see an angel. He has light blue eyes and curly light brown hair and full lips and a beauty spot on his cheek. He has the sweetest smile. I watch him swim up and down and then sit in the sun, talking with his friends. I wonder if he's a regular at the pool. I am too shy to talk to him but I think about him while I'm walking home. I imagine how nice it would be to wake up in the morning next to his face.

When I arrive home the answer machine goes off. Sade leaves another drunken message. *Sorry, Sade.* This time I'm waiting for an angel. I'm waiting to start again.